Spring and Autumn Annals of Wu and Yue

SUNY series, Translating China
Roger T. Ames and Paul J. D'Ambrosio, editors

Spring and Autumn Annals of Wu and Yue

A Literary Translation of the First Chinese Novel, *Wu Yue chunqiu*

OLIVIA MILBURN

Cover: Figure of a charioteer (bronze, Eastern Zhou dynasty, 4th–3rd century BCE). Metropolitan Museum of Art.

Published by State University of New York Press, Albany
© 2024 State University of New York
All rights reserved
Printed in the United States of America

No part of this book may be used or reproduced in any manner whatsoever without written permission. No part of this book may be stored in a retrieval system or transmitted in any form or by any means including electronic, electrostatic, magnetic tape, mechanical, photocopying, recording, or otherwise without the prior permission in writing of the publisher.

Links to third-party websites are provided as a convenience and for informational purposes only. They do not constitute an endorsement or an approval of any of the products, services, or opinions of the organization, companies, or individuals. SUNY Press bears no responsibility for the accuracy, legality, or content of a URL, the external website, or for that of subsequent websites.

For information, contact State University of New York Press, Albany, NY
www.sunypress.edu

Library of Congress Cataloging-in-Publication Data

Name: Milburn, Olivia, translator
Title: Spring and autumn annals of Wu and Yue : a literary translation of the first Chinese novel, Wu Yue chunqiu / Olivia Milburn, translator with an introduction and notes.
Description: Albany : State University of New York Press, [2024] | Series: SUNY series, Translating China | Includes bibliographical references and index.
Identifiers: ISBN 9781438499352 (hardcover : alk. paper) | ISBN 9781438499369 (ebook)
Further information is available at the Library of Congress.

10 9 8 7 6 5 4 3 2 1

Contents

Acknowledgments	vii
Introduction	ix
Textual History of the *Wu Yue chunqiu*	xv
The Reception of the *Wu Yue chunqiu*	xxvii
Narrative in the *Wu Yue chunqiu*	xxxv
Translator's Note	li
Timeline of the Kings of Wu and Yue	lv
Timeline of Events in the *Wu Yue chunqiu*	lvii
Chapter 1. The Traditions: The Story of the Great Lord Protector of Wu	1
Chapter 2. The Traditions: The Story of King Shoumeng of Wu	9
Chapter 3. The Traditions: The Story of How King Liao Employed Prince Guang	15
Chapter 4. The Inner Traditions: The Story of King Helü of Wu	37

Chapter 5.	The Inner Traditions: The Story of King Fuchai of Wu	77
Chapter 6.	The Outer Traditions: The Story of King Wuyu of Yue	117
Chapter 7.	The Outer Traditions: The Story of King Goujian of Yue Becoming a Vassal	129
Chapter 8.	The Outer Traditions: The Story of King Goujian Returning to His Country	157
Chapter 9.	The Outer Traditions: The Story of King Goujian's Conspiracy	173
Chapter 10.	The Outer Traditions: The Story of King Goujian's Attack on Wu	197
Appendix:	The Chinese Text	233
Bibliography		235
Index		247

Acknowledgments

Although I have now spent nearly twenty years studying the history of the kingdoms of Wu and Yue, I will admit to having long harbored considerable prejudices against the *Wu Yue chunqiu*. This is not a criticism of the book itself but the result of the fact that too many academics, in both China and the West, have chosen to study it as a factual source instead of considering it as fiction. This is the equivalent of deciding to learn the history of France from the works of Alexandre Dumas or studying the American Civil War in the pages of *Gone with the Wind*. However, having come to the conclusion that a translation of the *Wu Yue chunqiu* was needed, I now have a much-enhanced respect for the skill that the author has brought to his material and the remarkable ingenuity of the narrative.

This translation would not have been possible without the assistance of many people, and I would particularly like to thank the staff of the various libraries where I have worked, including the library at Seoul National University; the National Central Library, Taipei, Taiwan; the library of the School of Oriental and African Studies; the British Library; Shanghai Library; Suzhou Library; the library of Zhejiang University; and the library of Nanyang Technological University. In addition, I should give special thanks to my research assistant, Jiang Qingjun, for assisting me in dealing with the Rare Books Collection at Seoul National University. I would like to thank Bernhard Fuehrer, Thomas Hjørnet, Koh Keng We, Min Sunyoung, Tan Tianyuan, Maya Taneda, Marcus White, Ye Ye, and Yan Zinan for all their help. Finally, I gratefully acknowledge the financial assistance received from the Hsu Long-sing Research Fund at the University of Hong Kong to support the publication of this book.

Just before beginning work on this book, I was contacted by researchers in New Zealand, trying to trace the ancestry of the Māori Melbourne family, who indeed turned out to be my distant cousins. I am therefore honored to be able to dedicate this book to my cousin, Taiarahia Melbourne, and the rest of my relatives among the Tūhoe people.

Introduction

The *Wu Yue chunqiu* 吳越春秋 (Spring and Autumn Annals of the Kingdoms of Wu and Yue), which dates to the Eastern Han dynasty, is the earliest-surviving work of Chinese fiction that deserves to be considered as a novel. It takes as its subject the wars fought between the two ancient kingdoms of Wu and Yue, located in what is now southern Jiangsu and northern Zhejiang Provinces, respectively, during the first quarter of the fifth century BCE. Although there was a long history of low-level conflict involving these two countries stretching back into the mists of time, in the 490s BCE, this suddenly flared up into an appalling bout of violence. Taking advantage of the declaration of national mourning following the death of King Yunchang of Yue 越王允常 (d. 497 BCE), King Helü of Wu 吳王闔閭 (r. 514–496 BCE) invaded his southern neighbor, hoping for an easy victory. What happened next was truly disastrous. Meeting the Yue forces in battle at Zuili 檇李, the Wu Army suffered an ignominious defeat, and their king sustained such severe injuries that he was dead within days. Three years later, his successor, King Fuchai of Wu 吳王夫差 (r. 495–473 BCE), invaded Yue and, after a series of bloody battles, captured their capital city. King Goujian of Yue 越王勾踐 (r. 496–465 BCE), pinned down with what remained of his family and court at Mount Kuaiji, eventually negotiated a surrender that led to him being held as a prisoner of war in Wu for a number of years.[1] After this appalling calamity, King Goujian spent decades rebuilding his kingdom, and in 473 BCE, it was his turn to take revenge. After a series of

---

1. Hargett (2013) gives a detailed discussion of the vexed issue of the name of this mountain.

brutal campaigns, the kingdom of Wu was destroyed, and King Fuchai was forced to commit suicide.

Although at the time of this conflict, the kingdoms of Wu and Yue were located at the very edge of the Chinese world, and the population of this region would not be Sinicized until many centuries later, it is almost impossible to overstate the significance of these events within the history of Chinese culture. The wars between Wu and Yue are not particularly well recorded in the very earliest historical texts to cover this period, but this lack was soon offset by the fact that a whole literary genre grew up around this conflict during the late Warring States period and early imperial era.[2] In addition to the enormously famous *Sunzi bingfa* 孫子兵法 (Master Sun's Art of War), whose putative author, Sun Wu 孫武, was a general serving under King Helü of Wu, a number of other early texts are recorded in the catalog of the Han dynasty imperial library that were clearly related to these events but did not survive to the present day.[3] Unsurprisingly, these are also writings about warfare: the *Fan Li* 范蠡 and the *Dafu Zhong* 大夫種 (Grandee Zhong), named after two of King Goujian of Yue's most senior government officials, and the *Wu Zixu* 五(伍)子胥, which takes its name from the prime minister who served both Kings Helü and Fuchai of Wu.[4] By the end of the Han dynasty, it became clear that scholars from the Wu-Yue region were playing a particularly important part in the development of writings in this genre, since they collected material concerning the history of their own native place and ensured that documents that would not otherwise have survived have been transmitted to the present day. The *Wu Yue chunqiu* is itself believed to derive from this local tradition. The perception that what has been transmitted is only a fraction of the number of texts produced in antiquity is confirmed by regular archaeological discoveries of new material concerned with the conflict between these two kingdoms in early imperial-era tombs—though, to date, none of it has proved to be closely related to the *Wu Yue chunqiu*. For

---

2. As indicated by Su Tie (1990), early historical texts do not merely pay scant attention to Wu and Yue; the time frame of events covered is also extremely limited, focusing mainly on the reigns of Kings Helü, Fuchai, and Goujian.
3. The transmitted biography of Sun Wu is given in *Shiji*, 65.2161–62; this information is repeated in the text entitled "Jian Wuwang" 見吳王 (An Audience with the King of Wu), a previously unknown section of the *Sunzi bingfa*, excavated at Yinqueshan 銀雀山 in 1972; see Yinqueshan Hanmu zhujian zhengli xiaozu (1976): 106–8.
4. See *Hanshu*, 30.1757 and 30.1761, respectively.

example, a Han dynasty text recounting the story of Wu Zixu and his service with the kings of Wu was excavated from Tomb 77 in Shuihudi 睡虎地, while another Han dynasty military text entitled *Gailu* 蓋盧 (Helü) was discovered in Tomb 247 at Zhangjiashan 張家山.⁵ In addition, among the bamboo texts given to Tsinghua University in 2008, the *Yuegong qishi* 越公其事 (Deeds of the lord of Yue) focuses on the long struggle of King Goujian of Yue to achieve his revenge against Wu, in a text whose narrative complexity is already moving toward that found in other early Chinese fiction writings.⁶ Archaeological excavations have also affected our understanding of the early development of the saga of Wu and Yue in other ways. Art historians have shown that key events in the warfare between Wu and Yue were frequently depicted in Han dynasty art: ancient wall paintings, stone carvings, and some of the earliest-known pictorial bronzes.⁷ Furthermore, publication of details concerning newly discovered objects once owned by members of the Wu and Yue royal families is often the focus of keen public interest; for example, in 1995, the Shanghai Museum acquired a bronze vessel inscribed with a dedication stating that it had been made by order of King Fuchai of Wu for an unnamed woman.⁸ Naturally, this immediately resulted in feverish speculation that it had been made for Xi Shi 西施, King Fuchai's beloved consort from the kingdom of Yue, who is conventionally numbered among the four greatest beauties of ancient China.

---

5. The Shuihudi discovery has not been published; however, a preliminary discussion is found in Liu Lexian (2011). The text *Gailu* has been extensively studied; see, for example, Zhangjiashan ersiqi hao Hanmu zhujian zhengli xiaozu (2006): 159–68, Shao Hong (2007), and Milburn (2011).
6. Qinghua daxue chutu wenxian yanjiu yu baohu zhongxin and Li Xueqin (2017): 238–41. For studies of this text and its relationship with other transmitted accounts of these events, see Xie Naihe (2020), Li Shoukui (2017), and Xiong Xianpin (2018).
7. Among the earliest discoveries of Han dynasty wall paintings depicting events from the conflict between Wu and Yue are the Wu Zixu and Prince Qingji of Wu 吳王子慶忌 murals found in Inner Mongolia; see Neimenggu zizhiqu wenwu kaogu yanjiusuo (1978): 24. For a discussion of the representation of King Fuchai of Wu and Wu Zixu in Eastern Han dynasty stone carvings, see Thompson (1999): 20–21. All known bronze mirrors representing scenes from the history of Wu and Yue are discussed in Milburn (2013): 144–58; other important publications on these artistic representations include Zhang Honglin (2011) and Wang (1994).
8. This bronze vessel is discussed in Chen Peifen (2004): 194; Ye Wenxian (2007): 132–34; and Feng Puren (2007): 136.

The wars between the kingdoms of Wu and Yue and the personalities of the main protagonists have long fascinated Chinese writers and proved to be important and enduring sources of creative inspiration. It would be impossible to enumerate the poems written on the subject in the last two thousand years or so, but these would certainly number in the hundreds of thousands and include works by some of the most famous and significant of Chinese poets. Prose writers have also consistently reinterpreted this ancient conflict for new audiences; among the best-known modern reworkings are the short story entitled "Zhu jian" 鑄劍 (Forging the Swords) in the collection *Gushi xinbian* 故事新編 (Old Tales Retold) by Lu Xun 魯迅 (1881–1936) and the novella entitled *Yuenü jian* 越女劍 (The sword of the Yue maiden) by Jin Yong 金庸 (1924–2018).[9] In addition to these modern classics, there are also numerous popular novelizations on the same subject, such as the *Wu Yue chunqiu shihua* 吳越春秋史話 (Historical tales from the *Spring and Autumn Annals of the Kingdoms of Wu and Yue*) by Xiao Jun 蕭軍 or *Fan Li* 范蠡 by Xia Tingnan 夏廷楠.[10] The wars between Wu and Yue also have an important place in the history of Chinese performing arts. Discoveries at Dunhuang have revealed a medieval *bianwen* 變文 (transformation text) recounting the death of Wu Zixu.[11] *Bianwen* recitations, strongly associated with the transmission of Buddhism in China, involved storytelling to the accompaniment of large-scale illustrations. It is not surprising that with the rise of *zaju* 雜劇 drama during the Yuan dynasty, this subject was also popular in the theater: the earliest-known play based on these events is the *Kuaijishan Yuewang changdan* 會稽山越王嘗膽 (The king of Yue tastes gall at Mount Kuaiji) by Gong Tianting 宮天挺 (c. 1260–c. 1330).[12] This play was followed by numerous other dramatic interpretations, including the surviving *Shui Zhuan Zhu Wu Yuan chuixiao* 說鱄諸伍員吹簫 (To persuade Zhuan Zhu, Wu Yuan [i.e., Wu Zixu] plays the flute) by Li Shoujing 李壽卿, which takes as its subject

---

9. See Lu Xun (1973) and Jin Yong (1996): 659–90, respectively. The novella *Yuenü jian* is conventionally printed at the end of the longer novel *Xiake xing* 俠客行 (Ode to Gallantry) in collected editions of Jin Yong's works.
10. Xiao Jun (1980) and Xia Tingnan (1995).
11. Pan Zhonggui (1994): 831–68. For a translation of this transformation text, see Mair (1983): 123–66. See also Johnson (1980a, 1980b).
12. Gong Tianting's play is mentioned in a number of important early sources on Yuan dynasty drama; see, for example, Zhong Sicheng (2002), B: 156 and Yao Pinwen (2010): 22–24.

the assassination of King Liao of Wu 吳王僚 (r. 526–515 BCE).[13] Meanwhile, in the Ming dynasty, the *Huansha ji* 浣紗記 (Story of the girl who washed silk), concerning the relationship between King Fuchai of Wu and his beloved consort, by Liang Chenyu 梁辰魚 (c. 1521–94) is frequently cited as the first Kunqu 昆曲 opera; again, right up to the present day, similar new pieces are regularly commissioned, such as the award-winning modern opera *Xi Shi* 西施 in 2009.[14] During the course of the twentieth century, the story of King Goujian's revenge was an important narrative within discussions of national revival in China, and as a result, these events were interpreted for new audiences in popular performing arts mediums with specially written patriotic plays—for example, in 1935, a marionette play entitled *Woxin changdan* 臥薪嘗膽 ([King Goujian] tempers his steel) was written by Yu Zheguang 虞哲光 (1906–91), which presents a strongly nationalistic message.[15] Film and television have merely added to the ways in which people can enjoy representations of the rivalry between King Fuchai of Wu and King Goujian of Yue—since the year 2000, there have been six full-length dramatizations of the wars between Wu and Yue shown on Chinese television: *Xi Shi chuanqi* 西施傳奇 (The Tale of Xi Shi) in 2003, *Zhengba chuanqi* 爭霸傳奇 (The Tale of Competing Hegemons) in 2006, *Woxin changdan* 臥薪嘗膽 (The Great Revival) and *Yuewang Goujian* 越王勾踐 (King Goujian of Yue) in 2007, *Xi Shi mishi* 西施秘史 (The Secret History of Xi Shi) in 2011, and *Yingxiong* 英雄 (Heroes) in 2013. Many (if not most) of these later representations are directly derived from or inspired by the *Wu Yue chunqiu*. In contrast to earlier texts recording the history of the kingdoms of Wu and Yue that present their information in an unstructured or anecdotal format and are

---

13. Yang Jialuo (1985): 2899–986. Other Yuan dynasty plays on stories related to the history of the kingdoms of Wu and Yue that do not survive include *Gusutai Fan Li jin Xi Shi* 姑蘇臺范蠡進西施 (At Gusu Tower Fan Li presents Xi Shi) by Guan Hanqing 關漢卿 (1225–1320), *Mie Wuwang Fan Li gui hu* 滅吳王范蠡歸湖 (Having killed the king of Wu, Fan Li returns to the lakes) by Zhao Mingdao 趙明道 (dates unknown), *Tao Zhugong Wuhu chen Xi Shi* 陶朱公五湖沉西施 (Lord Zhu of Tao drowns Xi Shi in Lake Tai) by Wu Changling 吳昌齡 (dates unknown), and the anonymous *Fan Li yu Xi Shi* 范蠡與西施 (Fan Li and Xi Shi).
14. Liang Chenyu (2010): 445–581. The significance of this piece is considered in Guo Yingde (1998). The modern opera is discussed in Liu Wei (2008).
15. This is the subject of Cohen (2009). The script of Yu Zheguang's play is reprinted in its entirety in Ye Mingsheng (2017): 638–43, with photographs from a production in 1937.

much more difficult to read, this novel provides a tightly focused narrative with a well-developed plot and strongly individual characterizations of the main protagonists. It depicts men and women caught up in highly dramatic events, and these are presented in an approachable style. This means that the incidents described in the *Wu Yue chunqiu*, many of which were invented or changed beyond recognition by the author, have had a disproportionate effect on later accounts of this conflict.

A translation of the *Wu Yue chunqiu* into English has long been overdue.[16] There has previously been a complete translation of this novel into German—*Heldensagen aus dem unteren Yangtze-Tal* by Werner Eichhorn.[17] However, until recently, this novel has only been available to English-language readers in short excerpts given in anthologies and quotations found in studies of the history of this period. In addition to these scattered references, a translation of the first half of the book was produced in 1975 by John Lagerwey for his PhD thesis, but this has never been made available to a general audience.[18] This book is intended to give a literary translation of the text—one that attempts to render in English something of the artistic skill and linguistic flair of the original novel. Annotations are present but have been kept to a minimum; where necessary, reference is made to the most significant scholarship that has been produced in China on this text in the last forty years and to the archaeological studies that have revolutionized our understanding of both the historical events described and the context in which this novel was written. The first half of this book provides a discussion of the history of this text, its critical reception during the imperial era, and the narrative techniques employed to make it such an effective and influential account of the wars between Wu and Yue. In this introductory section, I will also explore the connections between the *Wu Yue chunqiu* and its source texts to demonstrate the way in which the latter have been adapted and transformed in the creation of the novel. The second half of the book comprises the complete translation of the *Wu Yue chunqiu*, with annotations to explain problematic passages, discuss important textual variants, and identify the historical individuals concerned.

---

16. This translation was completed in 2017; however, thanks to delays in publication, another translation was published first: see He (2021). My book represents a completely independent translation project.
17. Eichhorn (1969). Lagerwey (1993): 476 notes the problems with this translation.
18. Lagerwey (1975).

Textual History of the *Wu Yue chunqiu*

The present text of the *Wu Yue chunqiu* is attributed to the authorship of a man named Zhao Ye 趙曄 (fl. 60–80 CE). A very short biography of Zhao Ye appears in the "Rulin liezhuan" 儒林列傳 (Biographies of Confucian Scholars) chapter of the *Hou Hanshu* 後漢書 (History of the Later Han dynasty), which provides all the information that is known about him:

> Zhao Ye had the style name Changjun, and he was a native of Shanyin [County] in Kuaiji [Commandery]. As a young man, he served as prefectural clerk, but having received an order to go to meet the Local Inspector, Ye was insulted by his servants. Therefore, he simply walked away from [the Inspector's] chariot and horses. He moved to Zizhong [County] in Qianwei [Commandery], where he studied the Han recension of the *Shijing* (Book of Songs) under Du Fu (fl. 57–80) and became completely conversant in this academic tradition.[19] He was away for more than twenty years, and since he did not come back and there was no news of him, his family went into mourning. When Ye finished [his studies], he went home. [The administration] in this district summoned him for appointment as a Retainer, but he refused to go. Although he was recommended for office as a man of principle, he died at home. Ye wrote the *Wu Yue chunqiu*, and the *Shixi lishenyuan*

---

19. For the biography of this major scholar of the period; see *Hou Hanshu*, 69B.2573.

(Finer points of the *Book of Songs* with full explanations).[20] When Cai Yong (132–192) was in Kuaiji, he read the *Shixi* and sighed in amazement, because he considered this a finer piece of work than the *Lunheng* (Doctrines Weighed).[21] When Yong returned to the court, he ensured that it was transmitted, and scholars all recited it until they knew it off by heart.[22]

This biography provides a few useful pieces of information for understanding the cultural and intellectual context in which Zhao Ye lived and worked. First, he is said to be a native of Shanyin (modern-day Shaoxing 紹興), which five centuries earlier had been the site of King Goujian of Yue's capital city. As with many other people in the early imperial era who wrote about the wars between Wu and Yue, his interest is likely to have been the outcome of a strong sense of pride in the glorious history of his hometown.[23] (After the unification of China, Shaoxing would not be a capital again until after the fall of the Northern Song dynasty in 1126, when the first Southern Song emperor temporarily established his residence in this city.) Furthermore, Zhao Ye's connection with this place may have provided access to oral and written traditions that were not known to people from outside the Shanyin-Shaoxing area. The transmitted text of the *Wu Yue chunqiu* certainly contains a number of stories that are not recorded in other early accounts: these may represent local tales incorporated into the narrative. The *Hou Hanshu* also states that Zhao Ye was an expert in the *Shijing*—although this text is only quoted a couple of times in the *Wu Yue chunqiu*, the novel is nevertheless characterized throughout by a very strong interest in music and song. This book contains the lyrics of many songs; in addition, there are

---

20. The *Shixi lishenyuan* does not survive to the present day and is thought to have been lost in the medieval period.
21. The official biography of Cai Yong appears in *Hou Hanshu*, 60B.1979–2013. As perhaps the foremost scholar official of his time, with a particular interest in music, Cai Yong left the capital in 179 to live for a decade in the Wu-Yue region after his criticisms of eunuch involvement in the government led to serious political problems.
22. *Hou Hanshu*, 79B.2575.
23. Wei Qiao et al. (1980): 12. In addition, some scholars note the general increase in interest in the conflict between Wu and Yue at the beginning of the Eastern Han dynasty; these events were apparently felt to have important contemporary resonances; see Lin Xiaoyun (2012): 97. See also *Hou Hanshu*, 69A.2560.

a number of descriptions of musical performances and dramatic recitations of verse that serve to punctuate the narrative.[24] This unusual characteristic, not found in any of the earlier source texts, suggests a strong personal interest on the part of the author. Finally, the comparison of Zhao Ye's scholarly work to the *Lunheng* is also extremely interesting. Wang Chong 王充 (27–100 CE), the author of the *Lunheng*, was a scholar of extraordinary attainments, whose work demonstrates an original and inquiring mind.[25] Like Zhao Ye, he was a native of Kuaiji—indeed, Wang Chong seems to have been familiar with the work of a number of leading local scholars, most notably Yuan Kang 袁康 and Wu Ping 吳平, the compilers of the *Yuejue shu* 越絕書 (The Lost Histories of Yue), a text that is one of the most important sources for the *Wu Yue chunqiu*.[26] Whether these men were personally acquainted or not is not clear; however, the *Wu Yue chunqiu* certainly makes extensive use of the texts incorporated into the *Yuejue shu*, and the *Lunheng* appears to be the first book to mention the *Yuejue shu* and its compilers by name. In addition, although the *Lunheng* does not quote the *Wu Yue chunqiu* directly, it does make reference to stories known only from this novel, suggesting that Wang Chong can be considered its first recorded reader.

The interrelationship between the *Wu Yue chunqiu*, the *Yuejue shu*, and the *Lunheng* has proved extremely important for dating the core text of the first two works, both of which have suffered later rewriting and interpolation.[27] The *Lunheng* is generally agreed to have been compiled in its present

---

24. Some of the songs found in the *Wu Yue chunqiu* have parallels in other texts, but still appear to have been rewritten by the author, while others are unique to this novel and are assumed to be the original work of Zhao Ye; see Liu Xiaozhen (2009a) and Yu Shujuan (2010).
25. The official biography of Wang Chong is preserved in *Hou Hanshu*, 49.1629–30. Among other achievements, he is noted for his pioneering scholarship on meteorology and astronomy.
26. The *Yuejue shu* was originally attributed to various historical figures; however, in the Ming dynasty, the riddle that forms the conclusion of the final chapter of the book was solved to give the names of two compilers living in the early Eastern Han dynasty—Yuan Kang and Wu Ping. The solution of the riddle is given in a number of texts; see, for example, Yang Shen (1985): 79 and Tian Yiheng (1992): 309.
27. The rewriting of the *Yuejue shu* to bring it into line with the *Wu Yue chunqiu*, and vice versa, is considered in Qian Peiming (1956): 5–13. For a more general study of the way in which texts were tidied up from the Han dynasty onward, focusing on the *Shijing*, see Kern (2005).

form somewhere between 70 and 80 CE, though this text is thought to also include essays written some years earlier.[28] Since Wang Chong was such a major figure in the intellectual life of Kuaiji Commandery at this time, it is not surprising that he would have had access to writings by other scholars in the region. The references to stories from the *Wu Yue chunqiu* in the *Lunheng* mean that parts of this text were already in circulation by the period 70–80 CE and must be regarded as of early Eastern Han dynasty origin. The fact that the *Wu Yue chunqiu* draws extensively on the *Yuejue shu* also provides useful information about the date of composition of this novel. According to the descriptions of the editorial process found in the opening and closing chapters of this collection, the *Yuejue shu* was compiled in two stages. The earliest material, which forms the core of the compilation, was put together first, possibly by Yuan Kang—these are the *neijing* 內經 (inner canonical) and *neizhuan* 內傳 (inner tradition) chapters. Subsequently, a number of other short texts concerned with the history and culture of the kingdoms of Wu and Yue were collected by Wu Ping, and the text assumed its present form—these later additions form the *waizhuan* 外傳 (outer tradition) chapters.[29] Although the text repeatedly makes reference to the completion of the book during the reign of the Gengshi emperor of the Han dynasty 漢更始帝 (r. 23–25 CE), the "Ji Wudi" 記吳地 (Records of the Lands of Wu) chapter of the *Yuejue shu* contains the most recent date in the entire text, with a reference to the events of 52 CE.[30] The *Wu Yue chunqiu* contains extensive references to the *Yuejue shu*, as well as some direct quotations, and these are derived from *neijing*, *neizhuan*, and *weizhuan* chapters, indicating the author was familiar with Wu Ping's completed compilation and not just the earlier core text. It is most likely that the *Yuejue shu* only entered circulation sometime after 52 CE; therefore, the oldest parts of the *Wu Yue chunqiu* are most likely to have been written at some point between the years 50 and 70 CE.[31]

---

28. The dating of the *Lunheng* is considered in Pokora and Loewe (1993); see also Shao Yiping (2009) and Zhong Zhaopeng (1983).
29. The history of the compilation of the various texts that make up the *Yuejue shu* is discussed in detail in Milburn (2010): 37–52. This discussion extends the analysis of the dating of the chapters as a whole found in Zhou Shengchun (1991).
30. *Yuejue shu*, 20 ["Ji Wudi"].
31. Cao Lindi (1982), working with the same materials, suggests the most likely date of composition for the *Wu Yue chunqiu* would be the period 58–75 CE.

The *Wu Yue chunqiu* consists of ten chapters in total, five dealing with events from the perspective of the kingdom of Wu and five dealing with Yue. However, this novel is conventionally printed in two different recensions: there is a ten-*juan* 卷 (fascicle) version of the text and a six-*juan* version. These two formats are effectively identical, since both contain the same number of chapters, and the text is not changed. Nevertheless, the arrangement of one text into a different number of *juan* does point to underlying problems with the received text of the *Wu Yue chunqiu*. The first references to the *Wu Yue chunqiu* in bibliographical literature are found in the catalog of the imperial library preserved in the *Suishu* 隋書 (History of the Sui dynasty). This lists the *Wu Yue chunqiu* in twelve *juan* by Zhao Ye, as well as the *Wu Yue chunqiu xiaofan* 吳越春秋削繁 (Abridged *Spring and Autumn Annals of the Kingdoms of Wu and Yue*) in five *juan* by Yang Fang 楊方 (fl. early fourth century), and a text entitled the *Wu Yue chunqiu* 吳越春秋 in ten *juan* by Huangfu Zun 皇甫尊 (fl. seventh century).[32] The same books are listed in the two catalogs of the Tang imperial library, preserved in the dynastic histories, though in the catalog given in the *Xin Tangshu* 新唐書 (New history of the Tang dynasty), the title of Huangfu Zun's book is given as *Wu Yue chunqiu zhuan* 吳越春秋傳 (Tales from the *Spring and Autumn Annals of the Kingdoms of Wu and Yue*): this book title is also sometimes known as *Wu Yue chunqiu zhu* 吳越春秋注 (Commentary on the *Spring and Autumn Annals of the Kingdoms of Wu and Yue*).[33] The existence of these other two related texts has caused considerable difficulties for later scholars; for example, Yang Shen 楊慎 (1488–1559), in his reading notes, states: "The *Hanshu* says that Zhao Ye compiled the *Wu Yue chunqiu*. The *Jinshu* (sic) says that Yang Fang also compiled the *Wu Yue chunqiu*. Is the text

---

32. *Suishu*, 33.960. These are merely the works that ended up in the imperial library; Chen Qiaoyi (1984) cites three similar texts recorded elsewhere: the *Wu Yue chunqiu waiji* 吳越春秋外紀 (Further accounts of the *Spring and Autumn Annals of the Kingdoms of Wu and Yue*) by Zhang Xia 張遐 dated to the Eastern Han; an anonymous text in seven *juan* entitled *Wu Yue chunqiu*; and an anonymous work in one *juan* entitled *Wu Yue chunqiu cilu* 吳越春秋次錄 (Additional records of the *Spring and Autumn Annals of the Kingdoms of Wu and Yue*). Meanwhile, Zhou Shengchun (1996) adds another two further similar books: the *Wu Yue chunqiu* by Zhao Qi 趙歧 (108–201) and *Wu Yue chunqiu ji* 吳越春秋記 (Accounts from the *Spring and Autumn Annals of the Kingdoms of Wu and Yue*) by Guo Fen 郭頒 of the Western Jin dynasty.

33. *Jiu Tangshu*, 26.1993, and *Xin Tangshu*, 58.1463.

circulating today that by Ye? Or that by Fang?"[34] As a result of this kind of confusion, the received text of the *Wu Yue chunqiu* has sometimes been dismissed as a medieval compilation rather than a genuine early Eastern Han dynasty work. Further problems have been caused by the references to this novel found in the *Chongwen zongmu* 崇文總目 (General Index of the Chongwen Imperial Library) by Wang Yaochen 王堯臣 (1001–56). This records two versions of the *Wu Yue chunqiu*, both in ten *juan*. The first has a note appended stating that previous catalogs of the imperial library said that the *Wu Yue chunqiu* had twelve *juan*. This must refer to Zhao Ye's book. The second reference states that this version of the *Wu Yue chunqiu* was produced by Huangfu Zun: he edited together Zhao Ye's original text with Yang Fang's abridgment to produce a new book, also in ten *juan*.[35] Whether Wang Yaochen had access to information about the textual history of this version of the *Wu Yue chunqiu* that otherwise does not survive or whether he was just trying to suggest an explanation for why this novel existed in radically different formats is not clear. However, it appears that two distinct versions of the text in ten *juan* were circulating in the Song dynasty, one that was believed to be the same as that produced by Zhao Ye in the Eastern Han and one that was a medieval recompilation. Many people have subsequently leaped to the assumption that the text that survives today must be the medieval one and seem to be unaware that Wang Yaochen also reported the existence of a ten-*juan* version of the Han dynasty novel that he believed to be the same as the twelve-*juan* one. Furthermore, even if the transmitted text is the medieval recompilation by Huangfu Zun, this was apparently based on a reedited version of the Eastern Han dynasty text, and the antiquity of the core material should not be in doubt. In the absence of further archaeological discoveries, it is unlikely that we will ever know whether the transmitted text of the *Wu Yue chunqiu* is that written by Zhao Ye or not, so at present, opinions rest largely on vocabulary and matters of style: should the presence of the occasional unconnected anecdote and stories within stories incorporated into the narrative be considered as evidence of interpolation? Or should they be regarded as intrinsic to the text, with an Eastern Han dynasty author struggling to produce a lengthy and coherent work of prose fiction, at a time when this was still a new and innovative concept?

---

34. Yang Shen (1993): 47.367.
35. Wang Yaochen (1985): 58.

Quite apart from the problems with determining the nature of the transmitted text, the *Wu Yue chunqiu* may have suffered some textual loss, since a number of early encyclopedias provide quotations from this book that do not appear in the novel as it stands at present—many modern editions of the *Wu Yue chunqiu* give selected passages as a "Shiwen" 失文 (lost material) addendum. However, the existence of these lost quotations should not be regarded as intrinsically problematic. First, given that there seem to have been a number of different books known as the *Wu Yue chunqiu*, we cannot be sure that all these quotations are in fact derived from one and the same text. Second, the compilers of the *Siku quanshu tiyao* 四庫全書提要 (General catalog of the complete library of the four branches of literature), who accept the *Wu Yue chunqiu* as an Eastern Han dynasty text, note that there is no reason to question its authenticity on the basis of it having suffered some loss over the course of two millennia of transmission.[36] There are a number of reasons why the *Wu Yue chunqiu* should be treated as an Eastern Han dynasty text. First, even those who believe that the transmitted text is in fact the medieval compilation agree that this was based on and included elements from Zhao Ye's work, produced during the early Eastern Han. Second, the language of the book is largely consistent with an early Eastern Han dynasty date. Within the *Wu Yue chunqiu*, there are many details and vocabulary terms that are anachronistic when applied to the fifth-century BCE date of the events described, but there is little evidence of any post–Han dynasty terminology intruding.[37] It is worth emphasizing this point, since in other cases where Han dynasty material was reworked in the medieval period, there is evidence of significant linguistic change. Whatever alterations have occurred during transmission, in this instance, they have not affected the language of the text. Third, the *Wu Yue chunqiu* is structurally an extremely complicated text, with numerous intertextual references. It is difficult to imagine that in the event of a significant reworking of the text (even if this did not affect the language

---

36. Ji Yun et al. (2000): 1778.
37. This point is also made in Cao Lindi (1982): 72; however, it is not regarded as conclusive evidence of dating, since she suggests that the text may have been altered in the medieval period and then subsequently reworked again to remove anachronistic or inappropriate vocabulary. However, given the manifest difficulties of achieving this satisfactorily, the possibility that this is what happened to the *Wu Yue chunqiu* is exceedingly remote.

used), it would be possible to preserve this complex structure undisrupted.[38] Fourth, if this text was so radically altered as to lose two *juan* of material, as it was recast from a twelve-*juan* to a ten-*juan* text, there ought to be something missing from this story.[39] In fact, this is not the case: the only major events that are not described in any detail in the novel as it now stands are the death of King Helü and the subsequent campaign of revenge by King Fuchai, which led to King Goujian's surrender at Mount Kuaiji. Chronologically, these events should fit at the end of chapter 4 and the beginning of chapter 5, respectively; hence, they are unlikely to have constituted a separate *juan*. Furthermore, an account of the burial of King Helü of Wu and the surrender of the king of Yue both appear in "Shiwen" quotations, and if this is anything to go by, the *Wu Yue chunqiu* dealt with these events in a couple of lines.[40] Finally, given the existence of the same text in ten- and six-*juan* versions in modern times, it is surely not beyond the bounds of possibility that the twelve-*juan* version simply involved splitting the same material somewhat differently. Here it is perhaps worth noting that chapters 5 and 10 of the present text are significantly longer than any others in the book and would be obvious candidates for division should the aim be to achieve a more equal chapter length. For these reasons, in the discussion of this novel given below, the book will be treated as an early Eastern Han dynasty text, and for convenience, Zhao Ye will be described as the author.

---

38. Liang Zonghua (1988), who accepts the theory that the present transmitted text is the Huangfu Zun medieval reworking, makes a similar point—the structure of the novel as it survives today argues for very minimal intervention.
39. Qian Fu 錢福, in his "Chongkan *Wu Yue chunqiu* xu" 重刊吳越春秋序 (Preface on the republication of the *Spring and Autumn Annals of the Kingdoms of Wu and Yue*), suggests that two *juan* are indeed missing from the transmitted text: one tentatively entitled "Xi Shi zhi zhi Wu" 西施之至吳 (Xi Shi's arrival in Wu) and the other entitled "Fan Li zhi qu Yue" 范蠡之去越 (Fan Li's departure from Yue); see Qian Gu (1935): 1.55a. The problem with this theory is that there is no evidence that there was ever significant coverage of these two topics in this novel, and therefore, it appears to be pure fantasy on the author's part. Nevertheless, Qian Fu's idea has had some support from modern scholars; see for example Feng Kunwu (2000).
40. In both cases, these quotations are originally derived from the Tang dynasty encyclopedia, the *Yiwen leiju* 藝文類聚 (Collection of literature arranged by categories); see Ouyang Xun (2007): 8.141 and 96.1672, respectively.

The *Wu Yue chunqiu* has traditionally been classified as a work of history and appears as such in early library catalogs, categorized as a miscellaneous work (*zashi* 雜史). In modern times, it has become common to describe it as a work of fiction (*xiaoshuo* 小說), comparable to other such early prose texts as the *Mu Tianzi zhuan* 穆天子傳 (Tale of Mu, the Son of Heaven) or the *Yan Danzi* 燕丹子 (Prince Dan of Yan).[41] The *Wu Yue chunqiu* differs from these in its much greater length, more complex plot, and great narrative skill in building psychologically plausible characters. Indeed, those modern scholars who categorize it as fiction have frequently chosen to describe it as the earliest *yanyi* 演義 (historical romance) or some other similar term.[42] This categorization has not yet achieved universal acceptance: there are still many scholars today who choose to view the *Wu Yue chunqiu* as a historical text and thus ignore the fictional elements, as though swordsmiths regularly forged magical weapons in the kingdom of Wu and men often transformed themselves into gibbons in the forests of Yue. These kinds of elements in the *Wu Yue chunqiu* have generally been passed over in silence by those who accept this as a historical work, or excuses have been found to avoid having to take them into account.[43] For example, in the Ming dynasty, the great scholar and compiler of the history of the previous dynasty, Song Lian 宋濂 (1310–81), discussing the similarities in the fictional qualities of the *Yan Danzi* and the *Wu Yue chunqiu*, chose to consider both texts as fundamentally historical in nature: "Researching these matters [and comparing them] to the *Records of the Grand Historian* of Sima Qian, they are almost always the same . . . the theory that [Sima] Qian cut these sections and removed

---

41. In late imperial sources, the *Wu Yue chunqiu* was still classified as history, but the fictional elements were increasingly stressed; see, for example, Ji Yun et al. (2000): 1779, which describes it as "nearly a novel" (*jin xiaoshuojia yan* 近小説家言). The same point is made in Wang Hengzhan (1999): 140–41. See also Yang Yi (1995): 84–89 for a comparison between the *Wu Yue chunqiu* and the *Yan Danzi* as early works of fiction on the theme of revenge.
42. Cao Lindi (1984).
43. This kind of practice occasionally results in bizarre works of scholarship, such as Chen Ying (1998): 24–26, where the *Yan Danzi* is described as the first work of Chinese fiction in the *wuxia* martial arts tradition, and then the discussion moves on smartly to the story of Gan Jiang 干將 and Mo Ye 莫邪 as it is given in the *Soushen ji* 搜神記 (Records in Search of the Supernatural) by Gan Bao 干寶 (286–336), ignoring entirely the fact that these characters appear first in the *Wu Yue chunqiu*!

them [from his own work] may well be correct."[44] The suggestion that what might otherwise be troublingly fictional passages were originally derived from sources incorporated into one of the most esteemed works of history in China allows Song Lian to ignore them. In modern times, some scholars have continued to dismiss these sections of the novel as "folklore," as if that means that the factual nature of the text can go unquestioned, although it is known to have been written many hundreds of years after the events occurred and contains many errors and anachronisms and any comparison with its source texts will reveal that in a choice between making a good story and sticking to the facts, the author of the *Wu Yue chunqiu* always chose the former course.

In this analysis, the *Wu Yue chunqiu* is consistently described as a novel. This classification is proposed in light of the recategorization of many other ancient works of literature from around the world that have also come to be described as novels during the course of the last fifty years: a development ultimately provoked by archaeological discoveries revealing just how old the roots of lengthy works of prose fiction really are.[45] The *Wu Yue chunqiu* is far from being the world's oldest novel, but it is the earliest-surviving work of Chinese literature that represents a sustained fictional narrative, written in prose, with strongly individualized characters who develop as the plot unfolds—that is the definition of a novel.[46] As with many other ancient cultures, China lacked a word for such works of literature, and hence, applying the term "novel" to such writings is anachronistic but also unavoidable.[47] By considering this text as a novel, the *Wu Yue chunqiu* assumes its proper place in the history of the development of Chinese fictional narratives as a significantly longer and more complex work than any other that survives from the pre- or early imperial era. Furthermore, the *Wu Yue chunqiu* is a historical novel—a

---

44. Song Lian (1983): 27.69b.
45. The process of recognizing ancient prose fiction as "novels" has been complex, and a vast literature exists on the subject. For useful overviews of the field, see, for example, Doody (1996), Whitmarsh (2008), and Bowie (1985). The importance of excavated fragments for demonstrating something of the range of ancient prose fiction that has been lost is considered in Stephens and Winkler (1995).
46. This broad characterization of what makes a novel is taken from Swain (2011).
47. The importance of applying modern terminology to ancient concepts, even when this might be considered anachronistic, is considered in detail in Futre Pinheiro (2014).

term that requires further clarification.[48] Here I follow the four defining characteristics proposed by Thomas Hägg when studying ancient Greek historical novels: time, characters, setting, and truth.[49] Time refers to the era in which the historical novel is set: this background must be the subject of research and not of memory. Characters refer to the presence of genuine historical individuals within the narrative, whether as major or minor protagonists. Setting indicates that historical events are not merely referenced in passing but form an integral part of the narrative and play a role in the character development of the protagonists. Finally, truth implies that the novel should not merely have a surface accuracy in the details but convince the reader that they are discovering something about the personalities of a different age. On all four counts, the *Wu Yue chunqiu* has to be considered a historical novel. It was written at least five hundred years after the events described. It incorporates characters such as the kings of Wu and Yue who are undoubtedly historical individuals. The events of the rise and fall of the kingdom of Wu are integral to the development of the various characters: the sufferings of King Goujian of Yue as a prisoner of war are portrayed as crucial in hardening his resolve to seek revenge. Finally, the world described in this novel is that of the late Spring and Autumn period, which by the time of the Eastern Han would have been unutterably alien, and the author does not flinch from including details that would have struck early imperial readers as strange—for example, the endless bloody conflicts between the neighboring kingdoms of Chu, Wu, and Yue had by this time long been confined to the past, yet here they form the cornerstone of the plot.

Much work remains to be done on the connections between the *Wu Yue chunqiu* and later works of fiction—at present, in studies of the history of Chinese literature, this novel is frequently simply cited on its own as an extremely early example of fiction writing, with little attempt to trace its influence on later writings about the conflict between Wu and Yue or indeed on other historical novels. An exception to this rule seems to be scholars interested in the relationship between this text and imperial-era martial arts (*wuxia* 武俠) fiction: a number of fine studies of the influence of the *Wu Yue*

---

48. Some Chinese scholars have also used the term "historical novel" (*lishi xiaoshuo* 歷史小說) to describe the *Wu Yue chunqiu*; see, for example, Huang Rensheng (1994).
49. Hägg (1987).

chunqiu on later novels and short stories have been produced.[50] It is possible that this lack of scholarship on the importance of this text in the history of Chinese fiction writing is partly due to the traditional characterization of this novel as a work of history, partly due to concerns over the date of its composition and uncertainties over whether it should be regarded as a genuine Eastern Han dynasty text or not, and partly due to the fact that no work of Chinese literature of comparable complexity would be produced until many centuries later.

---

50. For studies of the *Wu Yue chunqiu* and its influence on the history of *wuxia* fiction, see Liu (1967), Liang Qi (2006), and Zhang Chouping (2005).

The Reception of the *Wu Yue chunqiu*

A truly vast number of quotations from the *Wu Yue chunqiu* are preserved in the scholarship on other ancient texts and in medieval encyclopedias. These quotations are important, because many people who did not read the novel as a whole nevertheless became familiar with the most dramatic events and certain famous phrases or passages in this way. However, there are no surviving early commentaries or discussions of the text—the earliest commentary by Xu Tianhu 徐天祜 (*jinshi* 1262) dates to the Yuan dynasty and is associated with what is today the oldest-surviving version of the text.[51] As a result of this paucity, baffling as it is in light of the subsequent popularity of this novel, there are very few early accounts of the way in which the *Wu Yue chunqiu* was understood and interpreted by its readers. Therefore, the handful of surviving writings on this subject, most of which date to the late imperial era, are of particular importance for understanding the reception of this novel. The earliest writing recording the impressions of a reader is the poem entitled "Du *Wu Yue chunqiu*" 讀吳越春秋 (On reading the *Spring and Autumn Annals of the Kingdoms of Wu and Yue*) by Guanxiu 貫休 (832–912), which is preserved in his collected works, the *Chanyue ji* 禪月集 (Collected writings by the [Great Master of the] Chan Moon):

> People like [the kings of] Wu and Yue really should have been ashamed of themselves!

---

51. Xu Tianhu (1999). This recension is supposed to be based on various Song dynasty printings of the text that Xu Tianhu had access to; these have not survived.

> They turned their back on virtue, betrayed their allies, and
> believed slanderous gossip.
> Chancellor Pi, with just one conversation, was able to kill
> Wu [Zixu],
> Grandee [Zhong] came up with seven stratagems but only
> needed three.
> After their victory when toasts were offered, the songs flew like
> snowflakes [through the air],
> Who would have begrudged [Fan Li] his little boat when the
> waters ran so blue?
> Where are your plans for world domination today?
> Wildflowers here cover the spring paths as birds twitter
> and sing.[52]

Although Guanxiu's poem purports to be about the experience of reading, this poem is very closely related to the format associated with the genre of *huaigu* 懷古 (cherishing antiquity) verse, which takes as its subject a visit to a site of historical importance. *Huaigu* verse allows the poet to describe the stirring events that occurred at a particular location and then contrast this with the conditions prevalent in their own time, usually emphasizing desolation, loneliness, ruin, and loss.[53] In this way, the unity of place provides a poignant juxtaposition with the disjunction in time. This early poem on the subject of reading the *Wu Yue chunqiu* dates to the Five Dynasties and Ten Kingdoms period—later on, this was not a popular topic, possibly because of increasing concerns in this period about the authenticity of the text. It should be stressed that throughout much of the imperial era, the literati elite most likely knew of the contents of the *Wu Yue chunqiu* only through quotations or second- and thirdhand through other works of literature that it had inspired; hence, it is entirely possible that reading the whole novel was something left only to devoted fans. Subsequently, in the Ming dynasty,

---

52. Guanxiu (1985): 20.107. Guanxiu seems to have written a number of poems on the experience of reading literature, including the *Lisao* 離騷 (Encountering Sorrow), the collected works of Meng Jiao 孟郊 (751–814), and the *Xuanzong xing Shu ji* 玄宗幸蜀記 (Record of Xuanzong's journey to Shu).
53. To quote Paul Rouzer, *huaigu* is a "personal response to an ancient site," while *yongshi* 詠史 (poetry on history) is a "moral and political evaluation of events"; see Rouzer (1993): 95. For an in-depth analysis of this important literary theme, see Owen (1986).

a further small group of poetic works was produced that reflected on the experience of reading the whole book rather than merely selected passages. One such poem is the "Du *Wu Yue chunqiu*" composed by Wang Guangyang 汪廣洋 (d. 1379): for this minister, who played a key role in the founding of the Ming dynasty, the power struggles between different factions at court may well have resulted in a very personal reading of the novel.[54] Certainly the emphasis on the character of Fan Li, who saved his own life by leaving the service of King Goujian of Yue and going into reclusion, suggests that his determination to avoid conflict seems to have had a powerful message for a minister who by all accounts was both exceptionally competent and honest and yet found himself repeatedly demoted thanks to the machinations of his rivals. Wang Guangyang's admiration for Fan Li seems unusual; this is not an aspect of the novel that other late imperial readers of the *Wu Yue chunqiu* particularly chose to comment on:[55]

> Before the blood taken at the covenant is even dry, the campaign of revenge begins again.
> It is this lack of sincerity that defines the Eastern Zhou.
> Fuchai only cared about lovely ladies and sycophants;[56]
> So Goujian was the only person who could employ wise ministers.
> Having returned from Zuili, he expanded his territories,
> Thus, deer came to wander at the Gusu Tower.
> Persons of refinement can only admire Lord Zhu of Tao:[57]
> Setting out in a tiny boat across a vast expanse of billowing waves.[58]

---

54. The official biography of Wang Guangyang is given in *Mingshi*, 127. 3773–76.
55. There are a significant number of poems by Wang Guangyang that testify to his interest in the history of the Wu-Yue region and the key personalities of the conflict between these two kingdoms; his other writings include the "Fan Li miao" 范蠡廟 (The Fan Li Temple) and "Gusu Tai you gan" 姑蘇臺有感 (Emotions upon [visiting] the Gusu Tower).
56. Appropriately enough, the term here used for sycophants is originally derived from the *Wu Yue chunqiu*, where it is used to describe Chancellor Bo Pi 伯嚭, whom the text constantly criticizes for flattering and fawning on King Fuchai of Wu.
57. According to the *Shiji*, 41.1752–53, Lord Zhu of Tao was one of the identities assumed by Fan Li after he left the court of Yue, to preserve his anonymity.
58. Wang Guangyang (1991): 7.1a–1b.

There is every reason to think that Wang Guangyang saw a reflection of his own experience in the notorious injustices inflicted by the monarchs of Wu and Yue on their government officials. However, other Ming dynasty writers addressing the topic of reading the *Wu Yue chunqiu* clearly did so for quite different reasons. In the mid-Ming period, a large number of writings about the history and culture of the Wu-Yue region were produced by the *Wu menpai* 吳門派, under the auspices of important local patrons such as Wang Ao 王鏊 (1449–1524, *jinshi* 1475) and Wu Kuan 吳寬 (1435–1504, *jinshi* 1472), and many of these show a strong interest in the account of the wars between Wu and Yue given in this novel.[59] The final example of a poem about reading the *Wu Yue chunqiu* comes from this literary coterie and was produced by Shen Zhou 沈周 (1427–1509), a senior figure in the *Wu menpai*.[60] From the tenor of the contents, it is very likely that it was inspired not so much by the contents of the *Wu Yue chunqiu* itself as by an awareness of earlier poems on the same topic; however, it is unusual for anchoring the opening lines so very firmly in the experience of reading:

> On a spring day, all alone, but for the wind and rain
> By the window I open my book, oblivious to my own aging.
> In this text there is constant fighting, and resurgence after loss,
> An ancient kingdom where small-minded people [destroy others] with their gossip.
> As for the towers of Yue, I hear that deer really do walk there,
> While the ruins of Wu are in truth covered in paulownia trees today.
> I feel even more sorrowful that [Zi]xu and Zhong both killed themselves,
> Once the enemy was destroyed and their plots were useless, they met with the same disaster.[61]

---

59. Although the *Wu menpai* is now most famous for the paintings they produced, important publications on local history by this group include the *Gusu zhi* 姑蘇志 (Gazetteer for Gusu [Suzhou]) and *Zhenze bian* 震澤編 (Edited writings on the Trembling Marsh [Lake Tai]), produced under the auspices of Wang Ao, and the *Huqiushan zhi* 虎丘山志 (Gazetteer for Tiger Hill) by Wen Zhaozhi 文肇祉 (1519–87). See Milburn (2009) and Clunas (1996): 135–36.
60. The various commissions that Shen Zhou received from Wang Ao in particular are detailed in Ruan Rongchun (1996): 49–50.
61. Shen Zhou (1991): 5.614.

In addition to poems about the experience of reading the *Wu Yue chunqiu*, another important source of information about the reception of this novel lies in the prefaces that this book has accumulated over time. There are two important prefaces to the text: the first, the "*Wu Yue chunqiu* xu" 吳越春秋序 (Preface to the *Spring and Autumn Annals of the Kingdoms of Wu and Yue*) produced by Xu Tianhu when he compiled the earliest-surviving edition of the text in 1306; and the second, entitled "Chongkan *Wu Yue chunqiu* xu" 重刊吳越春秋序 (Preface on the reprinting of the *Spring and Autumn Annals of the Kingdoms of Wu and Yue*) by Qian Fu 錢福 (1461–1504, *jinshi* 1490) in 1501. In the opening section of the Yuan dynasty preface, Xu Tianhu particularly emphasizes the righteousness of the behavior of the monarchs of both Wu and Yue—an unusual reading of events that takes scant account of the actual contents of the *Wu Yue chunqiu*. This account draws on the traditions explored in the opening chapters of each half of the novel concerning the distinguished ancestry of the two royal houses and thus argues that the claims consistently made in Chinese ancient texts about the poverty and backwardness of Wu and Yue were grossly exaggerated:

> In antiquity, Wu and Yue were considered remote and backward countries located in the southeast; however, when they became powerful, they were in every way the equal of the Upper States.[62] At the meeting at Huangchi, Fuchai wanted to show his respect for the [Zhou] Son of Heaven, and so he omitted the [royal] title that he had usurped, and called himself an "Unratified Ruler" when he gave his commands to the other lords.[63] Likewise when Yue conquered Wu, Goujian held a great covenant involving four states, in order to show his support for the royal house.[64] The key to their ambitions lay

---

62. The rulers of Wu and Yue frequently used the term "Upper States" (*shangguo* 上國) to refer to the Zhou confederacy; see, for example, *Zuozhuan*, 835 [Cheng 7].
63. The title here translated as "Unratified Ruler" (*zi* 子) was applied to monarchs from outside the Huaxia realm in their dealings with the Zhou king and his aristocracy, to stress the distinctions between those inside and outside the confederacy; see *Gongyang zhuan*, 614–16 [Ai 13]. For a study of the terminology applied to the kings of Wu and the dissatisfaction expressed by King Fuchai that his royal title was not recognized, see Wu Enpei (2010).
64. King Goujian's efforts to offer tribute to the Zhou king and make other gestures of respect are mentioned in *Shiji*, 41.1746.

in giving their allegiance to Zhou: they knew what was right! When Confucius wrote the *Chunqiu* (Spring and Autumn Annals), even [the affairs of] a small country were documented and turned into a book.[65] How much more important are the descendants of the Sage-King Yu, and Houji (Lord Millet), who occupied the lands of Kuaiji and Juqu (Lake Tai) with their rivers and their watersheds, which the geographers of the Zhou dynasty stated to be the most important of the Nine Regions, and who have both dominated the entire world! How can their records be lost and not transmitted?[66]

Having made this strong claim for the reader's attention, Xu Tianhu then goes on to consider the ongoing value of reading the *Wu Yue chunqiu* thanks to the lesson that these historical events provide. Although many scholars have expressed great concern about the troubling behavior of the characters in this novel, and strong criticism of the morality of their actions is no doubt justified, Xu Tianhu nevertheless argues that there is a valuable message here. Given that these problems are elided by his earlier assertion that any action on the part of the members of the ruling elite of Wu and Yue may be considered morally justified because of their ongoing support for the Zhou royal family, it is possible to completely avoid the question of whether the main protagonists of the *Wu Yue chunqiu* offer suitable exemplars for later generations to study and emulate: "In this account, by making use of the plans [put forward by] Zhong, Fan Li and the other grandees, [King Goujian] become hegemon; while failing to listen to the remonstrance offered by [Wu] Zixu resulted in disaster [for King Fuchai]. Given how fresh and lively [this narrative is], it can encourage and warn people for many generations to come. Surely this is not merely the story of a country that existed two thousand years ago!"[67]

The preface by Qian Fu, written some two hundred years later, expresses quite different concerns. In particular, Qian Fu was clearly much puzzled

---

65. Given the prestige attached to the *Chunqiu* 春秋 (Spring and Autumn Annals), an annalistic history supposed to have been edited by Confucius, it is not surprising that there were many historical and pseudo-historical works that adopted the same title in the early imperial era; see Xu Fuguan (1989): 265.
66. Quoted in Xu Tianhu (1999): 1.
67. Quoted in Xu Tianhu (1999): 2.

The Reception of the *Wu Yue chunqiu* | xxxiii

by the contents of the *Wu Yue chunqiu*, which he regarded as quite different from other surviving Han dynasty literature with which he was familiar. He begins his list of problems by puzzling over the strong narrative line: "its words and phrases sometimes seem like a novel."[68] Although in modern times this problem has been resolved for some scholars by simply changing the categorization of the *Wu Yue chunqiu* from "history" to "historical novel," in the Ming dynasty, this development had not yet taken place. Qian Fu then goes on to express other concerns about the nature of the contents of this book—in particular, the many references to mysticism and prophecy—and the nomenclature accorded to the different chapters, which appears to give priority to Wu:

> Although there are many stories appended which belong to esoteric traditions, or which speak of dream divination and other mantic techniques, this was something that definitely still existed at this time [in the Han dynasty], and *Zuo's Tradition of the Spring and Autumn Annals* also contains many records of this kind of thing, so you cannot say that it is entirely without precedent. [Zhao Ye] praises the many wise ministers in Yue in order to add luster to the former capital city, yet in his writings, he makes Wu the "inner" and Yue the "outer," which is simply impossible to understand.[69]

However, although these passages in the text were evidently troubling for this Ming dynasty scholar, he could not deny the appealing qualities of the narrative. In the conclusion of the "Chongkan *Wu Yue chunqiu* xu," he lists some of his favorite characters in the novel and mentions some of the scenes that he most admired:

> As for what is recorded in this book, such as the loyalty of [Wu Zi]xu, the wisdom of [Fan] Li, the planning ability of [Grandee] Zhong, the account of the military strategies of [Shen] Baoxu, or the training of troops by Sun Wu, the discussion of

---

68. Quoted in Qian Gu (1935): 1.55a.
69. Quoted in Qian Gu (1935): 1.55a–55b. Modern scholars have shown much puzzlement over this chapter's terminology, which would clearly imply that Wu is being considered more important; see Xu Diancai (2007) and Jin Qizhen (2000).

swordsmanship by the Yue Maiden, the description of a crossbow given by Chen Yin, King Goujian's appalling suffering, the scene where he ends his servitude in Wu, the warnings he gives when he begins his attack on Wu, the promises made by his five Grandees—how can we be without them? ... This book records how [King Goujian] leaned against the bar of his chariot in respect for an angry frog, and this was enough to encourage his soldiers: how much better to read this book and discuss their world! Anyone who does not find themselves moved, isn't really a man![70]

The *Wu Yue chunqiu* is a book that has always attracted devoted fans; unfortunately, this has not been matched by attracting equally serious scholarship on the importance of this novel in the development of Chinese fiction writing. Part of the problem, no doubt, is the difficulty of fitting this exceptionally well-written and complex narrative into any kind of linear history of the Chinese novel, given that no comparable work would be produced until much later. However, the lack of other equally fine novels dating to the Han dynasty does not in any way invalidate the importance and influence of this great book.

---

70. Quoted in Qian Gu (1935): 1.56a–57b.

Narrative in the *Wu Yue chunqiu*

Any discussion of the narrative techniques employed in the *Wu Yue chunqiu* must begin with a consideration of the sources used in this novel because it is by appreciating the differences between the source texts and the finished novel that the author's skill in handling his material can be understood. As close reading of the *Wu Yue chunqiu* makes clear, the author had access to a wide range of source texts, many of which can be conclusively identified. Among ancient classical texts, in addition to the *Shijing*, Zhao Ye also cites the *Yijing* 易經 (Book of Changes) and the *Shangshu* 尚書 (Book of Documents). For historical sources, he draws on the *Zuozhuan* 左傳 (Zuo's Tradition), the *Guoyu* 國語 (Tales of the states of the Eastern Zhou dynasty), the *Shiji* 史記 (Records of the Grand Historian), and the *Yuejue shu*. He also quotes a number of preunification philosophical texts, such as the *Mengzi* 孟子 (Mencius) and the *Han Feizi* 韓非子 (Book of Master Han Fei). In addition to these sources, the author also utilizes a number of Han dynasty collections of earlier material that had been compiled in the imperial library, such as the *Xinxu* 新序 (New Prefaces) and *Shuoyuan* 說苑 (Garden of Stories). This is an extremely impressive list of source material—in fact, the author seems to have made use of every known transmitted text that documents the history of the kingdoms of Wu and Yue. It is not at all clear how Zhao Ye would have obtained access to all these books, given that his entire recorded life was spent in either Kuaiji or Qianwei Commanderies. Either these texts were significantly more widely diffused by the beginning of the Eastern Han dynasty than has previously been recognized or Zhao Ye's biography has failed to document an extended stay in the capital city: the one place where all these books would have been readily available to readers.[71] An understanding of the diversity of his source material is also important to appreciate the literary skill the author demonstrated in constructing his narrative—these various disparate sources have been knitted together into a powerful tale of relentless brutality in the quest for revenge. The *Wu Yue chunqiu* frequently places events out of their proper date order so as to provide a more effective narrative and also changes the account to make them much more dramatic: many of the most famous incidents in the conflict between Wu and Yue are actually derived from this novel and are not historical facts. It is well known that there is a significant increase in the level of brutality recorded in the *Wu Yue chunqiu* compared with earlier accounts; for example, older texts do not say that Prince Qingji of Wu was assassinated nor that Yao Li 要離 committed suicide out of shame because he had allowed his wife and children to be murdered nor that Grandee Zhong was eventually ordered to commit suicide by King Goujian of Yue after his ultimate victory. In addition to significantly increasing the level of violence experienced by his characters, Zhao Ye also frequently takes an event that is recorded in ancient texts and incorporates it into his novel, but the details are changed to make it more shocking to the reader and more dramatic in tone; thus, earlier works mention the humiliations experienced by King Goujian of Yue when a prisoner of war in Wu, but they do not say that he was forced to taste King Fuchai's diarrhea to convince him of his subjection. Furthermore, the author shows a particular penchant for ending the description of a confrontation between his characters with one protagonist asking a rhetorical question, which highlights the ethical dilemma or difficulty that he is faced with. This kind of narrative technique is not found in any of the source texts.

In addition to the material for which a source can be determined, there are also many passages in the *Wu Yue chunqiu* for which there is no known origin. Occasionally, this results in particular problems of interpretation, as can be seen from the numerous references to divination by day and hour

---

71. Liang Zonghua (1993) suggests that Zhao Ye may have gone with his teacher to Chang'an in 54 CE, when Du Fu was summoned to serve on the staff of Liu Cang, the king of Dongping 東平王劉蒼 (fl. 39–83 CE), the brother of Emperor Ming of the Han dynasty 漢明帝 (r. 57–75 CE). This suggestion has then been repeated as fact in some subsequent publications; see, for example, Knechtges and Shih (2010–14): 1385. That Du Fu did indeed move to the capital for a short time is recorded in *Hou Hanshu*, 79B.2573; however, nowhere does it state that Zhao Ye went with him, nor do we know exactly when Zhao Ye was Du Fu's student.

found in this book. These references are unique to the *Wu Yue chunqiu*—although there are various descriptions of different kinds of divination performed in Wu and Yue in other texts that document these kingdoms, they are unrelated to this kind of practice.[72] Han dynasty texts often mention that the people of the Kuaiji region were considered unusually superstitious and interested in mantic techniques: judging by this novel, this reputation is justified.[73] The *Wu Yue chunqiu* makes particular reference to two divination traditions (or perhaps books; it is not clear): one is called the *Yumen* 玉門 (Jade Gate) and the other the *Jinkui* 金匱 (Metal Casket). The former is otherwise completely unknown; in the case of the latter, some scholars have suggested a relationship with the *Huangdi jinhui yuheng jing* 皇帝金匱玉衡經 (Yellow Sovereign's Classic of the Metal Casket and Jade Scales)—a text that survives to the present day as part of the Daoist canon—while others argue that the *Huangdi jinhui yuheng jing* bears a mere superficial resemblance to the contents of the *Wu Yue chunqiu* and that this is the result of some common terminology.[74] It is certainly true to say that the author of the *Wu Yue chunqiu* considered divination to be an extremely important subject within his novel; hence, there are frequent references to astrology, divination according to hour and day, and also the interpretation of dreams. Recent archaeological excavations have shown that almanacs of auspicious and inauspicious days were common in the early imperial era; Han dynasty *rishu* 日書 or "daybooks" and other almanacs recording lucky and unlucky days have been excavated at Dunhuang, Juyan 居延, and Kongjiapo 孔家坡 among others.[75] However, so far, there has been no published discovery of any Qin or Han daybook that bears a demonstrably close relationship with the divinations given in the *Wu Yue chunqiu*, and the lack of understanding

---

72. *Yuejue shu*, 73–78 ["Ji Wuwang zhan meng" 記吳王占夢], describes dream divination, and 86–89 ["Ji junqi" 記軍氣] discusses military auras (*qi* 氣) and the constellations associated with particular kingdoms and states in the late Spring and Autumn period. In excavated material, the *Gailu* contains an account of various different astrological techniques used in determining auspicious days and directions for battle; for a study of this material, see Tian Xudong (2002) and Wang Sanxia (2008).
73. See, for example, *Fengsu tongyi*, 401 ["Guaishen" 怪神].
74. For an example of the former position, see Zhang Jue (2006) and Schipper and Verellen (2004): 86; for the latter, see Liu Xiaozhen (2009b).
75. Wei Desheng (2000), Hu Wenhui (1995), and Hubeisheng wenwu kaogu yanjiusuo and Suizhoushi kaogudui (2006): 129–85.

of these techniques means that any translation of these sections can only be tentative.

In its present form, the *Wu Yue chunqiu* consists of ten chapters, five devoted to the subject of the kingdom of Wu and five to the kingdom of Yue. Throughout the novel, the author creates the impression of impartiality, and this is embedded in the structure of the *Wu Yue chunqiu*: the two kingdoms receive equal space and attention, and the focus in each half is on the point of view of that country, meaning that the other becomes the enemy. This way of arranging the text is likely to be ultimately derived from historical texts, such as the "Shijia" 世家 (Hereditary Houses) section of the *Shiji*, or the division of material by country of origin found in the *Guoyu*, although in the *Wu Yue chunqiu*, the contrast in perspective is sharpened by the fact that only two kingdoms are considered rather than the many different states (fifteen in the *Shiji*, and eight in the *Guoyu*) recorded in these earlier historical texts. The feeling of authorial impartiality is further enhanced by the approach taken in the first chapter of each half, which focuses on the founding of the kingdom: the royal houses of both Wu and Yue are accorded an incredibly distinguished ancestry, traced back to culture heroes of enormous significance to East Asian civilization.[76] By opening with this kind of description, the author emphasizes that in this respect, he sees them as equal.

While it is true that the author of the *Wu Yue chunqiu* does not present the conflict between these two ancient kingdoms as a black-and-white one, with one side right and the other wrong, this is not an impartial account, and the way in which the author's perspective has influenced later understanding of the wars between Wu and Yue has often been misunderstood. Throughout his novel, Zhao Ye repeatedly returns to one unifying theme: Wu should have crushed Yue. The fact that they failed to do so is their own fault, and by refusing to destroy his enemy, King Fuchai signed his own death warrant. The author—writing some five centuries after the events described—does not support one side or the other, but he does present a very strong underlying theme in the narrative: in the 490s BCE, various individuals in the governments of both Wu and Yue decided that the fighting could only be resolved by eliminating the enemy, and this result took some

---

[76]. For an analysis of the importance of this narrative technique, which is also found in other major works of Han dynasty literature like the *Shiji*, see Zhang Yi (2004): 129.

twenty years to achieve. Throughout the *Wu Yue chunqiu*, these people are presented as being in the right. Any protagonist seeking some other kind of outcome, such as peaceful coexistence or one country accepting protectorate status from the other, is consistently shown to be in the wrong: the novel depicts them as stupid or corrupt or willfully blind to the realities of the situation. Since the *Wu Yue chunqiu* is much easier to read than earlier historical texts concerning this conflict, and the narrative is presented in a very accessible way, many scholars for the last two thousand years have had their understanding of these events warped by Zhao Ye's highly persuasive account and thus ignore the fact that right until the final conquest, other options remained available, and senior government figures on both sides attempted to explore them.

Having established the antiquity and distinguished ancestry of both the Wu and Yue royal families in the opening chapter of each section, the narrative does not immediately move on to cover the conflict between the two kingdoms. Instead, chapters 2 and 7, though very different in format and content, are linked by a common theme of missed opportunities. Chapter 2 takes as its subject the vexed topic of inheritance within the kingdom of Wu; King Shoumeng 吳王壽夢 (r. 586–561 BCE) wished the throne to go to each of his four sons in turn in order that it might be ultimately inherited by his youngest and favorite son, Prince Jizha 王子季札, but the prince refused to accept this arrangement and thus unleashed an orgy of violence within the ruling family as the other princes murdered each other and attempted to establish themselves as king—King Helü was the ultimate victor in this long-drawn-out struggle. In the absence of any clear heir to the throne, and with a number of equally qualified princes eager to take power, such violence was inevitable. The narrative at this juncture emphasizes that Prince Jizha was not merely the rightful heir, he is also the wisest of all the princes and would have made the most virtuous of kings. His repeated refusals to take the throne therefore forced the kingdom of Wu onto a different trajectory, which resulted ultimately in the downfall of the country. Chapter 7, by contrast, focuses on a very different set of missed opportunities, in that it describes the years King Goujian spent as a prisoner of war in Wu. The author presents King Fuchai being warned repeatedly of the consequences of allowing King Goujian of Yue to return alive to his kingdom; every opportunity to avert the coming disaster is thwarted by the king's decision to save his bitterest enemy. Again, this chapter serves to set the stage for the coming catastrophe: at each stage when something could have been done to prevent it, the king is distracted from his purpose. This structure allows the remaining chapters of the Yue section of the novel to form a narrative arc, moving inexorably from the depths of despair to ultimate victory. Indeed, in terms of the highly sophisticated presentation of a single chapter of the novel, chapter 7 is probably the finest in the entire book: the opening section, in which the religious ceremony blessing the king of Yue before he sets out on his dangerous journey to Wu is intercut with his instructions to his ministers on how to preserve the kingdom during his indefinite term of imprisonment, is a remarkably visual—even cinematic—passage, in a novel that is almost entirely devoid of description. King Goujian's years as an enslaved prisoner of war are then encapsulated in a series of powerful vignettes, each focusing on a situation in which he was profoundly humiliated or in immediate danger—in one particularly unpleasant sequence, the king of Yue lies face down on the floor of the Wu palace while King Fuchai attempts to force his last supporter, Fan Li, to abandon him, and it is only after the king of Wu has departed and King Goujian rises to his feet again that it is revealed that he has been crying from sheer terror all the while.[77] This chapter then concludes by bringing the king of Yue back to exactly the same location that he left all those years earlier, but he returns as a free man. The geographical journey in this chapter thus begins and ends at the same place, but the emotions of the people concerned are very different. During this time, wounds have been inflicted on King Goujian's psyche that will never be healed.

The impression of balance achieved within the narrative of the *Wu Yue chunqiu* is a particular achievement given the uneven coverage of events. Leaving on one side the opening chapters of each half of the book that deal with legendary heroes in remote antiquity, the fact remains that the Wu part of the novel covers 112 years, from 585 to 473 BCE, and the Yue part covers 22 years, from 492 to 469 BCE. (For a detailed description of the time period covered by each individual chapter, see the timeline below.) This means that the first half of the book describes the rise of the kingdom of Wu to a position of great power within the Chinese world at the same time as which the seeds of its eventual destruction were sown, and then the second half of the novel, in its four chapters on the life of King Goujian of Yue, covers exactly the same period as the one chapter on King Fuchai of Wu, which concludes the first half of the book. This interesting structuring,

---

77. For a detailed study of the highly effective narrative technique employed in this passage, see Lin Xiaoyun (2009a): 18–19. Another admiring account of this narrative is found in Chen Qiaoyi (1982): 16.

with a brief description of events from one side interlocking with a much more detailed account focusing on the other side of the conflict, no doubt posed great challenges for the author—the decision that events should only appear once, either on the Wu side or the Yue side, is probably a response to concerns that the reader might otherwise become bored. It is also entirely possible that Zhao Ye was forced to construct his novel in this way through the nature of his source material: the monarchs of the kingdom of Yue who reigned prior to King Goujian are not merely badly recorded; they do not appear in any surviving records at all. Given that earlier accounts, such as the *Shiji*, were also forced to begin their account of the kingdom of Yue abruptly with the accession of King Goujian, this was not a new problem: it seems that even in the Han dynasty, there simply were no extant records concerning the earlier history of Yue.

The characters, whether major or minor, in the *Wu Yue chunqiu* provide an unexpectedly rich and psychologically complex array of individualized personalities, which is unique in surviving preunification and early imperial-era fiction writing. This discussion of characterization will begin with the male protagonists. At best, the men in the *Wu Yue chunqiu* can be described as deeply flawed individuals. Although the reader may at some stage in the narrative feel sympathy for the pain they experience, this is immediately overlaid either by remembrance of a horrible act of cruelty they perpetrated on someone else earlier in the narrative or by their own subsequent appalling actions. As many Chinese scholars have noted, Wu Zixu is the most fully developed of these psychologically complex male characters and has the most dramatic career.[78] When he first appears in the novel, he is the cherished younger son of a hereditary ministerial family in Chu whose father is a trusted adviser of King Ping 楚平王 (r. 528–516 BCE); then after his father is executed due to the machinations of jealous rivals, Wu Zixu becomes a wanted criminal, who nearly falls into the hands of his enemies on several occasions. Seeking refuge in Wu, he plays a key role in the rise to power of King Helü and participates in the murder of a number of his rivals—the king of Wu responds by agreeing to invade Chu and help Wu Zixu take revenge on those who wronged him. Such is Wu Zixu's power at this point that he is able to override all the

---

78. The character of Wu Zixu found in this text is analyzed in detail in Cao Lindi (1986). The author notes particular similarities between the portrayal of Wu Zixu in the *Wu Yue chunqiu* and Guan Yu 關羽 in the *Sanguo yanyi* 三國演義 (Romance of the Three Kingdoms).

king's concerns and force him to appoint Fuchai as his heir. However, in the end, Fuchai turns against his benefactor and orders him to commit suicide. Through all these changes of fortune, Wu Zixu's intense misery is movingly portrayed, yet his response to the trauma he has experienced is to demand that others suffer and die. His own awareness of his shortcomings can be seen from the message he sends to an old friend in Chu who criticized his brutal campaign of revenge: "My day is almost done, and I still have far to go: all I can do is to carry on along my crooked path."[79]

Some would see Wu Zixu as the hero of this novel, and he is certainly the main protagonist in chapters 3–5, often overshadowing the kings of Wu that he served. However, the text does not shy away from recording the more problematic features of his career; throughout the imperial era, even those very strongly committed to the moral value of filial piety found Wu Zixu an extremely troubling character. In his relentless pursuit of revenge for the death of his father and older brother, Wu Zixu got a vast number of people killed—the atrocities he committed would now be designated as war crimes or even crimes against humanity. Such terms may be a modern invention, but the dreadful suffering that underlies them was only too familiar to the people of Chu, Wu, and Yue. Opinion in China has long been divided about the validity of blood feud or vendetta, where vengeance is exacted on persons merely tangentially related to the original offender.[80] From at least the time of the Eastern Han dynasty, the example of Wu Zixu was regularly cited in legal cases as justification for desecrating corpses and murdering friends and relatives in revenge for some wrong: the authorities were justifiably nervous of a precedent that might encourage people to view the duty owed to senior family members (particularly parents) as more important than the laws laid down by the monarch.[81] It is this tension that makes the character of Wu Zixu so fascinating: he never compromises in his prioritization of his family over his king, and that gives his actions a dangerous, transgressive appeal.

---

79. *Wu Yue chunqiu*, 63 ["Helü neizhuan" 闔閭內傳]. This line is taken from *Shiji*, 66.2177.
80. Blood feuds in early imperial China have been the subject of a number of studies; see Lee (1988) and Dalby (1981).
81. *Hou Hanshu*, 31.1107–9. The legal and ethical implications of the Li 李-Su 蘇 blood feud are considered in van Ess (1994): 162–64.

While some of the male characters in the *Wu Yue chunqiu* are straightforwardly brutal, others perpetrate evil deeds in the name of serving their monarch: the suffering inflicted on others is the same. All these characters are quite capable of condemning vast numbers of their fellow men to death without the slightest compunction—this can be seen in incidents such as when Grandee Zhong (otherwise portrayed as a staunch supporter of good administration within King Goujian's government) plans for how to worsen the famine affecting the kingdom of Wu. Even those individuals superficially portrayed as noble and virtuous, like Prince Jizha, do not actually stand up to any scrutiny; his refusal to take the throne when he is the rightful heir may seem righteous, but it is a selfish abrogation of his responsibilities, which condemns thousands of his countrymen to suffer and die at the hands of his violent and greedy relatives. Prince Jizha therefore has quite as much blood on his hands as any of the other members of the Wu royal family; he has simply avoided having to shed it personally. Furthermore, the brutality and cruelty found among the male characters in the *Wu Yue chunqiu* is not restricted to portrayals of members of the ruling elite: in chapter 4, King Helü commissions buckle-makers to produce items for his own personal use and offers a generous reward; to claim it, a metalworker in Wu kills his two sons and anoints the buckles he has made with their blood. Such is the selfishness and greed of even ordinary characters within the narrative—the moral bankruptcy of all the men caught up within this frenzy of violence is one of the major themes of the novel.

In terms of coverage within the *Wu Yue chunqiu*, King Goujian of Yue is by far the most important personage, since he is the focus of four chapters. He is also the most complex character of any of the kings portrayed in this novel, who goes through great changes in his fortunes.[82] King Goujian is followed in importance by King Helü of Wu with two chapters and King Fuchai with one.[83] In the author's conceit, King Goujian is on the right side

---

82. Chen Huixing (1995): 63 suggests that in this novel, King Helü is presented as a classic dynastic founder, King Fuchai as a stereotypical doomed last king, while King Goujian is—in his own remarkable way—both.
83. An alternative way of calculating the presence of the different royal characters is given in Lin Xiaoyun (2012): 97–98, who counts a total of eighteen thousand characters devoted to the two kings of Wu and seventeen thousand characters devoted to King Goujian of Yue to reach the same conclusion: King Goujian is the most important character and the major focus of the narrative.

since he has recognized that the survival of Yue depends on the complete elimination of Wu; King Fuchai is wrong because he consistently tries to engineer a less violent resolution to the ongoing warfare between these two countries. At the ministerial level, in the kingdom of Wu, Wu Zixu (serving in a very senior capacity in the government under two kings) is by far the most important figure: he is also frequently connected in the narrative to Grandee Zhong in Yue—these similarities appear to be largely the invention of the author of the *Wu Yue chunqiu*. While it is perfectly true that Wu Zixu was ordered to commit suicide by King Fuchai of Wu, the fate of Grandee Zhong is less clear: there are some accounts that state that he too was ordered to commit suicide by King Goujian, but others state that he died naturally after having presided over the postwar reconstruction of the kingdom of Yue and was honored for his loyal service by a grand burial in the capital city.[84] The repeated connection made in the *Wu Yue chunqiu* between Wu Zixu and Grandee Zhong: that both were gradually alienated from their monarch, that they made their final appeals in verse to their respective kings at the same location, and that they were subsequently ordered to commit suicide using exactly the same sword, only to become water deities after their deaths—these are all fictional details introduced to create the impression of a tragically parallel biography. A more subtle pairing is found in the figures of King Goujian of Yue and Fan Li, who experience great suffering and humiliation together over the course of several decades, only to go their separate ways in the concluding section of the novel. Although their experiences are the same at many junctures of the narrative, and both men survive the final conflict, King Goujian is destined to enjoy ever-increasing honors, while Fan Li turns his back on power and wealth to head off for a life of obscurity in hiding. However, even so, there remains a strong narrative connection between the two, since both characters are clearly so deeply traumatized by what has happened to them that neither will ever fully recover: King Goujian has been through too much to ever experience unalloyed joy in his success, and Fan Li's life in peaceful reclusion has come at an enormously high cost.

---

84. *Shiji*, 41.1746, states that Grandee Zhong was ordered to kill himself; this fate is also ascribed to him in *Yuejue shu*, 33 ["Ji cekao" 紀策考]. However, *Yuejue shu*, 47 ["Jidi zhuan" 記地傳], also records his grand burial in accordance with his dying instructions, not an ignominious suicide.

If the male characters in the *Wu Yue chunqiu* are cruel and violent, their motives and actions are nevertheless fully comprehensible to the reader, not least because the author takes some effort to explain them. By contrast, the women characters are mostly extremely baffling individuals—their actions are often difficult to understand and their motives totally obscure. This is an aspect of the novel that has not had nearly enough attention. It is likely that one of the reasons for this contrasting portrayal is that the women in this novel retain their moral compass—unlike the venal and cruel men with whom they are surrounded, the women characters in the *Wu Yue chunqiu* still show a strong perception of right and wrong. The single most important female character in the entire novel is the wife of King Goujian of Yue (a character who does not appear in other accounts of these events); however, she is not named at any juncture in the narrative. She appears at three critical passages: when going as a prisoner of war to Wu with her husband, she intones a song and a poetic lament about his poor judgment, which has brought the two of them to such dire straits. Subsequently, she is shown with Fan Li to have been King Goujian's staunchest supporter in his hour of need—her determination to show proper respect for her spouse allows him to retain some sense of identity and self-confidence even when he is a slave in Wu.[85] However, in the final confrontation between the two of them, her acute political sense and decades of loyal support for the king count for nothing, as he effectively places her under house arrest within the palace to prevent her from "interfering" in his final campaign against Wu. Some of the other female characters in the *Wu Yue chunqiu* show what may well be a similarly strong sense of confidence in their own political judgment—indeed, the very strange story of the princess of Wu who committed suicide after being humiliated by being given leftovers to eat has been read in this way. This is certainly the interpretation made by one Song dynasty scholar and expert on the history of the region, Zhu Changwen 朱長文 (1039–98), in his gazetteer of Suzhou entitled the *Wujun tujing xuji* 吳郡圖經續記 (Supplementary Records to the *Illustrated Guide to Wu Commandery*):

---

85. Wu Congxiang (2013): 76 notes that the *Han Shi waizhuan* 韓詩外傳 (Outer Tales of the Han Tradition of the *Book of Songs*) particularly praised queens for supporting their husbands; if this is a particular part of the Han tradition of the *Shijing*, it is not surprising that this interest is transferred into the *Wu Yue chunqiu*.

The *Wu Yue chunqiu* says that the youngest daughter of the king of Wu felt humiliated when her father gave her steamed fish to eat, and so she could not bear to live any longer and committed suicide. There is one account that says Fuchai's youngest daughter was called Youyu, and that she observed her father's mistakes and worried about the danger in which the country found itself, and so she wanted to marry Han Zhong, but her wishes bore no fruit, and thus she died of the pain.[86] Fuchai was deeply upset by this, and so he buried her outside the Chang Gate, inside a golden coffin and bronze outer coffin. After the funeral he performed a sacrifice for her, and thus his daughter metamorphized [into a bird] and sang:

> "On the South Mountain there lives a bird;
> On the North Mountain are spread some nets.
> Since the bird flies high in the sky,
> What use are the nets?
> It is my ambition to follow my lord;
> But slanderous gossip has created many problems.
> Sadness and anger brought about a terrible illness,
> Causing my body to be returned to the yellow earth."[87]

In my opinion, this poem also has a deeper meaning and must have been composed when this woman was still alive. "On the South Mountain there lives a bird" refers to Yue. "On the North Mountain are spread some nets" speaks of trying to control Yue from afar. "Since the bird flies high in the sky" is about King Goujian's success. "What use are the nets?" refers to Fuchai's inability to control Yue. "It is my ambition to follow my lord, but slanderous gossip has created many problems" speaks of the fact that even though she wanted to follow her father's orders, there was nothing that could be done about his

---

86. The changes in the name given to this princess in different texts are considered in Xu Haoran (2004).

87. This song consists of rhymed couplets in the pattern AAAB; throughout this book, reconstructed pronunciations are given in accordance with Schuessler (2009). It seems to have been a peculiarity of elite women in ancient Wu and Yue culture to perform songs that expressed their feelings in terms of bird behavior; see Wang Yu (2007).

listening to slanderous gossip and ignoring loyal advice. As for her pain over the situation with Han Chong and her anger at the steamed fish, I am afraid that both are wrong.[88]

It is very striking that in later versions of this story, rather than being presented as killing herself over a moral principle, the princess is said to have died when her father refused her permission to marry the man she loved.[89] Such a sentimental reading has no place in understanding the strong female characters in the *Wu Yue chunqiu*. At a lower social level than the Wu princess, there is also the unnamed woman who dies to preserve her reputation as a person of high moral standing after she has met Wu Zixu; when she throws herself into the river rather than live on with a sullied name, she shows a resolute defense of morality that no man in the novel even attempts to achieve. At the same time, Wu Zixu's vocal appreciation of her virtue, both on the occasion of her death and when he revisits the site when returning from the successful campaign against Chu in 506 BCE, is highly ironic given the way he treats other women—in particular, when he rewards the family of the dead woman; this occurs immediately after he has organized the gang rape of women in the Chu royal family as punishment for the way in which their male relatives treated him.

Although the portrayal of female characters in the *Wu Yue chunqiu* is generally positive, there are two women who are the subject of criticism: the first is the wife of Gongsun Sheng in Wu (who is anonymous in this novel but named as Dajun 大君 in the *Yuejue shu*) and the other the wife of Grandee Zhong in Yue.[90] In both cases, they are said by their husbands to be "stupid" (yu 愚) and "ignorant" (buzhi 不知). This criticism is interesting, because these wives are faced with situations in which their husbands' executions are imminent, and the women concerned express a clear conviction that in normal circumstances, they would not have to die. In this situation, their reaction serves to make the author's underlying purpose clearer—the men are correct in their understanding that death is inevitable. Hence, in accordance with the main theme of this novel, they are in the right. By accepting that they live in a world of relentless violence, Gongsun Sheng and Grandee

---

88. Zhu Changwen (1999): 66. Modern supporters of this theory include Chen Pengcheng (2014) and Lin Xiaoyun (2009b).
89. See, for example, Gan Bao (1979): 200 and Lu Guangwei (1999): 76.
90. *Wu Yue chunqiu*, 78 and 175–76.

Zhong come to terms with the fact that their lives are part of the price to be paid. In this reading, the women who protest are indeed "stupid." However, when considering these characters in the context of the portrayal of women throughout the novel, as the only protagonists who show any moral principles, the wives act as an important counterpoint to their husbands. It is hard to argue that their outrage over the executions of their husbands is unjustified—Gongsun Sheng is beaten to death for providing a divination of King Fuchai of Wu's dream, which is correct but which His Majesty happens not to like; while Grandee Zhong is ordered to commit suicide because King Goujian has become unjustly suspicious of him.[91] The women cannot prevent this outcome, but they can at least express the conviction that this is not how things should be. Furthermore, it is worth noting that while their husbands stigmatize them as "stupid" and "ignorant," in both cases, it is the women who survive, while their menfolk are killed.

Throughout the *Wu Yue chunqiu*, the conflict between the two kingdoms is presented in highly personal terms. This emphasis on the characters of the individual kings and ministers adds force to the dramatic confrontations between them, which then, in turn, stresses their determined opposition to each other. This highly persuasive narrative, arranged with considerable skill by the author, has created the impression that Yue's ultimate victory over Wu was the result of the steely will of the king of Yue and his resolute determination to pursue his revenge—his years of modest living and self-abnegation standing in marked contrast to the luxurious lifestyle attributed to King Fuchai of Wu. Given that the facts and figures provided in the *Wu Yue chunqiu* have often been treated entirely uncritically by historians, as though this were not a work of fiction, the wars between Wu and Yue have often been considered as a kind of David-and-Goliath battle between the mighty yet over-arrogant forces of King Fuchai and the puny yet righteous armies of King Goujian.[92] This is likely to be a very serious distortion of the facts. First, we do not know whether the figures attributed to the Yue Army in the *Wu Yue chunqiu*

---

91. The account of the divination of King Fuchai's dream is taken from *Yuejue shu*, 73–78 ["Ji Wuwang zhan meng"]. What is very striking about this account is that two separate divinations are made, by Chancellor Pi and Gongsun Sheng, and both are correct: the first auspicious divination is a short-term prediction and the second inauspicious one more long term.

92. Zhu Zhaoju (2006): 36 lists the many ancient texts containing pejorative remarks about the backwardness of Yue.

are correct—furthermore, the fact that Yue won and utterly annihilated the kingdom of Wu means that they must have had a highly effective military force.[93] Attempts to calculate the population of Yue in the 470s BCE have generally been made on the principle that the *Wu Yue chunqiu* figures for the size of King Goujian's forces are correct and that this represents the largest army that it was possible for them to raise, creating a circular argument.[94] In addition, we know nothing about immigration and population growth in Yue: some suggestive information is recorded in historical texts, but this conflicts with the portrayal of events that Zhao Ye wished to give in the *Wu Yue chunqiu*, and hence, this is not utilized in the novel.[95] In recent years, some historians of this period have attempted to get away from the personalities of those involved to consider the economic causes of the conflict, particularly the way in which Wu built fortifications throughout the reign of King Helü with a view to dominating trade through the Yangtze delta region—this new way of considering the underlying motives for these two kingdoms to engage in such appalling warfare has allowed for a quite different understanding of why King Goujian was so determined to eliminate his rivals.[96] No doubt, with further archaeological discoveries of textual material and bronze inscriptions in the future, it will be possible to make further refinements to our understanding of these events. It is perhaps time to set Zhao Ye's account of events aside when considering what happened in the wars between Wu and Yue in the early fifth century BCE. At the same time, a proper consideration of the role of the *Wu Yue chunqiu* in the history of the Chinese novel, and beyond that, in world literature, is long overdue.

---

93. The problems with understanding the Yue administration under King Goujian, a function of the inadequacy of our sources, are discussed in detail in Fu Zhenzhao (2002): 201–42.
94. Chen Qiaoyi and Yan Yuehu (2004): 28 suggests that in the reign of King Goujian, the entire population of Yue was approximately three hundred thousand people. Zhao Gang (2006): 84 and Ren Guiquan (2011) both consider this too small.
95. The *Guoyu*, 635 ["Yueyu shang" 越語上], describes King Goujian's policies to encourage population growth; likewise, the newly discovered *Yuegong qishi* text contains multiple references to this and inward immigration into Yue during this time.
96. Xie Chen (2000): 61–69.

Translator's Note

This translation is based on the critical edition of the *Wu Yue chunqiu* by Zhou Shengchun 周生春 published in 1997, entitled the *Wu Yue chunqiu jijiao huikao* 吳越春秋輯校匯考 (A collated edition of the *Spring and Autumn Annals of the Kingdoms of Wu and Yue*). In addition, I have made use of the Yuan dynasty commentary produced by Xu Tianhu: the *Wu Yue chunqiu yinzhu* 吳越春秋音注 (*Spring and Autumn Annals of the Kingdoms of Wu and Yue* with commentary and notes on pronunciation)—the preface to this recension of the text is dated 1306 and represents the earliest extant edition of this novel.[97] I have also made reference to textual variants preserved in the *Sibu congkan* 四部叢刊 (Compendium of the four branches of literature) edition of the text, which reprints the 1501 recension of the text prepared by Kuang Fan 鄺璠 (1458–1521). There are also three important modern commentaries on the text, the *Wu Yue chunqiu jiaozhu* 吳越春秋校注 (Annotated *Spring and Autumn Annals of the Kingdoms of Wu and Yue* with Commentary) and *Wu Yue chunqiu quanyi* 吳越春秋全譯 (Complete translation of the *Spring and Autumn Annals of the Kingdoms of Wu and Yue*) by Zhang Jue 張覺, and the *Xinyi Wu Yue chunqiu* 新譯吳越春秋 (New translation of the *Spring and Autumn Annals of the Kingdoms of Wu and Yue*) by Huang Rensheng 黃仁生.

Over the years, a great deal of scholarly effort has gone into trying to integrate the chronology given in the *Wu Yue chunqiu* with that recorded in

---

97. The earliest recorded edition of the *Wu Yue chunqiu* was published by Wang Gang 汪剛 (d. after 1228) in Shaoxing during the Song dynasty, but this does not survive; see Zhang Jinwu (1999): 357. In 1212, Wang Gang was also responsible for printing the earliest-known edition of the *Yuejue shu*; see Huang Wei (1983): 107.

earlier historical texts and in attempting to identify the place-names mentioned in this text. Both these have proved generally fruitless endeavors. It is impossible to explain away the differences in dating in any meaningful way; Zhao Ye rearranged events to suit his own chronology and then assigned the dates that he found appropriate. Therefore, in the translation given below, the dates will be converted into years BCE where appropriate, but no attempt will be made to reconcile them with the accounts given in historical writings such as the *Zuozhuan* or *Shiji*. Similarly, with the place-names, massive efforts have been expended to try and identify them—sometimes they appear to be garbled versions of names found in other texts, while on other occasions, commentators have been forced to conclude that they were probably invented. Therefore, the notes to this translation concentrate on discussing textual variants, identifying source texts or parallel passages in other early works of Chinese literature (particularly where this assists with understanding a line that is garbled in the present transmitted text of the *Wu Yue chunqiu*) and explaining the identity of the historical personages mentioned.

For those readers not familiar with the nomenclature for individuals from the kingdoms of Wu and Yue, it should be explained that this is quite different from contemporary practice in the Central States of the Zhou confederacy. In the late Spring and Autumn period and early Warring States era when the events of this novel take place, the people of Wu and Yue had not yet generally adopted Chinese-style naming practices, with clan name, personal name, style names for formal use, and posthumous titles. Instead, they seem to have had a mixed nomenclature. First, they could use their name in the Wu or Yue language, transliterated into Chinese characters, which would usually be multisyllabic. In the translation, these names are given as a single word, since it is not known whether the people of Wu and Yue had surnames or not at this time. Second, they could use a short form of their transliterated name, usually just two characters, which seems to have been designed to be easy for people from the Central States to be able to remember. Finally, they could use a translation of the meaning of their Wu or Yue language name as their Chinese name.[98] The royalty and nobility of the kingdoms of Wu and Yue also do not seem to have had any kind of system of posthumous titles, nor did they use name taboos. The *Wu Yue chunqiu* seems to generally favor using the short transliterated names—therefore, King Shoumeng of

---

98. This understanding of the nomenclature for these southern kings is derived from Dong Chuping and Jin Yongping (1998): 95–96.

Wu 壽夢 is known by this name rather than Gufa'nanshoumeng 姑發難壽夢 or Cheng 乘, the full transliteration of his Wu language name and the translation, respectively.[99] Characters from the Chinese world come with the full panoply of names: in situations where this is likely to be confusing for the reader, the identity of the individual concerned is clarified in the notes.

---

99. The full name of King Shoumeng is recorded on the "Qiegoushu *jian*" 叡[戈+句]郘劍, a sword made for a prince of Wu that was excavated in Shaoxing in 1997; see Cao Jinyan (2007) and Feng Puren (2007): 120. King Shoumeng's translated name is given in the *Zuozhuan*, 995 [Xiang 12].

Timeline of the Kings of Wu and Yue

Kings of Wu		
King Shoumeng	吳王壽夢	r. 585–561 BCE
King Zhufan	吳王諸樊	r. 560–548 BCE
King Yuji	吳王餘祭	r. 547–544 BCE
King Yumei	吳王餘昧	r. 543–527 BCE
King Liao	吳王僚	r. 526–515 BCE
King Helü	吳王闔閭	r. 514–496 BCE
King Fuchai	吳王夫差	r. 495–473 BCE

Kings of Yue		
King Yunchang	越王允常	d. 497 BCE
King Goujian	越王勾踐	r. 496–465 BCE

Timeline of Events in the *Wu Yue chunqiu*

Wu Chapters	Yue Chapters
1: The Story of the Great Earl of Wu (Mythological Time)	6: The Story of King Wuyu of Yue (Mythological Time)
2: The Story of King Shoumeng of Wu 585–527 BCE	—
3: The Story of How King Liao Employed Prince Guang 525–515 BCE	
4: The Story of King Helü of Wu 514–505 BCE	
5: The Story of King Fuchai of Wu 485–473 BCE	7: The Story of King Goujian Becoming a Vassal 492–490 BCE
	8: The Story of King Goujian Returning to His Country 490–488 BCE
	9: The Story of King Goujian's Conspiracy 487–484 BCE
	10: The Story of King Goujian's Attack on Wu 482–469 BCE

Chapter One

The Traditions

The Story of the Great Lord Protector of Wu

The first lord of Wu, the Great Lord Protector, was a descendant of Houji (Lord Millet). Houji's mother was a woman named Jiang Yuan from Tai, the chief consort of the monarch Diku. When still very young, before she ever had experienced a pregnancy, while she was traveling through the wilds, she saw the footprint of a giant. Looking at it, she felt deeply pleased; delighted by its appearance, she stepped on it. There was a movement in her body, and she felt as if she had indeed had sexual intercourse. Afterward, when she realized she was pregnant, she was afraid that other people would accuse her of immoral behavior, so she performed a sacrifice and prayed, saying that she did not want to have a baby. However, having stood in the footprint of God on High, Heaven demanded that she give birth to this child. Jiang Yuan believed this to be a sign of ill fortune, and so she abandoned him in a narrow lane, yet the horses and cattle passing through moved to one side to avoid him. Then she decided

《吳太伯傳》

吳之前君太伯者，后稷之苗裔也。后稷其母台氏之女姜嫄，為帝嚳元妃。年少未孕，出游於野，見大人跡而觀之，中心歡然，喜其形像，因履而踐之。身動，意若為人所感。後妊娠。恐被淫泆之禍，遂祭祀以求，謂無子，履上帝之跡，天猶令有之。姜嫄怪而棄于阸狹之巷，牛馬過者折易而避之。復棄于林中，適會伐木之人多。復置于澤中冰上，眾鳥以羽覆之。后稷遂得不死。姜嫄以為神，收而養之，長因名棄。為兒時，好種樹，禾、黍、桑、麻五穀，相五土之宜，青、

to abandon him in the forest instead, but she met too many woodcutters there. After that, she placed him on the ice in the marshes, but flocks of birds protected him with their wings.[1] Thus, Houji was able to escape death. Jiang Yuan thought this a miracle, and so she took her baby and raised him—once he was grown, she named him Qi (Abandoned) because of these events.

While still a child, [Qi] was skilled at planting foxtail millet and panic millet, mulberry trees, hemp, and the five grains. He investigated what would be appropriate to the five different types of terrain, according to whether the soil was pale, red, brown, or black and the level of the water table, for different principles apply to the cultivation of sacrificial grain, panic millet and foxtail millet, lotus, wheat, beans, and rice. When in the time of Yao, there was a terrible flood; the people found themselves inundated, and so they were forced to live on high ground.[2] Yao employed Qi to teach people how to live in their mountain homes, building their houses according to the lie of the land and learning the techniques necessary to survive there. After the passage of three years, there was nobody who appeared to be starving or exhausted. Accordingly, [Yao] appointed Qi as master of agriculture, granting him the lands of Tai and giving him the title "Houji" and the surname Ji.

Houji now had his own state and was ranked among the lords of the land. When he died, his son Buzhu was established. He lived at a time when the Xia dynasty was going from bad to worse, and so he lost his official position and fled to live amid the Rong and Di people. His grandson was Gongliu.[3] Gongliu was a most kind and benevolent man: when he walked, he

赤、黃、黑，陵水高下，粱、稷、黍、禾、蕖、麥、豆、稻，各得其理。堯遭洪水，人民泛濫，遂高而居。堯聘棄使教民山居，隨地造區，研營種之術。三年餘，行人無飢乏之色。乃拜棄為農師，封之台，號為后稷，姓姬氏。

后稷就國，為諸侯，卒。子不窋立，遭夏氏世衰，失官，奔戎、狄之間。其孫公劉。公劉慈仁，行不履生草，運車以避葭葦。公劉避夏桀於戎、狄，變易風俗，民化其政。公劉卒，子慶節立。其後八世，而得古公亶甫。脩公劉、

---

1. This passage is closely related to the description of Jiang Yuan's three attempts to abandon her baby, recorded in the ode "Shengmin" 生民 (She Gave Birth to the People); see *Shijing*, 1055–65.
2. Xu Tianhu (1999): 2 argues that *sui* 遂 (then) in the original text should be read as *zhu* 逐 (to be forced to do something). This suggestion has been incorporated into the translation.
3. The family tree given here is somewhat different from that found in *Shiji*, 4.112, which gives Houji's son as Buzhu, his grandson as Ju 鞠, and his great-grandson as Gongliu.

would not trample the grass, and when he traveled by chariot, he would avoid any stands of reeds. Gongliu avoided the troubles caused by King Jie of the Xia dynasty by living with the Rong and Di, transforming their customs so that people found their lives greatly improved under his rule. When Gongliu died, his son Qingjie was established. Eight generations later, we come to the "Old Lord" Danfu.[4] He restored the regime originally founded by Gongliu and Houji, accumulating virtue and acting in a just manner, so he was greatly admired by the Di. The Xunyu and Rong people were jealous and attacked him; even though the Old Lord presented them with dogs and horses, cattle and sheep, their attacks did not stop. He gave animal furs and silks, gold, jade, and other precious treasures to them, but still the attacks did not stop.

"What is it that you want?" the Old Lord asked.

"We want your land," they replied.

"A gentleman does not harm people with that which he uses to nourish people," the Old Lord declared.[5] "If harm is done to that which should nourish, then the country will be destroyed. A place that is so dangerous to me is not somewhere that I can live."

The Old Lord grabbed hold of his whip and departed from Bin, traversing Mount Liang and stopping at the plain at the foot of Mount Qi.

"What is the difference," he asked, "between their ruler and myself?"

However, the people of Bin—fathers and sons, older brothers and younger brothers—carrying their older relatives on their backs, leading their children by the hand, and bearing their cooking equipment with them, followed in the wake of the Old Lord. After they had been living there for three months, they had constructed an inner and an outer city wall. After they had been living there for a year, they had built houses; and after two years, they

后稷之業，積德行義，為狄人所慕。薰鬻、戎姤而伐之。古公事之以犬馬牛羊，其伐不止；事以皮幣金玉重寶，而亦伐之不止。古公問：「何所欲？」曰：「欲其土地。」古公曰：「君子不以養害。害所養，國所以亡也，而為身害，吾所不居也。」古公乃杖策去邠，踰梁山而處岐周，曰：「彼君與我何異？」邠人父子兄弟，相帥負老攜幼，揭釜甑而歸古公。居三月，成城郭；一年成邑；二年成都，而民五倍其初。

---

4. Elsewhere, the name of this individual is given as Danfu 亶父. See, for example, *Shijing*, 980 ["Mian" 緜], and *Shiji*, 4.123.

5. This line is a slightly garbled quotation from *Mengzi*, 51 ["Liang Huiwang xia" 梁惠王下].

had not only established an ancestral shrine for the ruling family but the people had also quintupled the property with which they had arrived.[6]

The Old Lord had three sons: the eldest was the Great Lord Protector, the second was Zhongyong *also known as Wu Zhong*, and the youngest was Jili.[7] Jili was married to a wife named Tai Ren, and she gave birth to a son named Chang.[8] Chang was attended by all the auspicious signs of a sage. The Old Lord knew that Chang was a sage, and he wanted his state to be inherited by him.

"Will it not rest with Chang to establish a kingdom?" he asked.

Accordingly, he changed his name to Jili. The Great Lord Protector and Zhongyong saw the way that the wind was blowing and said: "Li means 'legitimate.'" They were well aware that the Old Lord wanted the state to go to Chang.

When the Old Lord became ill, the two men made the excuse that they wanted to go and gather medicinal herbs on Mount Heng, but instead, they traveled to the lands of the Man people in Jing, where they cut their hair and tattooed their bodies and dressed like the Yi and Di people to make it clear that they did not intend to dispute the succession. When the Old Lord died, the Great Lord Protector and Zhongyong returned home. Once their period of mourning was over, they went back to the Man people

古公三子。長曰太伯，次曰仲雍，雍一名吳仲，少曰季歷。季歷娶妻太任氏，生子昌。昌有聖瑞。古公知昌聖，欲傳國以及昌，曰：「興王業者，其在昌乎？」因更名曰季歷。太伯、仲雍望風知指，曰：「歷者，適也。」知古公欲以國及昌。古公病，二人託名採藥於衡山，遂之荊蠻。斷髮文身，為夷狄之服，示不可用。古公卒，太伯、仲雍歸。赴喪畢，還荊蠻。國民君而事之，自號為勾吳。吳人或問：「何像而為勾吳？」太伯曰：「吾以伯長居國，

---

6. This translation follows *Zuozhuan*, 242 [Zhuang 28], in understanding that a city only qualified as a *du* 都 if ancestral shrines were constructed within it for sacrifices to the ruling house.

7. In the text of the *Wu Yue chunqiu*, there are a number of occasions where annotations appear to have become integrated into the main text. In this translation, these annotations (usually clarifying the identity or nomenclature of individual characters) will be given in italics.

8. Lady Tai Ren had the clan name Ren and came from the state of Zhi 摯. She is identified elsewhere as the second daughter of the ruler of this state; see, for example, *Shijing*, 967 ["Daming" 大明], and *Lienü zhuan*, 14 ["Muyi" 母儀].

in Jing. The people of this country treated the Great Lord Protector as their ruler, and he took the title "Gouwu."⁹

"By what means did you become Gouwu?" a Wu person once asked him.

"I united the country in my capacity as the oldest and most senior within my generation, but I have no children," the Great Lord Protector said. "The person who ought to have received these lands is Wu Zhong. That is the reason that I took the title of Gouwu. Is that not appropriate?"

The Man people in Jing considered him to be very righteous, and so more than one thousand families gave their allegiance to him and together established him as Gouwu. Over the course of the next few years, his people became increasingly prosperous. When the Yin were in decline in the reign of their last monarch, the lords of the Central States attacked him on several occasions. Being afraid that these troubles would affect the Man people in Jing, the Great Lord Protector constructed a city wall three *li* and two hundred *bu* in diameter and an outer city wall of more than three hundred *li* in the northwestern part of the country.¹⁰ This was called "Old Wu." The people were all able to farm their fields within these walls.

When the Old Lord became critically ill and was about to die, he ordered Jili to yield the state to the Great Lord Protector. He tried to hand it over three times, and each time he refused it. Therefore, it is said: "The Great Lord Protector refused to accept the world three times."¹¹ It was only after this that Jili took charge of the government and restored the regime of the former kings, strictly maintaining the principles of benevolence and justice. When Jili died, his son Chang was established, and he assumed the title

絕嗣者也，其當有封者，吳仲也。故自號勾吳，非其方乎？」荊蠻義之，從而歸之者千有餘家，共立以為勾吳。數年之間，民人殷富。遭殷之末世衰，中國侯王數用兵，恐及於荊蠻，故太伯起城，周三里二百步，外郭三百餘里。在西北隅，名曰故吳，人民皆耕田其中。古公病，將卒，令季歷讓國於太伯，而三讓不受，故云：太伯三以天下讓。於是季歷蒞政，脩先王之業，守仁義之道。季歷卒，子昌立，號曰西伯。遵公劉、古公之術，業於養老，天下歸之。

---

9. For an interesting consideration of the meaning of this term; see Henry (2007): 20–22.
10. Following the conversion figures given in Wu Chengluo (1984), this equates to a city wall approximately 1,525 meters in length.
11. This is a quotation of *Lunyu*, 78 ["Taibo" 泰伯].

"Western Lord Protector." He respected the systems of government already established by Gongliu and the Old Lord and made the care for the elderly his priority; hence, the entire world gave their allegiance to him.[12] Having brought about a universal peace, Bo Yi arrived from the shores of the sea.[13] When the Western Lord Protector died, his heir, Fa, was established, and he employed [the dukes of] Zhou and Shao and attacked the Yin.[14] The world was thus at peace, and he was able to take the title "King," posthumously granting the Old Lord the title "Great King." He also enfeoffed the Great Lord Protector in Wu.

When the Great Lord Protector died, he was buried amid the wastes of Meili.[15] Zhongyong was established, and he became Zhongyong of Wu. When Zhongyong died, he was succeeded by his son Jijian; Jijian was succeeded by his son Shuda; [Shu]da was succeeded by his son Zhouzhang; [Zhou]zhang was succeeded by his son Xiong; Xiong was succeeded by his son Sui; Sui was succeeded by his son Kexiang; [Ke]xiang was succeeded by his son Qiangjiuyi; [Qiangjiu]yi was succeeded by his son Yuqiaoyiwu; [Yuqiaoyi]wu was succeeded by his son Kelu; [Ke]lu was succeeded by his son Zhouyao; [Zhou]yao was succeeded by his son Quyu; [Qu]yu was succeeded

西伯致太平，伯夷自海濱而往。西伯卒，太子發立，任周、召而伐殷，天下已安，乃稱王。追謚古公為大王，追封太伯於吳。

太伯祖卒，葬於梅里平墟。仲雍立，是為吳仲雍。仲雍卒，子季簡；簡子叔達；達子周章；章子熊；熊子遂；遂子柯相；相子彊鳩夷；夷子餘喬疑吾；吾子柯盧；盧子周繇；繇子屈羽；羽子夷吾；吾子禽處；處子專；專

---

12. This again is a reference to *Mengzi*, 174 ["Li Lou shang" 離婁上].
13. Bo Yi was a virtuous exemplar who, in spite of his position as legitimate heir, refused to take the throne after his father expressed the wish that his younger brother should succeed him. Rather than become involved in the events of the Zhou conquest, Bo Yi chose to live as a recluse and eventually starved to death; see *Shiji*, 61.2121–29.
14. Fa was the personal name of the future King Wu of Zhou 周武王 (r. 1049/1045–1043 BCE). The two dukes of Zhou and Shao played a key role during his administration and served as regents to his son after the untimely death of King Wu.
15. A "tomb" of the Great Lord Protector is today located at Hongshan 鴻山 near Wuxi—the present structures nearby date to the Qing dynasty. Meicun 梅村, which is the site of the temple to the Great Lord Protector (Taibo miao 泰伯廟) thought to have originally been founded in 154 CE, is frequently described as the site of the Lord Protector's walled city and the earliest capital of Wu; see Guojia wenwu ju (2008): 320 and 306, respectively.

by his son Yiwu; [Yi]wu was succeeded by his son Qinchu; [Qin]chu was succeeded by his son Zhuan; Zhuan was succeeded by his son Pogao; [Po]gao was succeeded by his son Jubi.[16] At this time, Lord Xian of Jin destroyed Yu because Yu had assisted Jin to attack Guo.[17] [Ju]bi was succeeded by his son Quqi; and [Qu]qi was succeeded by his son, Shoumeng. During this period Wu became increasingly powerful, and they assumed the title of king. From the time of the Great Lord Protector to the reign of Shoumeng, [Wu] from time to time was in contact with the Central States, paying court to the king and attending meetings; afterward, this state became the most powerful of them all.

子頗高；高子句畢立。是時晉獻公滅周北虞虞公，以開晉之伐虢氏。畢子去齊、齊子壽夢立，而吳益彊，稱王。凡從太伯至壽夢之世，與中國時通朝會，而國斯霸焉。

---

16. Alternative genealogies for the Wu royal family are given in *Shiji*, 31.1447, and Lu Guangwei (1999): 107–9. To date, none of these names have been verified by archaeological discoveries of inscribed bronzes.

17. It is interesting to see this reference to the state of Yu here, because some scholars argue that it is this country that was actually established by the Great Lord Protector when he left Zhou; see, for example, Huang Shengzhang (1983) and Li Xueqin (1993). This state was destroyed by Lord Xian of Jin 晉獻公 (r. 677–651 BCE) in 655 BCE; see *Zuozhuan*, 311 [Xi 5].

Chapter Two

The Traditions

The Story of King Shoumeng of Wu

In the first year of King Shoumeng [585 BCE], His Majesty paid court to Zhou and met with Chu, which allowed him to observe the rituals and music of the other lords. Lord Cheng of Lu met with him at Zhongli.[1] He took this opportunity to inquire deeply into the rituals and music of the duke of Zhou. Lord Cheng explained carefully to him the rituals and music used by the former kings and had the airs of the three dynasties sung for him.[2]

"I live with the Yi and the Man people," King Shoumeng said, "and we only have the custom of wearing our hair in a mallet-shaped bun—how

《吳王壽夢傳》

壽夢元年，朝周，適楚，觀諸侯禮樂。魯成公會於鍾離，深問周公禮樂，成公悉為陳前王之禮樂，因為詠歌三代之風。壽夢曰：「孤在夷蠻，徒以椎髻為俗，豈有斯之服哉！」因歎而去，曰：「於乎哉，禮也！」

---

1. Lord Cheng of Lu 魯成公 reigned from 590 to 573 BCE, and his meeting with the king of Wu is recorded in *Zuozhuan*, 876–77 [Cheng 15]. However, these events occurred in the tenth year of the reign of King Shoumeng, and not the first.
2. This parallels the famous concert of the songs of the *Shijing* performed by musicians in the service of Shusun Muzi 叔孫穆子, a government minister in Lu, for Prince Jizha of Wu, as recorded in *Zuozhuan*, 1161–65 [Xiang 29].

could we have clothing like this?" Then he sighed and departed, saying: "What an amazing thing ritual is!"

In the second year of his reign [584 BCE], Grandee [Qu] Wuchen, the duke of Shen, arrived in Wu as a refugee from Chu.[3] His Majesty appointed him as chief of staff, and he taught the Wu people about archery and charioteering before leading them in an attack on Chu. King Zhuang of Chu was furious at this and appointed Zifan as general, whereupon he defeated the Wu Army.[4] From this point onward, the two kingdoms found themselves locked in conflict. Furthermore, Wu for the first time established regular contact with the Central States and began to fight with the other lords.

In the fifth year of his reign [581 BCE], His Majesty attacked Chu and defeated Zifan.

In the sixteenth year of his reign [570 BCE], King Gong of Chu was infuriated that Wu had attacked them for Wu Chen's sake, so he raised an army and invaded Wu—he reached as far as Mount Heng before he turned homeward.[5]

In the seventeenth year of his reign [569 BCE], King Shoumeng appointed [Qu] Wuchen's son, Huyong, as prime minister, entrusting the government of the country to him.[6]

二年，楚之亡大夫申公巫臣適吳，以為行人。教吳射御，導之伐楚。楚莊王怒，使子反將，敗吳師。二國從斯結讎。於是吳始通中國而與諸侯為敵。

五年，伐楚，敗子反。

十六年，楚恭王怨吳為巫臣伐之也，乃舉兵伐吳，至衡山而還。

十七年，壽夢以巫臣子狐庸為相，任以國政。

---

3. The quarrels among the Chu ruling elite, which led to this highly distinguished minister being forced into exile, are recorded in *Zuozhuan*, 833–35 [Cheng 7].
4. King Zhuang of Chu ruled from 693 to 591 BCE; hence, he had been dead for some years by the time this conflict began. It was King Zhuang's son, King Gong of Chu 楚共王 (r. 590–560 BCE), who was actually in power at this point.
5. King Gong's campaign against Wu is described in *Zuozhuan*, 925 [Xiang 3].
6. Other accounts of the career of Qu Huyong note his role as an ambassador from Wu to Jin in 542 BCE and as a senior government minister; see *Zuozhuan*, 1189 [Xiang 31], and *Guoyu*, 539 ["Chuyu shang" 楚語上], respectively. An interesting bronze inscription on the "Luo'er yi" 羅兒匜 excavated in 1988, which seems to have belonged to Qu Huyong, suggests that his mother was a Wu princess; see Xu Bohong (1991). This may have a bearing on why Huyong was trusted so highly; however, the *Wu Yue chunqiu* is unique in suggesting that he served in so important a position as prime minister of Wu.

In the twenty-fifth year of his reign [561 BCE], King Shoumeng became ill and was about to die. He had four sons: the oldest was named Zhufan, the second was Yuji, the third was Yumei, and the fourth was Jizha. Jizha was wise, and so King Shoumeng wanted to establish him. Jizha refused this honor, saying: "There are long-established rules concerning this in the canons of ritual. How can you destroy the principles of our former rulers to satisfy the selfish love of a father for his son?"

King Shoumeng then gave the following orders to Zhufan: "I want the kingdom to pass to [Ji]zha; do not forget what I have told you!"

"The Great King of Zhou understood how wise the Western Lord Protector was," Zhufan said, "and so he set aside the claims of his oldest son to establish the younger; this is how the Royal Way began. Now you want the country to pass to [Ji]zha, so I promise you that I will go and plow the borderlands."

"In the past," the king said, "the virtues practiced by the Zhou royal house reached to the four seas. Now ours is but a tiny state, inhabited by the Man people of Jing—how can we accomplish the achievements of a Son of Heaven? All that I ask is that you do not forget what I told you; you must hand on the state according to birth order until it reaches Jizha."

"I would not dare to refuse to obey your commands!" Zhufan said.

When King Shoumeng died, Zhufan took charge of the government in his capacity as the legitimate heir and oldest son, and it was he who ruled the country.

In the first year of the reign of King Zhufan of Wu [560 BCE], once he had removed his mourning garb, he was determined to yield the throne to Jizha.

"In the past," he said, "when our former king was still alive, he was uncomfortable from morning until night. I watched him closely and realized that he wanted better things for you. Returning from court, he would sigh sadly and say to me: 'I know how clever Prince [Ji]zha is.' It was his intention to set my claims aside and have you, the younger son, succeed to the throne; this is something that he mentioned repeatedly. Furthermore, in my heart, I agreed with him. However, in the end His Late Majesty could not bear to put this private plan into action, and so the country was entrusted

二十五年，壽夢病，將卒。有子四人：長曰諸樊，次曰餘祭，次曰餘昧，次曰季札。季札賢，壽夢欲立之。季札讓曰：「禮有舊制，奈何廢前王之禮，而行父子之私乎？」壽夢乃命諸樊曰：「我欲傳國及札，爾無忘寡人之言。」諸樊曰：「周之太王，知西伯之聖，廢長立少，王之道興。今欲授國於札，臣誠耕於野。」王曰：「昔周行之，德加於四海。今汝於區區之國，荊

to me. How could I dare to disregard his true intentions? Right now, the country is yours. I am happy to be able to bring His Late Majesty's wishes to fruition."

Jizha refused. "For the oldest son and legitimate heir to rule the country is not a selfish wish on the part of the late king but an established precedent for the ancestral shrines and state altars," he said. "How can this be changed?"

"Are there not many occasions when former kings have ordered things on the grounds that they would be beneficial to the country?" Zhufan asked. "The Great King changed the succession for Jili's sake, and the two Lords Protector came to join the Man people in Jing; they built a city here and established a state, and the Way of the Zhou dynasty was thus accomplished. You know perfectly well that the late king was endlessly praising this."

Jizha again refused. "In the past, when the Lord of Cao died, his legitimate heir had died, but his other children were still living.[7] The other lords joined with the people of Cao in establishing a ruler with no righteous claim to take charge of the country. Zizang heard about this and traveled homeward, singing dirges. The ruler of Cao was frightened and wanted to establish Zizang instead, but Zizang ran away since he wanted Cao to be able to survive.[8] I have no particular talents, but I would like to follow the just principles of Zizang. I insist on being allowed to leave."

蠻之鄉，奚能成天子之業乎？且今子不忘前人之言，必授國以次，及于季札。」諸樊曰：「敢不如命。」壽夢卒，諸樊以適長攝行事，當國政。

吳王諸樊元年，已除喪，讓季札曰：「昔前王未薨之時，嘗晨昧不安，吾望其色也，意在於季札。又復三朝，悲吟而命我曰：『吾知公子札之賢，欲廢長立少。』重發言於口。雖然我心已許之。然前王不忍行其私計，以國付我。我敢不從命乎？今國者，子之國也，吾願達前王之義。」季札謝曰：「夫適長當國，非前王之私，乃宗廟社稷之制，豈可變乎？」諸樊曰：「苟可施於國，

---

7. Lord Xuan of Cao 曹宣公 reigned from 595 to 578 BCE. His son and heir was murdered by one of his other children, the Honorable Fuchu 公子負芻, who then established himself as Lord Cheng of Cao 曹成公 (r. 578–555 BCE); see *Zuozhuan*, 867 [Cheng 13].
8. Zizang was also known as the Honorable Xinshi of Cao 曹公子欣時. As noted by the *Zuozhuan*, 873 [Cheng 15], he fled into exile in Song to avoid being appointed as the new ruler.

The people of Wu were determined to establish Jizha, but he refused, going to plow the borderlands, at which point the people of Wu gave up on him. Zhufan proved to be an arrogant man who disrespected the ghosts and spirits, and so he looked up at the sky and begged to die. When he was dying, he ordered his younger brother Yuji: "You must pass the country to Jizha." Accordingly, he enfeoffed Jizha in Yanling and gave him the title "Master Ji of Yanling."

In the twelfth year of the reign of King Yuji [532 BCE?], King Ling of Chu held a meeting of the lords to arrange an attack on Wu.[9] They laid siege to Zhufang, executing Qing Feng.[10] Qing Feng had repeatedly probed other states on Wu's behalf, and this is the reason that Jin and Chu attacked him.

King Yuji of Wu was furious. "Qing Feng came to us when he was desperate," he said, "and Wu enfeoffed him in Zhufang, to make it clear that we appreciate men of talent." He immediately raised an army and attacked Chu, and he did not leave until after he had captured two cities.

In the thirteenth year of his reign [531 BCE?], Chu was so angry that Wu had attacked them for Qing Feng's sake that they could not overcome their rage; hence, they invaded Wu, advancing to Qianxi. Wu counterattacked, and the Chu Army was defeated and ran away.

何先王之命有！太王改為季歷，二伯來入荊蠻，遂城為國，周道就成。前人誦之，不絕於口，而子之所習也。」札復謝曰：「昔曹公卒，廢存適亡，諸侯與曹人不義而立於國。子臧聞之，行吟而歸。曹君懼，將立子臧。子臧去之，以成曹之道。札雖不才，願附子臧之義，吾誠避之。」吳人固立季札，季札不受，而耕於野，吳人舍之。諸樊驕恣，輕慢鬼神，仰天求死。將死，命弟餘祭曰：「必以國及季札。」乃封季札於延陵，號曰延陵季子。

---

9. Since King Yuji of Wu reigned for only four years, these dates are assumed to pertain to the reign of his younger brother, Yumei.
10. Qing Feng (d. 538 BCE) had previously held the title of prime minister in Qi and ruled the country as virtual dictator following the assassination first of Lord Zhuang of Qi 齊莊公 (r. 553–558 BCE) and then of his co–prime minister, Cui Shu 崔杼, in 538 BCE. King Ling of Chu 楚靈王 (r. 540–529 BCE) attacked him in the hope of establishing a better reputation and quietening gossip about the circumstances of his own rise to power, only to see his ignoble motives pointed out by Qing Feng himself; see *Zuozhuan*, 1253 [Zhao 4]. The same story is also found in other ancient texts; see, for example, *Guliang zhuan*, 606–7 [Zhao 4].

In the seventeenth year of his reign [527 BCE?], King Yuji died. Yumei was then established, but after four years, he too died. The people wished the throne to pass to Prince Jizha. However, Jizha refused and fled.

"It should be clear to everyone," he said, "that I will not take the throne. In the past, our former monarch did command that I should do so, but I have already shown my wish to follow the righteous behavior of Zizang. I would like to keep myself pure, my eyes fixed on the horizon, and my feet walking tall. The only thing that I care about is that my actions should be benevolent. To me, wealth and nobility are as the passing autumn winds."

He ran away back to his home in Yanling. The people of Wu established Yumei's son Zhouyu as their ruler, and he took the title "King Liao of Wu."

餘祭十二年，楚靈王會諸侯伐吳，圍朱方，誅慶封。慶封數為吳伺祭，故晉、楚伐之也。吳王餘祭怒曰:「慶封窮，來奔。吳封之朱方，以效不恨士也。」即舉兵伐楚，取二邑而去。

十三年，楚怨吳為慶封故伐之，心恨不解，伐吳，至乾谿。吳擊之，楚師敗走。

十七年，餘祭卒。餘昧立，四年，卒。欲授位季札，季札讓，逃去，曰:「吾不受位，明矣。昔前君有命，已附子臧之義。潔身清行，仰高履尚，惟仁是處，富貴之於我，如秋風之過耳。」遂逃歸延陵。吳人立餘昧子州于，號為吳王僚也。

Chapter Three

The Traditions

The Story of How King Liao Employed Prince Guang

In the second year of his reign [525 BCE], King Liao sent Prince Guang to attack Chu, in order to punish them for the earlier occasion on which they invaded and executed Qing Feng. The Wu Army was defeated, and they lost their boat; Prince Guang was frightened and retreated. However, he recaptured the royal boat before returning home.

It was Guang's intention to assassinate King Liao, but he did not have anyone with whom he could discuss this matter. Hence, he secretly recruited wise men into his service and appointed as the official in charge of the marketplace in Wu someone good at telling people's fortunes from their faces.

In the fifth year [522 BCE], Wu Zixu came as a refugee to Wu, fleeing from disaster in Chu. Wu Zixu came from Chu, and his personal name was Yun. His father was named She, and his older brother was named Shang. His grandfather's name was Wu Ju; he had served King Zhuang of Chu by

《王僚使公子光傳》

二年，王僚使公子光伐楚，以報前來誅慶封也。吳師敗而亡舟。光懼，因捨，復得王舟而還。光欲謀殺王僚，未有所與合議，陰求賢，乃命善相者為吳市吏。

五年，楚之亡臣伍子胥來奔吳。伍子胥者，楚人也，名員。員父奢，兄尚。其前名曰伍舉。以直諫事楚莊王。王即位三年，不聽國政，沉湎於酒，淫於聲色。左手擁秦姬，右手抱越女，身坐鐘鼓之間，而令曰：「有敢諫者，死！」於是伍舉進諫曰：「有一大鳥，集楚國之庭，三年不飛，亦不鳴。此何鳥也？」

offering remonstrance.[1] During the first three years of this monarch's reign, he did not pay any attention to the government of the country but spent his time sunk in an alcoholic stupor and was debauched with women and song. With his left hand, he grabbed a courtesan from Qin, while his right arm cuddled a lady from Yue. Sitting amid the drums and the bells, he commanded: "Anyone who dares to remonstrate with me will die!"

It was then that Wu Ju stepped forward to remonstrate. "There is a great bird that roosts in the palace of the kingdom of Chu," he said. "For three years, it has not flown, nor has it made its cry. What kind of bird is this?"

"This bird has not yet flown," King Zhuang replied, "but when it does, it will soar high into the sky; it has not made its cry, but when it does, it will startle all men."

"That it has not flown or made any cry means that it is the prey of huntsmen," Wu Ju said. "Once the arrow has been shot, how can it possibly soar high into the sky and startle all men?"

The king then sent away the courtesan from Qin and the lady from Yue; he stopped the music [being played] on bells and drums, and he employed Sunshu Ao, entrusting him with the government of the country. He ruled the entire world as a hegemon, and the other lords bowed down to his authority.

When King Zhuang died, King Ling was established.[2] He built the Zhanghua Tower and climbed up on it [with his ministers].[3]

"How beautiful this tower is!" the king said.

"I have heard that a ruler should think being given clothing as a gift of appreciation by the Zhou king is a beautiful thing," Wu Ju responded, "and

於是莊王曰:「此鳥不飛,飛則沖天;不鳴,鳴則驚人。」伍舉曰:「不飛不鳴,將為射者所圖。絃矢卒發,豈得沖天而驚人乎?」於是莊王棄其秦姬、越女,罷鐘鼓之樂;用孫叔敖,任以國政。遂霸天下,威伏諸侯。莊王卒,靈王立,建章華之臺。【羣臣】與登焉。王曰:「臺美!」伍舉曰:「臣聞國君服寵以為美,安民以為樂,克聽以為聰,致遠以為明。不聞以土木之崇高,蟲鏤之

---

1. The story of King Zhuang of Chu's refusal to take any role in the government during the early part of his rule is also recorded in *Shiji*, 40.1700; see also *Han Feizi*, 412–13 ["Yulao" 喻老], and *Xinxu*, 271–76 ["Zashi er" 雜事二].
2. King Ling of Chu reigned from 541 to 529 BCE; rather than being King Zhuang of Chu's son, he was actually his grandson.
3. The words "his ministers" (*qunchen* 群臣) are missing in the transmitted text but are given in a quotation of this passage of the *Wu Yue chunqiu* preserved in the *Taiping yulan* 太平御覽 (Imperial Readings of the Taiping Reign Era). See Zhang Jue (1994): 60 n. 11.

that he takes pleasure from making sure his people are at peace; he regards weighing up what he hears as a measure of intelligence and bringing in people of talent from far away as a sign of enlightenment. I have not heard of anyone considering piling up earth and timber, ornamenting with carving and painting, the pure sounds of metal and stone, or the plaintive notes of strings and bamboo as something to be proud of! In the past, King Zhuang built the Baoju Tower, and it was only just high enough that he could observe the celestial omens affecting his country, and it was only just large enough to allow for banqueting.[4] The timbers were not taken from defensive works, the use of labor did not cause problems in any other branches of the government, the people were not prevented from engaging in their usual seasonal employment, and government officials did not have to change their routine attendance at court. Today you, Your Majesty, have spent seven years on this tower—the people of the kingdom hate it, you have used up all your wealth on it, years' worth of harvests have been wasted on it, the ordinary people have been put to great trouble over it, other lords are furious, and your officials complain relentlessly—surely this is not something that our former kings would have praised, or that you, as the ruler, should be pleased about! I am indeed stupid, for I really do not know what to say!"

King Ling immediately stopped the work and sent away the workmen, and he did not spend any more time at the tower. In this way, the Wu family members were loyal ministers in Chu for three generations.

King Ping of Chu had a crown prince named Jian.[5] King Ping appointed Wu She as the crown prince's grand mentor and Fei Wuji as his junior mentor. King Ping appointed Wuji as his ambassador to arrange a

刻畫，金石之清音，絲竹之淒唳，以之為美。前莊王為抱［匏］居之臺，高不過望國氛，大不過容宴豆，木不妨守備，用不煩官府，民不敗時務，官不易朝常。今君為此臺七年，國人怨焉，財用盡焉，年穀敗焉，百姓煩焉，諸侯忿怨，卿士訕謗，豈前王之所盛，人君之美者耶？臣誠愚，不知所謂也。」靈王即除工去飾，不遊於臺。由是伍氏三世為楚忠臣。

---

4. The Baoju tower is also mentioned in *Guoyu*, 541 ["Chuyu shang" 楚語上], where it is called the Paoju Tower 匏居臺. *Fen* 氛, here translated as "celestial omens," refers specifically to predictions obtained from clouds, an important branch of early Chinese divination practice; see Loewe (1994): 191–213.

5. King Ping of Chu reigned from 528 to 516 BCE. The ongoing controversies of his reign would continue to cause serious problems many decades after his death and form one of the major themes in the *Wu Yue chunqiu*.

marriage alliance for the crown prince in Qin. The lady from Qin was very beautiful, so Wuji reported to King Ping: "The lady from Qin is the most beautiful woman in the world—you ought to take her for yourself, Your Majesty."

The king then took the lady from Qin as his consort, and he favored and loved her; she gave birth to Prince Zhen.[6] He arranged an alternative marriage alliance for the crown prince with a lady from Qi. Because of these events, [Fei] Wuji had to leave the service of the crown prince and go to work for King Ping. He was very concerned that one day King Ping would die and the crown prince would come to the throne, at which point he was going to be in serious trouble. He therefore repeatedly slandered Crown Prince Jian. Jian's mother, Lady Cai, had lost all favor, so he was able to get the crown prince sent to guard Chengfu, to train troops along the border.[7] A short time later, Wuji began complaining about the crown prince day and night.

"The crown prince has not been able to overcome his anger and resentment over what happened with the lady from Qin," he said. "I hope that you will take measures to protect yourself, Your Majesty. The crown prince is stationed at Chengfu, and he is in command of troops; furthermore, if he makes contact with the other lords beyond the borders, he could invite them in to launch a coup!"

King Ping summoned Wu She and questioned him about this. Wu She knew that this was all malicious gossip on the part of [Fei] Wuji, and so he remonstrated with him: "How can Your Majesty possibly only listen to the evil slanders of this small-minded man to the detriment of your own flesh and blood?"

楚平王有太子，名建。平王以伍奢為太子太傅，費無忌為少傅。平王使無忌為太子娶於秦。秦女美容，無忌報平王曰：「秦女天下無雙，王可自取。」王遂納秦女為夫人，而幸愛之，生子珍；而更為太子娶齊女。無忌因去太子，而事平王。深念平王一旦卒，而太子立，當害己也，乃復讒太子建。建母蔡氏無寵，乃使太子守城父，備邊兵。頃之，無忌日夜言太子之短曰：「太子以秦女之故，不能無怨望之心，願王自備。太子居城父，將兵，外交諸侯，

---

6. The personal name of the future King Zhao of Chu 楚昭王 (r. 515–489 BCE) is variously given as *zhen* 軫 and *zhen* 珍.
7. A number of historical texts record the way in which King Ping sent his son away from the court at this time; see *Zuozhuan*, 1402 [Zhao 19], and *Shiji*, 40.1712.

Wuji took advantage of a moment of leisure to repeat: "If you do not deal with him now, when he brings off his plan, Your Majesty will find your hands tied."

King Ping was furious and threw Wu She into prison. He ordered the commander in chief at Chengfu, Fen Yang, to go and kill the crown prince. Fen Yang sent someone to warn the crown prince ahead of time: "Leave as quickly as you can! Otherwise, you will be executed!"

In the third month, the crown prince fled to Song.

[Fei] Wuji again spoke to King Ping: "Wu She has two sons, both of whom are remarkably clever men. If you do not execute them, they are sure to cause trouble for Chu. You could use their father as a hostage and call them back."

The king sent a messenger to tell [Wu] She: "If you can bring your two sons back, you will live. Otherwise, you will die."

"I have two sons," Wu She said. "The older is called Shang, and the younger is called Xu. Shang has a kindly and trusting personality—if he hears that I want to call him back, he will immediately come. Xu's personality is such that when he was young, he became learned in books, and later on, he studied to become a very fine warrior. With books, you can rule a country well; with martial arts, you can conquer the world. He will hold to his principles at all costs—even if wronged, he will not be deflected; such a person can achieve great things. A knight with that kind of foreknowledge cannot be called back!"

King Ping reflected on the praise Wu She had heaped on his two sons, and so he sent an envoy riding a carriage drawn by a team of four horses, with an official letter of accreditation and seals, to go and summon Zishang and Zixu, tricking them to their deaths. He ordered him to say: "Congratulations to you two gentlemen! Your father, She, has been found not guilty of all charges, since his loyalty and trustworthiness has been proved—his troubles are over! King Ping feels deeply ashamed that he imprisoned such a fine minister, and foreign lords now treat him with distain, so he would now like to appoint She as prime minister and make you two gentlemen marquises. Shang will be appointed marquis of Hongdu, while Xu will be given the title

將入為亂。」平王乃召伍奢而按問之。奢知無忌之讒，因諫之曰：「王獨奈何以讒賊小臣而疏骨肉乎？」無忌承宴，復言曰：「王今不制，其事成矣，王且見擒。」平王大怒，因囚伍奢，而使城父司馬奮揚往殺太子。奮揚使人前告太子：「急去！不然將誅。」三月，太子奔宋。無忌復言平王曰：「伍奢有二子，皆賢。不誅，且為楚憂。可以其父為質而召之。」王使使謂奢曰：「能

'marquis of Gai'—these lands are just over three hundred *li* apart.[8] She was in prison for a long time, and he has been worried about you, so he sent me to give you your seals of office."

"During the three years that my father has been in prison," Shang said, "it has been so distressing that my food has lost all flavor, and I have experienced the bitterness of hunger and thirst. Day and night I have been worried, fearful lest my father not survive. The only thing that matters is that my father is pardoned; how could I dare to covet these seals of office?"

"Your father was in prison for three years," the envoy said, "and now thanks to His Majesty's grace, he has been released from captivity. His Majesty cannot give him anything, so he is enfeoffing you two gentlemen as marquises. Now that you have received this message, you ought to go back—or is there something else you want to complain about?"

Shang then went into the house and reported this to Zixu. "Our father has been so fortunate as to escape the death penalty, and we have been appointed as marquises; the envoy is at the gate with credentials and seals of office. You should meet him."

"Just sit there, and I will perform a divination about it for you," Zixu said. "Today is Jiazi Day, and we are in the hour Si.[9] The latter is harmed by being situated below this day sign, and the *qi* is blocked thereby; hence, rulers will oppress their subjects, and fathers will bully their sons.[10] If you go now, you will die—how can you expect to become a marquis?"

致二子，則生；不然，則死。」伍奢曰：「臣有二子，長曰尚，少曰胥。尚為人慈溫仁信，若聞臣召，輒來。胥為人少好於文，長習於武，文治邦國，武定天下，執綱守戾，蒙垢受恥，雖冤不爭，能成大事。此前知之士，安可致耶？」平王謂伍奢之譽二子，即遣使者駕馴馬，封函印綬往，詐召子尚、子胥。令曰：「賀二子，父奢以忠信慈仁，去難就免。平王內慚囚繫忠臣，外愧諸侯之恥，反遇奢為國相，封二子為侯。尚賜鴻都侯，胥賜蓋侯，相去不遠三百

---

8. Zhang Jue (2006): 37–38 n. 10–11 argues that these two place-names are invented by the author of this text and do not reflect genuine locations in the kingdom of Chu.
9. Jiazi Day is the first day in the sixty-day cycle used within the Chinese calendar. According to the commentary by Zhang Jue (2006): 38 n. 16, the use of Si to designate the hour reflects Han dynasty usage and, hence, was probably an invention of the author of the text.
10. As stated by the *Huainanzi* 淮南子 (Book of the Master of Huainan), the sign Zi in the Earthly Branches system represents the phase Water, while Si represents Fire. Since in Five Phase cosmology, Water overcomes Fire, the day sign is here understood as being in conflict with the hour sign; see *Huainanzi*, 277 ["Tianwen xun" 天文訓].

"Surely you understand that I don't care about being a marquis!" Shang exclaimed. "I am worried about our father! If I can see him just once and say goodbye, it will be worth it even if it costs my life."

"Shang, do not go!" Zixu said. "Our father is alive because of us. Chu is afraid of us and in the circumstances will not dare to kill him. If you make the mistake of going back, you are going to die!" After saying this, Zixu sighed. "If you are executed with our father," he continued, "how will people know what happened? If our wrongs are not avenged, the humiliation will grow greater day by day. If you go back, I will have to say goodbye forever."

Shang burst into tears. "If I survive but end up as a laughingstock for the entire world," he said, "even if I live to be old, what would be the point? If I cannot avenge the insults heaped on us, I am useless. You are talented at writing and martial arts; you are good at coming up with stratagems and schemes—it will be up to you to avenge father and myself. If I am able to return alive, it is because Heaven has protected me. If I end up dead and buried, this is still a price I am happy to pay."

"Go then, Shang!" [Zi]xu said. "I will leave with no regrets. I hope that nothing will happen to you, for otherwise you might be prey to vain remorse."

Still weeping, they said goodbye, and then he departed with the envoy. Once Chu got their hands on Shang, they arrested him and threw him into prison.

Again [the king] sent people to hunt down and capture [Wu] Zixu. He fled from Chu, holding his bow and arrows at the ready. Chu pursed him and found his wife, who said: "Xu is gone—he must be three hundred *li* away."[11]

餘里。奢久囚繫，憂思二子，故遣臣來，奉進印綬。」尚曰：「父繫三年，中心切怛，食不甘味，嘗苦飢渴，晝夜感思，憂父不活，惟父獲免，何敢貪印綬哉？」使者曰：「父囚三年，王今幸赦，無以賞賜，封二子為侯。一言當至，何所陳哉？」尚乃入報子胥曰：「父幸免死，二子為侯，使者在門，兼封印綬，汝可見使。」子胥曰：「尚且安坐，為兄卦之。今日甲子，時加於巳，支傷日下，氣不相受。君欺其臣，父欺其子。今往方死，何侯之有？」尚曰：

---

11. The *Yuejue shu*, 70 ["Waizhuan Jini" 外傳計倪], mentions the estrangement between Wu Zixu and his wife and children caused by his distress at the death of King Helü of Wu. It is not clear whether Wu Zixu was believed to have married again in exile in Wu or whether this was thought to be the same woman.

The envoy chased after him and caught up with him in an uninhabited wilderness. Xu then drew his bow and nocked his arrow, wanting to shoot the messenger. The man fell flat on the ground and started to wriggle away.

"Tell your King Ping that if he does not want his country to be destroyed, he has to release my father and older brother," [Zi]xu said.[12] "Otherwise I am going to turn Chu into a wasteland."

The messenger returned and reported this to King Ping. When His Majesty heard this, he immediately out sent the main army. They chased Zixu all the way to the Yangtze River, where they lost all trace of him. They had to turn back empty-handed.

When Zixu reached the Yangtze River, he looked up at the sky, walking and wailing his pain amid the forests and the marshes. "How wicked is the king of Chu," he cried. "He has killed my father and older brother! I hope that one of the foreign lords will take revenge on him for me!"

Having heard that Crown Prince Jian was living in Song, Xu determined to go there.

When Wu She was first informed that Zixu had escaped, he said: "The king and ministers of Chu are going to suffer some terrible military defeats."

After Shang arrived in Chu and joined his father, they both were tortured to death in the marketplace.

Wu Yuan fled to Song, and on the road, he met Shen Baoxu.[13] "The king of Chu has killed my father and older brother," he said. "What should I do?"

「豈貪於侯，思見父耳！一面而別，雖死而生。」子胥曰：「尚且無往。父當我活，楚畏我勇，勢不敢殺。兄若誤往，必死不脫。」尚曰：「父子之愛，恩從中出，徼倖相見，以自濟達。」於是子胥歎曰：「與父俱誅，何明於世？冤讎不除，恥辱日大。尚從是往，我從是決。」尚泣曰：「吾之生也，為世所笑，終老地上，而亦何之！不能報仇，畢為廢物。汝懷文武，勇於策謀，父兄之讎，汝可復也。吾如得返，是天祐之；其遂沉埋，亦吾所喜。」胥曰：「尚且行矣，

---

12. Some commentators argue that the words *Pingwang* 平王 (King Ping) in this sentence are extraneous; see, for example, Xu Tianhu (1999): 18. However, they may also be included to emphasize Wu Zixu's sense of alienation.

13. The name Shen Baoxu is also given in some texts as Shen Baoxu 申鮑胥; see *Shiji*, 40.1716. Alternatively, this individual is also known as Fenmao Bosu 棻冒勃蘇, with the last two characters being nearly homophonous to Baoxu; see *Zhanguo ce*, 769–70 ["Chuce yi" 楚策一]. It is thought that he was descended from the older brother of King Wu of Chu 楚武王 (r. 689–677 BCE).

"Alas!" Shen Baoxu replied. "If I were to tell you to take revenge on Chu, then I would be disloyal. If I tell you not to take revenge, then I would be showing myself a heartless friend. You should go on your way! I am not going to say a word."

"I have heard it said that you should not share the same sky or stand on the same earth as the person who killed your parents nor stay in the same country as the person who killed your brother," Zixu said. "You should not share the same neighborhood or live in the same village as he who killed your friend. Now I am going to take revenge for the crime committed by Chu and expunge the humiliation inflicted on my father and older brother."

"If you can destroy Chu, I can save it," Shen Baoxu declared. "If you can threaten it, I can bring it peace."

[Wu Zi]xu then fled to Song.

Lord Yuan of Song had lost any authority within the country, and the people of the capital despised him.[14] Various grandees of the Hua family conspired against and murdered Lord Yuan, and thus, there was a serious civil war involving the Hua family and the people of the capital.[15] Zixu and Crown Prince Jian both had to flee to Zheng, and the people of Zheng treated them with the greatest respect. Crown Prince Jian then traveled on to Jin. Lord Qing of Jin said to him:[16] "You are living in Zheng, and they trust you. If you would be prepared to act as our agent on the inside, when we have destroyed Zheng, we will enfeoff you with these lands."

吾去不顧，勿使臨難，雖悔何追！」旋泣辭行，與使俱往。楚得子尚，執而囚之。復遣追捕子胥。胥乃貫弓執矢，去楚。楚追之，見其妻。曰：「胥亡矣，去三百里。」使者追及無人之野。胥乃張弓布矢，欲害使者。使者俯伏而走。胥曰：「報汝平王，欲國不滅，釋吾父兄。若不爾者，楚為墟矣。」使返報平王。王聞之，即發大軍，追子胥至江，失其所在，不獲而返。子胥行至大江，仰天行，哭林澤之中，言：「楚王無道，殺吾父兄，願吾因於諸侯，以報讎

---

14. Lord Yuan of Song ruled from 531 to 517 BCE; according to the historical texts that record his difficult reign, it was the murder of a number of members of his own family that brought about the serious political troubles of this period; see *Zuozhuan*, 1409 [Zhao 20], and *Shiji*, 38.1630.
15. The rebellion of the Hua family, in particular Hua Hai 華亥 and Hua Ding 華定, is recorded in *Zuozhuan*, 1409–10 [Zhao 20].
16. Lord Qing of Jin ruled from 525 to 512 BCE; this account of his attempt to bribe Crown Prince Jian to assist his campaign against Zheng is derived from *Shiji*, 66.2173.

The crown prince returned to Zheng. Before he was able to act, it so happened that he wanted [to kill] one of his followers because of a private quarrel.[17] This follower knew of his plans and reported them to Zheng. Lord Ding of Zheng plotted the murder of Crown Prince Jian with Zichan.[18]

Jian had a son named Sheng, and Wu Yuan then fled to Wu with Sheng. When he arrived at the border pass of Zhao, the official in charge of the pass wanted to arrest him. Wu Yuan tricked him, saying: "The reason why his lordship wants to arrest me is because I owned a beautiful pearl. Now I have already lost it, but I will [tell them that] you took it for yourself."[19]

The border official then let him go.

He set out with Sheng, but their pursuers were close behind, and they nearly did not escape. When they arrived at the Yangtze River, there was a fisherman out in the middle of the river, moving against the current. Zixu shouted to him, bellowing: "Fisherman, take us across!"

He called twice, and the fisherman wanted to take him across, but it happened that there were some people watching them, so instead, he sang a song:

The sun shines brightly as it gradually moves toward the west,
I will wait for you in the reeds along the riverbank.[20]

矣。」聞太子建在宋，胥欲往之。伍奢初聞子胥之亡，曰：「楚之君臣，且苦兵矣！」尚至楚就父，俱戮於市。伍員奔宋，道遇申包胥，謂曰：「楚王殺吾兄父，為之奈何？」申包胥曰：「於乎！吾欲教子報楚，則為不忠；教子不報，則為無親友也。子其行矣，吾不容言。」子胥曰：「吾聞父母之讎，不與戴天履地；兄弟之讎，不與同域接壤；朋友之讎，不與鄰鄉共里。今吾將復楚辜，以雪父兄之恥。」申包胥曰：「子能亡之，吾能存之；子能危之，吾能安之。」胥遂奔宋。

---

17. The word "to kill" (*sha* 殺), which is not found in the original text, is taken from *Shiji*, 66.2173.
18. Lord Ding of Zheng ruled from 529 to 514 BCE; Zichan (d. 522 BCE) served as prime minister of Zheng from 544 BCE until his death. This account of the involvement of both men in the death of Crown Prince Jian is taken from *Shiji*, 66.2173, since other accounts only mention Lord Ding of Zheng by name.
19. This line does not make sense in the original text and, hence, is translated following the quotations preserved in Xu Jian (2004): 7.160 and Ouyang Xun (2007): 6.103.
20. These two lines rhyme in the *-ai, *-wai (*ge* 歌) rhyme group.

Zixu immediately hid himself among the reeds on the bank of the river. The fisherman then sang:

The sun is setting; you must be getting worried,
The moon is rising; why do you not cross the river?
In this crisis, what is to be done?[21]

Zixu got onto the boat, and the fisherman knew exactly what he wanted. He ferried him across the Qianxun Ford.[22]

When Zixu was being carried over the ford, the fisherman scrutinized him and thought that he looked half-starved. "Wait for me under this tree," he said, "and I will go and get something for you to eat."

After the fisherman had gone, Zixu became suspicious and hid himself amid a dense clump of rushes. A short time later, the fisherman returned, clutching a bowl of wheat with some fish stew and a jug of wine. He looked under the tree but could not find him, and so he sang out to him: "Man in the reeds! Man in the reeds! Are you not a gentleman in trouble?"

He called this way twice, and then Zixu emerged from the reeds and responded.

"I saw that you looked hungry," the fisherman said, "so I got some food for you. Why were you hiding from me?"

"My ultimate fate will be determined by Heaven," Zixu said, "but right now my life is in your hands. How could I possibly suspect you?"

When the two of them had finished eating and drinking and wanted to be on their way, [Wu Zi]xu undid a sword worth one hundred pieces of gold and gave it to the fisherman. "This sword belonged to our former king,"

宋元公無信於國，國人惡之。大夫華氏謀殺元公，國人與華氏因作大亂。子胥乃與太子建俱奔鄭，鄭人甚禮之。太子建又適晉。晉頃公曰：「太子既在鄭，鄭信太子矣。太子能為內應而滅鄭，即以鄭封太子。」太子還鄭，事未成，會欲私其從者，從者知其謀，乃告之於鄭。鄭定公與子產誅殺太子建。建有子，名勝。伍員與勝奔吳。到昭關，關吏欲執之。伍員因詐曰：「上所以索我者，美珠也。今我已亡矣，將去取之。」關吏因舍之。與勝行去，追者在後，幾不得脫。至江，江中有漁父，乘船從下方泝水而上。子胥呼之，

---

21. With the first two lines of the fisherman's song included, the rhyme pattern is AABAA; these three lines have final characters from the *-əi (*wei* 微), *-ai, and *-wai (*ge*) groups, respectively.
22. Zhang Jue (2006): 42 n. 9 argues that the name of the Qianxun Ford 千潯之津 should be understood as the epithet *qianxun* 千尋, meaning "unfathomable."

he said, "and it was forged from seven stars.[23] It is worth one hundred pieces of gold. I would like you to have this in return for your kindness."

"I have heard that Chu has issued an order saying that whoever captures Wu [Zi]xu will be given fifty thousand bushels of grain and an appointment at court," the fisherman responded. "How could I possibly want a sword worth a mere one hundred pieces of gold?"

He absolutely refused to take it. "Get away from here as fast as you can!" he told Zixu. "Do not stay any longer! Otherwise, you will be captured by Chu."

"Can I know your name?" Zixu asked.

"These are turbulent times," the fisherman replied, "and we both are criminals in cahoots with one another—I am talking about my actions in ferrying a traitor to Chu across the river. Since we have met, we should keep quiet about these things. What is the point of using our real names? You are the man in the reeds; I am the fisherman. When you are rich and noble, do not forget me."

"Okay," said Zixu.

When he was about to set off, he warned the fisherman. "You should hide that jug of wine. Do not let anyone find it."

The fisherman agreed. Zixu walked a couple of paces and then turned his head back to look at the fisherman, but he had already overturned his boat and sunk beneath the waters of the river.

Wu Zixu was silent, but after a while, he set off and proceeded toward Wu. He got sick on the journey and ended up begging for food in Liyang. He happened to meet a woman washing silk on the upper reaches of the Lai River, and she had some rice in her basket. Zixu approached her and said: "My lady, can I have something to eat?"

謂曰：「漁父渡我！」如是者再。漁父欲渡之，適會旁有人窺之，因而歌曰：「日月昭昭乎侵已馳，與子期乎蘆之漪。」子胥即止蘆之漪。漁父又歌曰：「日已夕兮，予心憂悲；月已馳兮，何不渡為？事寖急兮，當奈何？」子胥入船。漁父知其意也，乃渡之千潯之津。子胥既渡，漁父乃視之，有其飢色。乃謂曰：「子俟我此樹下，為子取餉。」漁父去後，子胥疑之，乃潛身於深葦之中。有頃，父來，持麥飯、鮑魚羹、盎漿，求之樹下，不見，因歌而呼之曰：「蘆中人，蘆中人，豈非窮士乎？」如是至再，子胥乃出蘆中而應。漁父曰：「吾

---

23. It has been suggested that this description should be taken literally; see Schafer (1977): 160, given that a number of ancient Chinese swords are known to have been produced from meteoritic iron.

"I live alone with my mother," the woman replied, "and I am not yet married at thirty years of age. I cannot give you anything to eat."

"If you can rescue a traveler in serious trouble with a little bit of food, my lady, why would you refuse?" said Zixu.

The woman realized that he was no ordinary man, and so she agreed to his request. She opened up her basket, in which there was food with a jug of wine. Then kneeling down, she gave it to him. Zixu ate two meals and then stopped.

"You have far to go, my lord, so why do you not eat your fill?" the woman said.

Having eaten, Zixu departed. However, he said to the woman: "You should hide that jug of wine. Do not let anyone find it."

The woman sighed. "Alas!" she said. "I have lived alone with my mother for thirty years, preserving my purity, unwilling to get married. How could it be right that I give this food to a man? I could not bear to do anything that contravenes ritual propriety. You had better go."

Zixu set off, and then he turned his head back to look at the woman, but she had already thrown herself into the Lai River. Alas! This heroine was indeed determined to preserve her purity!

Zixu arrived in Wu, and then he untied his hair and pretended to be mad. He walked around barefoot, his face plastered with mud, and begged in the marketplace. The people in the marketplace looked at him, but nobody knew who he was. On the second day, the official in charge of the marketplace at Wu who was good at telling people's fortunes from their faces saw him and said: "I have told the fortunes of many men from their faces, but I have never seen anyone like this! Must he not be an exiled minister from a foreign country?"

He reported this to King Liao and explained the situation. "You ought to summon this man for an audience, Your Majesty."

見子有飢色，為子取餉，子何嫌哉？」子胥曰：「性命屬天，今屬丈人，豈敢有嫌哉？」二人飲食畢，欲去，胥乃解百金之劍，以與漁者，【曰】：「此吾前君之劍，中有七星，價直百金，以此相答。」漁父曰：「吾聞楚之法令：得伍胥者，賜粟五萬石，爵執圭。豈圖取百金之劍乎？」遂辭不受。謂子胥曰：「子急去，勿留，且為楚所得！」子胥曰：「請丈人姓字。」漁父曰：「今日凶凶，兩賊相逢，吾所謂渡楚賊也。兩賊相得，得形於默，何用姓字為？子為蘆中人，吾為漁丈人，富貴莫相忘也。」子胥曰：「諾。」既去，誡漁父：「掩子之盎漿，無令其露。」漁父諾。子胥行數步，顧視漁者，已覆船自沉於江水之中矣。子胥默然，遂行。至吳，疾於中道，乞食溧陽。適會女子擊綿於瀨水之上，筥中有飯。子胥遇之，謂曰：「夫人，可得一餐乎？」女子曰：「妾獨與母居，

"I want you to come with him," King Liao said.

Prince Guang heard about this and was secretly delighted. "I have heard that Chu murdered their loyal minister Wu She and that his son Zixu is brave and wise—he must want to avenge his father, and that is why he has come to Wu," he said.

He secretly desired to recruit this man into his own service.

Then the official from the marketplace entered [the palace] to have an audience with the king together with [Wu] Zixu. King Liao was amazed at his impressive physique: he was one *zhang* tall, his waist was ten *wei* in circumference, and the space between his eyebrows was one *chi* in length.[24] King Liao spoke with him for three days, and he never once repeated himself.

"What a clever man!" the king said.

Zixu knew that His Majesty was pleased with him. Every time he went into the palace to speak with him, he would appear impressively brave; when he worked the conversation around to the discussion of his wrongs, he gave a strong impression of urgency. King Liao understood this and wanted to raise an army to take revenge for him. The prince wanted to assassinate King Liao, and he was afraid that his plan would be put in jeopardy should Zixu become close to the king beforehand, so he slandered him. "Zixu is remonstrating in favor of an attack on Chu, not for the sake of Wu, but because he wants revenge for a private enmity. You should not employ him in the government, Your Majesty."

Zixu was aware that Prince Guang intended to kill King Liao. "Given that Guang's ambitions are focused on internal matters, it is at present useless to speak to him about foreign affairs," he said.

He went into the palace and had an audience with King Liao. "I have heard that a lord would not raise an army and turn their forces against another country for the sake of a mere commoner," he said.

三十未嫁，飯不可得。」子胥曰：「夫人，賑窮途少飯，亦何嫌哉？」女子知非恆人，遂許之，發其簞筥飯其盎漿，長跪而與之。子胥再餐而止。女子曰：「君有遠逝之行，何不飽而餐之？」子胥已餐而去，又謂女子曰：「掩夫人之壺漿，無令其露。」女子歎曰：「嗟乎！妾獨與母居三十年，自守貞明，不願從適，何宜饋飯而與丈夫，越虧禮儀，妾不忍也。子行矣。」子胥行，反顧女子，已自投於瀨水矣。於乎！貞明執操，其丈夫女哉！子胥之吳，乃被髮佯狂，

---

24. This implies that in modern measurements, Wu Zixu was over two meters tall, his waist was over a meter in circumference, and the space between his eyebrows was about twenty centimeters, according to the conversions given by Wu Chengluo (1984).

"What are you talking about?" asked King Liao.

"A ruler should concentrate on the government of the country; you should save those who need your help, and only after that has been done should you engage in offensive warfare," Zixu said. "Your Majesty has only recently ascended the throne, and you are still establishing your authority; if you were to go to war for the sake of a mere commoner, it would not be right. I would not dare to obey your commands in this matter, Your Majesty."

The king of Wu then stopped.

[Wu] Zixu left and plowed the fields, while seeking out brave knights that he could recommend to Prince Guang, hoping thereby to ingratiate himself. This was how he discovered the assassin Zhuan Zhu. Zhuan Zhu came from Tangyi. At the time when Wu [Zi]xu fled from Chu to Wu, he met him on the way. Zhuan Zhu happened to be fighting with someone and was just about to defeat his opponent; he was angry enough to fight ten thousand men with irresistible force, but the moment his wife called to him, he immediately turned back.

Zixu thought this was most peculiar and asked what was going on. "Why did you turn in your tracks the moment you heard a woman's voice, sir, even though you were clearly furious? Were you just trying to please her?"

"Look at me; do you really think I am that stupid?" Zhuan Zhu asked. "Why did you say such a silly thing? Even though I obey one person, I can impose my authority on ten thousand others."

Zixu then performed a divination from his appearance. [Zhuan Zhu] had a high forehead and deep-set eyes, shoulders like a tiger, and a back as broad as a bear's. He would clearly be courageous in rescuing those in trouble, and so he realized this was a brave knight. He wanted to make use of him. When [Wu Zixu] joined Prince Guang's conspiracy, he presented him to Prince Guang.

跣足塗面，行乞於市。市人觀，罔有識者。翌日，吳市吏善相者見之，曰：「吾之相人多矣，未嘗見斯人也，非異國之亡臣乎？」乃白吳王僚，具陳其狀：「王宜召之。」王僚曰：「與之俱入。」公子光聞之，私喜曰：「吾聞楚殺忠臣伍奢。其子子胥，勇而且智，彼必復父之讎，來入於吳。」陰欲養之。市吏於是與子胥俱入，見王。王僚怪其狀偉：身長一丈，腰十圍，眉間一尺。王僚與語三日，辭無復者。王曰：「賢人也。」子胥知王好之，每入語語，遂有勇壯之氣，稍道其讎，而有切痛之色。王僚知之，欲為興師復讎。公子謀殺王僚，恐子胥前親於王而害其謀，因讒：「伍胥之諫伐楚者，非為吳也，但欲自復私讎耳。王無用之。」子胥知公子光欲害王僚，乃曰：「彼光有內志，未可說以外事。」入見王僚曰：「臣聞諸侯不為匹夫興師用兵於比國。」王僚曰：「何以言之？」

Once Guang had obtained the services of Zhuan Zhu, he treated him with all due ceremony. "Heaven sent you to help me at a time when I have lost all support," Prince Guang said.

"When our former king, Yumei, died, Liao was established; this is his position," Zhuan Zhu said. "Why do you want to harm him?"

"His Late Majesty, Shoumeng, had four sons, of whom the oldest was called Zhufan—he was my father," Guang replied. "The second was Yuji, the third Yumei, and the youngest was called Jizha. [Ji]zha was the wisest of all. When His Late Majesty was about to die, he demanded that the throne go to his oldest son and legitimate heir, passing in turn until it reached Jizha. You may remember that Jizha was then on a diplomatic mission visiting various foreign lords and had not yet returned. When Yumei died, the country was empty, but it would have been right to establish the oldest son and legitimate heir. I am the son of the legitimate heir. Why should Liao have been crowned in my stead? I found myself powerless, helpless in this dangerous situation—without strong supporters, how can I achieve my ambition? If I were able to take the throne, even if Master Ji returned from the east, he would not be able to dispossess me!"

"Why don't you get some important minister to put in a word for you with the king at the right moment?" Zhuan Zhu asked. "He could explain His Late Majesty's will and thus sound out his intentions, letting him know to whom the country should belong. Why should you have to employ an assassin? Will this not make His Late Majesty look bad?"

"Liao is a greedy and arrogant man—he will think only of the benefits that accrue to his present position and could not care less that he ought to give way to the rightful heir," Guang explained. "That is the reason why I am looking for a knight who shares my concerns and is willing to throw in his lot with mine. You, sir, are the only person who can fully appreciate the rightness of my cause."

子胥曰：「諸侯專為政，非以意救急後興師。今大王踐國制威，為匹夫興兵，其義非也。臣固不敢如王之命。」吳王乃止。

子胥退耕於野，求勇士薦之公子光，欲以自媚。乃得勇士專諸。專諸者，堂邑人也。伍胥之亡楚如吳時，遇之於途。專諸方與人鬥，將就敵，其怒有萬人之氣，甚不可當。其妻一呼，即還。子胥怪而問其狀：「何夫子之怒盛也，聞一女子之聲而折道，寧有說乎？」專諸曰：「子視吾之儀，寧類愚者也？何言之鄙也？夫屈一人之下，必伸萬人之上。」子胥因相其貌：磓顙而深目，虎膺而熊背，戾於從難。知其勇士，陰而結之，欲以為用。遭公子光之有謀也，而進之公子光。光既得專諸而禮待之。公子光曰：「天以夫子輔孤之失根也。」專諸曰：「前王餘昧卒，僚立，自其分也。公子何因而欲害之乎？」光曰：

"You have explained yourself very clearly," Zhuan Zhu said. "But what have I got to do with all this, my prince?"

"No, no," Guang said. "I have been telling you about something that affects the destiny of the entire country—this is not something that a small-minded person can become involved in. You are the only person I can trust with my orders."

"I am willing to obey your commands, my prince," Zhuan Zhu affirmed.

"The time is not yet ripe," Prince Guang said.

"If you want to kill the king, you must first discover his interests," Zhuan Zhu pointed out. "What does the king of Wu enjoy?"

"He is a gourmet," Guang replied.

"And what type of food does he particularly like?" Zhuan Zhu asked.

"He most enjoys roasted fish," Guang informed him.

Zhuan Zhu then went away and studied how to roast fish at Lake Tai. After three months, he could do so successfully, and then he settled down to await the prince's commands.

In the eighth year of his reign, King Liao ordered the prince to attack Chu, and he inflicted a terrible defeat on the Chu Army. As a result, he was able to escort the mother of the former Crown Prince Jian back from Zheng.[25] The ruler of Zheng gave Jian's mother earrings and hairpins made of pearls and jade, since he hoped by these means to be excused for his offense in murdering Jian.

In the ninth year of his reign [518 BCE], [King Liao of] Wu ordered Guang to attack Chu, and he razed and occupied Chao and Zhongli. The reason why Wu attacked them was that previously a woman from Jialiang, a frontier town of Chu, had been raising silkworms alongside a woman from Chǔ, a frontier town of Wu, and they had come to blows over the mulberry

「前君壽夢有子四人：長曰諸樊，則光之父也；次曰餘祭；次曰餘眛；次曰季札。札之賢也。將卒，傳付適長，以及季札。念季札為使，亡在諸侯，未還，餘眛卒，國空，有立者，適長也。適長之後，即光之身也。今僚何以當代立乎？吾力弱。無助於掌事之間，非用有力徒，能安吾志？吾雖代立，季子束還，不吾廢也。」專諸曰：「何不使近臣從容言於王側，陳前王之命，以諷其意，令知國之所歸？何須私備劍士，以捐先王之德？」光曰：「僚素貪而恃

---

25. According to *Zuozhuan*, 1447 [Zhao 23], it was Prince Guang's father, King Zhufan, who rescued the late Crown Prince Jian's mother from Zheng.

trees on the border.[26] The two families had started fighting, but the kingdom of Wu had not won, and so they then attacked each other again, resulting in the destruction of the Wu frontier town. Wu was furious about this and, as a result, invaded Chu, capturing two towns before the army turned back.

In the winter of the twelfth year [515 BCE], King Ping of Chu died.[27] Wu Zixu said to Sheng, [the future] duke of Bai:[28] "King Ping died before I achieved my revenge! Even though the kingdom of Chu survives, how can I not be sad?" The duke of Bai was silent and made no reply; Wu Zixu sat weeping in his room.

In the thirteenth year, in the spring, Wu wanted to attack Chu to take advantage of this period of [mourning].[29] His Majesty commanded Princes Gaiyu and Zhuyong to lay siege to Chu with their troops, while Jizha went to Jin to observe any changes among the other lords.[30] Chu sent out soldiers to cut the retreat behind the Wu Army, which made it impossible for them to make their way back.

Right at this moment, Prince Guang became excited. Wu Zixu realized that Guang had spotted his opportunity, and so he persuaded him: "At present,

力，知進之利，不睹退讓。吾故求同憂之士，欲與之并力。惟夫子詮斯義也。」專諸曰：「君言甚露乎，於公子何意也？」光曰：「不也。此社稷之言也，小人不能奉行，惟委命矣。」專諸曰：「願公子命之。」公子光曰：「時未可也。」專諸曰：「凡欲殺人君，必前求其所好。吳王何好？」光曰：「好味。」專諸曰：「何味所甘？」光曰：「好嗜魚之炙也。」專諸乃去，從太湖學炙魚，三月得其味，安坐待公子命之。

---

26. In *Shiji*, 31.1462, the name of the Chu frontier town involved is given as Beiliang 卑梁.
27. The *Zuozhuan*, 1474 [Zhao 26], gives these events as occurring in the ninth month of the eleventh year of King Liao's reign.
28. Eventually, Sheng would be allowed to return to the kingdom of Chu during the reign of King Hui 楚惠王 (r. 488–432 BCE), his nephew, and he was given the lands of Bai as his fief; see *Shiji*, 40.1718.
29. Xu Tianhu (1999): 26 suggests that *zang* 葬 (to bury) should be understood as a graphic error for *sang* 喪 (mourning) in this sentence. This suggestion has been followed in the translation. Also, King Liao of Wu only reigned twelve years, so the dating here is wrong.
30. In *Zuozhuan*, 1482 [Zhao 27], these two princes are named as Yanyu 掩餘 and Zhuyong 燭庸. They are identified as King Liao's younger full brothers in the *Chunqiu jingzhuan jijie*, 1552 n. 2.

the king of Wu is attacking Chu, and his two younger brothers are commanding the army—we do not yet know whether they will win or lose. It is crucial that Zhuan Zhu should go into action right now. This opportunity will not come again, so you must not let it slip."

The prince then gave an audience to Zhuan Zhu. "Right now, His Majesty's two younger brothers are attacking Chu, and Jizha has not yet returned," he said. "At this moment, if nothing is ventured, nothing will be gained! This opportunity cannot be lost . . . and I am the true heir to the throne."

"Liao can be killed," Zhuan Zhu replied. "His mother is old, his son is too young, and his younger brothers are attacking Chu, and Chu has cut their retreat. Given that at this moment Wu is in trouble with Chu abroad and has no senior ministers to hold the country together at home, His Majesty will not be able to do anything about us!"

In the fourth month, Prince Guang had soldiers lie in ambush in the cellars of his mansion and then arranged a banquet with wine to which he invited King Liao. Liao mentioned this to his mother. "Prince Guang has laid in wine and come to invite me on a certain day—does this not show he has completely changed?"

"Prince Guang is not a man who is easy to quell, and he always looks angry and resentful," his mother said. "You must be careful!"

King Liao then put on his triple-layered armor made from iron from Tang and ordered soldiers to line up along the road leading from the gate of the palace to the gate of Prince Guang's mansion. On the stairs, by his seating mat, to the left and right, there were King Liao's bodyguards, and he gave orders that all of them, whether standing or seated, should hold long spears with their blades crossed. When the wine was drunk, Prince Guang pretended that his foot was paining him, and so he went down

八年，僚遣公子伐楚，大敗楚師，因迎故太子建母於鄭。鄭君送建母珠玉簪珥，欲以解殺建之過。

九年，吳使光伐楚，拔居巢、鍾離。吳所以相攻者：初，楚之邊邑卑梁之女與吳邊邑處女蠶，爭界上之桑。二家相攻，吳國不勝。遂更相伐，滅吳之邊邑。吳怒，故伐楚，取二邑而去。

十二年冬，楚平王卒。伍子胥謂白公勝曰：「平王卒，吾志不悉矣。然楚國有，吾何憂矣？」白公默然不對，伍子胥坐泣於室。

十三年春，吳欲因楚葬而伐之。使公子蓋餘、燭傭以兵圍楚。使季札於晉，以觀諸侯之變。楚發兵絕吳後，吳兵不得還。於是公子光心動。伍胥知光之見機也，乃說光曰：「今吳王伐楚，二弟將兵，未知吉凶，專諸之事於斯急矣。

to the cellars to have his foot bandaged. He ordered Zhuan Zhu to place the blade named Yuchang inside a roast fish and present it to His Majesty.[31] When he arrived before King Liao, Zhuan Zhu ripped open the roast fish and pulled out this dagger. The spears held crossed were then thrust into Zhuan Zhu's chest, whereby his breast was ripped open and his ribs pulled apart; nevertheless, the dagger had already stabbed King Liao, cutting through his armor until it protruded from his back. King Liao died immediately. His guards killed Zhuan Zhu, and all those present were thrown into complete confusion. Prince Guang had his own soldiers lying in ambush, and they now attacked Liao's men and killed every single one of them. He then crowned himself as King Helü of Wu. He appointed Zhuan Zhu's son as a [senior minister].[32]

When Jizha completed his mission and returned to Wu, Helü tried to yield his position to him.

"Whoever ensures that the [sacrifices] to our former kings are not abandoned and that the proper ceremonies are carried out at the altars of soil and grain is my king," Jizha assured him.[33] "Whom should I be angry with? I mourn the dead, but I serve the living; in this way, I await the Mandate of Heaven. It is not my place to foment a civil war—I will obey whoever takes the throne, for this is the way of our forefathers."

時不再來，不可失也。」於是公子見專諸曰：「今二弟伐楚，季子未還，當此之時，不求何獲？時不可失。且光真王嗣也。」專諸曰：「僚可殺也。母老，子弱，弟伐楚，楚絕其後。方今吳外困於楚，內無骨鯁之臣，是無如我何也。」四月，公子光伏甲士於窟室中，具酒而請王僚。僚白其母曰：「公子光為我具酒，來請期，無變悉乎？」母曰：「光心氣怏怏，常有愧恨之色，不可不慎。」王僚乃被棠鐵之甲三重，使兵衛陳於道，自宮門至於光家之門，階席左右皆王僚之親戚，使坐立侍，皆操長戟交戟。酒酣，公子光佯為足疾，入窟室裹足，使專諸置魚腸劍炙魚中進之。既至王僚前，專諸乃擘炙魚，因推匕首，立戟

---

31. The name of this sword means "fish belly" and is probably derived from the appearance of the blade; see Hayashi Minao (1975): 225.
32. The original text says *keqing* 客卿, implying that the Zhuan family members were not natives of Wu. This translation follows *Shiji*, 86.2518, which says *shangqing* 上卿 (senior minister).
33. Some versions of the text lack the word *si* 祀 (sacrifices); see, for example, Zhang Jue (2006): 50. In others, it has been restored by analogy with the *Shiji*, 31.1465.

He made an official report on his mission, wept at the tomb of King Liao, and then he resumed his former position and awaited His Majesty's commands.

Prince Gaiyu and Prince Zhuyong, having commanded their troops to lay siege to Chu, now heard that Prince Guang had murdered King Liao and crowned himself as king. They then surrendered to Chu with their entire army, and Chu enfeoffed them with the lands of Shu.[34]

交戟倚專諸胸。胸斷臆開，匕首如故，以刺王僚，貫甲達背，王僚既死。左右共殺專諸，眾士擾動。公子光伏其甲士，以攻僚眾，盡滅之。遂自立，是為吳王闔閭也。乃封專諸之子，拜為客卿。季札使還，至吳。闔閭以位讓，季札曰：「苟前君無廢，社稷以奉，【乃吾】君也。吾誰怨乎？哀死【事】生，以俟天命。非我所亂，立者從之，是前人之道。」【復】命，哭僚墓，復位而待。公子蓋餘、燭傭二人，將兵遇圍於楚者，聞公子光殺王僚自立，乃以兵降楚，楚封之於舒。

---

34. The *Zuozhuan*, 1484 [Zhao 27], provides quite a different account of these events. First, it is only the princes who are said to have surrendered, and not the entire army. Furthermore, the two princes initially fled to Xu 徐 and Zhongwu 鐘吾, respectively, and only went to Chu after the king of Wu tried to have them arrested.

Chapter Four

The Inner Traditions
The Story of King Helü of Wu

In the first year of the reign of King Helü [514 BCE], he began to employ the able and use capable men; he showed his benevolence and enacted generous policies; and he became famous among the lords for his righteousness and fine sense of justice. However, in the period before his benevolence could be displayed and his generous policies could be enacted, he was afraid that the people would not obey him and the other lords would not trust him, so he appointed Wu Zixu as his chief of staff, treating him with the rituals proper to an honored guest and discussing the government of the country with him.

"I would like to make my kingdom powerful and become a hegemon-king, but how can I achieve this?" Helü inquired of Zixu.

Wu Zixu came forward on his knees, crying and kowtowing. "I am but an escaped prisoner from the kingdom of Chu," he wailed. "My father and

《闔閭內傳》

闔閭元年，始任賢使能，施恩行惠，以仁義聞於諸侯。仁未施，恩未行，恐國人不就，諸侯不信，乃舉伍子胥為行人，以客禮事之，而與謀國政。闔閭謂子胥曰：「寡人欲彊國霸王，何由而可？」伍子胥膝進垂淚頓首曰：「臣楚國之亡虜也。父兄棄捐，骸骨不葬，魂不血食。蒙罪受辱來歸命於大王，幸不加戮，何敢與政事焉？」闔閭曰：「非夫子，寡人不免於繁禦之使；今幸奉一言之教，乃至於斯。何為中道生進退耶？」子胥曰：「臣聞謀議之臣，

older brother were killed, but their bodies have not been buried, and their souls do not receive blood sacrifice. Accused of terrible crimes and suffering agonies of humiliation, I came here to entrust my life to you, Your Majesty. I was lucky enough not to be tortured to death here, but how could I dare to participate in the government of your country?"

"If it were not for you, sir," King Helü replied, "I would never have been able to escape from my unendurable bondage. That I hold my present position today is entirely due to having received but one line of instruction from you. How can you stop now, midway?"

"I have heard it said that a minister who advises his ruler should not stay in a place of great danger," said Zixu. "This being the case, I am concerned that once I have settled things to your satisfaction, Your Majesty is sure to become alienated from me."

"That will not happen," King Helü said. "There is no one to whom I can talk completely freely other than yourself—why should you refuse this opportunity? My kingdom is remote, located as it is far to the southeast, amid difficult and waterlogged terrain; we suffer from flooding from both the Yangtze River and the sea. I have no place of refuge; my people have nowhere to turn; we have no granaries or storehouses; and our fields are not under cultivation. What can I do about this?"

After a long pause, Zixu answered: "I have heard it said that when ruling the country, the most important thing is to ensure that the ruler is secure and that the people are properly governed."

"What techniques can ensure that I am secure and my people well governed?" asked King Helü.

"If you would make your position secure and govern your people well," Zixu said, "to raise yourself to the position of hegemon and confirm your position as king, to dominate everyone near and far, you must begin by laying out a city wall and outer fortifications, establishing your defenses, filling your granaries and storehouses, putting your armories in good order—this is the only way to achieve this."

何足處於危亡之地？然憂除事定，必不為君主所親。」闔閭曰：「不然。寡人非子無所盡議，何得讓乎？吾國僻遠，顧在東南之地，險阻潤濕，又有江海之害；君無守禦，民無所依；倉庫不設，田疇不墾。為之奈何？」子胥良久對曰：「臣聞治國之道，安君理民，是其上者。」闔閭曰：「安君治民，其術奈何？」子胥曰：「凡欲安君治民，興霸成王，從近制遠者，必先立城郭，設守備，實倉廩，治兵庫。斯則其術也。」闔閭曰：「善。夫築城郭，立倉庫，因地制宜，豈有天氣之數，以威鄰國者乎？」子胥曰：「有。」闔閭曰：

"Good!" cried King Helü. "But if we are going to build a city wall and outer fortifications, setting up granaries and armories, according to what is appropriate for the lie of the land, surely we also need to follow the patterns of the constellations and the circulation of *qi* to strike awe into neighboring countries."

"You are right," Zixu said.

"I will leave the planning for this to you," King Helü responded.

[Wu] Zixu accordingly surveyed the lands and tasted the waters, and then with Heaven and Earth as his model, he built a great city wall, forty-seven *li* in circumference. There were eight land gates, to correspond to the eight winds of Heaven. There were eight water gates, to match the eight entrances of Earth. He also constructed a citadel, ten *li* in circumference, with three land gates. There was no opening to the east, to make clear that he was determined to destroy the kingdom of Yue. He created the Chang Gate, to correspond to the Gate of Heaven, which lets loose the Changhe wind.[1] He created the Snake Gate, to correspond to the Door of Earth.[2] King Helü wanted to go west and crush Chu, *Chu being located to the northwest,* so he created the Chang Gate to allow beneficent *qi* to circulate. *This was also known as the Destruction of Chu Gate.* He wanted to conquer Greater Yue to the

「寡人委計於子。」子胥乃使相土嘗水，象天法地，造築大城。周迴四十七里，陸門八，以象天八風。水門八，以法地八聰。築小城，周十里，陵門三。不開東面者，欲以絕越明也。立閶門者，以象天門，通閶闔風也。立蛇門者，以象地戶也。閶闔欲西破楚，楚在西北，故立閶門以通天氣，因復名之破楚門。欲東并大越，越在東南，故立蛇門，以制敵國。吳在辰，其位龍也，故小城南門上反羽為兩鯢鱙，以象龍角。越在巳地，其位蛇也，故南大門上有木蛇，

---

1. The Changhe wind is the West wind; see *Huainanzi*, 196–97 ["Tianwen xun"], and *Shiji*, 25.1248. The Gate of Heaven (Tianmen 天門), represented by the stars 53 and 69 in the constellation Virgo, was therefore also sometimes known as the Changmen 閶門 or "Gate of the Chang[he Wind]" and was seen as a key numinous location in the northwest. See Sun and Kistemaker (1997): 174 for the identification of the relevant stars and *Chuci*, 68 ["Jiuge" 九歌. "Da Siming" 大司命], for an example of the later usage, respectively.

2. By analogy with the Gate of Heaven, the Door of Earth represents the southeast; see *Yuejue shu*, 49 ["Fan Bo" 范伯]. According to some accounts of the construction of the old city of Suzhou, the Snake Gate was actually built by Lord Chunshen 春申君 (d. 239 BCE) and would thus significantly postdate the time of Wu Zixu; see Lu Guangwei (1999): 23.

east, *Yue being located to the southeast.* Thus, he constructed the Snake Gate to control this enemy kingdom. Wu corresponded to the Earthly Branch Chen, which is the Dragon.[3] For this reason, the tiled eaves above the south gate to the citadel formed two crescents, to correspond to the horns of a dragon. Yue corresponded to the Earthly Branch Si, which is the Snake.[4] Therefore, a wooden snake was placed facing north with its head inside [the walls] above the main gate leading to the south, to show that Yue belonged to Wu.

Once the city wall and outer fortifications had been built, and the granaries and storehouses filled, King Helü had [Wu] Zixu, Qu Gaiyu, and [Qu] Zhuyong train his soldiers in the finer points of technique for doing battle, riding, shooting, and driving a chariot.[5]

Before he ever had any need for them, His Majesty invited Gan Jiang to make two fine swords for him. *Gan Jiang was a man from Wu, who had trained under the same master as Ou Yezi, and they both were exceptionally talented at making swords.*[6] In earlier times, Yue had presented three swords, which Helü treasured greatly after he had obtained them, and for this reason, he commissioned a swordsmith to make another two: one to be called "Gan Jiang" and the other to be called "Mo Ye." *Mo Ye was Gan Jiang's wife.* When Gan Jiang made these swords, he selected the finest iron from five famous mountains

北向首內，示越屬於吳也。城郭以成，倉庫以具，闔閭復使子胥、屈蓋餘、燭傭習術戰騎射御之巧。未有所用，請干將鑄作名劍二枚。干將者，吳人也，與歐冶子同師，俱能為劍。越前來獻三枚，闔閭得而寶之，以故使劍匠作為二枚：一曰干將，二曰莫耶。莫耶，干將之妻也。干將作劍，來五山之鐵精，六合之金英。候天伺地，陰陽同光，百神臨觀，天氣下降，而金鐵之精，不銷淪流。於是干將不知其由。莫耶曰：「子以善為劍聞於王，使子作劍，三月不成，其有意乎？」干將曰：「吾不知其理也。」莫耶曰：「夫神物之化，

---

3. The earthly branch Chen, as part of a twelve-part division based on the orbit of Jupiter, where each division was represented by an animal or a mythological beast, was commonly equated with the dragon; see, for example, *Lunheng*, 457 ["Yandu" 言毒].
4. The Earthly Branch Si was usually equated with the snake; see, for example, *Lunheng*, 457 ["Yandu" 言毒].
5. These two men have the same name as King Helü's cousins, the younger brothers of King Liao of Wu. It is not clear whether the same individuals are indeed being mentioned here or whether these were included, perhaps, as "typical" Wu language names.
6. Master Ou Yezi is mentioned in many early Chinese texts as an exceptionally fine craftsman; see, for example, *Huainanzi*, 797 ["Qisu xun" 齊俗訓], *Lüshi chunqiu*, 1600 ["Zanneng" 贊能], and *Yantie lun*, 43 ["Tongyou" 通有].

Chapter Four: The Inner Traditions | 41

and the best bronze in the entire world. He waited until conditions in Heaven and on Earth were right, *yin* and *yang* shone in harmony, the myriad deities came to watch, and the *qi* of Heaven descended, but this finest of all iron and bronze did not melt. Gan Jiang did not know the reason for this.

"Your excellence in making swords has been reported to His Majesty, and that is why he has commissioned you to make weapons for him," Mo Ye said. "However, though three months have gone by, you have not completed them; are you doing this on purpose?"

"I do not understand why this is happening," Gan Jiang replied.

"The transformation of divine objects is achieved when in accord with human beings," Mo Ye pointed out. "Today you are trying to make a sword; is this not something that can only be accomplished when you have obtained the right person?"

"In the past when my master was working at the forge," Gan Jiang said, "it happened that the bronze and iron did not melt, and so he and his wife both entered the furnace, whereupon it was possible to create the required objects. Right up to the present day, those going into the mountains or working the forge wear mourning garb with hempen hat and belt—it is only afterward that they dare to smelt metal amid the mountains. Now I am trying to make these swords, and yet they fail to meld: should I do likewise?"

"Your master understood that it was only by immolating himself that he would be able make these objects, so why would I have any difficulty in following his example?" Mo Ye asked.

Thereupon, Gan Jiang's wife cut short her hair and clipped her nails, throwing these items into the furnace.[7] Then she ordered three hundred virgin boys and girls to blow the bellows and make charcoal, and the bronze

須人而成【之】。今夫子作劍，得無得其人而後成乎？」干將曰：「昔吾師作冶，金鐵之類不銷，夫妻俱入冶爐中，然後成物。至今後世即山作冶，麻絰葌服，然後敢鑄金於山。今吾作劍不變化者，其若斯耶？」莫耶曰：「師知爍身以成物，吾何難哉！」於是干將妻乃斷髮剪爪，投於爐中，使童女、童男三百人，鼓橐裝炭，金鐵乃濡，遂以成劍。陽曰干將，陰曰莫耶。陽作龜文，陰作漫理。干將匿其陽，出其陰而獻之。闔閭甚重。既得寶劍，適會魯使季孫聘於吳，闔閭使掌劍大夫以莫耶獻之。季孫拔劍之，鍔中缺者大如黍

---

7. Huang Rensheng (1996): 72 n. 21 suggests that *Gan Jiang qi* 干將妻 (Gan Jiang's wife) in this line should be read as *Gan Jiang fuqi* 干將夫妻 (Gan Jiang and his wife). The strong connection made throughout this passage between sexual connection and the smelting of metal suggests that both male and female should be involved in this sacrifice.

and iron began to melt, whereupon it was possible for him to make the swords. The *yang* sword was called Gan Jiang, and the *yin* sword was called Mo Ye. The *yang* one was decorated with a pattern like tortoiseshell and the *yin* one with a meander design. Gan Jiang concealed the *yang* sword and presented the *yin* one, which King Helü valued very much.

Just when he had obtained this precious sword, it happened that Lu sent a member of the Jisun family as an ambassador to Wu, so King Helü had his grandee in charge of swords bring out Mo Ye and present it to him.[8] Master Jisun drew the sword, but there was a flaw in the middle of the blade the size of a grain of rice. "What an amazing sword!" he said with a sigh. "Even the masters of the Upper States would not be able to improve on it! That you were able to make such a sword shows that Wu will become hegemon. However, the fact that it has a flaw means that you will be destroyed. Although I admire it greatly, I could not possibly keep it!" He left, having refused to accept this gift.

Since King Helü so much treasured Mo Ye, he now again commanded people in the country to make metal belt buckles.[9] His order said: "Anyone who can make a fine belt buckle will be rewarded with one hundred pieces of gold." There were a great many people in Wu who could make belt buckles, of whom there was one man who was so greedy for the king's generous reward that he killed his two sons and used their blood to anoint the metal, with which he then made two belt buckles and presented them to King Helü. This man came to the palace gate and demanded his reward.

米。歎曰：「美哉！劍也。雖上國之師，何能加之！夫劍之成也，吳霸。有缺，則亡矣。我雖好之，其可受乎？」不受而去。

　　闔閭既寶莫耶，復命於國中作金鉤。令曰：「能為善鉤者，賞之百金。」吳作鉤者甚眾，而有人貪王之重賞也，殺其二子，以血釁金，遂成二鉤，獻於闔閭，詣宮門而求賞。王曰：「為鉤者眾而子獨求賞，何以異於眾夫子之鉤乎？」作鉤者曰：「吾之作鉤也，貪而殺二子，釁成二鉤。」王乃舉眾鉤以示之：「何者是也？」王鉤甚多，形體相類，不知其所在。於是鉤師向鉤而

---

8. The Jisun family were the descendants of the youngest son of Lord Huan of Lu 魯桓公 (r. 711–694 BCE). Zhang Jue (2006): 60 n. 15 argues that this is Jisun Pingzi 季孫平子, who had the personal name Yiru 意如 (d. 505 BCE).
9. This passage has been much discussed in histories of Chinese metalworking, because originally it was thought that the people of the southeast did not wear belt buckles at this time; see, for example, Wagner (1993): 114 n. 50. However, thanks to the discovery of three buckles, with inscriptions recording that they were made for the personal use of King Helü of Wu, this issue has now been resolved; see Cao Jinyan (2013).

"There are many people who have made belt buckles, but you are the only one to demand a reward," the king said. "What makes your belt buckles different from all the rest?"

"When I made these buckles," the maker said, "I was so very greedy that I killed my two sons. By anointing the metal [with blood], I completed these two belt buckles."

The king held up a handful of belt buckles and showed them to him. "Which ones are yours?" he asked.

The king had a great many belt buckles, and they were all the same shape and size, so he did not know which they were. Therefore, the master buckle-maker turned to the heap of buckles and shouted the names of his two sons. "Wuhong! Huji! Here I am! The king does not know where your spirits rest!"

As the sounds died in his throat, two belt buckles flew toward their father's breast.

The king of Wu was greatly amazed. "Alas!" he said. "I have indeed failed to appreciate you."

He then rewarded him with one hundred pieces of gold. He always wore these two, and they never left his person.

In the sixth month, just when he wanted to mobilize his troops, it happened that Bo Pi of Chu arrived, seeking refuge.[10] "Who is this Bo Pi?" the king of Wu asked Zixu.

"Bo Pi is the grandson of Bo Zhouli of Chu," he said. "When King Ping executed [Bo] Zhouli, Pi had to flee for his life—having heard that I am in Wu, he came here too."

"What crime did Zhouli commit?" King Helü asked.

呼二子之名：「吳鴻、扈稽！我在於此，王不知汝之神也。」聲【未】絕於口，兩鉤俱飛著父之胸。吳王大驚，曰：「嗟乎！寡人誠負於子。」乃賞【之】百金。遂服而不離身。

六月，欲用兵，會楚之白喜來奔。吳王問子胥曰：「白喜何如人也？」子胥曰：「白喜者，楚白州犁之孫。平王誅州犁，喜因出奔，聞臣在吳而來也。」闔閭曰：「州犁何罪？」子胥曰：「白州犁，楚之左尹，號曰郤宛，事平王。平王幸之，常與盡日而語，襲朝而食。費無忌望而妒之，因謂平王曰：『王愛幸宛，一國所知。何不為酒，一至宛家，以示羣臣於宛之厚？』平王曰：『善。』

---

10. The individual known as Bai Xi 白喜 in this chapter of the *Wu Yue chunqiu* is elsewhere always called Bo Pi 伯嚭. In the interests of comprehensibility, he is called Po Bi throughout this translation.

"Bo Zhouli held the position of minister of the left in the kingdom of Chu, and he had the title of Xiwan," Zixu said.[11]

"He served under King Ping. King Ping favored him and often spoke with him for an entire day at a time; having talked through the night, they would then eat breakfast together. Fei Wuji observed this and was jealous of him. Therefore, he said to King Ping: 'The entire country knows how much you love and favor [Xi]wan, so why do you not prepare some wine and then we will all go round to his house to demonstrate to your other ministers how generously you treat him?'

"King Ping said: 'What a good idea!' Then he prepared wine and went to Xiwan's residence.

"Wuji had earlier instructed [Xi]wan: 'King Ping is a very militaristic man and much enjoys weaponry, so you must make sure to station soldiers on the stairs and at your gate.' [Xi]wan believed what he was told and acted accordingly.

"When King Ping arrived, he was very shocked and said: 'What on earth does [Xi]wan think he is doing!'

"Wuji told him: 'I am afraid that he may be planning to assassinate you in a coup—you had better leave here immediately, Your Majesty, for we do not yet know what is going on.' King Ping was furious and had Xiwan executed. When the other lords heard about this, they were all deeply upset. Pi had been informed that I was living in Wu, and for that reason, he decided to come here. I hope that you will grant him an audience."

King Helü had an audience with Bo Pi. "My country is located far away to the eastern seaboard, but I have heard about the dreadful violence inflicted on your family in Chu and the slander you suffered from Fei Wuji," he said. "You did not consider my country to be too far away and arrived here anyway; what can you instruct me about?"

乃具酒於郤宛之舍。無忌教宛曰：『平王甚毅猛而好兵，子必前陳兵堂下門庭。』宛信其言，因而為之。及平王往而大驚，曰：『宛何等也？』無忌曰：『殆且有篡殺之憂，王急去之，事未可知。』平王大怒，遂誅郤宛。諸侯聞之，莫不歎息。喜聞臣在吳，故來請見之。」闔閭見白喜而問曰：「寡人國僻遠，東濱海。側聞子前人為楚荊之暴怒，費無忌之讒口，不遠吾國，而來於斯，將何以教寡人？」喜曰：「楚國之失虜，前人無罪，橫被暴誅。臣聞大王收

---

11. The *Wu Yue chunqiu* here conflates two individuals. Xiwan was in fact the name of Bo Zhouli's son, that is, Bo Pi's father. The *Zuozhuan*, 1223 [Zhao 1] and 1486 [Zhao 27], makes it clear that Bo Zhouli (d. 541 BCE) and Bo Xiwan (d. 515 BCE) were two different people.

"I am but an escaped prisoner from the kingdom of Chu," Pi said. "My family was innocent of any crime, and yet they were cruelly executed. I heard that Your Majesty took in Wu Zixu when he was in dire straits, and so I did not consider a thousand *li* too far to come to throw in my lot with yours—only you, Your Majesty, can decide whether I live or die."

King Helü felt very sorry for him and appointed him as a grandee, discussing matters of state with him.

Grandee Bei Li of Wu took advantage of a leisure moment to ask Zixu: "Why do you trust [Bo] Pi?"

"I have suffered from the same injustice that Pi has," Zixu replied. "Have you never heard the 'Song of the River'?

> "'Those who suffer the same disease feel sorry for one another;
> Those who experience the same sorrow help each other.
> The birds that are startled into flight
> Will wheel around each other and then form a flock.
> The waters of the bubbling stream
> Will flow together again in the end.
> Hu horses stand facing the north wind,[12]
> Yue swallows roost facing the sun.'[13]

"Who does not love those close to him and worry about those for whom he cares?"

伍子胥之窮厄，不遠千里，故來歸命。惟大王賜其死。」闔閭傷之，以為大夫，與謀國事。吳大夫被離承宴問子胥曰：「何見而信喜？」子胥曰：「吾之怨，與喜同。子不聞河上歌乎？『同病相憐，同憂相救。驚翔之鳥，相隨而集；瀨下之水，因復俱流；胡馬望北風而立，越鷰向日而熙。』誰不愛其所近，悲其所思者乎？」被離曰：「君之言外也，豈有內意，以決疑乎？」子胥曰：「吾不見也。」被離曰：「吾觀喜之為人，鷹視虎步，專功擅殺之性，不可親也。」子胥不然其言，與之俱事吳王。

---

12. Zhang Jue (2006): 63 n. 5 argues that the character *feng* 風 (wind) in this line should be omitted, noting that this was a proverbial expression, and very similar ideas are recorded in other texts; for example, *Qianfu lun*, 282 ["Shibian" 實邊], gives *Daima wang bei* 代馬望北 (Dai horses [stand] facing north).

13. The last two lines are usually given as part of Wu Zixu's speech, but the ABCA rhyme scheme of the couplets, with final characters from the *-ə (*zhi* 之), *-əp, *-ip (*ji* 緝), and *-u (*you* 幽) groups, respectively, makes it likely that it should be considered as the conclusion of the song.

"What you say is beside the point," Bei Li replied. "Surely you cannot set aside your suspicions because of your personal feelings?"

"I don't understand," Zixu said.

"I have observed how [Bo] Pi comports himself," Bei Li told him. "He has the gaze of an eagle and paces like a tiger, with all the appearance of a man who will claim all credit for any success and kill others without any regard for due legal process. This is not a man you can hold dear."

Zixu did not believe what he said and continued to serve the king of Wu with [Bo Pi].

In the second year of his reign [513 BCE], the king of Wu continued to worry that although he had already murdered King Liao, Prince Qingji was still resident in a neighboring country and he might join forces with the other lords and come attack him.[14] He asked Zixu about this: "In the past, you were very helpful to me in the matter of Zhuan Zhu. Now I have heard that Prince Qingji is plotting with the other lords, and so I find I cannot enjoy the flavors of my food nor can I sleep well at night; I am going to have to entrust this problem to you."

"I would never behave in a disloyal fashion, and yet I plotted against the life of King Liao with Your Majesty in that secret room," Zixu said. "Now you want to execute his son as well, but I am afraid that this goes against the will of Heaven."

"In the past, King Wu executed King Zhou [of the Shang dynasty] and then later on killed Wugeng, but the people of Zhou did not show the

二年，吳王前既殺王僚，又憂慶忌之在鄰國，恐合諸侯來伐。問子胥曰：「昔專諸之事於寡人厚矣。今聞公子慶忌有計於諸侯，吾食不甘味，臥不安席，以付於子。」子胥曰：「臣不忠無行，而與大王圖王僚於私室之中。今復欲討其子，恐非皇天之意。」闔閭曰：「昔武王討紂，而後殺武庚，周人無怨色。今若斯議，何乃天乎？」子胥曰：「臣事君王，將遂吳統，又何懼焉？臣之所厚其人者，細人也，願從於謀。」吳王曰：「吾之憂也，其敵有萬人之力，豈細人之所能謀乎？」子胥曰：「其細人之謀事，而有萬人之力也。」王曰：「其

---

14. In the previous references to King Liao's son and heir in the *Wu Yue chunqiu*, he is not named. According to one version of events, documented in *Zuozhuan*, 1715–16 [Ai 20], Prince Qingji was not killed by King Helü but was murdered late in the reign of King Fuchai for supporting a policy of appeasement toward Yue.

slightest resentment," King Helü said.[15] "If today I were to follow the same plan, I do not see what it has to do with Heaven!"

"In serving Your Majesty," Zixu said, "I am continuing the traditions of Wu; I have nothing to be afraid of! I have been cultivating the acquaintance of a tiny little man, because I hope he can deal with this situation for you."

"I am worried because my enemy has the strength of ten thousand men," the king of Wu said. "How can a tiny little man deal with him?"

"When this tiny little man plans something, he is the match for ten thousand men," Zixu replied.

"Who is he? Tell me!" the king said.

"His name is Yao Li," Zixu replied. "Some time ago, I watched him humiliate the famous knight Jiao Qiuxin."

"How did he humiliate him?" the king asked.

"Jiao Qiuxin was a man from the East Sea who was sent as an ambassador to Wu by the king of Qi," Zixu said.

"He was passing the ford on the Huai River and wanted to water his horses at the ford, but the official in charge warned him: 'There is a god in these waters that emerges when it sees a horse to kill it. You had better not water them here.'

"[Qiu]xin said: 'I am a famous knight; what god would dare to interfere with me?' Then he commanded his followers to water his horses at the ford. Just as you might expect, the River God snatched his horse, and it drowned. Jiao Qiuxin was furious, so he removed his clothes and went into

為何誰？子以言之。」子胥曰：「姓要名離。臣昔嘗見曾折辱壯士椒丘訢也。」王曰：「辱之奈何？」子胥曰：「椒丘訢者，東海上人也。為齊王使於吳，過淮津，欲飲馬於津。津吏曰：『水中有神，見馬即出，以害其馬。君勿飲也。』訢曰：『壯士所當，何神敢干？』乃使從者飲馬於津。水神果取其馬，馬沒。椒丘訢大怒，袒裼持劍，入水求神決戰，連日乃出，眇其一目。遂之吳，會於友人之喪。訢恃其與水戰之勇也，於友人之喪席而輕傲於士大夫，言辭不遜，有陵人之氣。要離與之對坐，合坐不忍其溢於力也。時要離乃挫訢曰：『吾

---

15. According to early Chinese historical texts, Wugeng was a son of the last monarch of the Shang dynasty. According to Han dynasty texts, he subsequently participated in the rebellion by Guan Shu and Cai Shu against the authority of the Zhou king, for which he was executed by the duke of Zhou; see, for example, *Hanshu*, 28B.1647. Earlier texts do not name Wugeng as a participant in this rebellion.

the water to fight with the god, his sword drawn. It was several days before he emerged, and he had lost one eye. When he arrived in Wu, he was called on to attend the funeral of a friend. [Qiu]xin was very proud of how brave he had been in the fight with the River [God], and so when he attended his friend's funeral, he behaved arrogantly toward the other knights and grandees present, speaking disrespectfully to them, with a really offensive air.[16] Yao Li was sitting opposite him and, like his companions, found he could not bear his self-satisfaction.

"At this point Yao Li humiliated [Jiao Qiu]xin by saying: 'I have heard that when a brave man fights with the sun, he does not turn a hair; when he fights with a god, he does not step back; and when he fights with a person, he does not make a sound. Whether he lives or dies, he accepts no humiliation. Now you have been fighting in the water with this god: you lost the horse that you were riding, and you had one eye put out. A true knight would be ashamed to call himself brave when he has been injured like that. Rather than fighting to the death with your enemy, you ran away to save your own skin, and you have the arrogance to look down on us!'

"Finding himself suddenly being criticized like that, Jiao Qiuxin was both angry and upset, and he decided that night he would go and attack Yao Li. After the funeral, Yao Li returned home and warned his wife: 'I humiliated the famous knight Jiao Qiuxin in front of everyone at the funeral, so he is feeling very angry with me. He is sure to come here tonight. Whatever you do, do not shut the gate!'

"That night, just as he had anticipated, Jiao Qiuxin arrived and saw that his gate was open. When he climbed the stairs to the main hall, it was open too. When he went into the bedroom, no one was on guard. [Yao Li] was lying on his back with his hair untied, looking completely

聞勇士之鬭也，與日戰不移表，與神鬼戰者不旋踵，與人戰者不達聲，生往死還，不受其辱。今子與神鬭於水，亡馬失御，又受眇目之病，形殘名勇，勇士所恥。不即喪命於敵，而戀其生，猶傲色於我哉！』於是椒丘訢卒於詰責，恨怒並發，暝即往攻要離。於是，要離席闌至舍，誡其妻曰：『我辱勇士椒丘訢於大家之喪，餘恨蔚恚，暝必來也，慎無閉吾門。』至夜，椒丘訢果往，見其門不閉；登其堂不關；入其室不守；放髮僵臥，無所懼。訢乃手劍而捽要離曰：『子有當死之過者三，子知之乎？』離曰：『不知。』訢曰：『子辱我

---

16. The word *shen* 神 (god) is missing in the transmitted text. This amendment is made in accordance with Xu Tianhu (1999): 36.

unconcerned. [Qiu]xin put one hand on his sword and pinned Yao Li down. He said: 'You have committed three transgressions that merit death—do you know that?'

"'No,' said Li.

"[Qiu]xin said: 'You deserve to die for humiliating me in front of everyone at the funeral. You deserve to die for not shutting your doors when you got home. You deserve to die for lying in bed when you should have been on guard. You have made three terrible mistakes, so you can't blame me for what happens next.'

"'I have not committed three transgressions that merit death, but you have certainly humiliated yourself by doing three ignoble things; do you know that?' Yao Li responded.

"[Qiu]xin said: 'No.'

"Yao Li said: 'I made fun of you in front of a vast crowd, but you did not dare to answer back: that is the first dreadful thing that you did. You entered my gate without knocking; you climbed the stairs to the main hall without making a sound: that is the second. It was only after you drew your sword and grabbed me by the neck that you dared to raise your voice: that is the third. Having made these three ignominious errors, don't you think that everyone will despise you if you try and threaten me now?'

"Jiao Qiuxin then threw his sword onto the ground and said with a sigh: 'Everyone admires me for my courage, but you are a much braver man than I—you should be one of the most famous knights in the world.' This is what I have heard of Yao Li, and I have told you all that I know."

"I would be happy to hold a banquet in his honor," the king of Wu said.

[Wu] Zixu then went to see Yao Li and said to him: "The king of Wu has heard of your great sense of honor and would like to meet you."

於大家之眾，一死也；歸不關閉，二死也；臥不守御，三死也。子有三死之過，欲無得怨。』要離曰：『吾無三死之過，子有三不肖之愧，子知之乎？』訢曰：『不知。』要離曰：『吾辱子於千人之眾，子無敢報，一不肖也。入門不咳，登堂無聲，二不肖也。前拔子劍，手挫捽吾頭，乃敢大言，三不肖也。子有三不肖，而威於我，豈不鄙哉？』於是椒丘訢投劍而嘆曰：『吾之勇也，人莫敢眥占者，離乃加吾之上，此天下壯士也。』臣聞要離若斯，誠以聞矣。」吳王曰：「願承宴而待焉。」

子胥乃見要離曰：「吳王聞子高義，惟一臨之。」乃與子胥見吳王。王曰：「子何為者？」要離曰：「臣國東千里之人。臣細小無力，迎風則僵，負風則伏。

He went with Zixu to have an audience with the king of Wu. "What can you do?" His Majesty inquired.

"I come from a place one thousand *li* to the east of your capital," Yao Li responded. "Even though I am small and weak, to the point where I can be blown about by the wind, if Your Majesty commands me to do something, how could I fail to do my very best?"

The king of Wu was privately annoyed at Zixu for introducing this man, and he stayed silent for a long time. Yao Li then stepped forward and said: "Are you worried about Qingji, Your Majesty? I can kill him."

"Everyone in the world knows how brave Qingji is," the king said. "With his thews and sinews, he could stand against ten thousand men—he can run fast enough to overtake any beast and catch a flying bird with his bare hands.[17] He is incredibly strong and can run several hundred *li* in a single bound. I once tried to have him arrested at the Yangtze River, and even those driving a team of four blood horses were not able to catch up with him. When they shot at him, he simply caught them, so not a single arrow touched him. You are not strong enough to deal with him."

"If this is what you want, Your Majesty," Yao Li said, "I can kill him."

"Prince Qingji is a clever man," the king responded. "Although he went abroad in dire straits, he is the equal of any knight."

"I have heard that delighting in the company of your wife and children to the point where you no longer put forth every effort in the service of the ruler is to fail in loyalty," Yao Li said, "while to enjoy the affections of your family when at the same time ignoring the dangers that threaten the monarch is wrong. If I pretend to have offended you and run away, having had

大王有命，臣敢不盡力？」吳王心非子胥進此人，良久默然不言。要離即進曰：「大王患慶忌乎？臣能殺之。」王曰：「慶忌之勇，世所聞也。筋骨果勁，萬人莫當；走追奔獸，手接飛鳥，骨騰肉飛，拊膝數百里。吾嘗追之於江，駟馬馳不及；射之闇接，矢不可中。今子之力不如也。」要離曰：「王有意焉，臣能殺之。」王曰：「慶忌明智之人，歸窮於諸侯，不下諸侯之士。」要離曰：「臣聞：『安其妻子之樂，不盡事君之義，非忠也。懷家室之愛，而不除君之患者，非義也。』臣詐以負罪出奔，願王戮臣妻子，斷臣右手，慶忌必信臣矣。」王曰：「諾。」要離乃詐得罪，出奔。吳王乃取其妻子，焚棄於市。要離乃奔諸侯，

---

17. This description of Prince Qingji's physical prowess seems to result from a confusion between him and a deity named Qingji, who is mentioned in a number of ancient texts; see, for example, *Guanzi*, 827 ["Shuidi" 水地].

my right hand cut off, you can torture my wife and children to death, and then Prince Qingji will definitely believe me."[18]

"Okay," the king said.

Yao Li then pretended that he had escaped into exile after offending the monarch, and the king of Wu arrested his wife and children, burning then to death and afterward exposing their bodies in the marketplace. Yao Li fled abroad and traveled around, proclaiming his wrongs and making his innocence known to the entire world. When he arrived in Wei, he begged for an audience with Prince Qingji. When he saw him, he said: "You know how cruel Helü is—now he has tortured my wife and children to death, burning them alive in the marketplace! He executed them when they were innocent of any crime! I know all about the government of the kingdom of Wu, and I hope that you will pluck up your courage to depose King Helü. Why don't you travel east with me to Wu?"

Qingji believed in the value of his advice. Three months later, he selected the finest officers and men to join him on the journey to Wu. Just when they were in midstream, crossing the Yangtze River, Yao Li took his seat upwind, because he was so feeble. Then he used the force of the wind to bring the hook of a halberd down on the prince's hat, and the following in the slipstream, he stabbed Qingji. Meanwhile, Prince Qingji turned his head and hit him, holding his head beneath the waters three times. Then he fished [Yao Li] out and placed him on his knee.

而行怨言，以無罪聞於天下。遂如衛，求見慶忌。見曰：「闔閭無道，王子所知。今戮吾妻子，焚之於市，無罪見誅。吳國之事，吾知其情，願因王子之勇，闔閭可得也。何不與我東之於吳？」慶忌信其謀。後三月，揀練士卒，遂之吳。將渡江於中流，要離力微，坐與上風，因風勢，以矛鉤其冠，順風而刺慶忌。慶忌顧而揮之，三捽其頭於水中，乃加於膝上【曰】：「嘻【嘻哉】！天下之勇士也！乃敢加兵刃於我。」左右欲殺之，慶忌止之曰：「此是天下勇士，豈可一日而殺天下勇士二人哉？」乃誡左右曰：「可令還吳，以旌其忠。」於是，

---

18. Some editions of the text give this line as: "If I pretend to have offended you and run away, you can torture my wife and children to death, burning them alive in the marketplace at Wu so that their ashes are spread to the four winds. Then you should offer a reward of one thousand pieces of gold and fief of one hundred *li* of land for me, for thus Prince Qingji will definitely believe me" (臣詐以負罪出奔，願王戮臣妻子，焚之吳市，飛揚其灰. 購臣千金與百里之邑，慶忌必信臣矣); see for example Zhang Jue (2006): 67. This additional text is derived from a quotation preserved in the *Taiping yulan*.

"Ah! This is one of the bravest knights in the world, for he has dared to raise his sword against me!"

His entourage wanted to kill him, but Qingji stopped them, saying: "This is the bravest man in the world. How could you want to see two great knights die by violence on the same day! Let him go back to Wu," he warned his entourage, "to make it clear that he was loyally obeying orders."

After that, Prince Qingji died.[19]

Yao Li crossed the river and arrived at Jiangling, by which time he was too depressed to travel any further. His servants asked: "Why do you not proceed, sir?"

"To kill my wife and children to serve His Majesty's purpose was not benevolent," Yao Li said, "and to murder the late king's son for the sake of our new monarch was unjust. To decide that I must survive at all costs would be both ignoble and unjust. Furthermore, it would be wrong of me to give up my principles to survive. If I commit three such wicked deeds so as to make my name, how could I look a true knight in the eyes?"

Having said this, he threw himself into the Yangtze River. However, before he could drown, his followers pulled him out.

"How can I fail to die?" Yao Li said.

"Do not die, sir!" his servants cried. "You have but to wait to receive titles and emoluments!"

But Yao Li cut off his own hands and feet before falling on his sword—thus, he died.

In the third year [512 BCE], the military high command in Wu wanted to attack Chu. Before the start of this campaign, Wu Zixu and Bo Pi discussed the matter among themselves. "We have been training soldiers for the king,

慶忌死。要離渡至江陵，慭然不行。從者曰：「君何不行？」要離曰：「殺吾妻子，以事吾君，非仁也；為新君而殺故君之子，非義也。重其死，不貴無義。今吾貪生棄行，非義也。夫人有三惡，以立於世，吾何面目以視天下之士？」言訖，遂投身於江。未絕，從者出之。要離曰：「吾寧能不死乎？」從者曰：「君且勿死，以俟爵祿。」要離乃自斷手足，伏劍而死。

三年，吳將欲伐楚，未行。伍子胥、白喜相謂曰：「吾等為王養士，畫其策謀，有利於國，而王故伐楚。出其令，託而無興師之意，奈何？」有頃，吳王問子胥、白喜曰：「寡人欲出兵，於二子何如？」子胥、白喜對曰：「臣

---

19. It is worth noting that the earliest-surviving account of Yao Li's attempt to assassinate Prince Qingji states that the prince survived; see *Lüshi chunqiu*, 594–95 ["Zhonglian" 忠廉].

and we have been planning this campaign that will be of great benefit to the country, but in spite of the fact that the king has attacked Chu in the past and says that he wants to give orders to the same effect again, he is delaying and clearly has no intention to mobilize the army. What should we do about it?"

A short time later, the king of Wu asked Zixu and Bo Pi: "I am going to send my soldiers out on campaign. What do you think?"

"We will obey your commands," Zixu and Bo Pi replied.

The king of Wu reckoned that both these men hated Chu, and he was deeply concerned that they were merely using his soldiers to crush them. His Majesty climbed a tower and screamed out at the south wind; then after a short time, he sighed. None of his officials understood the king's feelings. Zixu realized that the king could not make up his mind, and so he recommended Master Sun to the ruler.

Master Sun was named Wu, and he came from the kingdom of Wu. He was good at all military arts, but he lived very retired, and so no one knew of his remarkable abilities.

However, Wu [Zi]xu was an exceptionally intelligent man, and he was fully aware that Master Sun would be able to turn back any host and defeat any enemy. In the course of one morning, when discussing military matters with the king of Wu, he recommended Master Sun seven times.

"Since you have made such a fuss about this man, I am willing to take him into my service," the king of Wu said.

He summoned Master Sun to ask him about the military arts. Each time he explained one chapter from his book, the king could not stop himself from acclaiming it, and he was more than pleased. "Could I have a small demonstration of your military skills?" he asked.

"Of course!" Master Sun replied. "We could use the women of your harem for this test!"

"Fine," His Majesty said.

"I would like your two favorite consorts to act as captains," Master Sun said, "and they each will be in command of one company."

願用命。」吳王內計二子皆怨楚，深恐以兵往，破滅而已。登臺向南風而嘯，有頃而嘆。羣臣莫有曉王意者。子胥深知王之不定，乃薦孫子於王。孫子者，名武，吳人也。善為兵法，辟隱深居，世人莫知其能。胥乃明知鑒辯，知孫子可以折衝銷敵。乃一旦與吳王論兵，七薦孫子。吳王曰子胥託言進士，欲以自納。而召孫子，問以兵法。每陳一篇，王不知口之稱善。其意大悅。問曰：「兵法寧可以小試耶？」孫子曰：「可。可以小試於後宮之女。」王曰：「諾。」孫子曰：「得大王寵姬二人以為軍隊長，各將一隊。」令三百人皆被甲兜鍪，操劍盾而立。告以軍法；隨鼓進退，左右迴旋，使知其禁。乃令曰：「一鼓皆

Then he ordered three hundred women to put on armor and helmets and take their positions holding a sword and a shield.[20] He explained military law to them and taught them that they should advance and retreat, turn to left or right, according to the beating of the drums and made sure that they knew what was forbidden. Then he gave his orders: "When you hear the first drumroll, you should all move into lines; when you hear the second drumroll, you should march forward holding your weapons at the ready; and when you hear the third drumroll, you should go into battle formation."

At this point, the palace women all covered their mouths and laughed.

Master Sun took hold of the sticks himself and sounded the drums: he gave his commands three times and explained them five times, but they laughed just as hard as before. Master Sun turned to look at all these women in fits of giggles. He was absolutely furious. His eyes now suddenly opened wide, his voice was like the roaring of a tiger, and the hair on his head prickled beneath his hat as he broke the strings that tied it under his chin.

Now turning to look at the adjutant, he said: "Get the guillotine!"[21]

"It is the general's fault when orders are not clear and when men do not understand his explanations and commands," Master Sun announced. "However, if orders have been given, once commands have been issued three times and explanations made five times, it is the fault of the officers if the troops still do not move. What is the penalty under military law for this?"

"Beheading!" the adjutant exclaimed.

[Sun] Wu then gave orders to behead the two captains—that is, the king of Wu's favorite consorts.

The king of Wu had climbed a tower and was watching these events in the distance. When he saw that his two beloved consorts were about to

振，二鼓操進，三鼓為戰形。」於是宮女皆掩口而笑。孫子乃親自操枹擊鼓，三令五申，其笑如故。孫子顧視諸女連笑不止，孫子大怒，兩目忽張，聲如駭虎，髮上衝冠，項旁絕纓，顧謂執法曰：「取鈇鑕。」孫子曰：「約束不明，申令不信，將之罪也。既以約束，三令五申，卒不卻行，士之過也。軍法如何？」執法曰：「斬！」武乃令斬隊長二人，即吳王之寵姬也。吳王登臺觀望，正見斬二愛姬，馳使下之令曰：「寡人已知將軍用兵矣。寡人非此二姬

---

20. Huang Rensheng (1996): 89 incorrectly gives this line as part of Master Sun's speech.
21. The term here translated as "guillotine" is *fuzhi* 鈇鑕. This form of execution equipment was particularly heavy duty, since it was also used for chopping people in half at the waist.

be beheaded, he quickly sent one of his subordinates to put a stop to this: "I know that you, general, are a very fine commander, but without these two consorts, my food will lose its flavor, so you should not cut their heads off."

"I have already been appointed as general," Master Sun said, "and I uphold military law among my soldiers.[22] Even though Your Majesty has given other orders, I cannot obey them."

Master Sun again sounded the drums, and they now turned to the left and the right, moved forward and backward, wheeling around in perfect formation, not even daring to blink their eyes. The two companies were completely silent, and nobody dared to even look about.

[Master Sun] then reported back to the king of Wu: "The troops have been trained, and I hope Your Majesty will review them. They will do whatever you want; you can order them to brave fire or flood, and they will not refuse. You can now conquer the world."

At that moment, the king of Wu felt deeply displeased. "I know that you are a very fine commander," he said, "but even if it were possible to become hegemon in this way, this is not right. Dismiss your troops, general, and go back to your quarters. This is not what I want."

"You only like fine words, Your Majesty," Master Sun said, "and do not care about reality."

"I have heard that weapons are terrible things," Zixu remonstrated.[23] "They cannot be employed in a frivolous way. Therefore, a person who takes command of the army must punish those who have failed in their duties during the attack, for otherwise the Way of warfare will not be upheld. Today Your Majesty has considered the plight of your troops, and so you want

食不甘味，宜勿斬之。」孫子曰：「臣既已受命為將，將法：在軍，君雖有令，臣不受之。」孫子復撝鼓之，當左右進退，迴旋規矩，不敢瞬目。二隊寂然，無敢顧者。於是乃報吳王曰：「兵已整齊，願王觀之。惟所欲用，使赴水火，猶無難矣，而可以定天下。」吳王忽然不悅曰：「寡人知子善用兵，雖可以霸，然而無所施也。將軍罷兵就舍，寡人不願。」孫子曰：「王徒好其言，而不用其實。」子胥諫曰：「臣聞兵者凶事，不可空試。故為兵者，誅伐不行，兵道

---

22. Early military texts make it clear that commanders in the field did not have to obey orders from headquarters; see, for example, *Sunzi*, 136 ["Jiubian" 九變].
23. This is a proverbial expression in ancient China and is recorded in many other texts, also in the form *bingzhe xiongqi ye* 兵者凶器也 (weapons are terrible objects); see, for example, *Lüshi chunqiu*, 435 ["Lunwei" 論威], *Shiji*, 122.3141, and *Guoyu*, 643 ["Yueyu xia" 越語下].

to raise an army to punish the violence Chu has inflicted on us, thus making yourself hegemon over the entire world and striking awe into foreign rulers. Without Sun Wu in command, who would dare to ford the Huai River or cross the Si, traveling one thousand *li* to fight for you?"

The king of Wu was delighted by this. He had the drums beaten and held a muster of battle-chariots, gathering them together for an attack on Chu. Master Sun was appointed as general, and he razed Shu to the ground, killing the two exiled princes, Gaiyu and Zhuyong of Wu. However, just as His Majesty was planning a campaign against Ying, Sun Wu said:[24] "Your people are exhausted to the point where they can go no further."

Chu heard that Wu had appointed Master Sun, Wu Zixu, and Bo Pi as generals. The kingdom of Chu was deeply concerned by this. The government ministers were all furious, and with one voice, they proclaimed that Fei Wuji had brought about the deaths of Wu She and Bo Zhouli with his slanders—this was why Wu invaded their borders and caused ceaseless problems with their raids, so the ministers of the kingdom of Chu were facing this extraordinary crisis.

Marshal Cheng then said to Zichang:[25] "Everyone in the entire country believes that the grand mentor, Wu She, and the minister of the left, Bo Zhouli, were innocent of any crime. You, sir, plotted with His Majesty to kill them, spreading slanderous rumors throughout the kingdom—right up to the present day, gossip has not stopped. People have indeed been led

不明。今大王虔心思士，欲興兵戈，以誅暴楚，以霸天下，而威諸侯。非孫武之將，而誰能涉淮、踰泗，越千里而戰者乎？」於是吳王大悅，因鳴鼓會軍，集而攻楚。孫子為將，拔舒，殺吳亡將二公子蓋餘、燭傭。謀欲入郢，孫武曰：「民勞，未可恃也。」楚聞吳使孫子、伍子胥、白喜為將，楚國苦之。羣臣皆怨，咸言費無忌讒殺伍奢、白州犁，而吳侵境不絕於寇，楚國羣臣有一朝之患。於是，司馬成乃謂子常曰：「太傅伍奢，左尹白州犁，邦人莫知其罪，

---

24. Ying at this time was the capital of the kingdom of Chu, having been moved to this location during the reign of King Wen of Chu 楚文王 (r. 689–677 BCE). Attacks by Wu would eventually force Chu to move the capital city elsewhere.

25. Marshal Cheng is known in other accounts of these events as Marshal Xu 司馬戌; see, for example, *Zuozhuan*, 1488 [Zhao 27]. This individual is identified in the *Chunqiu jingzhuan jijie*, 1444 n. 1 [Zhao 19], as the great-grandson of King Zhuang of Chu. Zichang is also known as Nangwa 囊瓦, who played an important role in the conflict with Wu at this period.

astray![26] I have heard that a benevolent person will sanction the death of another man to put a stop to evil-minded gossip: this is not what you have done. Now you have killed people to encourage slander—how wrongheaded can you be? Fei Wuji has been the source of all this malice in Chu, but the people do not know that this is his fault. He has now killed three wise ministers—innocent of any offense—and caused us to become the sworn enemies of Wu. He has injured the feelings of loyal subjects within the country and made us a laughingstock abroad. The families of Xi[wan] and Wu have escaped to the kingdom of Wu, so they now have Wu Yuan and Bo Pi. This has not only made them more terrifying and sharpened their ambitions; they are also now locked in conflict with Chu: this is why the army of this powerful enemy state becomes more formidable by the day. If the kingdom of Chu gets into trouble, you will be in danger too. A wise man eliminates slanderous rumor to make his own position secure; a stupid man surrounds himself with sycophants and thus brings about his own destruction. Right now, you have surrounded yourself with these flatterers, and the country is indeed in danger."

"This is entirely my fault!" Zichang replied. "How could I refuse to deal with the problem?"

In the ninth month, Zichang joined forces with King Zhao to execute Fei Wuji. His entire family was also killed. This put a stop to the gossip circulating within the kingdom.

The king of Wu had a daughter named Tengyu; because he was planning an attack on Chu, he held a banquet attended by his wife and daughter, at which they ate steamed fish. The king first tasted half of it and then gave the rest to his daughter. She was angry and said: "His Majesty ate and then

君與王謀誅之，流謗於國，至于今日，其言不絕，誠惑之。蓋聞仁者殺人以掩謗者，猶弗為也。今子殺人以興謗於國，不亦異乎？夫費無忌，楚之讒口，民莫知其過。今無辜殺三賢士，以結怨於吳；內傷忠臣之心，外為鄰國所笑。且郤、伍之家出奔於吳，吳新有伍員、白喜，秉威銳志，結讎於楚，故彊敵之兵日駭。楚國有事，子即危矣。夫智者除讒以自安，愚者受佞以自亡。今子受讒，國以危矣。」子常曰：「是囊之罪也，敢不圖之！」九月，子常與昭王共誅費無忌，遂滅其族，國人乃謗止。

---

26. Zhang Jue (2006): 73 n. 4 suggests reading this line as "Even I have been led astray by this!" (誠惑之) on the basis of a parallel line found in *Zuozhuan*, 1488 [Zhao 27].

gave me the leftover fish. He has humiliated me—I cannot endure living any longer!"[27] She then killed herself.

King Helü was very upset about this, and he buried her west of the capital city, outside the Chang Gate. He dug a lake and piled up earth, making an outer coffin of striped stone inside a wooden mortuary chamber, into which was placed treasures such as bronze ding-vessels, jade cups, silver goblets, and a pearl-encrusted coverlet—all these things were gifts to his dead daughter. He had white cranes dance in the marketplace in Wu, and he ordered a myriad people to follow and watch them.[28] He subsequently commanded that the men and women and the cranes should all enter the tomb, whereupon he pulled the trigger mechanism to bury them.[29] The people of the capital were appalled that he killed the living to follow the dead.

The sword Zhanlu was horrified by King Helü's cruel deeds, so it left and traveled through the waters until it came to Chu. King Zhao of Chu was fast asleep, and when he woke up, he discovered the sword Zhanlu, which belonged to the king of Wu, in his bed. King Zhao did not know the reason for this, and so he summoned Feng Huzi and asked him:[30] "I was fast asleep

吳王有女滕玉，因謀伐楚，與夫人及女會，【食】蒸魚。王前嘗半而與女。女怒曰：「王食【我殘】魚，辱我，不忘久生。」乃自殺。闔閭痛之，葬於國西閶門外。鑿池積土，文石為槨，題湊為中，金鼎、玉杯、銀樽、珠襦之寶皆以送女。乃舞白鶴於吳市中，令萬民隨而觀之，還使男女與鶴俱入羨門，因發機以掩之。殺生以送死，國人非之。

湛盧之劍，惡闔閭之無道也，乃去而出，水行如楚。楚昭王臥而寤，得吳王湛盧之劍於床。昭王不知其故，乃召風湖子而問曰：「寡人臥，覺而

---

27. There are numerous stories preserved in early Chinese texts that indicate that being given leftovers to eat was considered an appalling insult in this period; see, for example, *Han Feizi*, 223 ["Shuinan" 說難].
28. The tradition in this region that funeral processions included a dance performed by persons costumed as cranes is discussed in Yin Zhiqiang and Ding Bangjun (1993): 30.
29. The author here seems to envisage a mechanism known from some major Han dynasty tombs, where the stone doors were fitted with a single-use fitting that would close and lock the doors in such a way that they could not be opened again from the outside. Such a mechanism was found in the tomb of Zhao Mo, king of Nanyue 南越王趙眛 (r. 137–122 BCE); see Guangzhoushi wenwu guanli weiyuanhui et al. (1991): 12–14.
30. This individual also appears in the *Yuejue shu*, 80 ["Ji baojian" 記寶劍], under the name Feng Huzi 風胡子.

and when I awoke, I found this precious sword, of which I do not know the name. What sword is this?"

"This is the sword Zhanlu," Feng Huzi replied.

"Why do you say that?' King Zhao asked.

"I have heard that the king of Wu obtained three precious swords, which were presented to him by Yue: the first was called Yuchang, the second was called Panying, and the third was called Zhanlu," Feng Huzi said. "The sword Yuchang has already been used to kill King Liao of Wu, Panying was given to his dead daughter, and now Zhanlu has come to Chu."

"Why did Zhanlu leave him?" King Zhao asked.

"I have heard that when King Yunchang of Yue commissioned Ou Yezi to make five swords," Feng Huzi said. "He showed them to Xue Zhu.[31] 'The sword Yuchang is unprincipled and disobedient, so it cannot be made to obey,' Zhu said. 'Hence, vassals will use it to kill their lords, and sons will use it to kill their fathers.' That is the reason why Helü used this sword to murder King Liao. 'The one named Panying, also known as Haocao, is an improper object, and will be of no benefit to people.' That is the reason why it was given to the dead. 'The one named Zhanlu was made from the finest of the five metals, and the essence of *yang*—it is overflowing with *qi* and has numinous powers.[32] Brandishing it, you can summon the gods; wearing it, you can strike awe into all around you. It can repel a host and defeat an enemy army. However, if the ruler has evil intentions, this sword will immediately depart.' That means that it will leave the bad to go to the good. Now the king of Wu has behaved in a wicked way, killing his ruler and plotting against Chu; hence, Zhanlu has come to Chu."

得寶劍，不知其名，是何劍也？」風湖子曰：「此謂湛盧之劍。」昭王曰：「何以言之？」風湖子曰：「臣聞吳王得越所獻寶劍三枚：一曰魚腸；二曰磐郢；三曰湛盧。魚腸之劍，已用殺吳王僚也，磐郢以送其死女，今湛盧入楚也。」昭王曰：「湛盧所以去者，何也？」風湖子曰：「臣聞越王元[允]常使歐冶子造劍五枚，以示薛燭。燭對曰：『魚腸劍逆理不順，不可服也。臣以殺君，子以殺父。』故闔閭以殺王僚。『一名磐郢，亦曰豪曹，不法之物，無益於人。』故以送死。『一名湛盧，五金之英，太陽之精，寄氣託靈，出之有神，服之

---

31. King Yunchang of Yue, who died in 497 BCE, is consistently designated in the transmitted text of the *Wu Yue chunqiu* as Yuanchang 元常, thanks to a Song dynasty name taboo. However, in this translation, the correct standard name of this king will be used.

32. According to the commentary by Yan Shigu 顏師古 (581–645) on *Hanshu*, 24A.1118 n. 3, the five metals are of five different colors: yellow is represented by gold, white is silver, red is copper, blue is lead, and black is iron.

"How much is this sword worth?" King Zhao asked.[33]

"I have heard that when this sword was still in Yue, there was a visitor who tried to put a price on it," Feng Huzi said. "He said that it was worth thirty market towns, one thousand fine horses, and two cities of ten thousand households. Xue Zhu replied to this: 'The mines in Mount Chijin are already closed, while the Ruoye Stream is too deep to be plumbed. The myriad deities have ascended to Heaven, and Ou Ye[zi] is dead. Even if you were to give all the gold in the entire capital and every pearl and piece of jade to be found in your streams, you would still not be able to obtain a treasure such as this—so why are you talking about market towns, one thousand fine horses, and cities of ten thousand households?'"[34]

King Zhao was delighted and treated it as a true treasure. However, when King Helü heard that Chu had gained possession of the sword Zhanlu, he was furious about this and ordered Sun Wu, Wu [Zi]xu, and Bo Pi to attack Chu. Zixu secretly gave orders to spread the word in Chu: "If Chu appoints Ziqi as the general, I will capture him and kill him.[35] If Zichang takes command of the troops, I will withdraw."

When Chu heard this, Zichang was indeed put in command, and Ziqi was ordered to withdraw. Wu razed to the ground the two cities of Liu and Qian.[36]

有威，可以折衝拒敵。然人君有逆理之謀，其劍即出。』故去無道，以就有道。今吳王無道，殺君謀楚，故湛盧入楚。」昭王曰：「其直幾何？」風湖子曰：「臣聞此劍在越之時，客有酬其直者：有市之鄉三十，駿馬千匹，萬戶之都二，是其一也。薛燭對曰：『赤堇之山已令［合］無雲，若耶之溪深而莫測，羣臣［神］上天，歐冶死矣。雖傾城量金，珠玉盈河，猶不能得此寶。而況有市之鄉、駿馬千匹、萬戶之都，何足言也！』」昭王大悅，遂以為寶。闔閭

---

33. This translation reads *zhi* 直 (straight) as *zhi* 值 (to be worth), following the commentary by Huang Rensheng (1996): 99 n. 12.
34. This represents a cut-down version of the highly poetic valuation of the sword given in *Yuejue shu*, 80–81 ["Ji baojian"].
35. Ziqi is also known as Prince Jie of Chu 楚公子結, the son of King Ping; see *Guoyu*, 558 n. 1 ["Chuyu shang" 楚語上]. His death in 479 BCE is described in *Zuozhuan*, 1702 [Ai 16].
36. These events are described in *Zuozhuan*, 1512 [Zhao 31]. The destruction of Liu and Qian occurred in the fourth year of the reign of King Helü, though this date is not given in the *Wu Yue chunqiu*.

In the fifth year of his reign [510 BCE], the king of Wu went south and attacked Yue because they had not participated in the campaign against Chu. King Yunchang of Yue said: "Wu does not keep faith with the blood covenants they made in the past, they have abandoned us in spite of all the tribute we have paid them, and they are proposing to destroy their closest neighbors."

King Helü did not accept the justice of his complaint. He did indeed make an attack and crushed them at Zuili.[37]

In the sixth year of his reign [509 BCE], King Zhao of Chu ordered Prince Nangwa to attack Wu, to take revenge for the campaign against Qian and Liu.[38] Wu ordered [Wu] Zixu and Sun Wu to attack him, and they laid siege to Yuzhang.

"I want to take advantage of this critical situation to enter the Chu capital city and crush it," the king of Wu said. "If I am not able to enter Ying, what will the two of you actually have achieved?"

Then His Majesty surrounded the Chu Army at Yuzhang and inflicted a terrible defeat on them. Following that, he laid siege to Chao and conquered it, taking Prince Fan of Chu captive.[39] His Majesty took him home to be held as a hostage.

In the ninth year of his reign [506 BCE], the king of Wu said to Zixu and Sun Wu: "To begin with, you said it would be impossible to capture Ying, but what about now?"

"When fighting battles," the two generals responded, "it would not be possible to ensure victory on every occasion by building on the fear inspired by previous successes."

聞楚得湛盧之劍，因斯發怒，遂使孫武、伍胥、白喜伐楚。子胥陰令宣言於楚曰：「楚用子期為將，吾即得而殺之。子常用兵，吾即去之。」楚聞之，因用子常，退子期。吳拔六與灊二邑。

五年，吳王以越不從伐楚，南伐越。越王元[允]常曰：「吳不信前日之盟，棄貢賜之國，而滅其交親。」闔閭不然其言，遂伐破檇里。

---
37. The *Zuozhuan*, 1516 [Zhao 32], claims that this was the first campaign against Yue launched by the kingdom of Wu. Meanwhile, *Chunqiu jingzhuan jijie*, 1596 n. 1, suggests that previous conflicts had occurred but were too minor to be mentioned.
38. According to the *Chunqiu jingzhuan jijie*, 1504 n. 1, Nangwa (otherwise known as Zichang) was the son of Prince Zhen of Chu, and hence, he should be referred to as *wangsun* 王孫 (royal grandson).
39. The identity of this individual within the Chu royal house is not known.

"Why do you say that?" His Majesty asked.

"Chu's army is the strongest in the entire world," the two generals replied. "If we were to fight with them today, we would have a one in ten chance of survival. If you are able to enter Ying, Your Majesty, it would be by the will of Heaven. We would never dare to guarantee such a thing."

"I want to attack Chu again," the king of Wu said. "How do I make victory assured?"

"Nangwa is a greedy man," Wu [Zi]xu and Sun Wu pointed out, "and he has committed many offenses against the other lords: Tang and Cai loathe him. If you must attack [Chu], it is with the help of Tang and Cai [that you can achieve your heart's desire]."[40]

"Why do they hate him?"

"In the past," the two generals explained, "Lord Zhao of Cai was paying court to Chu, and he owned two beautiful fur cloaks and two fine jade pendants—he gave one of each to King Zhao.[41] His Majesty wore one set to hold court, and Lord Zhao himself wore the other. Zichang wanted them, but Lord Zhao refused to part with them. Zichang held him captive for three years and would not allow him to go home. Meanwhile, Lord Cheng of Tang paid court to Chu, and he had two beautiful dappled horses.[42] Zichang wanted one, but the lord refused to part with it, so he was also held for three years. The prime minister serving Lord Cheng of Tang came up with a plan, and he decided to get the horse from Lord Cheng's servants to ransom his ruler. What he did was to give the servants wine to drink and got them

六年，楚昭王使公子囊瓦伐吳，報潛、六之役。吳使伍胥、孫武擊之，圍於豫章。吳王曰：「吾欲乘危入楚都，而破其郢．不得入郢，二子何功？」於是圍楚師於豫章，大破之。遂圍巢，克之，獲楚公子繁以歸，為質。

九年，吳王謂子胥、孫武曰：「始子言郢不可入，今果何如？」二將曰：「夫戰，借勝以成其威，非常勝之道。」吳王曰：「何謂也？」二將曰：「楚之為兵，天下彊敵也。今臣與之爭鋒，十亡一存，而王入郢者，天也。臣不敢必。」

---

40. Some commentaries indicate a loss of text at this point; see, for example, Huang Rensheng (1996): 104 n. 1.
41. Lord Zhao of Cai ruled from 598 to 481 BCE. His unjust treatment at the hands of Nangwa is mentioned in many ancient texts; see, for example, *Chunqiu fanlu*, 124 ["Wangdao" 王道], *Xinxu*, 1142–53 ["Shanmou" 善謀], and *Zuozhuan*, 1531 [Ding 3].
42. Lord Cheng of Tang ruled from 510 to 505 BCE. The story of his troubles in Chu seems to be derived from a unique account preserved in *Zuozhuan*, 1531–32 [Ding 3].

drunk so that he could steal the horse and give it to Zichang. [Zi]chang then sent Lord Cheng back to his country. However, all his ministers were very critical of him. They said: 'Our lord imprisoned himself for three years for the sake of a horse. We ought to be rewarding the person who thought to steal it!' Lord Cheng has been racking his brains for a way to take revenge on Chu's king and his ministers; he never stops talking about it. When the people of Cai heard about this, they asked permission to present the cloak and pendant to Zichang: that is how the marquis of Cai was able to go home. He went to Jin to complain and sent his son, Yuan, and the children of various grandees as hostages, when asking for assistance in attacking Chu.[43] That is why we said if you get the help of Tang and Cai, you can attack Chu."

The king of Wu then sent an ambassador to Tang and Cai to inform them: "Chu has behaved in a barbaric way: they have tortured and killed loyal ministers, conquered territory from other rulers, and imprisoned and humiliated you two lords. I intend to raise an army to attack Chu, and I hope that you will join in this campaign."

The marquis of Tang sent his son, Qian, as a hostage to Wu.[44] The three countries plotted a joint attack on Chu. They rested their armies overnight at the bend on the Huai River, and then having passed Yuzhang, they went into battle formation opposite the Chu Army on either side of the Han River.[45]

吳王曰：「吾欲復擊楚，奈何而有功？」伍胥、孫武曰：「囊瓦者，貪而多過於諸侯，而唐、蔡怨之。王必伐，得唐、蔡何怨？」二將曰：「昔蔡昭公朝於楚，有美裘二枚，善珮二枚，各以一枚獻之昭王。王服之以臨朝，昭公自服一枚。子常欲之，昭公不與。子常三年留之不使歸國。唐成公朝楚，有二文馬，子常欲之，公不與，亦三年止之。唐成相與謀，從成公從者請馬，以贖成公。飲從者酒，醉之，竊馬而獻子常。常乃遣成公歸國。羣臣誹謗曰：『君以一馬之故，三年自囚，願賞竊馬之功。』於是成公常思報楚君臣，未嘗

---

43. The original text reads: "[He] sent his son Yuan, and his heir as hostages" (以子元與太子質). This is here being understood as a garbled version of the line: "[He] sent his son, Yuan, and the children of various grandees as hostages" (以其子元與大夫之子爲質), found in *Zuozhuan*, 1532 [Ding 3].
44. The *Zuozhuan*, 1532 [Ding 3], actually states that it was the marquis of Cai who sent his son as a hostage to Wu.
45. Xu Tianhu (1999): 47 suggests that this line should be understood as: "They abandoned their boats at the bend on the Huai River," reading "they rested their armies" (*she bing* 舍兵) in the original text as a graphic error for *she zhou* 捨舟.

Zichang forded the Han River and went into battle formation. Advancing from Mount Xiaobie to Mount Dabie, he fought three times but was not victorious. Realizing that it would be impossible to proceed any further, he wanted to run away. The court historian Huang said: "You helped His Late Majesty kill three loyal ministers for no reason; now Heaven is punishing you for that! This disaster was created by our former king."

Zichang did not respond.

In the tenth month, the two armies went into battle formation at Boju.[46] Prince Fugai, the younger brother of King Helü, got up at dawn to discuss the matter with him. "Zichang is not a benevolent man; he is greedy and cruel," he said. "None of those under his command will risk their lives in his service. If we chase after them, we will crush them; have no doubt about that!"

King Helü did not agree.

"When people talk about subordinates acting on their own initiative and not waiting for orders, they mean this kind of situation," Prince Fugai proclaimed. He then attacked Zichang with his regiment of five thousand men, inflicting a terrible defeat on him. [Zichang] fled toward Zheng, and the Chu Army was thrown into complete confusion. The Wu forces took advantage of this situation and crushed the main body of the Chu Army. The Chu soldiers paused to eat before crossing over the Han River, and just at that moment, the Wu troops attacked and defeated them at Yongzhi.[47] These five battles opened the way to Ying.

The king was hard-pressed by the Wu invaders, and so he left his capital and fled into exile with his younger sister, Princess Ji Mi. When he journeyed between the Yellow River and the Sui River, Grandee Yin Gu of Chu was traveling on the same boat as the king.[48] When the Wu Army entered Ying,

絕口。蔡人聞之，固請獻裘、珮於子常。蔡侯得歸，如晉告訴，以子元與太子質，而請伐楚。故曰得唐、蔡而可伐楚。」吳王於是使使謂唐、蔡曰：「楚為無道，虐殺忠良，侵食諸侯，困辱二君，寡人欲舉兵伐楚，願二君有謀。」唐侯使其子乾為質於吳。三國合謀伐楚，舍兵於淮汭，自豫章與楚夾漢水為

---

46. The character Chu 楚 in the original text is extraneous and has been omitted; see Zhang Jue (2006): 83 n. 2.
47. In *Zuozhuan*, 1544 [Ding 4], this place-name is given as Yongshi 雍澨.
48. According to *Zuozhuan*, 1545 [Ding 4], this individual was named Gu, but his title was *zhenyin* 鍼尹 (also given as *zhenyin* 箴尹), an official in charge of remonstrating with the king. The last character of this title has apparently been misunderstood by the author of the *Wu Yue chunqiu* as a surname.

they were looking for King Zhao, but by this time His Majesty had forded the Sui River and crossed the Yangtze, entering the Yunmeng Marshes. That night when they paused to rest, a group of bandits attacked them. They thrust their halberds at the king's head, but Grandee Yin Gu protected His Majesty, turning his back to them and taking the points in his own shoulder.[49] The king was terrified and fled to Yun. Grandee Zhong Jian followed him, carrying Princess Ji Mi on his back.[50]

When Xin, duke of Yun, found he had been joined by King Zhao, he was delighted and wanted to restore him to power. His younger brother, Huai, was furious. "King Zhao is our enemy!" he shouted. He wanted to kill him, so he said to his older brother, Xin: "In the past, King Ping killed our father, and now I will kill his son—what is wrong with that?"[51]

"When a ruler punishes his minister, would you dare to treat him as an enemy?" Xin demanded. "Besides which, it is not benevolent to take advantage of someone else's misfortunes; it is not filial to destroy an entire family line and put an end to the ancestral sacrifices; and it is not wise to act without good reason."

Huai's anger was not assuaged. Therefore, Xin secretly fled with the king and his younger brother, Chao, to Sui. The Wu Army pursued them there and said to the lord of Sui: "All the branches of the Zhou royal family living on the upper reaches of the Han River have been destroyed by Chu. You could say that Heaven has now paid them back for their crimes and is punishing Chu. Why are you protecting these people?[52] What did these members of the

陣。子常遂濟漢而陣，自小別山至於大別山。三不利，自知不可進，欲奔亡。史皇曰：「今子常無故與王共殺忠臣三人，天禍來下，王之所致。」子常不應。十月，楚二師陣於柏舉。闔閭之弟夫概，晨起請於闔閭曰：「子常不仁，貪而少恩。其臣下莫有死志。追之，必破矣。」闔閭不許。夫概曰：「所謂臣行其志，不待命者，其謂此也。」遂以其部五千人擊子常。大敗，走奔鄭，楚

---

49. In *Zuozhuan*, 1546 [Ding 4], the man who saved King Zhao's life is named as Royal Grandson Youyu 王孫由于.
50. Although not mentioned in the *Wu Yue chunqiu*, the princess subsequently insisted on marrying Grandee Zhong Jian because of his behavior on this occasion; see *Zuozhuan*, 1554 [Ding 5].
51. King Ping had executed Dou Chengran 鬥成然, the father of Xin, Huai, and Chao, in 528 BCE; see *Zuozhuan*, 1366 [Zhao 14].
52. This translation follows the annotations by Xu Tianhu (1999): 49, that *bao* 寶 (to treasure) should be read as *bao* 保 (to protect).

Zhou royal house do wrong? Why are you giving succor to these criminals? If you could hand over King Zhao, we would very much appreciate it."

The lord of Sui performed an oracle-bone divination about handing over King Zhao to the king of Wu, but it was not auspicious. He therefore refused the king of Wu's request.

"Sui is small and remote," he said, "but we are located close to Chu—in truth they have saved us from peril, and we have been allied through blood covenants right up to the present time. How can we now abandon them in their hour of need? Everything is peaceful in Chu under your control now; would anyone there dare to disobey your orders?"

The Wu Army respected his refusal and withdrew. At this time, Grandee Ziqi—in spite of the fact that he had fled with King Zhao—was secretly doing a deal with the Wu Army to hand over King Zhao. His Majesty discovered this and was able to escape. He cut out Ziqi's heart and performed a blood covenant with the lord of Sui with it; then he departed.[53]

The king of Wu entered Ying and stayed there. Since Wu [Zi]xu proved unable to lay his hands on King Zhao, he dug up the tomb of King Ping and took out his corpse, whipping it three hundred lashes. With his left foot, he stamped on his stomach, and with his right hand, he gouged out his eyes, as he berated him: "Who told you to believe those lying sycophants and kill my father and older brother? Surely you deserve all this!" He also told King Helü that he should rape King Zhao's wife; Wu [Zi]xu, with

師大亂。吳師乘之，遂破楚眾。楚人未濟漢，會楚人食，吳因奔而擊破之雍澨，五戰徑至於郢。王追於吳寇，出固將亡，與妹季羋出河、灘之間，楚大夫尹固與王同舟而去。吳師遂入郢，求昭王。王涉灘濟江，入于雲中。暮宿，羣盜攻之，以戈擊王頭，大夫尹固隱王，以背受之，中肩。王懼，奔鄖。大夫鍾建負季羋以從。鄖公辛得昭王大喜，欲還之。其弟懷怒曰：「昭王是我讎也！」欲殺之，謂其兄辛曰：「昔平王殺我父，吾殺其子，不亦可乎！」辛曰：「君討其臣，敢讎之者？夫乘人之禍，非仁也；滅宗廢祀，非孝也；動無令名，

---

53. This passage has caused commentators considerable problems, since Ziqi is elsewhere said to have been totally loyal to King Zhao until his death in 479 BCE. Therefore, commentators including Huang Rensheng (1996): 109 n. 17–19 and Zhang Jue (2006): 86 n. 15 argue that Prince Ziqi's plot was entirely benign and that blood was taken from the region of his heart, in a process that he was intended to survive. This interpretation, however, involves completely ignoring what it actually says in the *Wu Yue chunqiu*.

Sun Wu and Bo Pi, also raped the wives of Zichang and Marshal Cheng to humiliate the king of Chu and his ministers.[54]

His Majesty then ordered his army to attack Zheng. *Lord Ding of Zheng had earlier killed Crown Prince Jian and forced [Wu] Zixu into exile, for which he hated Zheng.* Troops were just about to cross the border. Lord Ding of Zheng was terrified, and so he issued the following message to the country: "If there is anyone who can turn back the Wu Army, I will share the government of the country with him."[55]

The son of the fisherman responded to this proclamation. "I can turn them back," he said, "and I will not need any weapons or provisions. Give me an oar, and let me sing as I travel: they will leave immediately!"

His lordship then gave the fisherman's son an oar.

The arrival of [Wu] Zixu's army was imminent. He blocked the road, thumping his oar and singing out: "Man in the reeds!"

He did this twice. Zixu heard him and was struck dumb with surprise. "Who are you?" he asked. "Sir, what is your name?"

"I am the fisherman's son," he said. "The ruler of our country was so frightened that he issued a nationwide proclamation: 'If there is anyone who can turn back the Wu Army, I will share the government of the country with him.' I remembered that my late father once met you, sir, on the road, so today I came to beg you to have mercy on the state of Zheng."

Zixu heaved a sigh. "How sad!" he said. "I owe everything that I have today to your father's kindness. Heavens, how could I forget?"

非智也。」懷怒不解。辛陰與其季弟巢以王奔隨。吳兵逐之，謂隨君曰：「周之子孫在漢水上者，楚滅之。謂天報其禍，加罰於楚，君何寶？周室何罪而隱其賊？能出昭王，即重惠也。」隨君卜昭王與吳王不吉，乃辭吳王曰：「今隨之僻小密近於楚，楚實存我，有盟至今未改。若今有難而棄之。今且安靜楚，敢不聽命？」吳師多其辭，乃退。是時大夫子期雖與昭王俱亡，陰與吳師為市，欲出昭王。王聞之，得免，即割子期心，以與隨君盟而去。

吳王入郢，止留。伍胥以不得昭王，乃掘平王之墓，出其屍，鞭之三百。左足踐腹，右手抉其目，誚之曰：「誰使汝用讒諛之口，殺我父兄，

---

54. The term *qi* 妻, literally "to treat as a wife," is often used to mean "rape" in texts dealing with the conflict between Wu and Yue; see also *Yuejue shu*, 106 ["Pianxu waizhuan" 篇叙外傳].

55. Lord Ding of Zheng died in 514 BCE. It was Lord Xian of Zheng 鄭獻公 (r. 513–501 BCE) who was in power when this state was attacked by Wu.

He then gave up his attack on the state of Zheng and returned with his army to place Chu under close guard, searching for King Zhao's place of refuge with ever-renewed vigor.

Shen Baoxu was hiding in the mountains. When he heard about this, he sent someone to take a message to Zixu: "Your vengeance has been terrible indeed! However, you used to be a vassal of King Ping; you faced north and served him as a minister. Now you have subjected him to the humiliation of having his corpse mutilated—is this not enough?"

"Thank Shen Baoxu on my behalf," Zixu said, "and tell him: 'My day is almost done, and I still have far to go; all I can do is to carry on along my crooked path.'"

Shen Baoxu understood that there was nothing he could do, so he traveled to Qin to beg that they rescue Chu. He journeyed day and night; his feet were cut and swollen, his clothes in rags, but still he stood like a crane and wept in the main courtyard of the Qin palace. His wailing continued without a break for seven days and seven nights. Lord Huan of Qin was a drunken sot who did not concern himself in the government of the country.[56] Thus, Shen Baoxu stopped crying and began to sing:

> How wicked is the king of Wu:
> Like a pig; like a snake!
> He is eating away at the Upper States,
> And wants to take control of the entire world:
> Chu is just the beginning!
> Our monarch is out in the marshes;
> He sends me to report this emergency,
> And I have cried like this for seven days.[57]

豈不冤哉？」即令闔閭妻昭王夫人，伍胥、孫武、白喜亦妻子常、司馬成之妻，以辱楚之君臣也。遂引軍擊鄭。鄭定公前殺太子建，而困迫子胥，自此【怨】鄭。【兵將入境】，定公大懼，乃令國中，曰：「有能還吳軍者，吾與分國而治。」漁者之子應募曰：「臣能還之。不用尺兵斗糧，得一橈而行歌道中，即還矣。」公乃與漁者之子橈。子胥軍將至，當道扣橈而歌，曰：「蘆中人！」如是再。子胥聞之，愕然大驚，曰：「何等謂？」與語：「公為何誰矣？」曰：「漁父者子。吾國君懼怖，令於國：有能還吳軍者，與之分國而治。臣念前人與君相逢於途，

---

56. Lord Huan of Qin ruled from 603 to 577 BCE. At the time of these events, it was Lord Ai of Qin 秦哀公 (r. 536–501 BCE) who was in power.
57. This song is characterized by a complete lack of rhyme and irregular line length.

Lord Huan was amazed: "Wu wants to destroy Chu even though the country has such a fine minister! None of my vassals can be compared to him—we can expect disaster at any moment!"

He recited the ode "You Have No Clothes," which runs as follows:

How can you say you have no clothes?
I will share my robe with you.
The king will raise an army . . .
He has the same enemies as you.[58]

"I have heard that those who turn their backs on virtue are insatiable in their demands," Baoxu said, "so even if you do not care about a disaster striking a neighboring country, you could yet get your share of the spoils by moving before Wu has consolidated their conquest. In what way would it benefit Qin to see Chu destroyed? It will simply be land that has lost its ruler. I hope that you will use your numinous powers to save us, for then we will serve you from one generation to the next."

The earl of Qin sent someone to make his excuses to him: "I understand the situation. You should return to the guesthouse, and we will inform you once we have completed our deliberations."

"At this very moment, His Majesty is out in the wilderness," Baoxu said, "without anywhere to lay his head. How can I enjoy the comforts of being safe and sound here?"

He went back to stand in the courtyard, where he leaned against the wall and wept ceaselessly day and night, without so much as a sip of water. The earl of Qin was moved to tears by this, and so he sent his army to escort him out of the country.

今從君乞鄭之國。」子胥歎曰：「悲哉！吾蒙子前人之恩，自致於此。上天蒼蒼，豈敢忘也？」於是乃釋鄭國，還軍守楚，求昭王所在日急。申包胥亡在山中，聞之，乃使人謂子胥曰：「子之報讎，其以甚乎？子故平王之臣，北面事之。今於僇屍之辱，豈道之極乎！」子胥曰：「為我謝申包胥：『日暮路遠，【吾故】倒行而逆施之於道也。』」申包胥知不可，乃之於秦，求救楚。晝馳夜趨，足踵蹠劈，裂裳裹膝，鶴倚哭於秦庭，七日七夜，口不絕聲。秦桓公素沉湎，不恤國事。申包胥哭已，歌曰：「吳為無道，封豕長蛇，以食上國。欲有天下，政從楚起。寡君出在草澤，使來告急。」如此七日。桓公大驚：「楚有賢臣如

---

58. This is the first verse of this ode; see *Shijing*, 431 ["Wuyi"]. This quotation omits the fourth line of this verse.

In the tenth year [505 BCE], the Qin Army had still not yet set out. King Yunchang of Yue was furious over the defeat King Helü had inflicted on him at the battle of Zuili, so he raised an army to attack Wu.[59] Since Wu was occupied with Chu, the invading forces of Yue were able to make a surprise attack on them.

In the sixth month, Shen Baoxu arrived with the Qin Army. Qin ordered the Honorable Zipu and Zihu to lead a force of five hundred chariots to rescue Chu by making an attack on Wu. The two men said: "We do not know the roads to Wu."[60] They had the Chu Army go on ahead and do battle with Wu, and then they joined them, inflicting a terrible defeat on Prince Fugai.

In the seventh month, Marshal Zicheng of Chu and the Honorable Zipu of Qin found themselves locked in a stalemate with the king of Wu. They secretly sent soldiers to attack Tang and destroyed it. [Wu] Zixu remained in Chu for a long time, refusing to depart, because he was searching for King Zhao.

When Prince Fugai's army was defeated, he withdrew. In the ninth month, the prince returned home in secret and crowned himself as the king of Wu. When King Helü was informed of this, he stopped skirmishing with the Chu Army because he wanted to kill Fugai. He then fled to Chu, where King Zhao enfeoffed him with the lands of Tangxi. King Helü then returned home.

[Wu] Zixu, Sun Wu, and Bo Pi stayed behind, and they fought with the Chu at Yongshi, where the Qin Army again defeated the Wu Army.

是，吳猶欲滅之？寡人無臣若斯者，其亡無日矣。」為賦無衣之詩，曰：「豈曰無衣，與子同袍。王于興師，⋯與子同仇。」包胥曰：「臣聞庆德無厭，王不憂鄰國疆場之患，逮吳之未定，王其取分焉。若楚遂亡，於秦何利？則亦亡君之土也。願王以神靈存之，世以事王。」秦伯使辭焉，曰：「寡人聞命矣。子且就館，將圖而告。」包胥曰：「寡君今在草野，未獲所伏，臣何敢即安？」復立於庭，倚牆而哭，日夜不絕聲，水不入口。秦伯為之垂涕，即出師而送之。

---

59. This attack by Yue is also documented in *Zuozhuan*, 1550 [Ding 5].
60. This line is a direct quotation from *Zuozhuan*, 1551 [Ding 5]. The *Chunqiu jingzhuan jijie*, 1638 n. 2, explains *dao* 道 as meaning not literally "road" but "method" (*fashu* 法術). This interpretation has been followed by many modern commentators; see, for example, Zhang Jue (2006): 91 n. 3 and Huang Rensheng (1996): 117 n. 4. However, it is quite possible to take this term entirely literally. At this stage, the commanders of the Qin Army would not yet have been familiar with best routes through the Yangtze River delta region.

Ziqi of Chu was about to use fire against the Wu forces, when Zixi said:[61] "The bodies of our men—young and old men—killed in battle lie exposed throughout this desolate wilderness.[62] Instead of collecting them for burial, you are going to burn them—how can you do such a thing?"

"The fate of the country, the survival of our people, life and death itself are going to be decided right here," Ziqi said. "How can I get the living killed to save some dead bodies? If the dead have consciousness, they will leap through this smoke to help us! If they are without consciousness, why should we begrudge a few bones lying the wilderness if we can destroy the kingdom of Wu?"

They then fought a battle after firing the area, and the Wu Army suffered a terrible defeat.

[Wu] Zixu and the others said to themselves: "Even though Chu has defeated our reinforcements, they have not yet inflicted any real damage on us."

"With the Wu Army, we have gone west to crush Chu, we have chased down King Zhao and destroyed the tomb of King Ping of Chu, tormenting and humiliating his corpse—that ought to be enough now," Sun Wu said.

"Ever since the time of the first hegemons, there has never been another vassal who was able to take such a revenge! We can leave!" Zixu replied.

After the Wu Army had departed, King Zhao returned to his capital. Music Master Hu had been horrified when the king of Chu had been led

十年，秦師未出，越王元［允］常恨闔閭破之檇里，興兵伐吳。吳在楚，越盜掩襲之。六月，申包胥以秦師至，秦使公子子蒲、子虎率車五百乘救楚擊吳。二子曰：「吾未知吳道。」使楚師前，與吳戰，而即會之，大敗夫概。七月，楚司馬子成、秦公子子蒲，與吳兵相守，私以間兵伐唐，滅之。子胥久留楚，求昭王，不去。夫概師敗，卻退。九月，潛歸，自立為吳王。闔閭聞之，乃釋楚師，欲殺夫概。奔楚，昭王封夫概於棠溪，闔閭遂歸。子胥、孫武、白喜留，與楚師於淮澨，秦師又敗吳師。楚子期將焚吳軍，子西曰：

---

61. Zixi, also known as Prince Shen (d. 479 BCE), was the oldest son of King Ping of Chu by junior consort; see *Zuozhuan*, 1474 [Zhao 26]. Meanwhile, the *Shiji*, 40.1714, incorrectly suggests that he was King Ping's younger brother.

62. As noted by Zhang Jue (2006): 92 n. 4, this passage garbles a story derived from *Zuozhuan*, 1552 [Ding 5]. During this campaign, the Wu Army occupied the city of Jun 麇, and many corpses of Chu soldiers had to remain unburied because they were located within its purlieus, which would have been far too dangerous to approach. It was therefore necessary to set fire to the place and cremate the remains rather than try and collect them for burial. By misunderstanding the place-name Jun as meaning "wilderness," the author of the *Wu Yue chunqiu* made this discussion incomprehensible.

by his trust in malicious lies to murder Wu She and Bo Zhouli, which had resulted in endless military incursions at the border and eventually led to the desecration of King Ping's tomb, the mutilation of his corpse, and the rape of his widow to shame the ruler of Chu and his vassals.[63] He was also upset by the travails experienced by King Zhao, who had been rendered a laughingstock to the entire world, and he felt personally humiliated by this. He strummed his *qin* and composed a "Song of Suffering" for Chu, to express his pain at the dangers threatening his ruler and make this situation more widely known.[64] The words ran as follows:

> How perverse was this king—how perverse!
> Since his interest was in slander, he paid no attention to the ancestral shrines.
> Employing Wuji meant that murders were many,
> He butchered the Bo family until almost all were dead.
> These two men fled east to Wu and Yue:
> Shocked and horrified, the king of Wu helped them in their pain.
> Still crying, they raised an army and attacked to the west—
> This was the plan of Wu [Zi]xu, Bo Pi, and Sun Wu.
> After three battles they crushed Ying and our king ran away;
> The soldiers in control raced to plunder the Chu palace.
> The bones of the Chu king were dug from their grave,
> The humiliation of whipping and exposing the corpse will be hard to expunge!

「吾國父兄身戰暴骨草野焉，不收，又焚之，其可乎？」子期曰：「亡國失眾，存沒所在，又何殺生以愛死？死如有知，必將乘煙起而助我。如其無知，何惜草中之骨，而亡吳國？」遂焚而戰，吳師大敗。子胥等相謂曰：「彼楚雖敗我餘兵未有所損者。」孫武曰：「吾以吳干戈西破楚，逐昭王而屠荊平王墓，割戮其屍，亦已足矣。」子胥曰：「自霸王以來，未有人臣報讎如此者也。行去矣！」吳軍去後，昭王反國。樂師扈子非荊王信讒佞，殺伍子奢、白州

---

63. This translation follows the commentary by Lu Wenchao 盧文弨 (1717–95), cited in Zhang Jue (2006): 93 n. 2, in reading *xi* 喜 (pleasure) in the original text as *qi* 妻 (wife or, in this case, widow).
64. The translation of this line, garbled in the original text, follows the commentary by Xu Tianhu (1999): 54.

Almost were the ancestral shrines toppled, the state altars destroyed,
What crime did our king commit that his country should face ruin?
Our knights have suffered appallingly, our people have been terrorized,
Although the Wu Army has gone, their fears have not been assuaged,
I hope Your Majesty will now offer succor to the loyal and honest:
Do not allow slanderous mouths to spread their foul lies.[65]

King Zhao had tears rolling down his cheeks, for he understood the deep feelings that this song for the *qin* was intended to express. Afterward, Master Hu did not play it again.

[Wu] Zixu and the others crossed the upper reaches of the Lai River at Liyang. At this time, he heaved a great sigh and said: "Once, I was starving here, and I begged for food from a woman. She gave it to me, but afterward she threw herself into the river and drowned."

He wanted to repay her with a gift of one hundred pieces of gold, but he did not know where her family lived. He could only throw the gold into the river before leaving.

A short time later, an old woman came passed, weeping. Someone asked her: "Why are you crying so bitterly?"

"I had a daughter who stayed at home unmarried for thirty years," the old woman explained. "Some years ago, she was here washing silk when she happened to meet a gentleman in dire straits. She gave him food but was afraid that other people would find out about it, so she threw herself into the Lai

犁，而寇不絕於境，至乃掘平王墓，戮屍奸喜，以辱楚君臣。又傷昭王困迫，幾為天下大鄙，然已愧矣。乃援琴為楚作窮劫之曲，以暢君之迫厄之暢達也。其詞曰：「王耶王耶何乖烈，不顧宗廟聽讒孽。任用無忌多所殺，誅夷白氏族幾滅。二子東奔適吳、越，吳王哀痛助切怛。垂涕舉兵將西伐，伍胥、白喜、孫武決。三戰破郢王奔發，留兵縱騎虜荊闕。楚荊骸骨遭發掘，鞭辱腐屍恥難雪。幾危宗廟社稷滅，嚴王何罪國幾絕。卿士悽愴民惻悷，吳軍雖去怖不歇。

---

65. This song consists of rhymed couplets; in each case, the rhyme is derived from the *yue-ji* 月祭 group.

River. Now I have heard that Lord Wu has come back, but I was not able to get any reward, so I was upset that she died in vain! That is why I was so sad."

"Zixu wanted to reward you with one hundred pieces of gold," the person told her, "but he did not know where you lived. He threw the gold into the river before leaving."

The old woman then collected the gold and went home.

[Wu] Zixu returned to Wu. When the king of Wu heard that the three commanders in chief were about to arrive, he had a banquet of sashimi fish prepared.[66] On the day that they were due to arrive, time passed, and they did not come, so the fish began to stink. A short time later, Zixu arrived. Helü had the sashimi presented, and they ate it, not noticing the foul smell. Afterward, when the king had this dish made again, it was with the same flavor. The tradition of the people in Wu making sashimi began with King Helü.

The various generals also returned from Chu at this time, and so they changed the name of the Chang Gate to the "Destruction of Chu Gate." His Majesty now plotted an attack on Qi, but the ruler of Qi sent his daughter as a hostage to Wu.[67] The king of Wu afterward sent a diplomatic mission to request the hand of the lady of Qi in marriage for Crown Prince Bo. This lady was very young, and she was homesick for Qi, so she cried day and night and ended up making herself sick. King Helü ordered a city gate to be built to the north, which he called the "Looking Toward Qi Gate." He commanded that the lady go and spend time on top of it. The lady could not control her feelings of homesickness, and her health became worse by the day: in the end she died. "In case the dead have awareness," she said, "I want you to be sure to bury me on the peak of Mount Yu, so that I may look toward the country of Qi."

願王更隱撫忠節，勿為讒口能謗襲。」昭王垂涕，深知琴曲之情，扈子遂不復鼓矣。子胥等過溧陽瀨水之上，乃長太息曰：「吾嘗飢於此，乞食於一女子。女子飼我，遂投水而亡。」將欲報以百金，而不知其家，乃投金水中而去。有頃，一老嫗行哭而來。人問曰：「何哭之悲？」嫗曰：「吾有女子，守居三十不嫁。往年擊綿於此，遇一窮途君子而輒飯之，而恐事泄，自投於瀨水。今聞伍君來，不得其償，自傷虛死，是故悲耳。」人曰：「子胥欲報百金，不知其家，投金水中而去矣。」嫗遂取金而歸。子胥歸吳，吳王聞三師將至，治魚為鱠。

---

66. The importance of thinly sliced raw fish, now usually associated with Japanese cooking, within the haute cuisine of this region in antiquity is considered in Despeux (1999) and Xiao Fan (1990).
67. The distress of Lord Jing of Qi 齊景公 (r. 547–490 BCE) at having to send his daughter to Wu is recorded in *Mengzi*, 168 ["Li Lou shang"].

King Helü was very upset about this and did as she had requested; thus, she was buried on the peak of Mount Yu.

At this time, the crown prince also became sick and died. King Helü considered which of the other princes he could choose to replace him, but he had not made a decision. Crown Prince Bo's [son], Fuchai, spoke day and night to Zixu:[68] "His Majesty wants to establish a crown prince; who could be more suitable than myself? What happens next is entirely in your hands, sir."

"The appointment of the crown prince has not yet been settled," Wu Zixu said, "but once I enter the palace, it will be."

A short time later, King Helü summoned Zixu to discuss establishing a crown prince.

"I have heard that when no sons are born, sacrifices to the ancestors will be cut off," Zixu said. "Hence, having many children is the sign of a flourishing state. Now the crown prince has died young.[69] Having lost your son and heir, Your Majesty wants to appoint a new crown prince; who could be more suitable than Bo's son, Fu[chai]?"[70]

"Fu[chai] is stupid and not benevolent," King Helü replied.[71] "I am afraid that he will not be able to uphold the traditions of the kingdom of Wu."

"Fuchai keeps his word and is an affectionate character," Zixu said. "He is also honest and upright and behaves with propriety and justice toward

將到之日，過時不至，魚臭。須臾子胥至，闔閭出鱠而食，不知其臭。王復重為之，其味如故。吳人作鱠者，自闔閭之造也。諸將既從還楚，因更名閶門曰破楚門，復謀伐齊。齊子使女為質於吳。吳王因為太子波聘齊女。女少，思齊，日夜號泣，因乃為病。闔閭乃起北門，名曰望齊門，令女往游其上。女思不止，病日益甚，乃至殂落。女曰：「令死者有知，必葬我於虞山之巔，以望齊國。」闔閭傷之，正如其言，乃葬虞山之巔。是時太子亦病而死。闔閭謀擇諸公子可立者，未有定計。波太子夫差日夜告於伍胥曰：「王欲立太子，非我而誰當立？此計在君耳。」伍子胥曰：「太子未有定，我入，則決矣。」闔閭有頃召子胥謀立太子，子胥曰：「臣聞祀廢於絕後，興於有嗣。今太子不祿，早失侍御，今王欲立太子者，莫大乎波秦之子夫差。」闔閭曰：「夫愚

---

68. This translation follows the annotations by Xu Tianhu (1999): 56 in reading the line *Bo Taizi Fuchai* 波太子夫差, which makes no sense at all, as *Taizi Bo zhi zi Fuchai* 太子波之子夫差 (Crown Prince Bo's son, Fuchai).
69. The term *bulu* 不祿 was used in Han dynasty writings specifically to indicate an untimely demise; see *Liji*, 157 ["Quli xia" 曲禮下].
70. The character *qin* 秦 in this line is thought to be extraneous and has been omitted.
71. The translation here follows the commentary by Xu Tianhu (1999): 56 in reading the character *fu* 夫 at the beginning of this line as the first part of the name Fuchai 夫差.

others. Furthermore, it is clearly written in the ancient classical texts that a father should be succeeded by his son when he dies."

"I will do as you suggest," King Helü responded.

He established Fuchai as crown prince. Afterward, he ordered the crown prince to encamp his army and protect against incursions by Chu.[72] Meanwhile, His Majesty rebuilt the palace. He constructed the Archery Tower at An Village, the Flower Pool at Pingchang, and the Southern City Palace at Changle.[73] King Helü came and went: sometimes he traveled, and sometimes he rested. Autumn and winter would be spent running the country from within the walls, while in the spring and summer, he governed from outside the city. He constructed the Gusu Tower. He would eat breakfast at Mount Shan and then spend the day enjoying himself at the [Gu]su Tower. He went shooting at Seagull Bank and raced his horses at Traveler's Tower. He made music at Shi City and raced his dogs at Long Island. At this time, King Helü was at the peak of his powers as hegemon.

Having settled the matter of the crown prince, His Majesty attacked Chu, inflicting a crushing defeat on their army and razing the city of Po. Chu was afraid that the Wu Army would return yet again, so they abandoned Ying and moved the capital to Weiruo.[74] At this time, thanks to the stratagems of [Wu] Zixu, Bo Pi, and Sun Wu, the kingdom of Wu was able to crush the powerful state of Chu to the west, strike fear into Qi and Jin to the north, and attack the Yuyue people to the south.

而不仁，恐不能奉統於吳國。」子胥曰：「夫差信以愛人，端於守節，敦於禮義，父死子代，經之明文。」闔閭曰：「寡人從子。」立夫差為太子，使太子屯兵守楚留止。自治宮室，立射臺於安里，華池在平昌，南城宮在長樂。闔閭出入游臥，秋冬治於城中，春夏治於城外，治姑蘇之臺。旦食鉏山，晝游蘇臺，射於鷗陂，馳於游臺，興樂石城，走犬長洲。斯止闔閭之霸時。於是太子定，因伐楚，破師拔番。楚懼吳兵復往，乃去郢，徙于蔿若。當此之時，吳以子胥、白喜、孫武之謀，西破彊楚，北威齊晉，南伐於越。

---

72. Huang Rensheng (1996): 124 n. 14 suggests that this line has been garbled, probably as the result of a misplaced bamboo strip, and in fact pertains to the description of the moving of the Chu capital at the end of this chapter.
73. This section of the text is derived from the *Yuejue shu*, 9 ["Ji Wudi"].
74. The decision to move the capital city of the kingdom of Chu to a new location, usually named as Ruo, is described in *Zuozhuan*, 1557 [Ding 6].

Chapter Five

The Inner Traditions
The Story of King Fuchai of Wu

In the eleventh year of his reign [485 BCE], King Fuchai went north to attack Qi. Thereupon, Qi sent Grandee Gao to apologize to the Wu Army.[1]

"Qi is isolated among the Central States; our granaries are bare and our storehouses empty, while our people have scattered and dispersed," he said. "We consider Wu as our most powerful support, but before we have ever had cause to report an emergency to you, you attacked us. Let us send the people of the capital out to the suburbs to prostrate themselves, to proclaim the message that we would not dare to go into battle formation and fight with you—may it be that Wu shows their understanding of the fact that Qi has never stepped out of bounds."

《夫差內傳》

十一年，夫差北伐齊。齊使大夫高氏謝吳師，曰：「齊孤立於國，倉庫空虛，民人離散。齊以吳為彊輔，今未往告急，而吳見伐。請伏國人於郊，不敢陳戰爭之辭。惟吳哀齊之不濫也。」吳師即還。

十二年，夫差復北伐齊。越王聞之，率眾以朝於吳，而以重寶厚獻太宰嚭。嚭喜，受越之賂，愛信越殊甚，日夜為言於吳王。王信用嚭之計，伍胥大懼，

---

1. This individual is identified in Xu Tianhu (1999): 61 as Gao Wuping 高無平, at this time general in command of the upper army of Qi. Xu Naichang (1906): 5.1a suggests this name should be Gao Wupi 高無丕, following *Zuozhuan*, 1662 [Ai 11].

The Wu Army immediately turned back.

In the twelfth year of his reign [484 BCE], King Fuchai again went north to attack Qi.[2] The king of Yue heard about this and led his forces to pay court to Wu and generously presented many treasures to Chancellor Pi. Pi was delighted and accepted these bribes from Yue, and this greatly strengthened his love and faith in Yue. Day and night, he spoke to the king of Wu on their behalf. His Majesty trusted him and made use of the stratagems suggested by Pi. Wu [Zi]xu was horrified by this.

"He has abandoned Wu!" he exclaimed.[3] Then he stepped forward and remonstrated: "Yue is a disease of the heart and vitals, and you should have removed this cancer already. However, instead you have now chosen to believe these false words and lying schemes, because you hope to profit from Qi. Crushing Qi can be compared to plowing a field of stones—it will yield no crops. I hope that Your Majesty will give up on Qi and prioritize the situation with Yue. Otherwise, when you regret your decision, it will be too late."

The king of Wu did not listen to him, sending [Wu] Zixu as an ambassador to Qi to communicate the date set for the coming battle. Zixu said to his son: "I have repeatedly remonstrated with His Majesty, but the king does not follow my advice. Now we are going to see the destruction of Wu!

曰：「是棄吾也。」乃進諫曰：「越在心腹之病，不前除其疾，今信浮辭偽詐而貪齊。破齊，譬由磐石之田，無立其苗也。願王釋齊而前越。不然，悔之無及。」吳王不聽，使子胥使於齊，通期戰之會。子胥謂其子曰：「我數諫王，王不我用。今見吳之亡矣。汝與吾俱亡，亡無為也。」乃屬其子於齊鮑氏而還。太宰嚭既與子胥有隙，因讒之曰：「子胥為強暴力諫，願王少厚焉。」王曰：「寡人知之。」未興師，會魯使子貢聘於吳。

十三年，齊大夫陳成恆欲弑簡公，陰憚高、國、鮑、晏，故前興兵伐魯。魯君憂之。孔子患之，召門人而謂之曰：「諸侯有相伐者，丘常恥之。夫魯，父母之國也，丘墓在焉。今齊將伐之，子無意一出耶？」子路辭出，孔子止

---

2. This campaign is also mentioned in *Zuozhuan*, 1661 [Ai 11], and *Shiji*, 31.1471.
3. Here *wu* 吾 is being understood as an error for Wu 吳, following the commentary by Lu Wenchao, quoted in Zhang Jue (2006): 104 n. 5. There is a parallel line in *Shiji*, 31.1472: "This is abandoning Wu" (是棄吳也). It is a peculiarity of this chapter that the author has introduced wordplay, whereby the text reads equally well whether it is understood as *wu* 吾 (I) or Wu 吳 meaning the kingdom of Wu. I am grateful to the anonymous reviewer who pointed this out.

However, there is no point in getting you killed with Wu!"[4] He entrusted his son to the Bao family in Qi and then went home.[5]

Chancellor Pi had now long been alienated from [Wu] Zixu, and accordingly, he slandered him. "Zixu is offering such determined remonstrance because he is in the pay of those violent and wicked people," he said. "I hope that Your Majesty will be less indulgent of him."

"I am well aware of that," His Majesty said.

However, before he was able to raise an army, it so happened that Lu sent Zigong as an ambassador to Wu.[6]

In the thirteenth year [483 BCE], Grandee Chen Cheng Heng of Qi wanted to assassinate Lord Jian, but he was secretly afraid of the Gao, Guo, Bao, and Yan families; hence, he began by raising an army and attacking Lu.[7] The ruler of Lu was worried about this.[8] Confucius

之。子張、子石請行，孔子弗許。子貢辭出，孔子遣之。子貢北之齊，見成恆，因謂曰：「夫魯者，難伐之國，而君伐，過矣。」成恆曰：「魯何難伐也？」子貢曰：「其城薄以卑，其池狹以淺，其君愚而不仁，大臣無用，士惡甲兵，不可與戰。君不若伐吳。夫吳，城厚而崇，池廣以深，甲堅士選，器飽弩勁，又使明大夫守之，此易邦也。」成恆忿然作色曰：「子之所難，人之所易。子

---

4. Again, as above, *wu* 吾 is being understood as an error for Wu 吳.
5. The Bao family here is said to refer to Bao Mu 鮑牧 according to Xu Tianhu (1999): 62. However, the *Zuozhuan*, 1651 [Ai 8], states that Bao Mu was executed by Lord Dao of Qi 齊悼公 (r. 488–485 BCE) in 487 BCE. After taking up residence in Qi, Wu Zixu's son adopted the surname of Wangsun 王孫—given the known marriage practices of the Wu royal family who frequently selected senior government ministers as marriage partners, it is likely that he was indeed the son of a Wu princess.
6. Zigong, also known as Duanmu Ci 端木賜, was one of the most famous of the disciples of Confucius; his biography is given in *Shiji*, 67.2195–201. His diplomatic efforts are summed up in the expression: "Zigong's one trip resulted in the preservation of Lu, civil war in Qi, the destruction of Wu, the strengthening of Jin and the hegemony of Yue" (子貢一出存魯，亂齊，破吳，彊晉而霸越), which appears to have been virtually proverbial in early China.
7. Grandee Chen Cheng Heng, also known as Tian Chang 田常, dominated the government of the state of Qi at this time. His great-grandson would become the first Tian ruler of the state of Qi; see *Shiji*, 46.1883–86. Lord Jian of Qi (r. 484–481 BCE) was indeed eventually murdered by Chen Cheng Heng, and the other senior ministerial families purged.
8. The ruler of Lu at this point would have been Lord Ai of Lu 魯哀公 (r. 494–467 BCE).

believed that disaster was imminent, so he summoned his disciples and said to them: "I have always found the way in which the lords attack each other is deeply shameful. Lu is the country of my parents—their tombs are here. Now Qi is going to invade us; do you intend to do nothing about this?"

Zilu said that he would go, but Confucius stopped him. Zizhang and Zishi asked permission to set out, but Confucius refused.[9] Then Zigong said that he would go, and Confucius sent him on his way.

Zigong went north to Qi, where he had an audience with Cheng Heng and said to him: "Lu is a country that is very difficult to attack. However, you have undertaken a campaign against it, my lord, and that is a mistake."

"In what way is Lu difficult to attack?" Cheng Heng asked.

"Its walls are thin and low, its moats are narrow and shallow, its ruler is stupid and unkind, the most senior government ministers are not consulted in matters of state, and its soldiers loathe the very sight of weapons and armor—you cannot fight them," Zigong said. "It would be much better for you to attack Wu. Wu has strong and high walls, its moats are broad and deep, they have strong armor and handpicked officers, abundant weaponry and bowstrings at the ready—not to mention that they have employed enlightened officials to guard their cities. This is a country that would be easy to attack."

Cheng Heng looked angry. "The things that you say are difficult everyone else considers to be easy," he said, "while the things that you say are easy everyone else considers to be difficult. What are you trying to tell me?"

"I have heard that you have sought enfeoffment three times and failed three times; this is because some of the senior ministers are opposed to you," Zigong said. "Now you want to destroy Lu in order to enlarge Qi, to pull Lu down in order to strengthen your own position, but your success will not

之所易，人之所難。而以教恆，何也？」子貢曰：「臣聞君三封而三不成者，大臣有所不聽者也。今君又欲破魯以廣齊，墮魯以自尊，而君功不與焉。是君上驕下恣羣臣，而求以成大事，難矣！且夫上驕則犯，臣驕則爭，此君上於王有邅，而下與大臣交爭。如此，則君立於齊，危於累卵。故曰不如伐吳。且吳王剛猛而毅，能行其令，百姓習於戰守，明於法禁，齊遇，為擒必矣。今君悉四境之中，出大臣以環之，人民外死，大臣內空，是君上無彊敵之臣，下無黔首之士，孤主制齊者，君也。」陳恆曰：「善。雖然吾兵已在魯

---

9. The biographies of these three disciples of Confucius are found in *Shiji*, 67.2191–94, 2201–2, and 2219–20.

achieve this for you—all you will do is to make your ruler arrogant on the one hand and make government ministers even more difficult to control on the other. It will be much harder to try to achieve great things after that! Furthermore, if your lord becomes arrogant, it will be much easier for you to offend him; if the other ministers become prideful, they will fight with you for power. This means that you will find yourself alienated from your ruler on the one hand and locked in conflict with other ministers on the other, in which case your position in Qi will be as parlous as that of a stack of eggs.[10] That is why I said that you would do better to attack Wu. The king of Wu is a brave and redoubtable man, who can make his orders obeyed: his people are used to both offensive and defensive fighting, and they know the laws and regulations—it is self-evident that when Qi goes up against them, it will be in serious trouble. Now if your lordship were to remove all soldiers from within the four borders and send the senior government ministers out with them as their commanders, this would mean that people would die abroad and ministers will leave the country empty, so you would have no powerful enemies, and they would have no soldiers to fight under them. Only one person would then be in control of Qi, and that would be your lordship."

"Great!" Chen Heng said. "However, my soldiers are already in place at the foot of the walls of Lu. If I send them to Wu, the grandees here are sure to suspect my actions.[11] What can I do?"

"Order your troops to stay where they are and not to attack," said Zigong. "I will go south to see the king of Wu on your behalf and request that he rescues Lu by launching an attack on Qi; you can then send your army to intercept them."

之城下矣，吾去之吳，大臣將有疑我之心，為之奈何？」子貢曰：「君按兵無伐，請為君南見吳王，請之救魯而伐齊，君因以兵迎之。」陳恆許諾。子貢南見吳王，謂吳王曰：「臣聞之，王者不絕世，而霸者無彊敵。千鈞之重，加銖而移。今萬乘之齊，而私千乘之魯，而與吳爭彊，臣竊為君恐焉。且夫救魯，顯名也。伐齊，大利也。義存亡魯，害暴齊而威強晉，則王不疑也。」吳王曰：「善。雖然，吾嘗與越戰，棲之會稽，入臣於吳，不即誅之。三年，使歸。夫越君，賢主，苦身勞力，夜以接日，內飾其［兵］政，外事諸侯，

---

10. The original text here gives *wang* 王 (king), but this character is understood as a graphic error for *zhu* 主 (ruler), following the commentary by Xu Tianhu (1999): 63.
11. The punctuation of this line by Huang Rensheng (1996): 134 gives it as the grandees of Wu that will become suspicious. This is not correct.

Chen Heng agreed to this.

Zigong then went south and had an audience with the king of Wu. He told the king of Wu: "I have heard that a true king does not allow another ruling house to be destroyed, while a hegemon has no powerful enemies.[12] When a weight of a thousand *jun* is in equilibrium, add a single grain to one side, and it will tip. Right at this moment, Qi, a state of ten thousand chariots, hopes to profit from the destruction of Lu, a state of a thousand chariots, which would allow them to vie for dominance with Wu; I am concerned about this situation on Your Majesty's behalf. Furthermore, if you were to save Lu, it will make you famous; if you attack Qi, you will benefit greatly thereby. If you show your fine sense of justice by saving the dying state of Lu, while at the same time putting a spoke in the wheel of the cruel state of Qi, and striking awe into the powerful state of Jin, you will be considered a true king, make no mistake about that!"

"Good!" His Majesty cried. "However, in the past, I had to fight a battle with Yue whereupon [King Goujian] took refuge in Kuaiji, after which he came to Wu as a vassal. I did not execute him, and after three years, I allowed him to go home. The king of Yue is a wise ruler—he works incredibly hard day and night, he has improved both the army and the civilian government out of all recognition, and he is in contact with other lords abroad. I am sure that he wants to take revenge on me. If you would attack Yue on my behalf, I would be happy to listen to you."

"No," Zigong said. "Yue is not as strong as Lu, and Wu is not as strong as Qi. Your Majesty has refused to listen to me because you are concentrating on the idea of making an attack on Yue—this is the same as Qi hoping to profit from Lu. Besides which, to fear little Yue while worrying about the

必將有報我之心。子待我伐越而聽子。」子貢曰:「不可。夫越之彊,不過於魯。吳之彊,不過於齊。主以伐越而不聽臣,齊亦已私魯矣。且畏小越而惡彊齊,不勇也。見小利而忘大害,不智也。臣聞仁人不因厄以廣其德,智者不棄時以舉其功,王者不絕世以立其義。且夫畏越如此,臣誠東見越王,使出師以從下吏。」吳王大悅。子貢東見越王,王聞之,除道郊迎,身御至舍,問曰:「此僻狹之國,蠻夷之民,大夫何索然若不辱乃至於此?」子貢曰:「君處,故來。」越王勾踐再拜稽首,曰:「孤聞禍與福為鄰,今大夫之弔,孤之

---

12. The issue of preserving foreign ruling houses when under threat was a key problem of this period, when many states were at loggerheads; this topic was regularly broached in interstate meetings throughout the Spring and Autumn period.

great state of Qi is not brave; to keep an eye on some minor profit and ignore a terrible danger is not wise. I have heard that a benevolent person would not make other people suffer to show off his own virtue; a wise person would not let slip any opportunity to achieve success, while a true king would not allow another ruling line to be cut off when he could instead demonstrate his fine sense of justice by preserving it. Since you are so very afraid of Yue, I am willing to go east and have an audience with the king of Yue and make him send out an army to serve under your command."

The king of Wu was delighted.

Zigong went east to have an audience with the king of Yue. When His Majesty heard this, he cleared the roads and welcomed him in the suburbs. Having personally driven him to the guesthouse, he inquired: "Mine is a remote kingdom, inhabited by the Man and the Yi people, so why have you come here, sir, as cheerfully as if this were no humiliation to you?"

"This is where you live, Your Majesty," Zigong said, "and that is why I have come."[13]

King Goujian of Yue bowed twice, kowtowed, and said: "I have heard that good luck and bad depend on each other—for you, sir, to come here to condole with me is my good fortune. How could I dare to neglect to inquire into what you have to tell me?"

"Recently," Zigong replied, "I had an audience with the king of Wu, begging him to rescue Lu and attack Qi, but he is far too frightened of Yue. It is stupid of you to make him so suspicious if you do not intend to take your revenge on him. If you do intend to take your revenge on him and he already knows it—your situation is dangerous indeed! For people to hear about things before they even happen places you at great risk. These are three things that anyone wanting to achieve results must avoid."

福矣。孤敢不問其說？」子貢曰：「臣今者見吳王，告以救魯而伐齊，其心畏越。且夫無報人之志，而使人疑之，拙也。有報人之意，而使人知之，殆也。事未發而聞之者，危也。三者舉事之大忌也。」越王再拜，曰：「孤少失前人，內不自量與吳人戰，軍敗身辱遁逃，上棲會稽，下守海濱，唯魚鱉見矣。今大夫辱弔而身見之，又發玉聲以教孤，孤賴天之賜也，敢不承教？」子貢曰：「臣聞明主任人不失其能，直士舉賢不容於世。故臨財分利，則使仁；涉患犯難，則使勇；用智圖國，則使賢；正天下定諸侯，則使聖。兵強而不能行

---

13. The parallel passage in *Yuejue shu*, 52 ["Chen Cheng Heng" 陳成恒], gives this line of Zigong's speech as: "I have come to condole with Your Majesty" (弔君故來).

The king of Yue bowed twice. "I lost my father when I was still very young," he said. "I had no idea of my own strengths and weaknesses, so I tried to fight the people of Wu—my army was defeated, and I suffered great humiliation. I escaped to take refuge amid the peaks of Mount Kuaiji beside the sea, with only the fish and turtles as my companions. Now you have been so gracious as to come and see me, and you have put yourself to the trouble of offering me instruction—I consider this to be a gift from Heaven! How could I dare to refuse to follow your advice?"

"I have heard that an enlightened ruler employs people in situations where he can make full use of their abilities and appoints knights and wise men to places where they will be useful to their society," Zigong replied. "When it comes to supervising your financial affairs and making sure that profits are divided equitably, you should employ the benevolent; when dealing with difficult and dangerous situations, you should employ the brave; when planning for national affairs, you should employ the wise; when putting the world to rights and settling problems among the other lords, you should employ a sage. How many rulers are there who have a strong army but cannot make use of their awe-inspiring might, who are placed on the throne and yet cannot make their commands obeyed by their subordinates? How difficult this all is! How many ministers are there who can select the right person to build up to become a successful monarch? Right now, the king of Wu's ambitions are focused on attacking Qi and Jin. You should not begrudge sending expensive military equipment to delight him, Your Majesty, nor should you resent using humble words to express your respect for him. When he attacks Qi, Qi will most assuredly fight back. If [King Fuchai of Wu] does not win, this would indeed be a blessing for you. If he does battle and is victorious, he will then use his troops to put pressure on Jin. When his finest regiments of cavalry and infantry have been killed off by Qi, when his chariots and horses have all been used up against Jin, I am sure that you can deal with the remainder!"

The king of Yue bowed twice. "In the past, the king of Wu raised a large army to destroy my country, massacring my people, forcing my

其威勢，在上位而不能施其政令於下者，其君幾乎？難矣！臣竊自擇，可與成功而至王者，惟幾乎？今吳王有伐齊、晉之志。君無愛重器以喜其心，無惡卑辭以盡其禮。而伐齊，齊必戰。不勝，君之福也。彼戰而勝，必以其兵臨晉。騎士銳兵弊乎齊，重寶車騎羽毛盡乎晉，則君制其餘矣。」越王再拜曰：「昔者吳王分其民之眾以殘吾國，殺敗吾民，鄙吾百姓，夷吾宗廟，國為墟棘，身為魚鱉。孤之怨吳，深於骨髓。而孤之事吳，如子之畏父，弟之敬兄。此孤之死言也。今大夫有賜，故孤敢以報情。孤身不安重席，口不嘗厚味，目

subjects to become refugees, and razing my ancestral shrines," he said. "My capital city became a wasteland overgrown with brambles; the bodies of my people [became prey] for the fish and the turtles.[14] My anger against Wu has entered the very marrow of my bones, and yet I had to serve Wu like a son attending on his father or a younger brother respecting his older sibling. This is something I have sworn to avenge, even if it kills me. Today you, sir, have offered me advice, and so I dare to speak of my true feelings. It has now been three years since I last sat on a double mat or enjoyed spiced food or looked at a pretty face or listened to music.[15] I have worked myself to the bone, with cracked lips and blistered tongue, bringing good ministers into my service and nurturing my people. I hoped that thereby I would one day be able to fight with Wu out in the wilds on the plains of the Central States so that when I readied myself to attack Wu, the knights of Yue would rush into the breach, even though their liver and brains would be crushed into the mud. I have been planning this for three years, but nothing has been achieved so far. I have calculated that at present, my country cannot possibly defeat Wu, even with foreign assistance. Therefore, I was willing to give up my country, abandon my people, change my appearance, alter my name, and pick up a dustpan and brush and serve [King Fuchai of Wu] by raising cattle and horses. Even though I knew that I might be executed by being beheaded or cut in half at the waist or that I might be dismembered and have my body placed on display to be laughed at by the peasantry, I was determined

不視美色，耳不聽雅音，既已三年矣。焦脣乾舌，苦身勞力，上事羣臣，下養百姓；願一與吳交戰於天下平原之野，正身臂而奮吳、越之士，繼踵連死，肝腦塗地者，孤之願也。思之三年，不可得也。今內量吾國，不足以傷吳；外事諸侯，而不能也。願空國，棄羣臣，變容貌，易姓名，執箕帚，養牛馬以事之。孤雖知要領不屬，手足異處，四支布陳，為鄉邑笑，孤之意出焉。今大夫有賜，存亡國，舉死人，孤賴天賜，敢不待令乎？」子貢曰：「夫吳王為人，貪功名而不知利害。」越王愾然避位。子貢曰：「臣觀吳王為數戰伐，

---

14. This line is translated according to *Yuejue shu*, 53 ["Chen Cheng Heng"], which adds the word *er* 餌 (prey).
15. According to *Liji*, 632 ["Liqi" 禮器], the number of layers in the mat on which people sat was a sign of status: the Son of Heaven was the only person permitted to sit on a five-layered mat. Using a mat with fewer layers than that he was entitled to (a grandee would use a double mat) emphasizes King Goujian's frugality.

to do this. Today your advice has saved my country, has raised me from the dead—I consider this a gift from Heaven! How could I dare to refuse to obey your commands?"

"It is the nature of the king of Wu that he is only concerned with establishing his reputation as a brilliant military commander and has no idea of whether this has been achieved at too high a cost or not," replied Zigong.

The king of Yue was amazed and got up from his seat.

"I have observed the king of Wu's behavior during the course of several campaigns," Zigong said. "He does not care about his officers and men, his senior ministers are troublemakers, and he is surrounded by ever more sycophants. Zixu, on the other hand, is a sincere and honest man, who knows a great deal about what is going on and understands how to seize the moment—he would never hide his lord's mistakes even if he risks his life by so doing. He speaks out, because this is how he shows his loyalty to the king; he acts straight when this is in the interest of the country; he will not listen to anyone even if this brings about his own death. Chancellor Pi has brilliant moments but can also be quite stupid; he can be decisive but at another moment shows himself curiously weak. He has flattered and fawned to get himself into a position of power, and he serves his ruler by sycophantic lies—he can see the surface situation but is no good at understanding the underlying tensions, and he seeks to ingratiate himself by obeying the ruler even when he is in the wrong. This is the kind of wicked minister that brings about the destruction of the country and the death of the ruler."

The king of Yue was delighted. When Zigong departed, the king of Yue gave him one hundred ingots of gold, a fine sword, and two blood horses, but Zigong refused to accept them.

When he arrived back in Wu, he said to the king of Wu: "I suggested to the king of Yue that he should send an army to serve under your

士卒不恩，大臣內引，讒人益眾。夫子胥為人精誠，中廉外明而知時，不以身死隱君之過，正言以忠君，直行以為國，其身死而不聽。太宰嚭為人智而愚，彊而弱，巧言利辭以內其身，善為詭詐以事其君，知其前而不知其後，順君之過以安其私，是殘國傷君之佞臣也。」越王大悅。子貢去，越王送之金百鎰、寶劍一、良馬二，子貢不受。

至吳，謂吳王曰：「臣以下吏之言告於越王，越王大恐，曰：『昔者孤身不幸，少失前人，內不自量，抵罪於吳，軍敗身辱，逋逃出走，棲于會稽，國為墟莽，身為魚鱉。賴大王之賜，使得奉俎豆，修祭祀。死且不敢忘，何謀之敢？』其志甚恐，將使使者來謝於王。」子貢館五日，越使果來，曰：

command. The king of Yue was terrified, and he said to me: 'In the past, I was so unfortunate as to lose my father when I was still very young: I had no idea of my own strengths and weaknesses and thus committed a crime against Wu—my army was defeated, and I suffered great humiliation. I escaped to take refuge amid the peaks of Mount Kuaiji; my capital city became a wasteland overgrown with brambles, and the bodies of my people [were prey for] the fish and the turtles. Thanks to His Majesty's kindness, I was able to maintain my ancestral sacrifices and continue these ceremonies—even if the king were to order my death, I would not dare to forget his benevolence. How could I possibly be plotting against him?' He was clearly very shocked and will send an ambassador to apologize to Your Majesty."

Zigong spent five days in the official guesthouse, and then the Yue ambassador did indeed arrive. "Your humble servant by the Eastern Sea, Goujian, has sent me here as an ambassador," he said.[16] "I dare to place myself at your command, having heard something of what is afoot from your entourage. In the past, I was so unfortunate as to lose my father when I was still very young: I had no idea of my own strengths and weaknesses and thus committed a crime against Wu—my army was defeated, and I suffered great humiliation. I escaped to take refuge at Kuaiji. Thanks to Your Majesty's kindness, I was able to maintain my ancestral sacrifices. Even if I die, I will never forget this. Today I have been informed that Your Majesty is about to embark on a righteous campaign, executing a powerful criminal and saving the weak, punishing mighty Qi and rescuing the Zhou royal house. With this end in mind, let me present you with twenty suits of armor from the collection of His Late Majesty, the spear named Qulu and

東海役臣勾踐之使者臣種，敢修下吏，少聞於左右：『昔孤不幸，少失前人，內不自量，抵罪上國，軍敗身辱，逋逃會稽。賴王賜，得奉祭祀，死且不忘。今竊聞大王興大義，誅彊救弱，困暴齊而撫周室，故使賤臣以奉前王所藏甲二十領、屈盧之矛、步光之劍，以賀軍吏。若將遂大義，弊邑雖小，請悉四方之內士卒三千人以從下吏，請躬被堅執銳以前受矢石，君臣死無所恨矣。』」吳王大悅，乃召子貢曰：「越使果來，請出士三千，其君從之，與寡人伐齊，可乎？」子貢曰：「不可。夫空人之國，悉人之眾，又從其君，不仁也。受幣，許其師，辭其君即可。」吳王許諾。子貢去晉，見定公，曰：「臣聞慮

---

16. The terms of speech given here indicate that it was Grandee Zhong who served as King Goujian's ambassador on this occasion.

the sword Buguang, to reward your troops.[17] If I am indeed to be allowed to participate in this great endeavor, even though my state is small, I would like to send my entire army, to the number of three thousand men, to serve under your command, and I myself will go on ahead to take the slings and arrows of the enemy wearing armor and carrying a spear. Even if we die, we will have no regrets!"

The king of Wu was delighted. He then summoned Zigong and said: "The ambassador from Yue has arrived just as you said he would, and he is asking permission to send three thousand officers and men, with [King Goujian] following them, to join me in the attack on Qi. How would that be?"

"You can do no such thing," Zigong said. If you empty the national coffers, take their entire army, and insist that their ruler follow you—that would be most unkind. You can accept the money and agree to take their troops, but you should refuse to allow their lord to follow you. That would be the right thing to do."

The king of Wu agreed.

Zigong traveled to Jin, where he had an audience with Lord Ding.[18] "I have heard people say that if you do not make your preparations in advance, you cannot respond to any sudden emergency; if your soldiers are not ready, they cannot defeat the enemy," he said. "Right now, Wu and Qi

不預定，不可以應卒；兵不預辦，不可以勝敵。今吳、齊將戰，戰而不勝，越亂之必矣；與戰而勝，必以其兵臨晉。君為之奈何？」定公曰：「何以待之？」子貢曰：「修兵伏卒以待之。」晉君許之。子貢返魯，吳王果興九郡之兵，將與齊戰。道出胥門，因過姑胥之臺，忽晝假寐於姑胥之臺，而得夢。及寤而起，其心怵然悵焉。乃命太宰嚭，告曰：「寡人晝臥有夢，覺而怵然悵焉。請占之，得無所憂哉？夢入章明宮，見兩鬲蒸而不炊；兩黑犬嗥以南，嗥以

---

17. Qulu is sometimes understood as a person's name; according to the *Suoyin* 索隱 (Seeking the Obscure) commentary by Sima Zhen 司馬貞 (679–732), quoted in *Shiji*, 68.2236 n. 16, Qu Lu was a maker of spears comparable to Gan Jiang as a maker of swords. However, in *Yuejue shu*, 76 ["Ji Wuwang zhanmeng" 記吳王占夢], Qulu is said to be a bow, not a spear. Buguang, on the other hand, is always identified as one of the famous named swords belonging to the Yue royal house.

18. Lord Ding of Jin 晉定公 (r. 511–475 BCE) was the last ruler of this state to have any authority over the government. His successors saw the partition of Jin into Han 韓, Wei 魏, and Zhao 趙, thus marking the beginning of the Warring States era.

are about to do battle: if they fight and [Wu] is defeated, then Yue will definitely rise up in rebellion against them. However, if they fight and are victorious, they will move their soldiers to put pressure on Jin. What are you going to do about it, my lord?"

"What preparations should I make to deal with them?" Lord Ding asked.

"Put your weapons in good order, make your soldiers lie in ambush, and wait for them," Zigong said.[19]

The lord of Jin agreed to this. Zigong then returned to Lu.

The king of Wu did indeed raise an army from the nine commanderies, and he fought a battle with the state of Qi. His route took him out through the Xu Gate and past the Guxu Tower.[20] It so happened that at midday he took a nap at the Guxu Tower and had a dream. When he awoke and got up, he felt a strange sense of panic. Accordingly, he summoned Chancellor Pi and told him: "I was having a nap at midday, and when I woke up, I experienced an oddly panicked sensation. Please perform a divination about this; is this something I should be worried about or not? I dreamed that I entered the Zhangming Palace, and I saw two cauldrons placed on the fire, but their contents were not cooking. There were two black dogs: one barking to the north and one barking to the south. There were two plowshares leaning against the wall of my palace, and running water poured into the main hall. Meanwhile, there were blacksmiths in the back room

北；兩鋘殖吾宮牆；流水湯湯，越吾宮堂；後房鼓震簸簸，有鍛工；前園橫生梧桐。子為寡人占之。」太宰嚭曰：「美哉！王之興師伐齊也。臣聞章者，德鏘鏘也。明者，破敵聲聞，功朗朗也。兩鬲蒸而不炊者，大王聖德，氣有餘也。兩黑犬嗥以南，嗥以北者，四夷已服，朝諸侯也。兩鋘殖宮牆者，農夫就成，田夫耕也。湯湯越宮堂者，鄰國貢獻，財有餘也。後房簸簸鼓震，有鍛工者，宮女悅樂，琴瑟和也。前園橫生梧桐者，樂府鼓聲也。」吳王大悅，

---

19. The parallel line in *Shiji*, 67.2200, says *xiu zu* 休卒 (rest your troops) rather than *fu zu* 伏卒 (make your troops lie in ambush).

20. The Guxu or Gusu Tower 姑蘇臺 was a major prestige project undertaken by the kings of Wu; it is attributed to either King Helü or King Fuchai; for the former, see Ouyang Xun (2007): 1119; and Lu Guangwei (1999): 38; for the latter, see *Guoyu*, 599 ["Wuyu" 吳語], and *Yuejue shu*, 83 ["Jiushu" 九術]. Regardless of which monarch was responsible for the construction of this building, all accounts speak of vast landscaping works associated with it and considerable luxury in the internal decorations.

holding pincers and hammering with a thunderous noise, while out in the front garden, there were paulownia trees growing everywhere. I want you to perform a divination for me."

"How wonderful!" Chancellor Pi exclaimed. "You are going to raise an army to attack Qi, Your Majesty. I have heard people mention that the word *zhang* means that your virtue is resounding, while *ming* means that you will defeat the enemy and become famous thanks to your great successes. The two cauldrons placed on the fire where their contents were not cooking symbolizes Your Majesty's omnipotence. The two black dogs barking to the south and the north means that the barbarians living in all four directions will pay court to you. The plowshares leaning against the wall of the palace means that farmers will place land under cultivation. The flood pouring into the main hall of the palace represents neighboring countries coming to offer tribute and making us even wealthier than before. The blacksmiths in the back room holding pincers and hammering with a thunderous sound means that palace women will join together in singing joyous songs. Finally, the paulownia trees growing everywhere in the front garden means that the Music Bureau will compose paeans."

The king of Wu was delighted, but his mind was still not easy. He summoned Royal Grandson Luo. "I suddenly had a daydream, and I would like to tell you about it," His Majesty announced.

"I am afraid that I am rather ignorant," Royal Grandson Luo said, "and do not know much about that kind of thing. The dream that Your Majesty had today is not one that I can divine. If there is anyone who understands about it, it would be Gongsun Sheng, the disciple of Lord Changcheng, the elder of East Ye Gate Township. When Sheng was a young man, he was interested in travel; when he grew older, he enjoyed study. He has seen much and learned a great deal, and he has a good understanding of the ghosts and spirits. You should question him on this matter."

The king then sent Royal Grandson Luo to go and invite Gongsun Sheng. "The king of Wu was having a nap at the Guxu Tower, when suddenly

而其心不已，召王孫駱問曰：「寡人忽晝夢，為予陳之。」王孫駱曰：「臣鄙淺，於道不能博小，今王所夢，臣不能占。其有所知者，東掖門亭長長城公弟公孫聖。聖為人少而好游，長而好學，多見博觀，知鬼神之情狀。願王問之。」王乃遣王孫駱往請公孫聖，曰：「吳王晝臥姑胥之臺，忽然感夢，覺而悵然，使子占之，急詣姑胥之臺。」公孫聖伏地而泣，有頃而起。其妻從旁謂聖曰：「子何性鄙！希睹人主，卒得急召，涕泣如雨。」公孫聖仰天歎曰：「悲哉！非子所知也。今日壬午，時加南方，命屬上天，不得逃亡，非但自哀，誠傷

he had a strange dream," he explained. "When he woke up, he felt strangely nervous, and so he would like you to perform a divination about it. Please come immediately to the Guxu Tower."

Gongsun Sheng threw himself onto the ground and wept bitterly. A short time later, he got up, and then his wife, who was standing to one side, said to him: "How can you be so useless? You have always wanted to meet the king; now suddenly you get an urgent summons, and your tears fall like rain!"

Gongsun Sheng looked up at the sky and sighed. "Alas!" he said. "This is not something that you can understand. Today is Renwu Day, and the hour is in a southern constellation. My destiny is under the control of Heaven, and I will not escape! I am not only sad about my own fate; I am sincerely concerned about the king of Wu."

"You can go to the king protected by your esoteric knowledge," his wife said. "With that in hand, you can remonstrate with the king, and you can look after yourself. A wise man would not be so upset and confused at receiving an urgent summons like this."

"What stupid things women say!" Gongsun Sheng complained. "I have been studying for a decade, hiding myself away and avoiding trouble in the hope of prolonging my life span. I was not expecting to suddenly receive this urgent summons, which means that I will be killed right here and now—that is why I was so sad. This is where I say goodbye to you forever."

He set out and arrived at the Guxu Tower. The king of Wu said to him: "I was on my way north to rescue Lu by attacking Qi, and my road took me out through the Xu Gate and past the Guxu Tower. Suddenly I fell asleep and had a dream. I want you to divine it for me and tell me if this means good luck or bad?"

"If I say nothing, I will survive," Gongsun Sheng explained. "If I speak, I will die right here in front of you, Your Majesty, under a hail of blows. However, a loyal vassal should not consider his own fate." He looked up at the sky and sighed. "I have heard it said that a person who loves boats is sure to be drowned, while a person who loves fighting will definitely die by

吳王。」妻曰：「子以道自達於主，有道當行，上以諫王，下以約身。今聞急召，憂惑潰亂，非賢人所宜。」公孫聖曰：「愚哉！女子之言也。吾受道十年，隱身避害，欲紹壽命。不意卒得急召，中世自棄，故悲與子相離耳。」遂去，詣姑胥臺。吳王曰：「寡人將北伐齊、魯，道出胥門，過姑胥之臺，忽然晝夢。子為占之，其言吉凶。」公孫聖曰：「臣不言，身名全。言之，必死百段於王前。然忠臣不顧其軀。」乃仰天歎曰：「臣聞好船者必溺，好戰者必亡。臣好直言，不顧於命，願王圖之。臣聞章者，戰不勝，敗走偉偟也。明者，去昭昭，

violence," he said. "All I can do is to speak out, without caring what happens to me, in the hope that Your Majesty will make sensible dispositions. *Zhang* means that you will not be victorious in battle; worse, you will be routed. *Ming* means that you will leave the light and go toward the dark. When you entered the gate and saw the cauldrons placed on the fire, but the contents were not cooking, this means that Your Majesty will not be able to eat cooked food. Then there were the two black dogs, one barking southward and the other barking northward: black symbolizes *yin*, and the northward direction symbolizes the hidden. The two plowshares leaning against the wall of the palace means that the Yue Army will enter the kingdom of Wu, destroying the ancestral shrines and digging up the altars of soil and grain. The running waters pouring into the main hall of the palace means that the palace is going to be an empty ruin. The blacksmiths in the back room holding pincers and hammering with a thunderous sound means that they will experience a long rest. Finally, there were the paulownia trees growing everywhere in the front garden. Paulownia trees do not have heartwood, and so they are not used to make things, with the exception of funerary figures that are buried with the dead. I hope that Your Majesty will put down your weapons and rectify your virtue instead; do not attack Qi, for then this evil can be avoided! If you were to order Chancellor Pi and Royal Grandson Luo to set aside their official hats and walk barefoot with shoulders bared to kowtow in apology to King Goujian, the country might yet survive, and you yourself could avoid an ignominious death."

When the king of Wu heard what he had to say, he was absolutely furious. "I am born of Heaven!" he shouted. "The representative of the gods!"

He had the strong knight Shi Fan beat him to death with an iron cudgel. Sheng raised his head toward the sky. "Alas!" he said. "Heaven knows that I am innocent of any crime! My loyalty is being treated as an offense—I die even though I have done nothing wrong! You are killing me because my straightforward advice is disregarded in favor of echoing in blind obedience! Throw my body deep in the mountains, that later generations may hear my voice respond."

就冥冥也。入門見鬲蒸而不炊者，大王不得火食也。兩黑犬嗥以南，嗥以北者，黑者，陰也，北者，匿也。兩鋘殖宮牆者，越軍入吳國，伐宗廟，掘社稷也。流水湯湯越宮堂者，宮空虛也。後房鼓震簌簌者，坐太息也。前園橫生梧桐者，梧桐心空不為用器，但為盲僮，與死人俱葬也。願大王按兵修德，無伐於齊，則可銷也。遣下吏太宰嚭、王孫駱解冠幘，肉袒徒跣，稽首謝於勾踐，國可安存也，身可不死矣。」吳王聞之，索然作怒，乃曰：「吾天之所生，

Afterward, the king of Wu ordered his gatekeepers to dump his body at Mount Zheng.[21] "Dholes and wolves will eat your flesh; wildfires will burn your bones, and when the east wind rises, it will scatter your remains far and wide. Once your flesh and bones have rotted away, how can you make reply?"

Chancellor Pi rushed forward. "Congratulations, Your Majesty," he said. "The evil has been exorcised. Now let us raise our goblets in a toast, so your soldiers can march out."

The king of Wu then appointed Chancellor Pi as marshal of the right and Royal Grandson Luo as marshal of the left, and they attacked Qi in concert with the army provided by King Goujian.

Wu Zixu heard about this and remonstrated: "I have heard that to raise forces of one hundred thousand men and then take your army over a thousand *li* will cost thousands of pieces of gold per day—all of which has to be extracted from the common people or taken from national reserves. I think that it is very risky for the country, not to mention dangerous for yourself, if you do not care about the deaths of your soldiers and only strive for a single moment's victory. This is like going to live with a bandit and not expecting any trouble to arise from it. You have repeatedly engaged in risky foreign adventures, trying your luck in other countries, as if you are determined to cure the boil and leave the heart disease untouched, even though when it flares up, you will die. A boil is a skin disease, there is no need to treat it so seriously. Qi is located more than a thousand *li* away, and to get there, you have to cross the borders of Chu and Lu.[22] The problems that Qi

神之所使。」顧力士石番，以鐵鎚擊殺之。聖乃仰頭向天而言曰：「吁嗟！天知吾之冤乎？忠而獲罪，身死無辜。以葬我以為直者，不如相隨為柱，提我至深山，後世相屬為聲響。」於是吳王乃使門人提之蒸丘：「豺狼食汝肉，野火燒汝骨，東風數至，飛揚汝骸骨，肉糜爛，何能為聲響哉？」太宰嚭趨進曰：「賀大王喜，災已滅矣。因舉行觴，兵可以行。」吳王乃使太宰嚭為右校司馬，王孫駱為左校，及從勾踐之師伐齊。伍子胥聞之，諫曰：「臣聞興十

---

21. The name of the site where Gongsun Sheng's body was dumped varies during the course of the *Wu Yue chunqiu*; subsequently, his corpse is said to have been placed on one of the peaks of Mount Qinyuhang, which is not the same place.
22. The original text here names Chu 楚 and Zhao 趙, but it has been amended to Lu 魯, following the commentary by Zhang Jue (2006): 122 n. 8. At this time in Chinese history, Zhao did not yet exist.

cause you can be compared to those of a boil! Yue, on the other hand, is a disease of the heart: when it is quiescent, you are injured thereby, but when it is set off, you will die. I hope that you will settle the situation with Yue first, Your Majesty, and then turn your attention to Qi. These are my final words; how could I fail to provide the most loyal advice that I could? I am old, and my eyes and ears have become dull; with my growing senility, I cannot help the country anymore. I have inspected the eighth chapter of the *Metal Casket*, and danger is lurking."

"What does it say?" the king of Wu asked.

"Today is Xinhai Day in the seventh month, and it is sunrise," said Zixu, "and you are just about to begin on a major campaign, Your Majesty. Xin refers to the position of Jupiter, while Hai is the next position in which Counter-Jupiter is found. They will meet on Renzi Day, which is the next conjunction of the planets.[23] This day would be appropriate for engaging in warfare, and if you fight, you will be sure to be victorious. However, although the numinous powers are in accord, the constellation of the Dipper is attacking Chou.[24] Chou is the foundation for Xin.[25] Daji is known as the

萬之眾，奉師千里，百姓之費，國家之出，日數千金。不念士民之死，而爭一日之勝，臣以為危國亡身之甚。且與賊居不知其禍，外復求怨，徼幸他國，猶治救痟疥，而棄心腹之疾，發當死矣。痟疥，皮膚之疾，不足患也。今齊陵遲千里之外，更歷楚趙之界，齊為疾，其疥耳。越之為病，乃心腹也。不發，則傷。動，則有死。願大王定越而後圖齊。臣之言決矣，敢不盡忠？臣今年老，耳目不聰，以狂惑之心，無能益國。竊觀金匱第八，其可傷也。」吳王曰：「何謂也？」子胥曰：「今年七月，辛亥平旦，大王以首事。辛，歲位也。

---

23. According to *Huainanzi*, 279 ["Tianwen xun"], in the sixty-day cycle, there were eight days of conjunction: the *bahe* 八合. Renzi Day was the fifth of these eight days.

24. Chou is the Jupiter station also known as Chifenruo 赤奮若; see *Huainanzi*, 265 ["Tianwen xun"]. This particular station was located in the same area of the sky as the lunar lodges Dou 斗 (six stars of the constellation Sagittarius) and Niu 牛 (six stars of the constellation Capricorn). For the identification of these constellations, see Sun and Kistemaker (1997): 158. These two lunar lodges represented Wu and Yue in some versions of the *fenye* 分野 system; see, for example, *Yuejue shu*, 88 ["Ji junqi" 記軍氣].

25. According to *Huainanzi*, 277 ["Tianwen xun"], Chou is associated with the element Earth and Xin with Metal. Since Metal follows on from Earth, Chou precedes or is the foundation for Xin.

White Tiger, and it is located close to Xin.[26] Gongcao is known as Taichang and is located close to Hai.[27] When Daji moves toward Xin, it creates one of the Nine Evil Days, and it is also in mutual conflict with the White Tiger.[28] If someone begins a campaign on this day, even if they start with a few small victories, there is sure to be a serious defeat awaiting them. When Heaven and Earth send down calamities, disaster cannot be long averted."

The king of Wu paid no attention to this.

In the ninth month, [King Fuchai] ordered Chancellor Pi to begin the attack on Qi. As the army approached the northern suburbs of the capital, the king of Wu said to Pi: "Go ahead! Do not forget to reward the deserving, and do not pardon those who have committed a crime. You should love the people and care for your men as if they were your own children. Make your plans with clever men and make benevolent people your friends."

Chancellor Pi accepted his commands and set out.

The king of Wu summoned Grandee Bei Li. "You have always been very close to Zixu and been joined with him in many of his plans," he asked. "I have now raised an army and attacked Qi; what does Zixu have to say about that?"

"Zixu served His Late Majesty with the utmost sincerity," Bei Li replied. "Now he claims that he is senile and that his eyes and ears are dull, so

亥，陰前之辰也。合壬子歲，前合也，利以行武，武決勝矣。然德在合鬥擊丑。丑，辛之本也。大吉為白虎而臨辛，功曹為太常所臨亥。大吉得辛為九醜，又與白虎并重。有人若以此首事，前雖小勝，後必大敗。天地行殃，禍不久矣。」吳王不聽，遂九月使太宰嚭伐齊。軍臨北郊，吳王謂嚭曰：「行矣！無忘有功，無赦有罪。愛民養士，視如赤子。與智者謀，與仁者友。」太宰嚭受命，遂行。吳王召大夫被離，問曰：「汝常與子胥同心合志，并慮一謀。

---

26. During the course of the Han dynasty, the number of asterisms associated with the White Tiger increased significantly; see Sun and Kistemaker (1997): 117. However, at the heart of this system was the constellation Shen 參 (Tristar), consisting of the three stars of Orion's Belt. The association of Shen with the White Tiger is mentioned in many texts; see, for example, *Shiji*, 27.1306, and *Hanshu*, 26.1278.

27. Taichang here must from context be referring to an asterism, but which one is not clear.

28. The term *jiuchou* 九醜 (Nine Evil Days) is frequently seen in imperial-era almanacs and divinatory texts, but the appearance of this term in the *Wu Yue chunqiu* is the first known usage. Hence, the meaning of this term is not entirely clear.

he has lost touch with the world outside and does not know how to help the kingdom of Wu anymore."

His Majesty then attacked Qi. Qi fought a great battle with Wu at Ailing, and the Qi Army was utterly defeated. Since the king of Wu was victorious, he sent his chief of staff to make peace with Qi and tell them:[29] "His Majesty, the king of Wu, heard that Qi had suffered terrible flooding, so he brought his army to inspect the situation, only to discover that Qi had raised an army that was lurking in the reeds. Wu did not know what to do for the best, so they went into battle formation to be ready for any emergency. Although we did not intend this, the Qi Army suffered considerable damage. We would like to conclude a marriage alliance, and then we can leave."

"I live here on the northern borders," the king of Qi said, "and I have no intention of ever invading your country. Now Wu has crossed the Yangtze and the Huai Rivers, advancing one thousand *li* to occupy my lands and massacre my people. Thanks to the clemency of God on High, we have survived this, and our country is by no means on the point of collapse. Hence, if the king wants a marriage alliance, how could I dare to refuse?"

Wu and Qi then swore a blood covenant together, and [Wu] withdrew.

The king of Wu returned home and complained to [Wu] Zixu: "Our former ruler was an enlightened and virtuous monarch, whose excellences were noticed by God on High, and who achieved great things thanks to his own efforts—it was for your sake that he made a powerful enemy in Chu to the west. His Late Majesty can be compared to a farmer who has cut down tall reeds in all directions; he became famous in Chu and the surrounding regions. You played your part in this too! Now you are old, but you do not keep to your place; you go about causing trouble and giving rise to malicious gossip as a means of venting your disappointments and anger. You have caused trouble among my officers and men, you have thrown our laws

寡人興師伐齊，子胥獨何言焉？」被離曰：「子胥欲盡誠於前王，自謂老狂，耳目不聰，不知當世之所行，無益吳國。」王遂伐齊，齊與吳戰於艾陵之上，齊師敗績。吳王既勝，乃使行人成好於齊。曰：「吳王聞齊有沒水之慮，帥軍來觀。而齊興師蒲草，吳不知所安集，設陣為備，不意頗傷齊師。願結和親而去。」齊王曰：「寡人處此北邊，無出境之謀。今吳乃濟江、淮，喻千里而來我壞土，戮我眾庶。賴上帝哀存，國猶不至顛隕。王今讓以和親，敢不

---

29. The *Guoyu*, 600 ["Wuyu"], identifies this individual as Grandee Xisi 大夫奚斯 of Wu.

into confusion, and you have tried to ruin the morale of my army with your superstitious nonsense. Thanks to the blessings of Heaven, we were able to defeat Qi. Would I dare to take credit for this myself? This is all due to the accumulated virtue of our former kings and the protection and aid of the gods and spirits. What can someone like you do to help Wu?"

Wu Zixu was so furious that he waved his arms in the air, and then he threw down his sword. "In the past, the late king had ministers who would debate matters of state with him and who could solve his problems and come up with good plans so that he did not get into any serious trouble," he shouted. "Now you have got rid of these people, Your Majesty, and you ignore serious problems in the hope that they will go away—this is what a child would do and is not how a hegemon-king deals with matters of state. When Heaven has not yet quite abandoned you, it will still throw you some minor sops, but this means that a terrible disaster is approaching.[30] If you would come to your senses, then the kingdom of Wu could survive for many generations to come. If you do not understand this, then the kingdom of Wu will soon be destroyed. I cannot bear to simply avoid trouble by resigning on the grounds of ill-health and leave Your Majesty to your fate! I am prepared to die first, but you must hang my eyes above the gate that I may watch the destruction of the kingdom of Wu!"

The king of Wu did not pay any attention to him. He was sitting in the main hall of the palace, where he was the only person there to see four men standing with their backs toward him, facing the courtyard. The king thought this was rather odd, and he stared at them.

"What are you looking at, Your Majesty?" his ministers inquired.

"I was looking at the four men standing with their backs to me," the king said. "When they heard you begin to speak, they walked off in different directions."

如命？」吳、齊遂盟而去。吳王還，乃讓子胥曰：「吾前王履德明，達於上帝，垂功用力，為子西結彊讎於楚。今前王譬若農夫之艾，殺四方蓬蒿，以立名于荊蠻。斯亦大夫之力。今大夫昏耄而不自安，生變起詐，怨惡而出。出則罪吾士眾，亂吾法度，欲以妖孽挫衄吾師。賴天降哀，齊師受服。寡人豈敢自歸其功？乃前王之遺德，神靈之祐福也。若子於吳則何力焉？」伍子胥攘臂大怒，釋劍而對曰：「昔吾前王，有不庭之臣，以能遂疑計，不陷於大難，

---

30. Although the original text reads: "When Heaven has abandoned you" (天之所棄), which does not make sense in this context, it is translated in accordance with the parallel line in *Guoyu*, 602 ["Wuyu"]: "When Heaven has not yet quite abandoned you" (天未所棄).

"If it was as you said, Your Majesty," Zixu said, "you are going to lose the support of your people."

"Your words are inauspicious!" the king of Wu said angrily.

"Not just inauspicious," Zixu said. "You are going to die!"

Five days after these events, the king of Wu was again sitting in the main hall of his palace, when he caught sight of two men standing opposite each other in the distance; then the one facing north killed the one facing south. The king asked his ministers: "Did you see that?"

"See what?" they replied.

"What did you see, Your Majesty?" asked Zixu.

"The other day, I saw four people," the king said. "Today I saw two people standing opposite each other, and the one facing north killed the one facing south."

"I have heard," said Zixu, "that four people walking away means a rebellion will occur. That the man facing north killed the man facing south means that a vassal will murder his ruler."

The king of Wu made no reply.

Subsequently, the king of Wu held a banquet at the Wen Tower, and all his ministers attended. Chancellor Pi was in charge of the government at this time; the king of Yue was sitting in attendance; and Zixu was also present.

"I have heard people say that a ruler should not disregard a successful minister, and a father should not be angry with a hardworking son," His Majesty said. "Today Chancellor Pi has done great things in my service, so I am going to give him the highest possible rewards. The king of Yue has shown himself to be benevolent, loyal, and trustworthy, and he has served me as he would a parent. I am going to restore his country to him as his reward for helping me in this campaign. What do you think about that, gentlemen?"

His ministers congratulated him:

Our king is most virtuous, working hard to nurture his knights,
We advance together, rushing into the breach when we see the danger.

今王播棄，所患外不憂，此孤僮之謀，非霸王之事。天所未棄，必趨其小喜，而近其大憂。王若覺寤，吳國世世存焉。若不覺寤，吳國之命斯促矣。員不忍稱疾辟易，乃見王之為擒。員誠前死，掛吾目於門，以觀吳國之喪。」吳王不聽，坐於殿上，獨見四人，向庭相背而倚，王怪而視之，群臣問曰：「王何所見？」王曰：「吾見四人，相背而倚。聞人言，則四分走矣。」子胥曰：「如王言，將失眾矣。」吳王怒曰：「子言不祥！」子胥曰：「非惟不祥，王亦亡矣。」後五日，吳王復坐殿上，望見兩人相對，北向人殺南向人。王問群臣：「見

Your Majesty is famous; you have struck awe into all within the four seas!
The meritorious are rewarded, a doomed state lives again.
You are a hegemon-king, and we, your ministers, all support you![31]

However, [Wu] Zixu now sat down on the ground and chanted with tears rolling down his cheeks:

Alas! How sad! We have met with disaster, yet all are silent!
Loyal ministers have no way to speak; sycophants are everywhere.
The government is ruined, the system is collapsing, yet nothing puts a stop to slander;
Gossip and lies can make the crooked straight!
Let flatterers hold sway and attack the loyal; that will destroy the kingdom of Wu.
The ancestral shrines will be destroyed, the state altars will not be fed,
The city walls will turn into a wasteland, and brambles will grow in the palace halls![32]

"You have ruined Wu with your tricks and lies!" the king of Wu shouted. "You seem determined to monopolize all power; if you cannot dominate our

乎？」曰：「無所見。」子胥曰：「王何見？」王曰：「前日所見四人，今日又見二人相對，北向人殺南向人。」子胥曰：「臣聞四人走，叛也。北向殺南向，臣殺君也。」王不應。吳王置酒文臺之上，羣臣悉在，太宰嚭執政，越王侍坐，子胥在焉。王曰：「寡人聞之，君不賤有功之臣，父不憎有力之子。今太宰嚭為寡人有功，吾將爵之上賞。越王慈仁忠信，以孝事於寡人，吾將復增其國，以還助伐之功。於眾大夫如何？」羣臣賀曰：「大王躬行至德，虛心養士，

---

31. This recitation shows a pattern of rhyme ABACD, from the groups *-ə (*zhi* 之), *-i, *-əi (*zhi* 脂), *-ən (*wen* 文), and *-in (*zhen* 真). However, the C and D rhymes share a final *-n sound, making them somewhat alliterative.
32. Every line of Wu Zixu's recitation here rhymes in the group *-ək (*zhi* 職). Given that these seven lines all have the same rhyme, it suggests that there may be some textual corruption in the previous recitation, which has disrupted what was originally a more regular rhyme scheme.

country, you are happy to set everyone by the ears! The only reason I have not punished you is because of your service to our former king. I want you to go away and think about your position; do not stand in the way of our plans for Wu!"

"If I were disloyal and untrustworthy," Zixu pointed out, "I would never have become a minister under His Late Majesty! I do not care about my own fate, but I am afraid that our country is on the brink of disaster. In the past, Jie killed Guan Longfeng, and Zhou killed Prince Bigan.[33] Today Your Majesty will kill me, thus making a third with Jie and Zhou. Say no more, Your Majesty! I ask leave to speak my farewells now!"

[Wu] Zixu went home. He said to Bei Li: "I came here after barely escaping from Zheng and Chu with my life, crossing the Yangtze and the Huai Rivers. His Late Majesty listened to my suggestions, and that is how he crushed Chu, taking revenge on my behalf. I have stayed here to pay back the many kindnesses I received from our former king. I have nothing to regret, except that you are going to suffer disaster with me."

"If your repeated remonstrance is not listened to," Bei Li said, "what is the point of killing yourself? Why don't you go into exile?"

"Exile?" said Zixu. "Where could I go?"

When the king of Wu heard of Zixu's resentment and anger, he sent someone to bestow the sword Shulu on him. Zixu received the sword and walked barefoot out of the main hall of his residence, carefully lifting up his robe. When he got to the courtyard, he looked up at the sky. "I

羣臣並進，見難爭死，名號顯著，威震四海，有功蒙賞，亡國復存，霸功王事，咸被羣臣。」於是子胥據地垂涕，曰：「於乎哀哉！遭此默默。忠臣掩口，讒夫在側。政敗道壞，諂諛無極。邪說偽辭，以曲為直。舍讒攻忠，將滅吳國。宗廟既夷，社稷不食。城郭丘墟，殿生荊棘。」吳王大怒，曰：「老臣多詐，為吳妖孽。乃欲專權擅威，獨傾吾國。寡人以前王之故，未忍行法。今退自計，無沮吳謀。」子胥曰：「今臣不忠不信，不得為前王之臣。臣不敢愛

---

33. Guan Longfeng is supposed to have been a loyal minister at the end of the Xia dynasty, who was killed by the wicked last monarch, King Jie, because of his impassioned remonstrance. Likewise, Prince Bigan was murdered by the evil King Zhou of the Shang dynasty when he refused to keep quiet about his monarch's actions. These two men were frequently paired as moral exemplars in early Chinese political rhetoric; see, for example, *Zhuangzi*, 139 ["Renjian shi" 人間世], *Shuoyuan*, 207 ["Zhengjian" 正諫], and *Han Shi waizhuan*, 1.27.

was your father's most loyal minister right from the very beginning," he screamed. "I established the kingdom of Wu; I worked out the plan that brought about the destruction of Chu; I made Yue submit to our authority in the south; I struck awe into the other lords—I made you hegemon! Now you not only do not listen to my advice any longer, but you have also gone so far as to bestow this sword on me! I may die today, but all this means is that the Wu palace will become a wasteland, brambles will grow in your courtyards, and the people of Yue will destroy your altars of soil and grain. How could you forget what I have done for you? In the past, His Late Majesty did not want to establish you as his heir, but I fought for this at the risk of my own life and in the end made it possible for you to get what you wanted; many of the other princes still hate me for that. What I have done has all been to the benefit of Wu; now having forgotten that it was I who stabilized the country, you want me to die—how wicked you are!"

The king of Wu heard about what he said and was absolutely furious. "You have been neither loyal nor trustworthy," he retorted. "When I sent you as an ambassador to Qi, you entrusted your son to the Bao family in Qi—this proves that you are no longer on my side."

He gave orders for him to kill himself immediately. "I do not want you to be able to see me again."

Zixu drew the sword and looked up at the sky and sighed. "After I am dead, later generations will certainly know that I have been loyal. What has happened here is just like events in the Xia and Yin dynasties; I can call Longfeng and Bigan my friends." He then fell on his sword and died.

Afterward, the king of Wu collected Zixu's body, stuffed it in a horsehide sack, and threw it into the river. "[Zi]xu, now that you are dead, what can you know?" he asked.

He also cut off his head and placed it on top of a tall building. His Majesty proclaimed: "The sun and moon will burn your flesh, the winds will

身，恐吾國之亡矣。昔者桀殺關龍逢，紂殺王子比干，今大王誅臣，參於桀、紂。大王勉之，臣請辭矣。」子胥歸，謂被離曰：「吾貫弓接矢於鄭、楚之界，越渡江、淮，自致於斯。前王聽從吾計，破楚見凌之讎。欲報前王之恩，而至於此。吾非自惜，禍將及汝。」被離曰：「未諫不聽，自殺何益？何如亡乎？」子胥曰：「亡，臣安往？」

吳王聞子胥之怨恨也，乃使人賜屬鏤之劍。子胥受劍，徒跣褰裳，下堂中庭，仰天呼怨。曰：「吾始為汝父忠臣，立吳，設謀破楚，南服勁越，

dry your eyes, wildfires will burn your bones, and fish and turtles will eat your body. Once your bones have turned to ash, what will you see?"[34]

He then dumped his corpse, throwing it into the river. Zixu followed the current, rocked on the waves as the tide rolled in and out, until the waters deposited him on the riverbank.

The king of Wu said to Bei Li: "You have often discussed my shortcomings with Zixu." Then he had Bei Li's hair shaved off before executing him.

Royal Grandson Luo heard about these events and refused to attend court. The king summoned him and asked: "Why are you so upset with me that you are refusing to attend court?"

"I am afraid!" Luo admitted.

"Do you really think I went too far in having [Wu] Zixu killed?"

"You are very hasty-tempered, Your Majesty," Luo said, "and Zixu was in a subordinate position, so you could execute him. Will my fate be any different from that of Zixu? That is the reason why I am frightened!"

"If I had not listened to Chancellor Pi's advice and killed Zixu, he would have plotted against me!" His Majesty asserted.

"I have heard it said that a king must have ministers who dare to remonstrate with him," Luo replied. "A person in authority must have friends who are prepared to tell him the truth. Zixu was a senior minister who served under His Late Majesty—if he were indeed disloyal and untrustworthy, he would never have been employed by our former king."

The king of Wu felt very upset and regretted killing Zixu. "Can it be that Chancellor Pi was telling lies about Zixu?" [he asked himself], and then he wanted to execute him.

"You cannot do this," Luo said. "If you kill Pi, then you make him a second Zixu."

In the end, he was not executed.

威加諸侯，有霸王之功。今汝不用吾言，反賜我劍。吾今日死，吳宮為墟，庭生蔓草，越人掘汝社稷。安忘我乎？昔前王不欲立汝，我以死爭之，卒得汝之願，公子多怨於我。我徒有功於吳，今乃忘我定國之恩。反賜我死，豈不謬哉！」吳王聞之，大怒，曰：「汝不忠信，為寡人使齊，託汝子於齊鮑氏，有我外之心。」急令自裁：「孤不使汝得有所見。」子胥把劍仰天歎曰：「自

---

34. Zhang Jue (2006): 134 n. 8 suggests this speech is an interpolation. It is likely that this is a misplaced strip, originally derived from the story of the death of Gongsun Sheng.

In the fourteenth year of his reign [482 BCE], after King Fuchai had killed [Wu] Zixu, the crops did not ripen for several years, and the people were profoundly angry. The king of Wu again attacked Qi, so he had a deep canal dug between the lands of Shang and Lu. To the north, it stretched as far as Yi, while to the south, it reached to Ji.[35] He intended to launch a joint attack [on Qi] in concert with Lu and Jin, above Huangchi. However, [King Fuchai] was afraid that many of his ministers would again remonstrate against his plans, so he issued an order within the capital that stated: "I am going to attack Qi. Anyone who dares to remonstrate with me will die!"

Crown Prince You was well aware that [Wu] Zixu was loyal and yet he had gone unheeded, while Chancellor Pi was a mere sycophant who nevertheless dominated the government. He wanted to speak out against this, but he was afraid of getting into trouble. Instead, he thought of a riddle that might interest the king. Early one morning, he arrived at the palace from the rear garden, holding a slingshot with pellets at his side, his clothes daubed in mud, and his shoes sopping wet.

The king was amazed. "What have you been doing that your clothes are all muddy and your shoes soaked through like that?" he asked.

"Just now, when I was walking through the palace gardens, I heard the sound of an autumn cicada, so I went over to look at it," Crown Prince You said.[36] "This autumn cicada had climbed up a tall tree where it could drink the clearest of dew, following the wind as it waved the branches, singing its endless sad song, and all the while imagining itself to be quite safe. It had no idea that a praying mantis was holding onto the branch covered in green shoots, with its nipped-in waist and claws held high, hoping to

我死後，後世必以我為忠，上配夏、殷之世，亦得與龍逢、比干為友。」遂伏劍而死。吳王乃取子胥屍，盛以鴟夷之器，投之於江中，言曰：「胥，汝一死之後，何能有知？」即斷其頭，置高樓上，謂之曰：「日月炙汝肉，飄風飄汝眼，炎光燒汝骨，魚鱉食汝肉。汝骨變形灰，有何所見？」乃棄其軀，投之江中。子胥因隨流揚波，依潮來往，蕩激崩岸。於是吳王謂被離曰：「汝嘗與子胥論寡人之短。」乃髡被離而刑之。王孫駱聞之，不朝。王召而問曰：「子

---

35. The original text reads Qi 蘄, but Xu Tianhu (1999): 78 suggests that this is a graphic variant for Yi 沂, the name of a river in Shandong Province.
36. In other versions of this story, it is told to prevent King Zhuang of Chu from attacking Jin, see *Han Shi waizhuan*, 10.359–60; and to prevent King Xiang of Chu 楚襄王 (r. 298–263 BCE) from showing hubris, see *Zhanguo ce*, 818–19 ["Chuce si" 楚策四].

catch its prey. This mantis crept forward, thinking only about how it would launch itself on its target, but it had no idea that a sparrow was hidden in the dense foliage, hopping slowly toward it concealed within the shadow of the branches, hoping to get the mantis with its beak. The sparrow thought that it only had to keep an eye on the delicious mantis, completely oblivious to the fact that I had readied my slingshot and was just about to shoot, sending the pellet flying high with a flick of the wrist to strike it on the back. And I was concentrating so intently on the sparrow that I did not notice the gaping ditch beside me, and in a moment of inattention, I fell into it, dropping into a deep hole. That is the reason why I got coated in mud with my shoes squelching in such a way that Your Majesty almost burst out laughing."

"That is the stupidest thing in the entire world," the king said. "You were just thinking about the benefit right in front of you and completely ignoring the disaster lurking behind."

"There is something that is even more stupid," the crown prince stated. "Lu is ruled by the descendants of the duke of Zhou, and they have the benefit of the teachings of Confucius; they are benevolent and virtuous and have never cast greedy eyes on their neighbors, but Qi has raised an army and attacked them, not caring about how many of their own people will be killed and thinking only of what they will get out of it. Furthermore, Qi is attacking Lu without any further support, and they do not know that Wu is spending every last coin in our treasury to send all the soldiers found within our borders on a journey of a thousand *li* to attack them. Finally, Wu is only thinking of crossing the frontier and attacking other countries without considering that the king of Yue is going to use this occasion to select his finest warriors, go out of the mouth of the Yangtze delta, and sail into the Five Lakes to put the kingdom of Wu to the sword and destroy our royal palace. It is this that is the dumbest thing in the entire world."

The king of Wu did not listen to the crown prince's remonstrance but set off northward to attack Qi.

何非寡人而不朝乎？」駱曰：「臣恐耳。」曰：「子以我殺子胥為重乎？」駱曰：「大王氣高，子胥位下，王誅之。臣命何異於子胥？臣以是恐也。」王曰：「非聽宰嚭以殺子胥，胥圖寡人也。」駱曰：「臣聞人君者，必有敢諫之臣。在上位者，必有敢言之交。夫子胥，先王之老臣也。不忠不信，不得為前王臣。」吳王中心愴然，悔殺子胥：「豈非宰嚭之讒子胥？」而欲殺之。駱曰：「不可。王若殺嚭，此為二子胥也。」於是不誅。

十四年，夫差既殺子胥，連年不熟，民多怨恨。吳王復伐齊。闕為闌溝於商、魯之間，北屬沂［蘄］，西屬濟，欲與魯、晉合攻於黃池之上。恐

Chapter Five: The Inner Traditions | 105

The king of Yue heard that the king of Wu was attacking Qi, so he ordered Fan Li and Xieyong to lead the army to encamp at the delta where the Yangtze River flowed into the sea, thus cutting off Wu's retreat. He defeated Crown Prince You in battle at Guxiongyi and then proceeded back along the Yangtze and Huai Rivers to make a surprise attack on Wu.[37] He was able to enter the Wu capital, burning the Guxu Tower and sailing away their Great Boat.[38]

Wu had defeated the Qi Army in battle at Ailing, and then they turned back the army, putting pressure on Jin and competing for seniority with Lord Ding.[39] Before a peace treaty could be concluded, border officials reported what had happened. King Fuchai of Wu was horrified, and he called a meeting of his ministers to discuss what to do: "We are a very long way away. Should we leave without attending the meeting with the other lords, or should we move it forward?[40] Which would be more advantageous for us?"

"We had better bring it forward," Royal Grandson Luo said. "Then we have a means to control the other lords by appealing to their ambitions. I think that you should summon your officers, Your Majesty, and explain your orders to them. You can encourage them with offers of senior positions and heap humiliations on those who do not obey; that way, each of them will fight to the death."

羣臣復諫，乃令國中，曰：「寡人伐齊，有敢諫者，死！」太子友知子胥忠而不用，太宰嚭佞而專政，欲切言之，恐罹尤也，乃以諷諫激於王。清旦懷丸持彈，從後園而來，衣袷履濡。王怪而問之，曰：「子何為袷衣濡履，體如斯也？」太子友曰：「適游後園，聞秋蜩之聲，往而觀之。夫秋蟬登高樹，飲清露，隨風撝撓，長吟悲鳴，自以為安，不知螳蜋超枝緣條，曳腰聳距而稷其形。夫螳蜋翕心而進，志在有利，不知黃雀盈綠林，徘徊枝陰，踆躍微進，欲啄螳蜋。夫黃雀但知伺螳蜋之有味，不知臣挾彈危擲，蹭蹬飛丸而集

---

37. The original text reads Shixiongyi 始熊夷; however, this is being read here as Guxiongyi 姑熊夷, following the commentary by Xu Tianhu (1999): 80. Guxiongyi is mentioned in *Guoyu*, 604 ["Wuyu"], as the site of the battle where Crown Prince You was defeated.
38. This is thought to be a reference to the royal boat named Yuhuang 餘皇, which is named in *Zuozhuan*, 1393 [Zhao 17].
39. This refers to the events at the covenant at Huangchi in 482 BCE, when the king of Wu and Lord Ding of Jin competed over who would preside as the master of covenants (*mengzhu* 盟主).
40. The original text is somewhat garbled at this point. It has been translated according to the more extensive parallel passage in *Guoyu*, 605 ["Wuyu"]. This text, however, suggests that the second option was giving precedence to Jin.

That evening, Fuchai had fodder given to the horses and had his officers eat their fill. After that they all donned armor and took hold of their weapons, bridling their horses so that they would move in silence, extinguishing the fires in the stoves so that they would advance in pitch blackness. The Wu Army was all equipped with long shields of rhinoceros hide and Bianzhu swords; they now moved forward in formation. The central army all wore white robes, carried white flags, and wore plain armor, and their arrows were fletched with white feathers, so that from a distance they looked like bleached grass. The king himself was holding a battle-ax and stood in the middle of the phalanx, underneath a great battle standard. The army of the left wore vermilion robes, carried red flags, and wore lacquer-red armor, and their arrows were fletched with crimson feathers, so that from a distance they looked like flames. The army of the right wore black robes, carried black flags, and wore dark armor, and their arrows were fletched with crow feathers, so that from a distance they looked like a pool of ink. Thirty-six thousand men-at-arms went into battle formation at cockcrow, one *li* away from the Jin Army. Before the sky had even begun to get light, the king of Wu personally sounded a great bronze battle drum, and the three armies shouted their approval as they waved their flags, the noise resounding through the skies and shaking the very earth.

Jin was very alarmed and refused to go out to fight, retreating instead behind huge ramparts. They ordered Tong He to go to the enemy army and say:[41] "May our two armies set aside their weapons and make a peace treaty: let this take place at midday. However, we would like to ask why you have come all this way to where our army is encamped."

The king of Wu answered this himself. "The Son of Heaven gives his orders, but the Zhou royal house is so weak that even when he asks the lords

其背。今臣但虛心志在黃雀，不知空坎其旁，闇忽坎中，陷於深井。臣故袷體濡履，幾為大王取笑。」王曰：「天下之愚，莫過於斯：但貪前利，不睹後患。」太子曰：「天下之愚，復有甚者。魯承周公之末，有孔子之教，守仁抱德，無欲於鄰國，而齊舉兵伐之，不愛民命，惟有所獲。夫齊徒舉而伐魯，不知吳悉境內之士，盡府庫之財，暴師千里而攻之。夫吳徒知踰境征伐非吾之國，不知越王將選死士，出三江之口，入五湖之中，屠我吳國，滅我吳宮。天下之危，莫過於斯也。」吳王不聽太子之諫，遂北伐齊。越王聞吳王伐齊，使范蠡、

---

41. Tong He is identified in *Guoyu*, 610 n. 2 ["Wuyu"], as a grandee of Jin, Marshal Yan 司馬演. The *Zuozhuan*, 1677 [Ai 13], gives his title as Marshal Yin 司馬寅.

to offer tribute, none actually finds its way into the palace—he does not even have the means to hold sacrifices for God on High and the ghosts and spirits. Members of the Ji family suffer terror and fear; the messengers sent to report emergencies form an endless queue on the roads. To begin with, Zhou relied on Jin, and that is the reason why they could ignore the Yi and Di barbarians. Now Jin has betrayed the royal family like this; hence, I have come to beseech his lordship to rectify this. If he is not willing to accept that he is my junior, I am afraid we will have to determine it by a trial of strength. Having come this far, I would not dare to retreat; so, if your lord does not accept me as his senior, I will become a laughingstock to other rulers. If your lord agrees, then we can say goodbye today; if your lord does not agree, then he will die today. Can I put you to the trouble of going and telling him this, ambassador? I will wait outside the walls of your camp for his reply."

Tong He was about to leave when the king of Wu stamped down really hard with his left foot as he was saying goodbye.

When he reported back, the various lords and grandees were sitting in serried ranks in front of Lord Ding of Jin. Having explained what happened during his mission, he noted to Zhao Yang:[42] "I observed the king of Wu's appearance, and he seems to be deeply worried about something. If he were slightly worried, I would imagine that a favorite wife or perhaps one of his children had died... or that there is some sort of problem in Wu. However, if he is deeply worried, this must mean that the people of Yue have invaded, and he cannot go back to deal with them. That means that he has serious concerns elsewhere and is unsure whether he should advance or retreat; he cannot do battle with us. You ought to accept their demands at the earliest opportunity; do not fight with them over precedence because that could really put our country in danger. But you must be careful not to

洩庸率師屯海通江，以絕吳路。敗太子友於始熊夷，通江、淮轉襲吳，遂入吳國，燒姑胥臺，徙其大舟。

吳敗齊師於艾陵之上。還師，臨晉，與定公爭長。未合，邊候。吳王夫差大懼，合諸侯謀曰：「吾道遼遠，無會、前進，孰利？」王孫駱曰：「不如前進，則執諸侯之柄，以求其志。請王屬士，以明其令，勸之以高位，辱之以不從，令各盡其死。」夫差昏秣馬食士，服兵被甲，勒馬銜枚，出火於造，闇行而進。吳師皆文犀、長盾、扁諸之劍，方陣而行。中校之軍皆白裳、白髦、

---

42. Zhao Yang, a very senior government minister in the state of Jin (d. 475 BCE), would receive a gift of metal from King Fuchai of Wu for his part in the peace treaty negotiated with Jin at this time; see Dong Chuping (1992): 76–78.

seem to be agreeing to everything, for you must make them believe that we are sincere."

Zhao Yang agreed to this and went into the palace to inform Lord Ding. "Within the Ji clan of Zhou, Wu is the most senior," he said. "You should let him take charge, to show how seriously we take international diplomatic protocols."

Lord Ding accepted his recommendation and ordered Tong He to report back to this effect. The king of Wu felt shamed by Jin's show of magnanimity, so he went back to his tent, and that was where the meeting was held. The rulers and ministers of the two countries were all present when the king of Wu took charge of the proceedings and was the first [to smear his mouth with blood]; after that, the marquis of Jin was next, and then the ministers all participated in the blood covenant.[43]

[King Fuchai of] Wu turned back, having imposed his authority on Jin, but he had not yet traveled beyond Huangchi. When Yue heard that the king of Wu had been so long away with no sign of return, they sent all their troops to Mount Zhang; then they crossed the Yangtze River delta and began to make their attack. [King Fuchai of] Wu was afraid that he might also have to fight Qi and Song, so he ordered Royal Grandson Luo to report his success to Zhou.

"In the past, Chu did not offer tribute and treated states governed by members of the Ji family with great barbarity," he said. "Our former king, Helü, could not bear their wicked behavior, and so he buckled

素甲、素羽之矰，望之若荼。王親秉鉞，戴旗以陣而立。左軍皆赤裳、赤髦、丹甲、朱羽之矰，望之若火。右軍皆玄裳、玄輿、黑甲、烏羽之矰，望之如墨。帶甲三萬六千，雞鳴而定陣，去晉軍一里。天尚未明，王乃親鳴金鼓，三軍譁吟，以振其旅，其聲動天徙地。晉大驚，不出，反距堅壘。乃令童褐請軍，曰：「兩軍邊兵接好，日中無期。今大國越次而造弊邑之軍壘，敢請辭故。」吳王親對曰：「天子有命，周室卑弱，約諸侯貢獻，莫入王府，上帝鬼神而不可以告無，姬姓之所振，懼遣使來告，冠蓋不絕於道。始周依負於

---

43. The character *sha* 歃 (to smear the mouth with blood) is missing from the original text; it is understood here from the parallel line in *Guoyu*, 615 ["Wuyu"]. There seems to be some disagreement in ancient texts as to whether King Fuchai did preside over this covenant or not: *Zuozhuan*, 1677 [Ai 13], and *Shiji*, 31.1474, say Lord Ding of Jin took priority; other chapters in *Shiji*, 39.1685 and 43.1798, say that the king of Wu did.

on his sword and drew his saber, chasing King Zhao of Chu through the Central Plains. Heaven sent down its blessings, and the Chu Army suffered a terrible defeat. Today Qi has proved no wiser than Chu, and they have also refused to obey royal commands, treating other states governed by members of the Ji clan with barbarity. I could not stand their wickedness any longer, so I donned my armor and tied a sword by my side, marching on Ailing. Heaven has blessed Wu—the Qi Army pulled back and withdrew. I would not dare to claim any credit for these events myself—I have been assisted by the virtues of the great kings Wen and Wu. At the time when we returned to Wu, the harvest was not yet ripe, so instead we sailed down the Yangtze River and up the Huai, to dig a deep canal between Shang and Lu. Thus, I report the success of my mission to the Son of Heaven."

"Did my uncle send you here?" the king of Zhou asked.[44] "If you have sworn a blood covenant with another country, I am sure it can be relied on. I am indeed delighted! If my uncle is prepared to support me, then we both will enjoy perpetual blessings. What is there for us in the Zhou royal house to be worried about?" He then bestowed a bow and crossbow, together with meat from a royal sacrifice [upon King Fuchai], to augment his honors and titles.

After the king of Wu returned home from [Huang]chi, he allowed his people to rest and dismissed his troops.[45]

晉，故忽於夷、狄。會晉今反叛如斯，吾是以蒲服就君。不肯長弟，徒以爭彊。孤進，不敢去。君不命長，為諸侯笑。孤之事君，決在今日。不得事君，命在今日矣。敢煩使者往來，孤躬親聽命於藩籬之外。」童褐將還，吳王蹶左足，與褐決矣。及報，與諸侯、大夫列坐於晉定公前。既以通命，乃告趙鞅曰：「臣觀吳王之色，類有大憂。小則嬖妾、嫡子死，否則吳國有難；大則越人入，不得還也。其意有愁毒之憂，進退輕難，不可與戰。主君宜許之以前，期無以爭行而危國也。然不可徒許，必明其信。」趙鞅許諾，入謁定

---

44. The king of Zhou is here referring to King Fuchai as his uncle thanks to the putative blood relationship between them. All members of the Ji royal family used this kind of kin terminology when referring to members of the aristocracy; see *Yili*, 524 ["Jinli" 覲禮]. The monarch speaking, though not named in the *Wu Yue chunqiu*, was King Jing of Zhou 周敬王 (r. 519–476 BCE).
45. The character Huang 黃 is missing in the original text. This is indicated here in accordance with the commentary by Xu Tianhu (1999): 83.

In the twentieth year [476 BCE], the king of Yue raised an army and attacked Wu, and Wu fought a battle with Yue at Zuili. The Wu Army suffered a terrible defeat, and their forces were scattered—it was impossible to count the fatalities. Yue chased them down and crushed Wu. The king of Wu was in dire straits, so he sent Royal Grandson Luo to bow down and ask for a peace treaty, just like that which had once applied to Yue.

"In the past, Heaven bestowed Yue on Wu, but Wu did not take it," the king of Yue responded. "Now Heaven has bestowed Wu on Yue; how can I refuse this boon? I will give you the lands of Gou[zhang] and Yongdong: then you and I both will still be two rulers!"[46]

"According to my position in the Zhou hierarchy," the king of Wu said, "I get to eat my meal before the king does, as the demands of protocol dictate. If the king of Yue has not forgotten what he owes to the Zhou royal family, you will agree to let us become a subordinate state: that is my sincere wish. I have sent my chief of staff to you to ask for a peace treaty according to the rules for diplomacy among rulers; you must now make up your mind what it is that you want."

"Wu has behaved with great cruelty," Grandee Zhong said, "and today we have been lucky enough to capture them. I hope that Your Majesty takes control of their fate."

"I am going to destroy your state altars," the king of Yue said, "and raze your ancestral shrines to the ground."

公，曰：「姬姓於周，吳為先，老可長，以盡國禮。」定公許諾。命童褐復命。於是吳王愧晉之義，乃退幕而會。二國君臣並在，吳王稱公，前，晉侯次之，羣臣畢盟。吳既長晉而還，未踰於黃池，越聞吳王久留未歸，乃悉士眾將踰章山，濟三江而欲伐之。吳又恐齊、宋之為害，乃命王孫駱告勞于周，曰：「昔楚不承供貢，辟遠兄弟之國，吾前君闔閭不忍其惡，帶劍挺鈹，與楚昭王相逐於中原。天舍其忠，楚師敗績。今齊不賢於楚，又不恭王命，以遠辟兄弟之國。夫差不忍其惡，被甲帶劍，徑至艾陵。天福於吳，齊師還鋒而退。夫差豈敢自多其功？是文、武之德所祐助。時歸吳不熟於歲，遂緣江泝淮，開

---

46. The identification of Gou as Gouzhang 勾章縣 is derived from the commentary by Xu Tianhu (1999): 83. However, he suggests that Yongdong means east of Yong. According to *Chunqiu jingzhuan jijie*, 1842 n. 1 [Ai 22], Yongdong was a place-name, referring to what is now the islands of the Zhoushan 舟山 archipelago, located in Gouzhang county.

The king of Wu was silent. He asked for a peace treaty seven times, but the king of Yue refused.

In the tenth month of the twenty-third year [473 BCE], the king of Yue attacked Wu again. In the capital city of Wu, everyone was too exhausted to be able to fight; officers and ordinary soldiers had begun to flee; the gates to the walls ceased to be defended; therefore, [Yue] was able to put Wu to the sword. The king of Wu led his ministers to abandon the capital, and they traveled day and night for three days, until they arrived at Mount Qinyuhang. [King Fuchai] was deeply depressed, his eyes were glazed, his steps were stumbling, and his stomach was rumbling with hunger—having obtained some raw rice, he ate it, and then he lay down on the ground to drink some water. He turned his head to look at his entourage and asked: "What is this called?"

"It is raw rice," they said.

"This is what Gongsun Sheng meant when he said that I would not be able to eat cooked food and that I would be routed," the king of Wu said.

"Once you have eaten your fill, we should move on," Royal Grandson Luo said. "Mount Xu is just ahead. Once we get to the western slopes, we can stop and hide."

His Majesty proceeded on his way, and a short time later, having found a ripe vegetable gourd, the king of Wu picked it and ate it. "Why is this vegetable gourd growing here in the winter?" he asked his entourage. "Why don't people passing by on the road eat it?"

"This is grown using manure, so people don't eat it," his entourage explained.

"What do you mean by grown using manure?" the king of Wu asked.

"People eat raw vegetable gourds in the height of summer," his entourage explained. "However, since people relieve themselves by the side of the road, these plants grow an additional crop, which is then damaged by the autumn frosts. That is why it is not eaten."

溝深水，出於商、魯之間，而歸告於天子執事。」周王答曰：「伯父令子來乎！盟國一，人則依矣，余實嘉之。伯父若能輔余一人，則兼受永福，周室何憂焉？」乃賜弓弩王阼，以增號謚。吳王還，歸自池，息民散兵。

二十年，越王興師伐吳。吳與越戰於檇李。吳師大敗，軍散死者不可勝計。越追破吳，吳王困急，使王孫駱稽首請成，如越之來也。越王對曰：「昔天以越賜吳，吳不受也。今天以吳賜越，其可逆乎？吾請獻勾、甬東之地，吾

The king of Wu sighed. "That is what Zixu meant when he spoke about breakfast," he said.[47] Then he mentioned something to Chancellor Pi. "After Gongsun Sheng was tortured to death, his body was abandoned on the peak of Mount Xu. I cannot bear to go on myself, nor are my feet up to the journey, for I am afraid of being shamed in front of all the world."

"Is it possible to avoid the problems of life and death, victory and defeat?" Chancellor Pi asked.

"That is true," His Majesty said. "How could I fail to be aware of that? You should go on ahead and call to him. If Sheng is present, he will immediately reply."

The king of Wu stopped at Mount Qinyuhang. Meanwhile, [Chancellor Pi] shouted: "Gongsun Sheng!" Three times he called on Sheng, and from the midst of the mountains came the echo: "Gongsun Sheng!"[48]

The king of Wu looked up at the sky and shouted: "Surely I will not ever return to my country? In that case, I would hold sacrifices to Gongsun Sheng in perpetuity!"

A short time later, the Yue Army arrived. They surrounded the Wu party in three concentric circles.[49] Fan Li was in the middle, and with his left hand, he held up a drum, while with his right hand, he grasped the drumsticks with which he was hitting it. The king of Wu tied a message onto an arrow and shot it at the army led by [Grandee] Zhong and [Fan] Li. The message read: "I have heard that when the cunning hare is killed, the clever

與君為二君乎！」吳王曰：「吾之在周，禮前王一飯。如越王不忘周室之義，而使為附邑，亦寡人之願也。行人請成列國之義，惟君王有意焉。」大夫種曰：「吳為無道，今幸擒之，願王制其命。」越王曰：「吾將殘汝社稷，夷汝宗廟。」吳王默然。請成七反，越王不聽。

二十三年十月，越王復伐吳。吳國困不戰，士卒分散，城門不守，遂屠吳。吳王率羣臣遁去，晝馳夜走，三日三夕，達於秦餘杭山。胸中愁憂，目視茫茫，行步猖狂，腹餒口飢，顧得生稻而食之，伏地而飲水。顧左右曰：「此何名

---

47. Here *qie* 且 is being read as a graphic variant for *dan* 旦 (morning), as recorded in a Song dynasty recension of the text. Whatever story this refers to has not been preserved.
48. I am grateful to the anonymous reviewer who suggested a different way of punctuating the text here, to improve the logic at this juncture of the narrative.
49. Zhang Jue (2006): 231 modifies this line according to a quotation preserved in the *Taiping yulan*.

hunting dog is cooked; once enemy states are destroyed, the ministers who planned the conquest will certainly be killed. Now Wu is at death's door; should you gentlemen not consider your position?"

Grandee Zhong and Prime Minister [Fan] Li hastened to attack him. Grandee Zhong tied a message onto an arrow and shot it back to him. It read: "August Heaven is blue indeed: if you live, then you must die. I, the humble servant of King Goujian of Yue, have the temerity to inform you that in the past, Heaven bestowed Yue on Wu, but Wu was unwilling to take it—you went against the will of Heaven. King Goujian has exerted himself greatly in the respect that he has shown for Heaven; this is why he was able to return to his own country. Now Heaven has repaid Yue's exertions, and with all due respect, we will take our reward and not dare to forget what we owe to the gods. Furthermore, Wu has committed six terrible mistakes that have brought you to destruction; did you know that, Your Majesty? Your first great mistake was to kill your loyal minister Wu Zixu when he offered you loyal remonstrance. Your second great mistake was your treatment of Gongsun Sheng when he explained the situation. Chancellor Pi is stupid and a mere sycophantic flatterer, who would slander another man for the least little thing and speak any lie that came into his head, but you listened to him and employed him in your government: that was your third great mistake. Qi and Jin had not betrayed you, nor had they done anything wrong; they had been neither overbearing nor greedy, but Wu attacked these two states, humiliating their ruler and vassals and destroying their state altars: this was your fourth terrible mistake.[50] Above and beyond that, Wu and

也？」對曰：「是生稻也。」吳王曰：「是公孫聖所言：不得火食、走偟偟也。」王孫駱曰：「飽食而去，前有胥山，西阪中可以匿止。」王行。有頃，因得生瓜，已熟，吳王掇而食之。謂左右曰：「何冬而生瓜，近道人不食，何也？」左右曰：「謂糞種之物，人不食也。」吳王曰：「何謂糞種？」左右曰：「盛夏之時，人食生瓜，起居道傍，子復生秋霜，惡之，故不食。」吳王歎曰：「子胥所謂旦〔且〕食者也。」謂太宰嚭曰：「吾戮公孫聖，投胥山之巔。吾以畏責天下之慚，吾足不能進，心不能往。」太宰嚭曰：「死與生，敗與成，故有避乎？」王曰：「然。曾無所知乎？子試前呼之，聖在，當即有應。」吳王止

---

50. There are persistent suggestions in ancient Chinese texts that what occurred at Huangchi was not merely a covenant but that a battle was fought there between the forces of King Fuchai of Wu and Lord Ding of Jin; see *Yuejue shu*, 75 ["Ji Wuwang zhanmeng"], and *Guoyu*, 608 ["Wuyu"].

Yue are effectively one people; they are represented by the same constellation in the sky above and share the same region on earth below, and yet Wu attacked us: that was your fifth great mistake. In the past, Yue personally killed your predecessor as king of Wu; no crime could be greater than this. You were successful when you attacked us, but you did not follow the Mandate of Heaven and forgave your enemy, thus bringing disaster on yourself. This was your sixth great mistake. The king of Yue has the greatest respect for Heaven—he will obey its mandate!"

Grandee Zhong said to the king of Yue: "It is midwinter, and hence, *qi* has become settled; Heaven is about to begin the process of death and destruction. If you do not accord with Heaven in killing [King Fuchai], you will meet with disaster yourself."

The king of Yue bowed respectfully. "I agree," he said. "When dealing with the king of Wu, what should we do?"

"You should dress yourself in robes bearing the emblems of the Five Phases, clasping the sword Buguang to your belt and grasping the spear Qulu; then you should go to take him prisoner, glaring and shouting at him," Grandee Zhong said.

"Okay," said the king of Yue. He then did exactly as Grandee Zhong had said.

"I sincerely hope that you will decide my fate today," the king of Wu said. However, although a long time passed after he said this, the king of Wu was still refusing to commit suicide.

The king of Yue sent someone to repeat the following message: "Why are you so determined to experience humiliation and suffering, Your Majesty?

秦餘杭山，呼曰：「公孫聖！」三反呼。聖從山中應曰：「公孫聖！」三呼三應。吳王仰天呼曰：「寡人豈可返乎？寡人世世得聖也。」須臾，越兵至，三圍吳。范蠡在中行，左手提鼓，右手操袍而鼓之。吳王書其矢而射種、蠡之軍，辭曰：「吾聞狡兔以死，良犬就烹。敵國如滅，謀臣必亡。今吳病矣，大夫何慮乎？」大夫種、相國蠡急而攻。大夫種書矢射之，曰：「上天蒼蒼，若存若亡。越君勾踐下臣種敢言之：昔天以越賜吳，吳不肯受，是天所反。勾踐敬天而功，既得返國，今上天報越之功，敬而受之，不敢忘也。且吳有大過六，以至于亡，王知之乎？有忠臣伍子胥忠諫而身死，大過一也。公孫聖直說而無功，大過二也。太宰嚭愚而佞，言輕而讒諛，妄語恣口，聽而用之，大過三也。夫齊、晉無返逆行，無僭侈之過，而吳伐二國，辱君臣，毀社稷，大過四也。且吳與越同音共律，上合星宿，下共一理，而吳侵伐，大過五也。昔越親戕吳之前王，罪莫大焉，而幸伐之，不從天命，而棄其仇，後為大患，大過六

There is no ruler who has ever lived for ten thousand years—death comes to all. If you have any remaining self-respect, why should you want to force my army to kill you?"

The king of Wu was still unwilling to kill himself. King Goujian asked [Grandee] Zhong and [Fan] Li: "Why don't you two execute him?"

"We are but vassals," Zhong and Li replied. "We would not dare to execute a monarch. However, we hope that you will hurry up and give the necessary order, for such an execution ought to be carried out immediately. This cannot be delayed."

The king of Yue again glared [at King Fuchai]. "Death is something that everyone wishes to avoid," he said angrily. "However, it is only those who have not offended against Heaven nor betrayed their fellow man who have a right to feel this way. Now Your Majesty has committed six dreadful mistakes, and yet you seem determined to try and survive despite every shame and humiliation. How very ignoble!"

The king of Wu heaved a deep sigh and then turned his head to look into the distance in all directions. "I agree!" he said and then drew his sword and fell on it—thus, he died.

The king of Yue said to Chancellor Pi: "As a vassal, you have been disloyal and untrustworthy; you destroyed the country and brought about the death of your king." He then executed Pi, his wife, and children.[51]

也。越王謹上刻青天，敢不如命？」大天種謂越君曰：「中冬氣定，天將殺戮。不行天殺，反受其殃。」越王敬拜，曰：「諾。今圖吳王，將為何如？」大夫種曰：「君被五勝之衣，帶步光之劍，仗屈盧之矛，瞋目大言以執之。」越王曰：「諾。」乃如大夫種辭。吳王曰：「誠以今日聞命。」言有頃，吳王不自殺。越王復使謂曰：「何王之忍辱厚恥也？世無萬歲之君，死生一也。今子尚有遺榮，何必使吾師眾加刃於王！」吳王仍未肯自殺。勾踐謂種、蠡曰：「二子何不誅之？」種蠡曰：「臣人臣之位，不敢加誅於人主。願主急而命之。天誅當行，不可久留。」越王復瞋目怒曰：「死者，人之所惡。惡者，無罪於天，不負於人。今君抱六過之罪，不知愧辱，而欲求生，豈不鄙哉！」吳王乃太息，四

---

51. The execution of Chancellor Pi at the time of the fall of Wu is recorded in many ancient texts; see, for example, *Shiji*, 31.1475, and *Lüshi chunqiu*, 486 ["Shunmin" 順民]. Only *Yuejue shu*, 15 ["Ji Wudi"], and *Wu Yue chunqiu* mention that his wife and children were also killed.

When the king of Wu was just about to fall on his sword, he looked at his entourage and said: "I am too ashamed to live, but I am also humiliated by dying thus. If the dead have awareness, I will be embarrassed to appear before our former rulers in the Underworld—I will not be able to bear seeing my loyal ministers Wu Zixu and Gongsun Sheng. Even if the dead have no awareness, I have betrayed those who will survive me. Once I am dead, you must cover my eyes with my belt. I am afraid that even that may not be enough, so I want you to fold a piece of silk in three, so they are completely covered. That way I will not see the living, and the dead will not see me. What more can I ask for?"

The king of Yue buried the king of Wu according to the proper rituals at Beiyou on Mount Qinyuhang. The king of Yue ordered those army officers who had been successful in the campaign to each bring a lump of earth to bury him.[52] Chancellor Pi was also buried beside him at Beiyou.

顧而望，言曰：「諾。」乃引劍而伏之死。越王謂太宰嚭曰：「子為臣不忠無信，亡國滅君。」乃誅嚭并妻子。吳王臨欲伏劍，顧謂左右曰：「吾生既慚，死亦愧矣。使死者有知，吾羞前君地下，不忍睹忠臣伍子胥及公孫聖。使其無知，吾負於生。死必連縶組以罩吾目。恐其不蔽，願復重羅繡三幅，以為掩明。生不昭我，死勿見我形。吾何可［言］哉？」越王乃葬吳王以禮於秦餘杭山卑猶。越王使軍士集于我戎之功，人一隔土以葬之。宰嚭亦葬卑猶之旁。

---

52. This account of the burial of King Fuchai follows that given in *Yuejue shu*, 15 ["Ji Wudi"]. However, the *Wu Yue chunqiu* adds the detail that the soldiers who constructed the tomb were those who had performed deeds of valor in the campaign against Wu, thus emphasizing that although performed with all due ritual, this burial was also a posthumous humiliation for the last king of Wu.

Chapter Six

The Outer Traditions
The Story of King Wuyu of Yue

The former lord of Yue, Wuyu, was enfeoffed because he was a descendant of the sage-king Yu of the Xia dynasty.[1] Yu's father, Gun, was the descendant of the sovereign Zhuanxu.[2] Gun married a woman from the Youxin Clan, whose name was Nüxi. Although she was already fully adult, she had not yet given birth to a child. Then she went on a pleasure trip to Mount Zhi, where she found a pearl from a Job's tears plant and swallowed it, whereupon she felt as if she had indeed had sexual intercourse.[3] Because

《越王無余外傳》

越之前君無余者，夏禹之末封也。禹父鯀者，帝顓頊之後。鯀娶於有莘氏之女，名曰女嬉。年壯未孳，嬉於砥山，得薏苡而吞之，意若為人所感，因而妊孕，剖脅而產高密。家於西羌，地曰石紐。石紐在蜀西川也。帝堯之時，遭洪水滔滔，天下沉潰，九州閼塞，四瀆壅閉。帝乃憂中國之不康，悼黎元之罹咎，乃命四嶽，乃舉賢良，將任治水。自中國至於條方，莫薦人，帝靡

---

1. The name Wuyu 無余 is given in *Yuejue shu*, 57 ["Jidi zhuan"], as Wuyu 無餘.
2. The *Shiji*, 2.49, states that Gun was the son of Zhuanxu.
3. The choice of vocabulary in this account of the birth of Yu deliberately echoes the description of the birth of Houji in chapter 1 of the *Wu Yue chunqiu* and is not derived from the source texts for either chapter.

of this she became pregnant, and she gave birth to Gaomi by cutting open her belly. Her home was amid the Western Qiang, and these lands were called Shiniu.[4] *Shiniu is located in the Xichuan region in Shu.*

In the time of the sovereign Yao, it happened that floods poured across the land, and the world was inundated—the Nine Regions were blockaded, and the Four Drainageways choked. The sovereign then worried that the Central States would not be healthy and was concerned lest the common people suffer harm; hence, he ordered the Four Guardians to select wise and honorable men, who could be employed to control the waters.[5] From the Central States to the farthest-flung region, no one recommended anyone, and so the sovereign had nobody to be employed. The Four Guardians then selected Gun and recommended him to Yao.

"Gun disobeyed orders and destroyed his clan," the sovereign said. "He cannot do this."[6]

"Compared to your other vassals, there is no one as competent as Gun," the Four Guardians replied.

Yao did engage him to control the waters, but nine years after he had received this command, he had achieved nothing.

"I knew that he was incapable," the sovereign said angrily. Then he again sought out other men and obtained the services of Shun, ordering him to take over enacting the government of a Son of Heaven in his stead, while he went on progresses and held hunts. He observed that Gun's efforts to control the floods had achieved no concrete results and therefore executed Gun at Mount Yu. Gun was thrown into the river, and there he

所任。四嶽乃舉鯀而薦之於堯。帝曰：「鯀負命毀族，不可。」四嶽曰：「等之羣臣，未有如鯀者。」堯用治水，受命九載，功不成。帝怒曰：「朕知不能也。」乃更求之，得舜。使攝行天子之政，巡狩。觀鯀之治水無有形狀，乃殛鯀於羽山。鯀投於水，化為黃能，因為羽淵之神。舜與四嶽舉鯀之子高密。四嶽謂禹曰：「舜以治水無功，舉爾嗣考之勳。」禹曰：「俞！小子敢悉考績，以

---

4. The commemoration of Yu at this place is recorded in a number of early geographical texts; see, for example, *Shuijing zhu*, 36.827, and Li Jifu (2005): 32.812.
5. The Four Guardians feature in many discussions of the government of Yao; see, for example, *Shangshu*, 40–45 ["Yaodian" 堯典], and *Shiji*, 1.20.
6. This criticism is a quotation from the *Shangshu*, 40 ["Yaodian"].

transformed into a yellow turtle, which became the spirit of the Yuyuan watershed.⁷

Shun and the Four Guardians passed the mantle to Gun's son, Gaomi. The Four Guardians said to Yu: "Since previous efforts to control the floods have been to no avail, Shun has selected you to continue your late father's work."

"I understand!" Yu said. "I will follow the traces of my late father's endeavors to carry out the will of Heaven. In taking this job, I will do my best."

Yu was deeply pained that his father's hard work had achieved no results, so he followed downstream along the Yellow River and traveled up the length of the Yangtze, investigated the Ji, and checked on the Huai River, always working hard and racking his brains about how to proceed. For seven years, when he heard the sound of music, he did not listen; when he passed his gate, he did not go in; when his hat dropped off, he did not notice; nor did he put back on a shoe that had fallen from his foot, so worried and concerned was he that his work had not yet been completed. Then he read *The Yellow Sovereign's Most Important Almanac*, in which the sage recorded:⁸ "To the southeast of Mount Jiu[yi] stands the Pillar of Heaven, which is also known as Wanwei; the Red Sovereign once had his palace here, at the peak of this mountain escarpment. Here written on golden staves in characters of black jade in relievo and tied together with silver bands is what you need. It lies on a piece of fine jade, underneath a great boulder."

Yu then went on a progress to the east, where he climbed Mount Heng and performed a sacrifice using the blood of a white horse, but he did not receive the boon for which he asked. Yu then climbed the mountain and

統天意，惟委而已。」禹傷父功不成，循江泝河，盡濟甄淮，乃勞身焦思以行。七年聞樂不聽，過門不入，冠掛不顧，履遺不躡，功未及成，愁然沉思。乃案黃帝中經曆，蓋聖人所記，曰：「在於九山東南天柱，號曰宛委，赤帝在闕，其巖之巔。承以文玉，覆以磐石。其書金簡，青玉為字，編以白銀，皆瑑其文。」禹乃東巡，登衡嶽，血白馬以祭，不幸所求。禹乃登山仰天而嘯，忽然而臥。因夢見赤繡衣男子，自稱玄夷蒼水使者，聞帝使文命於斯，故來

---

7. Xu Tianhu (1999): 94 notes that some early versions of the text give *xiong* 熊 (bear) instead of *nai* 能 (mythical three-legged turtle). The posthumous transformation of Gun into a water deity is also mentioned in many ancient texts; see, for example, *Zuozhuan*, 1290 [Zhao 7], *Guoyu*, 478 ["Jinyu" 晉語 8], and *Shuoyuan*, 466 ["Bianwu" 辨物].

8. The title of this book is otherwise unrecorded and seems to have been invented for the occasion.

looked up toward the heavens with a deep sigh. Afterward he dreamed that he saw a man dressed in a red embroidered robe, who proclaimed himself to be an emissary from Lord Cangshui of Xuanyi.[9]

"His lordship heard that the sovereign sent you here," he said, "so I came to wait for you. However, this is not the right time, so let me tell you the correct date. Please do not imagine that this is a joke." Then he played his own accompaniment as he sang at Mount Fufu. Looking toward the east, he told Yu: "Anyone who wishes to obtain instructions from our mountain gods must perform a fast underneath the Yellow Sovereign's peak, and then in the third month on Gengzi Day, when you climb the mountain and lift the boulder, the golden book will be there."

Yu withdrew and performed the fast. On Gengzi Day in the third lunar month, he climbed Mount Wanwei, and there he uncovered the golden book, and from the jade characters written on staves of gold, he came to understand the principles of controlling the waters. After this he returned to his home mountains and loading up his four main methods of travel, he set off to patrol the rivers, beginning at Mount Huo.[10] He traveled all around the Five Marchmonts. As the *Book of Songs* says:

Extensive is the Southern Mountain, Yu made sure that it was put in order.[11]

Having walked around the Four Drainageways, he made his plans together with Yi and Kui.[12] As he traveled around the great mountains and

候之。非厥歲月，將告以期，無為戲吟。故倚歌覆釜之山，東顧謂禹曰：「欲得我山神書者，齋於黃帝巖嶽之下。三月庚子，登山發石，金簡之書存矣。」禹退，又齋。三月庚子，登宛委山，發金簡之書，案金簡玉字，得通水之理。

復返歸嶽【從三子】，乘四載以行川。始於霍山，徊集五嶽。詩云：「信彼南山，惟禹甸之。」遂巡行四瀆，與益、夔共謀。行到名山大澤，召其神

---

9. Zhang Jue (2006): 160 n. 22 suggests that this is the name of a mountain deity.
10. Some recensions of the text include the words *cong san zi* 從三子 (following the three sons), which makes no sense at all and, hence, have been omitted. The term here translated as "four main methods of travel" is *chengsizai* 四乘四載; according to *Shiji*, 2.51, this refers to the chariot for travel by land, the boat for travel by water, the sledge for travel over mud, and the palanquin for travel over mountains.
11. This is a quotation from the song "Xin Nanshan" 信南山 (Extensive Is the Southern Mountain); see *Shijing*, 824.
12. These two government officials are frequently mentioned in ancient texts describing the government of the sage-kings of antiquity; see, for example, *Shiji*, 1.38–39, and *Shuoyuan*, 10–11 ["Jundao" 君道].

vast marshes, he summoned the local deities and questioned them as to the positions of each peak and river; the presence of metal or jade deposits; the species of birds, beasts, and insects; and the customs of the people to be found in each place, not to mention the distances to and dimensions of foreign lands. He ordered Yi to record all this, and the name of the book was the *Guideways to the Mountains and Seas*.[13]

At thirty years of age, Yu was still unmarried. When he arrived at Mount Tu, he was afraid that time was getting late and he might not find a wife even though it was appropriate for him to do so. "If I am to get married, an omen must appear," he proclaimed.

Just at that moment, a white fox with nine tails came walking toward Yu.

"White is the color of my clothing," said Yu, "and that this beast has nine tails presages a true king. Furthermore, the people of Mount Tu have a folk song that runs:

> "'The white fox searches for a mate; how bushy are its nine tails!
> Our household is filled with joy, we treat our son-in-law like a king.
> They get married, they form a family; their happiness is down to us!
> Heaven and man are interconnected: when the time comes, you should act!'"[14]

而問之山川脈理，金玉所有，鳥獸昆蟲之類，及八方之民俗，殊國異域土地裏數，使益疏而記之，故名之曰：山海經。禹三十未娶，行到塗山，恐時之暮，失其度制，乃辭云：「吾娶也，必有應矣。」乃有白狐九尾，造於禹。禹曰：「白者，吾之服也。其九尾者，王之證也。塗山之歌曰：『綏綏白狐，九尾痝痝。我家嘉夷，來賓為王。成家成室，我造彼昌。』天人之際，於茲則行。明矣哉！」

---

13. The *Shanhai jing* or *Guideways to the Mountains and Seas*, an extremely ancient text that survives to the present day, describes the geography of the known world in fantastical terms: its authorship is unknown but is also assigned to Yu and Yi in other ancient texts; see *Lunheng*, 274 ["Bietong" 別通].

14. Every line in this song rhymes, with final characters taken from *-aŋ (*yang* 陽) group. This song is thought to derive from *Lüshi chunqiu* 呂氏春秋 (Spring and Autumn Annals of Lü Buwei). Although it is not found in the present transmitted text, there are numerous early quotations that attribute it to this book; see Liu Xiaozhen (2009a): 130.

"How clear it all is!"

Accordingly, Yu married a woman from Mount Tu, whose name was Nüjiao. He celebrated the wedding on the days Xin, Ren, Kui, and Jia; after that, Yu moved on.[15] In the tenth month, Nüjiao gave birth to a son named Qi. When Qi was born and did not see his father, day and night, he wailed and cried.

When Yu set off again, he ordered Dazhang to pace out the distances east to west and Shuhai to measure the distances north to south, going as far as they could in each of the eight directions, so that they would be able to calculate every dimension in Heaven and Earth.[16]

At the time when Yu crossed the Yangtze River delta region to inspect the waters there, a yellow dragon lifted the boat on its back. The other people in the boat were terrified, but Yu laughed silently. "I have received a mandate from Heaven," he said, "and I am putting forth my very best efforts to help the people of the world. Life is determined by natural forces, and death is a matter of fate. What can any of you do about it?"

His face did not change expression at all. He explained to the other people on board the boat: "It has been sent by Heaven to help me."

The dragon then released the boat with a flick of its tail and moved on.

They proceeded southward with their investigations until they arrived at Cangwu, where they saw a man tied up. Yu patted his back and began to cry.

"This man is a criminal," Yi said, "and he has brought this on himself. Why are you so upset?"

"When the world is in good order," said Yu, "people do not commit crimes. When things go wrong, then good people are forced into criminal activity. I have heard people say: 'When one man does not plow, other people will have to go hungry; when one woman does not raise silkworms,

禹因娶塗山，謂之女嬌，取辛壬癸甲。禹行十月，女嬌生子啟。啟生，不見父，晝夕呱呱啼泣。禹行，使大章步東西，豎亥度南北，暢八極之廣，旋天地之數。禹濟江，南省水理，黃龍負舟，舟中人怖駭。禹乃啞然而笑曰：「我受命於天，竭力以勞萬民。生，性也。死，命也。爾何為者？」顏色不變。謂舟人曰：「此天所以為我用。」龍曳尾舍舟而去。南到計於蒼梧，而見縛人。禹拊其背而哭。益曰：「斯人犯法，自合如此，哭之何也？」禹曰：「天下有道，民不罹辜。

---

15. This four-day marriage is mentioned in many accounts of the life of Yu; see, for example, *Shangshu*, 123 ["Yi Ji" 益稷], and *Shiji*, 2.80.

16. This section of the text is closely related to the account of Yu's travails found in *Huainanzi*, 321–26 ["Dixing xun" 墬形訓].

some people will have to go cold.' I have been put in charge of organizing the waters and land on behalf of the sovereign. I am supposed to be making sure that people have somewhere safe to live, where they can make a home, and yet now we see this kind of criminal! This is the proof that my virtue is so shallow that I have been unable to transform the people. That is why I was crying so sadly!"

After this he traveled throughout the realm, going as far as the edge of the world in the east and Mount Jishi in the west; to the south he traversed the Chi'an River, and to the north he passed beyond Mount Hangu. He journeyed around the Kunlun Mountains and investigated Xuanhu, checking on the lie of the land and naming each kind of metal and stone.[17] He pushed back the desert into the western regions and dammed the Ruo River in northern Han. The Qingquan and the Chiyuan Rivers were diverted to run into cave complexes. He carved a channel for the Yangtze River to flow to the east, reaching as far as Mount Jie. He diverted the Nine Rivers from forming stagnant pools and sent the Five Waterways into the northeast. He cut through Mount Longmen and established watchtower-like massifs at the Yi River. Having cleared these broad plains, he tested the soil; after observing the lie of the land, he divided them into provinces. Each of these different regions had their own characteristics and a means to offer tribute to the throne. The people then left the high peaks and returned home to the Central States.

"Well done!" Yao said. "We can indeed establish the realm here!"

He then gave Yu the title "Lord Protector" and appointed him as minister of works. The surname Si was bestowed on him, and he was put in charge of the regional administration, with remit over the twelve provinces.

天下無道，罪及善人。吾聞一男不耕，有受其飢。一女不桑，有受其寒。吾為帝統治水土，調民安居，使得其所，今乃罹法如斯，此吾得薄，不能化民證也。故哭之悲耳。」於是周行宇［寓］內，東造絕迹，西延積石，南踰赤岸，北過寒谷，徊崑崙，察六扈，脈地理，名金石。寫流沙於西隅，決弱水於北漢。青泉、赤淵，分入洞穴，通江東流，至於碣石。疏九河於涽淵，開五水於東北。鑿龍門，闢伊闕。平易相土，觀地分州。殊方各進，有所納貢。民去崎嶇，歸於中國。堯曰：「俞！以固冀於此。」乃號禹曰伯禹，官曰司空，賜姓姒氏，領統州伯，以巡十二部。堯崩，禹服三年之喪，如喪考妣，晝哭夜泣，氣不屬聲。堯禪位於舜，舜薦大禹，改官司徒，內輔虞位，外行九伯。

---

17. The original text reads Liuhu 六扈. However, the commentary on this line by Sun Yirang (1895): 3.14a indicates that this is a graphic error for Xuanhu 玄扈.

When Yao died, Yu wore mourning garb for three years, as if he were grieving for his own parents. He cried during the day and wept at night, wailing endlessly.

Since Yao had chosen Shun as his successor, Shun was then in a position to promote Yu—he now became minister of education, supporting the regime at court and making sure that the nine regional administrators did their job in the provinces.

When Shun died, he chose Yu as his successor. Yu wore mourning garb for three years, and his body was racked by suffering, his face burned black. He yielded his position to Shang Jun and withdrew to live in reclusion south of Mount Yang and north of Yin Hill.[18] The people did not obey Shang Jun, and they searched out Yu's place of hiding; they looked like birds frightened into flight through the sky or terrified fish forced deep into the gulf. During the day they sang, and at night they recited, climbing up onto the high hills, they called out: "Yu has abandoned us! Where is our ruler now?"

After completing his three years of mourning, Yu felt so sorry for the people that he believed he had no other choice than to accept the position of Son of Heaven. For three further years, he investigated the competence of his officials and, then after five years, established his own government. He traveled all over the realm, returning to the lands of Greater Yue, where he climbed Mount Mao to allow people from all four directions to pay court to him, with his ministers observing the ceremonies. One of the lords from the Central Region, Fangfeng, arrived late, so he was beheaded as a warning to others and to demonstrate that the entire world belonged to Yu.[19] Afterward

舜崩，禪位命禹。禹服三年，形體枯槁，面目黎黑。讓位商均，退處陽山之南，陰阿之北。萬民不附商均，追就禹之所，狀若驚鳥揚天，駭魚入淵。晝歌夜吟，登高號呼，曰：「禹棄我，如何所戴？」禹三年服畢，哀民不得已，即天子之位。三載考功，五年政定。周行天下，歸還大越。登茅山，以朝四方羣臣，觀示中州。諸侯防風後至，斬以示眾，示天下悉屬禹也。乃大會計治國之道，內美釜山州慎之功，外演聖德，以應天心。遂更名茅山曰會稽之山。

---

18. Shang Jun is identified as Shun's son in *Shiji*, 1.44; see also the commentary by Wei Zhao 韋昭 (204–73) quoted in *Guoyu*, 527 n. 4 ["Chuyu shang" 楚語上].

19. These events are mentioned in *Guoyu*, 213 ["Luyu xia" 魯語下], where the execution of Fangfeng was used to explain what appears to be the discovery of a dinosaur fossil at Mount Kuaiji in 494 BCE.

he held a great meeting at which he set out the Way to govern a country well. On the one hand, he elaborated on his success in showing respect at Mount Fu[fu]; on the other, he demonstrated how sagacious virtue could be used to respond to the will of Heaven. He then changed the name of Mount Mao to Kuaiji. He explained how the country would be governed, resting and nurturing his people. His dynasty was given the name: "Xia." He gave grants of land to those who had been successful in the service of the government and granted titles to the virtuous. All evil acts, no matter how minor, were now punished; all successes, no matter how small, were now rewarded. The entire world was dumbstruck; they were like infants mindful of their mother or like children obedient to their father.

[Yu] wanted to stay on in Yue, but he was afraid that his ministers would not agree.

"I have heard," he said, "that when eating the fruits, you should be careful not to injure the branches, and when drinking the waters, you should be sure not to muddy the flow. Having obtained that book at [Mount] Fufu, I was able to eliminate natural disasters across the entire realm; now the people have returned to their lanes and alleys. These virtues have indeed been demonstrated far and wide; how could any of us ever forget this?"

After that, he asked for advice and listened to remonstrances. To make his people secure, he constructed housing for them. He flattened a hill and cut down many trees to create a community, drawing lines as a pattern to follow and marking the gateways with twigs. He standardized weights and measures, establishing punishments to instruct his people, so they would obey the laws and statutes. After this, cock phoenixes perched in the trees, while hen phoenixes nested by their sides, qilins walked through the courtyard of the palace, and a myriad birds worked the fields in the marshlands.

When he was already over sixty and about to die, [Yu] sighed and said: "I am old, and my day is drawing to a close—my life will soon come

因傳國政，休養萬民，國號曰夏后。封有功，爵有德；惡無細而不誅，功無微而不賞；天下喁喁，若兒思母，子歸父；而留越。恐羣臣不從，言曰：「吾聞食其實者，不傷其枝。飲其冰［水］者，不濁其流。吾獲覆釜之書，得以除天下之災，令民歸於裏閭，其德彰彰若斯，豈可忘乎？」乃納言聽諫，安民治室。居靡山，伐木為邑，畫作印，橫木為門，調權衡，平斗斛，造井示民，以為法度。鳳凰棲於樹，鷥鳥巢於側，麒麟步於庭，百鳥佃於澤。遂已耆艾

to an end, and my reign will then be over. After I am dead," he ordered his ministers, "I want you to bury me at Mount Kuaiji. Make my inner coffin of paulownia wood and wrap it in reeds as an outer coffin and then dig a tomb for me seven *chi* deep so that it will not go down as far as the water table. Pile up a tomb mound three *chi* high and have three steps in the earth—after I am buried, I do not want fields to be taken out of cultivation.[20] That would only serve to make the tomb occupant happy, while those who have to live with it suffer greatly."

After Yu passed away, myriad auspicious omens were observed. Heaven had been moved by Yu's virtue and appreciated all he had achieved; hence, it sent myriad birds into people's fields. There were both little ones and large ones; they moved back and forward in good order; and when one left, another took its place, coming and going with perfect regularity.

When Yu died, he passed the throne to Yi. Yi wore mourning garb for three years, and he remembered what Yu had said all this time. When the mourning rituals were concluded, Yi sent Yu's son, Qi, away to live south of Mount Ji. The lords then abandoned Yi and went to pay court to Qi, saying: "It is Yu's son that should be our ruler."

It was thus that Qi assumed the position of Son of Heaven and was able to establish the Xia dynasty. He showed great respect to the principles laid out in the "Tribute of Yu," and he made sure that crops were planted throughout the Nine Regions so that harvests would always be abundant.[21] Qi sent envoys in the spring and autumn of every year to offer sacrifice to

將老，歎曰：「吾晏歲年暮，壽將盡矣，止絕斯矣。」命羣臣曰：「吾百世之後，葬我會稽之山，葦槨，桐棺；穿壙七尺，下無及泉；墳高三尺，土階三等。葬之後，曰〔田〕無改畝。」以為居之者樂，為之者苦。禹崩之後，眾瑞並去。天美禹德而勞其功，使百鳥還為民田，大小有差，進退有行，一盛一衰，往來有常。禹崩，傳位與益。益服三年，思禹，未嘗不言。喪畢，益避禹之子啟於箕山之陽，諸侯去益而朝啟，曰：「吾君帝禹子也。」啟遂即天子之位，

---

20. Some versions of this text give this line as *yue bugai mu* 曰不改畝, which does not make sense; see, for example, Huang Rensheng (1996): 212. Other editions of the text have corrected this to *tian bugai mu* 田不改畝 (I do not want fields to be taken out of cultivation).
21. See *Shangshu*, 132–71 ["Yugong"].

Yu in Yue, and he established his ancestral shrine on top of the Southern Mountain.[22]

Six generations after Yu, there was the sovereign Shaokang. Shaokang was concerned that the sacrifices to Yu were no longer being held, so he enfeoffed Wuyu, his son by a junior consort, in Yue. When [Wu]yu first received his fief, the people lived in the mountains, with only the profits from their "bird fields" to support them; rent and taxes were given to pay the expenses of the sacrifices at the ancestral temples.[23] Now again they began to plow and cultivate according to the lie of the land, while others made a living by hunting birds or deer. Wuyu lived a simple life and did not allow for the construction of such a conspicuous project as a palace, residing in the same way as his people. In the spring and autumn, he offered sacrifice at the tomb of Yu at Kuaiji. After Wuyu, the throne was handed down for more than ten generations, but the last ruler was insignificant and could not maintain his authority, so he was reduced to the status of a commoner and inscribed on the rolls of ordinary householders, and the sacrifices to Yu were discontinued.

Ten years or so after these events, a child was born who could speak [at birth].[24] He said: "The bird is captured!" and then he twittered. Pointing to the sky and then at the tomb of Yu, he said: "I am descended from Lord Wuyu. I have come to restore the sacrifices to our former rulers; to reestablish

治國於夏，遵禹貢之美，悉九州之土，以種五穀，累歲不絕。啟使使以歲時春秋而祭禹於越，立宗廟於南山之上。禹以下六世，而得帝少康。少康恐禹祭之絕祀，乃封其庶子於越，號曰無余。余始受封，人民山居，雖有鳥田之利，租貢纔給宗廟祭祀之費。乃復隨陵陸而耕種，或逐禽鹿而給食。無余質朴，不設宮室之飾，從民所居。春秋祠禹墓於會稽。

---

22. The Southern Mountain is another name for Mount Kuaiji; this is the site of a very ancient temple dedicated to Yu. The earliest reference to worship at this location is thought to be *Yuejue shu*, 57 ["Jidi zhuan"].
23. *Lunheng*, 83 ["Shuxu" 書虛]. According to *Shuijing zhu*, 40.941, "bird fields" referred to a form of agriculture, where the fields were weeded by birds in spring and the work of harvesting was also done by birds in the autumn.
24. Children who could speak at birth seem to have played a particularly important role in the mythology of the Wu-Yue region; another story of this kind is recorded in *Yuejue shu*, 64 ["Jidi zhuan"].

the rituals performed at the tomb of Yu; and to ask for blessings from Heaven on behalf of our people, thus opening the way for communication with the gods and spirits."

The people were delighted by this. They all agreed to give sacrificial offerings to Yu and offer tribute each season. They united to establish him to continue the family line of the rulers of Yue. They restored the sacrifices to the Xia kings and continued the practice of seeing "bird fields" as an auspicious omen, hoping to receive blessings for the common people thereby. From this time onward they gradually began to practice the proper respect between ruler and vassals, whereupon he took the title of Wuren.

[Wu]ren's son was named Wushi. [Wu]shi concentrated on protecting his country, and he never lost the Mandate of Heaven. When Wushi died, someone established Futan.[25] Futan in turn had a son named Yunchang. [Yun]chang was on the throne during the reigns of King Shoumeng, Zhufan, and Helü of Wu.[26] The rise of Yue to the position of overlord began with Yunchang.

無余傳世十餘，末君微劣，不能自立，轉從眾庶為編戶之民。禹祀斷絕十有餘歲，有人生而言語。其語曰［曰］「鳥禽呼」：嚁喋嚁喋，指天向禹墓曰：「我是無余君之苗末。我方修前君祭祀，復我禹墓之祀，為民請福於天，以通鬼神之道。」眾民悅喜，皆助奉禹祭，四時致貢。因共封立，以承越君之後，復夏王之祭，安集鳥田之瑞，以為百姓請命。自後稍有君臣之義，號曰無壬。壬生無瞫。瞫專心守國，不失上天之命。無瞫卒，或為夫譚。夫譚生元［允］常，常立，當吳王壽夢、諸樊、闔閭之時。越之興霸自元［允］常矣。

---

25. It is often presumed on the basis of the *Wu Yue chunqiu* king list that Futan, King Goujian's grandfather, was not actually related to earlier monarchs of Yue; see Xu Jianchun (2005): 107.
26. This chronology for King Yunchang of Yue gives him a reign of at least forty-five years, given that King Shoumeng of Wu died in 561 BCE and the king of Yue in 496 BCE. While clearly not impossible, it is usually considered unlikely that King Yunchang in fact reigned for this long.

Chapter Seven

The Outer Traditions
The Story of King Goujian of Yue Becoming a Vassal

In the fifth month of the fifth year of the reign of King Goujian of Yue [492 BCE], he went to Wu as a vassal, accompanied by Grandee Zhong and Fan Li. His ministers all escorted him to the upper reaches of the Zhe River, where they held a farewell banquet in his honor overlooking the waters. The army was arrayed in battle formation at Guling. Grandee Zhong stepped forward and performed the role of the supplicant, saying:[1]

> May August Heaven come to our aid and protect us;
> Let the obstacles before us be cleared away behind!

《勾踐入臣外傳》

越王勾踐五年五月，與大夫種、范蠡入臣於吳。羣臣皆送至浙江之上。臨水祖道，軍陣固陵。大夫文種前為祝，其詞曰：「皇天祐助，前沉後揚。禍為德根，憂為福堂。威人者滅，服從者昌。王雖牽致，其後無殃。君臣生離，感動上皇。眾夫哀悲，莫不感傷。臣請薦脯，行酒二觴。」越王仰天太息，舉杯垂涕，默無所言。種復前祝曰：「大王德壽，無疆無極，乾坤受靈，神祇輔翼。

---

1. The ritual role of the *zhu* 祝 or supplicant is discussed in *Zhouli*, 658–79 ["Chunguan Zongbo" 春官宗伯].

Disaster is the root of good fortune;[2]
Affliction builds the house of blessings.
May the vicious bully be destroyed—
While the obedient follower flourishes!
Although our king is held in chains,
May his descendants suffer no harm!
May this painful parting of lord and subjects
Move the heavens!
When all of us are sad and despondent;
Let no one remain unaffected!
I ask permission to make a sacrifice of dried meat,
And to pour a libation of two goblets of wine![3]

The king of Yue raised his face to the skies, sighing deeply; he raised his cup as tears coursed down his cheeks; and he was silent, for there was nothing he could say. Yet again Grandee Zhong stepped forward and performed the role of supplicant:

May Your Majesty's virtue and longevity,
Be without limit and without end.
May Heaven and Earth extend their numinous powers—
May the gods and spirits spread their protective wings.
Since Your Majesty has great merit,
May blessings and divine assistance be by your side.
Let virtue cause every misfortune to melt away;

我王厚之，祉祐在側。德銷百殃，利受其福。去彼吳庭，來歸越國。觴酒既升，請稱萬歲。」越王曰：「孤承前王餘德，守國於邊，幸蒙諸大夫之謀，遂保前王丘墓。今遭辱恥，為天下笑，將孤之罪耶，諸大夫之責也？吾不知其咎，願二三子論其意。」大夫扶同曰：「何言之鄙也！昔湯繫於夏臺，伊尹不離其側。文王囚於石室，太公不棄其國。興衰在天，存亡繫於人。湯改儀而媚於

---

2. Here *de* 德 (virtue) is read as *fu* 福 (good fortune) in accordance with the commentary by Zhang Jue (2006): 176 n. 8. This gloss is based on the commentary by Zheng Xuan 鄭玄 (127–200) on the line *baixing zhi de* 百姓之德 (the good fortune of the common people) in *Liji*, 1260 ["Aigong wen" 哀公問], where *de* is identified as a synonym for *fu*.
3. This recitation consists of seven couplets, with the rhyme words all belonging to the *-aŋ (yang* 陽) group.

That you may receive the benefit of this good luck.
Go to the court of Wu,
That you may return to the kingdom of Yue.
Since the goblet of wine has already been lifted,
I ask your permission to wish you a long life.[4]

"Thanks to what remains of my royal ancestor's virtues, I have been able to guard the borders of my kingdom," the king of Yue said. "Having been lucky enough to obtain the advice of my ministers, I have protected the tombs of our former kings. But now, I have suffered humiliation and become the laughingstock of the entire world—is this my fault? What is your responsibility in this, gentlemen? I do not understand who is to blame, and so I beg that you will explain it to me."

"How can you speak so pessimistically?" Grandee Futong said.[5] "In the past, Tang was held captive at the Xia Tower, but Yi Yin did not leave his side.[6] King Wen was imprisoned in a stone cell, and yet Taigong did not abandon his country.[7] The rise and fall of nations is due to Heaven; the survival or death of an individual is down to man. Tang changed his behavior

桀，文王服從而幸於紂。夏、殷恃力而虐二聖。兩君屈己，以得天道。故湯王不以窮自傷，周文不以困為病。」越王曰：「昔堯任舜、禹而天下治，雖有洪水之害，不為人災。變異不及於民，豈況於人君乎？」大夫若成曰：「不如君王之言。天有曆數，德有薄厚。黃帝不讓，堯傳天子。三王臣弒其君，五霸子弒其父。德有廣狹，氣有高下。今之世，猶人之市，置貨以設詐，抱謀以待敵。不幸陷厄，求伸而已。大王不覽於斯，而懷喜怒？」越王曰：「任

---

4. Grandee Zhong's second recitation also consists of six rhymed couplets, in this case taken from the *ək (zhi 職) group, with the exception of the final line, where the last character belongs to the yue-ji 月祭 group. This may indicate textual corruption.
5. This individual is usually identified as the same person as the Grandee Fengtong 大夫逢同 mentioned in other texts; see, for example, Shiji, 41.1743, and Han Feizi, 918 ["Shuoyi" 說疑].
6. These events are mentioned in a number of ancient texts; see, for example, Zhushu jinian, A.10a, and Shiji, 2.88. The Suoyin gloss on the Shiji states that the Xia Tower was the name of a prison.
7. The motif of imprisonment in a stone cell relates the experience of King Wen to that of King Goujian of Yue. However, most historical texts merely state that King Wen was held prisoner at a place named Youli 羑里; see Shiji, 4.116, Han Feizi, 824 ["Naner" 難二]; and Shuoyuan, 421 ["Zayan" 雜言].

and thus was loved by Jie; King Wen obeyed and thus became favored by Zhou.[8] The Xia and the Yin dynasties were overconfident of their might and maltreated these two great sages. The two lords humbled themselves to obtain the Heavenly Way. Therefore, the future king Tang did not despair simply because he was poor, nor did the future king Wen feel humiliated because he was held prisoner."[9]

"In the past, Yao employed both Shun and Yu, and hence, the world was well governed," said the king of Yue. "Even though there was a great flood, it did not cause a humanitarian crisis. If such terrible natural disasters did not affect the common people, then how could they afflict the ruler?"

"It is not as Your Majesty has stated," Grandee Kucheng said. "Just as Heaven has its own seasonal patterns, so there is a waxing and a waning in virtue. The Yellow Sovereign did not yield his place, but Yao handed on the position of Son of Heaven. In the time of the Three Kings, ministers assassinated their rulers; in the era of the Five Hegemons, children murdered their parents.[10] Virtue can spread and contract, just as qi can be high or low. The world today is like a market: goods are carefully placed so that they

人者不辱身，自用者危其國。大夫皆前圖未然之端，傾敵破讎，坐招泰山之福。今寡人守窮若斯，而云湯、文困厄，後必霸，何言之違禮儀！夫君子爭寸陰而棄珠玉。今寡人冀得免於軍旅之憂，而復反係獲敵人之手，身為傭隸，妻為僕妾，往而不返，客死敵國。若魂魄有，愧於前君。其無知，體骨棄捐。何大夫之言不合於寡人之意！」於是大夫種、范蠡曰：「聞古人曰：『居不幽，誌不廣；形不愁，思不遠。』聖王賢主，皆遇困厄之難，蒙不赦之恥，身拘

---

8. The *Han Feizi*, 691–92 ["Waichushuo zuo xia"] contains a story indicating that King Zhou of the Shang dynasty was indeed very fond of King Wen and refused to execute him when advised to do so by Fei Zhong 費仲.
9. The usage of the term *bing* 病 (to be humiliated) here suggests familiarity with *Han Feizi*, 403 ["Yulao" 喻老], where there is a related line: "The hegemony of the king of Yue resulted from him not being humiliated by being a vassal; the rule of King Wen resulted from him not feeling humiliated by being insulted" (越王之霸也不病宦文王之王也不病囚).
10. Each of the Three Kings (i.e., the founders of the Xia, Shang, and Zhou dynasties) is supposed to have been vassals who murdered the previous ruler, to whom they owed a duty of loyalty. In the case of the Five Hegemons, given that there is little agreement on who should be considered to be included in this category, it is hard to be sure whether they all came to power by parricide. However, whichever rulers are included, it is unlikely that this was in fact the case.

might snare the unwary, and people hone their schemes as they wait for their enemies.[11] The unlucky fall into these traps, whereby all they can do is to try to straighten themselves out.[12] Your Majesty has failed to understand this, and so you have remained overemotional about the situation."

"A ruler employs others so that he does not need to sully himself," the king of Yue said, "while one who insists on doing everything himself puts the country in danger. You gentlemen all claimed that following the plans of these former kings would allow me to bring to fruition the things they had failed to achieve, that it would enable me to topple all opposition and crush my enemies, and that I would find myself enjoying the blessings of Mount Tai. Instead, I find myself in the terrible situation that you see, and yet you still speak of how Tang and Wen became supremely powerful after having been held prisoner; how unprincipled and unkind your words are! A true gentleman should seize the moment, even if it means that he must abandon his pearls and jade.[13] Now when I hoped to escape from the troubles of a disastrous military campaign, I instead find myself bound hand and foot and delivered into

而名尊，軀辱而聲榮，處卑而不以為惡，居危而不以為薄。五帝德厚，而窮厄之恨，然尚有泛濫之憂。三守暴困之辱，不離三獄之囚，泣涕而受冤，行哭而為隸，演易作卦，天道祐之。時過於期，否終則泰。諸侯並救王命，見符朱鸇、玄狐。輔臣結髮，拆獄破械。反國修德，遂討其讎。擢假海內，若覆手背。天下宗之，功垂萬世。大王屈厄，臣誠盡謀。夫截骨之劍，無削剟之利。舀鐵之矛，無分髮之便。建策之士，無暴興之說。今臣遂天文，案墜籍，二氣共萌，存亡異處。彼興則我辱，我霸則彼亡。二國爭道，未知所就。

---

11. The concept of markets being stuffed with fake goods, sold by lying tradesmen, links this section of *Wu Yue chunqiu* with the rhetoric found in wide range of texts, including the *Han Feizi*, 1076 ["Wudu" 五蠹], and the "Zhenglun" 政論 (Discourse on Government) by the Eastern Han dynasty official Cui Shi 崔寔 (ca. 110–70 CE), quoted in Yan Kejun (1985): 46.722–23.
12. This expression seems to be derived from the *Yijing* 易經 (Book of Changes): "When the worm coils itself up, it is in order to straighten itself out again. When dragons and snakes go into hibernation, it is in order to survive." (尺蠖之屈，以求信也. 龍蛇之蟄，以存身也); see *Zhouyi*, 304 ["Xici xia" 繫辭下]. *Qiuxin* 求信 and *qiushen* 求伸 are used interchangeably.
13. The locus classicus of this expression is *Huainanzi*, 54 ["Yuandao xun" 原道訓]: "A sage does not value a jade disc a foot across, but he does take seriously the movements of the shadow [across the sundial], since time is difficult to obtain and easy to lose" (故聖人不貴尺之璧，而重寸之陰，時難得而易失也). The same expression is also seen in *Wenzi*, 46 ["Daoyuan" 道原].

the hands of my enemies; I am a slave and my wife likewise.[14] We leave with no hope of return, expecting to die [in] a hostile country.[15] If the souls of the dead have [consciousness], I am indeed ashamed to appear before our former kings.[16] If they have no awareness, then my corpse can simply be abandoned.[17] How much your words fail to take into account my feelings on this occasion!"

At this point, Grandee Zhong and Fan Li said: "We have heard that people in antiquity had the saying: 'A person who has never experienced trouble has no ambition. A person who has never worried cannot think deeply.'[18] The most sagacious kings and the wisest rulers were men who met the troubles of imprisonment and danger; they suffered the shame of being unable to help themselves. Nevertheless, they achieved a glorious reputation even while their bodies were in bonds, and their names were honored though they themselves were experiencing humiliation. These are men who could occupy a humble position without thinking it a disgrace; they could live amid danger without thinking it a hardship. The Five Sovereigns were possessed of great virtue and hence did [not] object when they found themselves in danger; in spite of this, they still worried that they might be overtaken by

君王之危，天道之數，何必自傷哉！夫吉者，兇之門。福者，禍之根。今大王雖在危困之際，孰知其非暢達之兆哉？」大夫計硯曰：「今君王國於會稽，窮於入吳，言悲辭苦，羣臣泣之。雖則恨悵之心，莫不感動。而君王何為謾辭譁說，用而相欺？臣誠不取。」越王曰：「寡人將去入吳，以國累諸侯大夫。願各自述，吾將屬焉。」大夫臯如曰：「臣聞大夫種忠而善慮，民親其知，士樂為用。今委國一人，其道必守。何順心佛命羣臣？」大夫曳庸曰：「大夫

---

14. The term for a female slave, *qie* 妾, would imply that she could be expected to provide sexual services for her master; this point is stressed in Barbieri-Low (2007): 248. Although in this case, the Yue queen does not seem to have been used in this way by King Fuchai, her position at this juncture of the narrative is extremely unenviable.
15. Xu Tianhu (1999): 114 indicates that the character *yu* 於 (in) is missing from this line.
16. Here the translation follows the annotations of Xu Tianhu (1999): 114, who argues that the character *zhi* 知 (consciousness) is missing from this line.
17. Concerns over the awareness of the dead and the feeling that an individual had failed with respect to his ancestors are reported with unusual frequency among the ruling elite of Wu and Yue.
18. Similar expressions are recorded in *Xunzi*, 527 ["Youzuo" 宥坐] and *Shuoyuan*, 421 ["Zayan"].

circumstances beyond their control.[19] [King Wen] experienced the humiliation of being the victim of cruelty and imprisonment, and yet he did not leave the cells where he was held captive.[20] He wept because he was punished in spite of being innocent, and he wailed because he was treated as a criminal. Then he used the *Book of Changes* to lay out the hexagrams, and the Heavenly Way protected him.[21] Time passed until the moment was ripe, and then all his bad luck turned to good.[22] The lords united to save him, and omens of a royal mandate appeared: a white horse with a vermilion mane and a black fox. His supportive ministers and his wife broke open his chains and smashed his fetters. Returning to his state, he rectified his virtue, and then he punished his enemies. He traveled throughout the realm, and his conquests were as easy as flipping his palm. The world was united under his command, and his achievements will be lauded until the end of time. Your Majesty, you are now suffering and in danger, so we will do our very best to plan for you. Thus, even the sharpest sword will have no chance to cut you, even the hardest spear will not be able to harm one hair on your head, and even the most eloquent of knights will have no opportunity to whip up violence against you. Today I have observed the patterns in the constellations and investigated the lie of the land: both kinds of *qi* are flourishing together, and success

文種者，國之梁棟，君之爪牙。夫驥不可與匹馳，日月不可並照。君王委國於種，則萬綱千紀無不舉者。」越王曰：「夫國者，前王之國。孤力弱勢劣，不能遵守社稷，奉承宗廟。吾聞父死子代，君亡臣親。今事棄諸大夫，客官於吳，委國歸民，以付二三子，吾之由也，亦子之憂也。君臣同道，父子共氣，天性自然。豈得以在者盡忠，亡者為不信乎？何諸大夫論事一合一離，令孤懷心不定也？夫推國任賢，度功績成者，君之命也。奉教順理，不失分者，臣之職也。吾顧諸大夫以其所能而雲委質而已。於乎，悲哉！」計硯曰：

---

19. Xu Tianhu (1999): 114 glosses *er* 而 (and) in the original text as the negative *wu* 無. At the end of the line, he suggests that some text is missing at this point.
20. This translation follows Zhang Jue (2006): 272 n. 25 in reading the character *san* 三 as a mistake for *wang* 王. This section of the text clearly refers to events in the life of King Wen of Zhou.
21. The story of King Wen telling his own fortune using the *Yijing* while imprisoned is found in many ancient texts; see, for example, *Shiji*, 4.119.
22. The term here translated as "bad luck" is Fou 否, and this is also the name of a hexagram in the *Yijing*. Likewise, "good luck" is actually the name of the hexagram Tai 泰; see *Zhouyi*, 66–72. These two hexagrams are often mentioned as a pair, symbolizing extreme bad luck and good fortune.

and failure are located in different places. As long as they flourish, we will suffer humiliation; when we achieve hegemony, they will be destroyed. Our two countries are locked in conflict, and we do not know yet who will win. The problems that we face are a necessary part of the Heavenly Way; there is no need to distress yourself! Good fortune is the gate to evil, and blessings are the root of disaster.[23] Although Your Majesty today finds yourself in a position of danger, who knows whether this is not an omen of future greatness?"

"Now although Your Majesty's kingdom is located in Kuaiji, you will have to enter Wu," Grandee Jini said. "The tragedy and bitterness of your words are such that we have all wept. There is no one here who has not been moved by your resentment. However, why do you speak wildly and use intemperate language, Your Majesty, as if you are blaming us for what has happened? I really do not understand."

"I am just about to leave on my journey to Wu, and I will be entrusting the country to your care, gentlemen," the king of Yue said. "I would like each of you to explain to whom I should assign my kingdom."

"I have heard that Grandee Zhong is loyal and good at making deliberations," Grandee Gaoru said. "The people appreciate his wisdom, and knights enjoy being employed by him. Now if you were to entrust your state to a single person, it would definitely be preserved. Why would you insist on employing many ministers?"

"Grandee Wen Zhong is a pillar of the state," Grandee Yeyong said. "He is our ruler's claws and teeth. A blood horse does not run with a nag, and the sun and moon do not shine in the same sky. If His Majesty entrusts the state to Zhong, then the warp and weft of government will remain in place."

"The kingdom is that of our former kings," the king of Yue said. "I have proved too weak in strength and insufficient in power; hence, I have not been able to preserve the state altars or support the ancestral temples. I have heard

「君王所陳者，固其理也。昔湯入夏，付國於文祀。西伯之殷，委國於二老。今懷夏將滯，誌在於邊。夫適市之妻，教嗣糞除。出亡之君，敕臣守禦。子問以事，臣謀以能。今君王欲士之所誌，各陳其情，舉其能者，議其宜也。」

越王曰：「大夫之論是也。吾將逝矣，願諸君之風。」大夫種曰：「夫內修封疆之役，外修耕戰之備；荒無遺土，百姓親附；臣之事也。」大夫范蠡曰：「輔危主，存亡國；不恥屈厄之難，安守被辱之地，往而必反，與君

---

23. The intimate connection between good luck and bad was a key part of early Daoist thought; see *Laozi*, 444 ["Dejing jia" 德經甲]: "Bad luck follows on from good; good fortune is hidden in bad" (禍福之所倚; 福禍之所伏).

that when a father dies, a son should inherit; and when a lord passes away, his ministers should act as kin. Now the government of the country will be left to you, gentlemen, as I go abroad to serve in Wu.[24] It is to you that I entrust my country and hand over my people. This is all that I can do, and it will be a worry to you all. When ruler and ministers follow the same path, when father and son share common values, the natural order is preserved. I do not expect those who are present to be completely loyal, nor do I stigmatize those who are gone as untrustworthy! Furthermore, of my most trusted officials, one will stay, and one will leave with me—how can you expect me not to be nervous? It is my duty as your ruler to hand over my country to the control of others and to give employment to wise men, to measure success and apportion merit. It is your job to educate the people and obey the rules, not overstepping the boundaries of your position. I am expecting that you will declare to the best of your abilities: 'We will obey you to the end.' Alas! How sad!"[25]

"What the king has just said is entirely logical," Jini replied. "In the past, when Tang was imprisoned by the Xia, he entrusted his country to Wen Si; when the Western Earl went to Yin, he turned over his state to the care of the Two Elders.[26] Now [King Goujian] will have to leave this summer—his thoughts are fixed on how to return.[27] Just as a woman going to the marketplace instructs her offspring to clean up the house, so a ruler in

復讎者；臣之事也。」大夫苦成曰：「發君之令，明君之德；窮與俱厄，進與俱霸；統煩理亂，使民知分；臣之事也。」大夫曳庸曰：「奉令受使，結和諸侯；通命達旨，賂往遺來；解憂釋患，使無所疑；出不忘命，入不被尤；臣之事也。」大夫皓進曰：「一心齊誌，上與等之；下不違令，動從君命；修德履義，守信溫故；臨非決疑，君誤臣諫；直心不撓，舉過列平；不阿親戚，不私於外；推身致君，終始一分；臣之事也。」大夫諸稽郢曰：「望敵設陣，

---

24. Zhang Jue (2006): 278 n. 9 argues that *guan* 官 (to serve as an official) in the original text is a mistake for *huan* 宦 (to be a vassal).
25. *Weizhi* 委質 refers to the practice in ancient China of individuals swearing loyalty to the death to their lord; see, for example, *Shiji*, 86.2521; *Han Feizi*, 87 ["Youdu" 有度], and *Guanzi*, 619 ["Sicheng" 四稱].
26. The Two Elders are the two government ministers appointed by the future king Wen of Zhou to manage his state while he was imprisoned; see *Mengzi*, 174 ["Li Lou shang"]. They are identified either as San Yisheng 散宜生 and Hong Yao 閎夭 or as San Yisheng and the Great Lord of Qi 齊太公.
27. This sentence is agreed by all scholars who have commented on the text to be corrupt in some way, and various suggestions have been made as to how to resolve the problem; see, for example, Xu Naichang (1906): 7.5a–5b and Zhang Jue (2006): 184 n. 20.

exile relies on his ministers to safeguard the country. Her children ask what they can do; his ministers plan how they can help. Now the king wants to know our intentions, so we should all explain our feelings and what we are capable of so that we can discuss appropriate measures."

"You are absolutely right!" the king of Yue said. "I am about to leave, and I would like [to hear] what you are planning to do."[28]

"It will be my business to ensure that work is carried out to repair boundaries and borders on the one hand and on the other that preparations are made for farming and warfare, that no land is left uncultivated, and that the people are friendly and obedient," Grandee Zhong said.

"It will be my business to support our ruler in his time of trouble and to preserve our country from harm," Grandee Fan Li said. "I will not be ashamed in any dangerous or difficult situation, and I will hold my peace in any place where I suffer humiliation. I will make sure that we will return from this journey so that together we will be able to take revenge on your enemies."

"It will be my business to issue Your Majesty's orders and make sure that everyone understands your virtue," Grandee Kucheng said. "I will suffer together with you now, and in the future, I will make you hegemon: dealing with every trouble and sorting out every problem, ensuring that the people comprehend their duties."

"It will be my business to receive ambassadors in accordance with your instructions, making peace with the rulers of other countries and ensuring that your orders are promulgated, maintaining a constant flow of gifts and bribes, resolving any difficulties and smoothing over problems on the way," Grandee Yeyong said. "This will be done so that no one suspects; outside the country, I will never forget your commands, and inside the country, I will never cause you any concern."

飛矢揚兵；履腹涉屍，血流滂滂；貪進不退，二師相當；破敵攻眾，威淩百邦；臣之事也。」大夫皋如曰：「修德行惠，撫慰百姓；身臨憂勞，動輒躬親；弔死存疾，救活民命；蓄陳儲新，食不二味；國富民實，為君養器；臣之事也。」大夫計硯曰：「候天察地，紀歷陰陽；觀變參災，分別妖祥；日月含色，五精錯行；福見知吉，妖出知兇；臣之事也。」越王曰：「孤雖入於北國，為吳窮虜，有諸大夫懷德抱術，各守一分，以保社稷，孤何憂焉？」

---

28. The character *wen* 聞 (to hear) has been added to the translation in accordance with the commentary by Xu Tianhu (1999): 110. Meanwhile, Zhang Jue (2006): 184–85 n. 23 suggests that no amendment is necessary here.

"It will be my business to make sure that everyone is united in a single cause, which ruler and subjects will achieve together," Grandee Haojin said. "Your subjects will not disobey orders, and they will follow whatever you command. I will rectify your virtue and restore your sense of justice, making sure that you are considered worthy of trust and that the wise ways of our former kings are resumed. I will make sure that wrongs are righted, and problems resolved, and if you make a mistake, Your Majesty, your ministers will remonstrate with you. I will neither bend nor break in upholding righteousness and showing where transgressions have occurred, without nepotism or favoritism. I will devote my life to your cause, Your Majesty, and I will never overstep the bounds of my position from beginning to end."

"It will be my business to check the movements of enemy armies and arrange our own forces in battle order—to deal with flying arrows and brandished swords," Grandee Zhujiying said.[29] "If it is necessary, I will walk across human entrails and tread on corpses, where blood is flowing in lakes, to make sure that our forces advance and never retreat. When our two armies confront each other, I will crush the enemy and attack their hosts, striking awe into all other countries."

"It will be my business to rectify your virtue and carry out good works, comforting your people," Grandee Gaoru said. "I will personally check on those in trouble, dealing with their issues myself. I will condole with the dead and cure the sick, rescuing people from disaster.[30] Likewise, I will ensure that surplus is stored, and preparations are made, while remaining frugal myself, so that the country is rich and its people satisfied, producing talented people for Your Majesty to employ."

遂別於浙江之上，羣臣垂泣，莫不咸哀。越王仰天歎曰：「死者，人之所畏。若孤之聞死，其於心胸中曾無怵惕？」遂登船徑去，終不返顧。越王夫人乃據船哭，顧烏鵲啄江渚之蝦，飛去復來，因哭而歌之，曰：「仰飛鳥兮烏鳶，淩玄虛號翩翩。集洲渚兮優恣，啄蝦矯翮兮雲間。任厥兮往還。妾無罪兮負地，有何辜兮譴天？驟驟獨兮西往，孰知返兮何年？心惙惙兮若割，淚泫泫兮雙懸。」又哀今曰：「彼飛鳥兮鳶烏，已迴翔兮翕蘇。心在專兮素蝦，

---

29. This individual is mentioned in *Guoyu*, 593 ["Wuyu"], as a senior figure in the Yue government at this time, who led the negotiations for surrender after the defeat of Yue at the Battle of Fujiao 夫椒. Zhang Jue (2006): 186 n. 7 reads Zhuji as a two-character surname.
30. Both Xu Tianhu (1999): 111 and Zhang Jue (2006): 185 give *diao* 吊 (to hang) for *diao* 弔 (to condole). This is a mistake.

"It will be my business to watch the skies and investigate the earth, tracing the movements of the stars, *yin* and *yang*; to observe changes and predict disaster, distinguishing between good and evil omens," Grandee Jini said. "I will investigate when the sun and moon change color or when any of the five planets move from their courses, spotting good fortune and identifying it as a favorable omen, while expelling evil, because it represents a bad omen."

"Even though I head to an enemy country to the north, and become a prisoner in Wu, with you to maintain virtuous conduct and govern properly, each keeping to your promises to preserve the state altars, what have I got to worry about?" said the king of Yue.

Then they said goodbye there, at the upper reaches of the Zhe River, with the ruler and his subjects in tears and all deeply saddened. The king of Yue looked up at the sky and sighed. "Death is something that everyone fears," he said. "But when I hear about death, there is not the slightest tremor in my heart." Then he climbed onto the boat and set off on his journey; right to the end, he never turned his head to look back.

The king of Yue's wife sat leaning against the side of the boat and wept. She turned her head back and saw the crows and magpies pecking at the shrimp on the sandbanks in the river, flying away and then coming back again. Thus, while she wept, she composed a song about them:

I raise my head to face the flying birds: the crows and the kites,
In the cold dark air, they flap their wings.[31]
Gathering on the islands and sandbanks, they enjoy themselves,
Pecking at the shrimp and spreading their wings: they soar amid the clouds.

何居食兮江湖？徊復翔兮遊颺，去復返兮於乎！始事君兮去家，終我命兮君都。終來遇兮何幸，離我國兮去吳。妻衣褐兮為婢，夫去冕兮為奴。歲遙遙兮難極，冤悲痛兮心惻。腸千結兮服膺，於乎哀兮忘食。願我身兮如鳥，身翱翔兮矯翼。去我國兮心搖，情憒愯兮誰識？」越王聞夫人怨歌，心中內慟，乃曰：「孤何憂？吾之六翮備矣。」於是入吳，見夫差，稽首再拜稱臣，曰：「東海賤臣勾踐，上愧皇天，下負後土，不裁功力，汙辱王之軍士，抵罪邊境。

---

31. In this line, the character *hao* 號 is understood as an error for *xi* 兮, following the commentary by Xu Tianhu (1999): 112.

They use their [one character missing in the original text] to come and go.[32]
I am innocent, but Earth has turned against me!
What crime have I committed, that Heaven punishes me so?
Traveling at high speed, alone, I head toward the west,
Who knows when I shall ever return?
My heart is pained, as if cut by a knife,[33]
My tears fall in two lines, like crystal pearls.[34]
Then she recited sadly:
The flying birds, here, are kites and crows,
They have already flown away; they gather and then disperse.
Their minds are concentrated on the pale shrimp,
Otherwise, why would they live by the rivers and lakes?
Wheeling around, they soar again, playing in the wind,
Leaving, they return again—alas!
When first I served my lord, and left my own home,
I thought I would end my life in my husband's capital.
A transgression in midlife has brought about such punishment,[35]
That I must leave my country and go to Wu!

大王赦其深辜，裁加役臣，使執箕帚。誠蒙厚恩，得保須臾之命，不勝仰感俯愧。臣勾踐叩頭頓首。」吳王夫差曰：「寡人於子，亦過矣。子不念先君之讎乎？」越王曰：「臣死則死矣，惟大王原之。」伍胥在旁，目若燻火，聲如雷霆，乃進曰：「夫飛鳥在青雲之上，尚欲繳微矢以射之。豈況近臥於華池，集於庭廡乎？今越王放於南山之中，遊於不可存之地，幸來涉我壤土，入吾梐梱，此乃廚宰之成事食也，豈可失之乎？」吳王曰：「吾聞誅降殺服，

---

32. In addition to the missing character found in this line as it stands, the disruption in the rhyme scheme suggests that there is also a further missing line here. Zhang Jue (2006): 188 n. 7 argues that the text should read: 任厥□□□□，□□□□兮往還, which would preserve the rhyme scheme.
33. The wording of this line references *Shijing*, 71 ["Caochong" 草蟲].
34. This song consists of rhyming couplets in the pattern AABBA (though this is disrupted by the missing first line in the fourth couplet). The A rhymes are derived from the *-en (*yuan* 元) group; the B rhymes from the *-in (*zhen* 真) group.
35. Here *xing* 幸 (good luck) is being read as an error for *gu* 辜 (punishment), following the annotations by Zhou Shengchun in *Wu Yue chunqiu*, 120, and this restores the rhyme of this recitation.

The wife wears coarse cloth and works as a maid;
The husband takes off his crown to become a slave.
The years have passed, and now the crisis has come,
The pain of undeserved suffering overwhelms my heart.
It ties my stomach in knots, and marks my every waking moment,
I am so sad that I even forget to eat!
I wish that I were like a bird,
That I might fly away, on outstretched wings.
On leaving my country, my heart is pained,
My feelings are outraged, but who understands?[36]

The king of Yue heard his wife's tragic song, and his heart was overwhelmed with sorrow. Then he said: "Why should I worry? My flight feathers are ready!"[37]

After this, [King Goujian of Yue] entered Wu, whereupon he had an audience with King Fuchai, at which he knocked his head on the ground, bowed twice, and acknowledged himself to be his vassal. "Your humble servant from the Eastern Sea, Goujian, has shamed himself before Heaven and betrayed himself before Earth," he said. "I failed to measure my own powers and thus humiliated myself in front of the officers of your army, receiving a richly deserved punishment at the border. Your Majesty has pardoned my terrible crimes and allowed me to become your servant, employing me to

禍及三世。吾非愛越而不殺也，畏皇天之咎教而赦之。」太宰嚭諫曰：「子胥明於一時之計，不通安國之道。願大王遂其所執，無拘羣小之口。」夫差遂不誅越王，令駕車養馬，祕於宮室之中。三月，吳王召越王入見。越王伏於前，范蠡立於後。吳王謂范蠡曰：「寡人聞貞婦不嫁破亡之家，仁賢不官絕滅之國。今越王無道，國已將亡，社稷壞崩。身死世絕，為天下笑，而子及主俱為奴僕，來歸於吳，豈不鄙乎！吾欲赦子之罪，子能改心自新，

---

36. The queen of Yue's recitation consists of rhymed lines in the complex pattern AAAABAAAAACADDEDFDGD. In this recitation, the A rhymes are from the *-a (yu 魚) group; B is the *-aŋ (yang 陽) group; C is the *-e (zhi 支) group; D is the *-ək (zhi 職) group; and E, F, and G are from the *-əŋ (zheng 蒸), *-u (you 幽), and *-au (xiao 宵) groups, respectively.

37. In Han dynasty rhetoric, flight feathers are often used as a metaphor for loyal ministers; see, for example, Han Shi waizhuan, 6.236.

hold a dustpan and brush.[38] I am indeed overwhelmed by a sense of your generosity and kindness, which means I have been able to preserve my insignificant life—I cannot overcome my awe and sense of personal inadequacy. I hereby kowtow and bow my head to the ground."

"We have also transgressed against you," King Fuchai of Wu said. "Do you not remember the enmity of our ancestors?"

"If I die, then I die," the king of Yue said. "It shall be as Your Majesty pleases."

[Wu] Zixu was standing to one side, with eyes like lambent flame and a voice of thunder. Now he stepped forward and said: "When a bird is flying high in the blue sky, amid the clouds, you will need a threaded arrow to shoot it. Surely it is no different when it is sleeping close to the garden pond or roosting on the corridors leading out from the main hall? The king of Yue was defending himself at the Southern Mountain, roaming in places where it would be impossible for us [to keep track of] him: luckily, he has been brought to our country and entered our trap.[39] This is like the cook being ready to get to work and make his dish; how can you possibly release him?"

"I have heard it said that to execute someone who has surrendered or to murder an obedient vassal will bring disaster even to the third generation," the king of Wu responded. "I do not refuse to kill him because I love Yue but because I am afraid of the punishments of Heaven. Therefore, I will instruct him about his crimes and then pardon him."

棄越歸吳乎？」范蠡對曰：「臣聞亡國之臣，不敢語政。敗軍之將，不敢語勇。臣在越，不忠不信，今越王不奉大王命號，用兵與大王相持，至今獲罪，君臣俱降。蒙大王鴻恩，得君臣相保，願得入備掃除，出給趨走，臣之願也。」此時越王伏地流涕，自謂遂失范蠡矣。吳王知范蠡不可得為臣，謂曰：「子既不移其誌，吾復置子於石室之中。」范蠡曰：「臣請如命。」吳王起入宮中，越王、范蠡趨入石室。越王服犢鼻，著樵頭；夫人衣無緣之裳，施左關之襦。夫斫剉養馬，妻給水除糞灑掃。三年不慍怒，面無恨色。吳王登遠臺望見

---

38. The use of the term *jizhou* 箕帚 (dustpan and brush) emphasizes the degrading treatment meted out to King Goujian. This is a common rhetorical technique in the *Wu Yue chunqiu*.

39. *Cun* 存 in the original text is here being read as *cha* 察 (to keep track of), following the reading given in *Erya*, 58 ["Shigu" 釋詁]. This translation thus follows the commentary on this line given in Zhang Jue (2006): 189 n. 11.

Chancellor Pi remonstrated: "[Wu] Zixu understands well how to plan for an emergency, but he knows nothing about the Way of bringing peace to the country. I hope Your Majesty will hold to your decision and not be constrained by the complaints of a host of small-minded persons."[40]

King Fuchai thus did not execute the king of Yue but ordered him to raise horses and break them in for chariot work, secreting him within the palace.[41]

In the third month, the king of Wu summoned the king of Yue for an audience. The king of Yue lay down on his face in front, while Fan Li stood behind him. The king of Wu said to Fan Li: "I have heard that a wise woman does not marry into a ruined family, and a clever minister does not serve a doomed state. Now the king of Yue has shown his wicked ways, and his country has been destroyed, the state altars have collapsed, and he himself faces death as a laughingstock for the entire world. However, you have come with your master into slavery, showing your obedience to Wu—surely this is more than servile! I would like to pardon you for your crimes. If you would but reform your way of thinking and behavior, would you be prepared to abandon Yue and serve Wu?"

"I have heard that a minister from a ruined country does not dare to speak of matters of government, while a general whose army has been defeated does not dare to speak of bravery," Fan Li replied. "I have failed in loyalty and trustworthiness during my service to Yue. It is my fault that the

越王及夫人、范蠡坐於馬糞之旁，君臣之禮存，夫婦之儀具。王顧謂太宰嚭曰：「彼越王者，一節之人。范蠡，一介之士。雖在窮厄之地，不失君臣之禮，寡人傷之。」太宰嚭曰：「願大王以聖人之心，哀窮孤之士。」吳王曰：「為子赦之。」後三月，乃擇吉日而欲赦之。召太宰嚭謀曰：「越之與吳，同土連域。勾踐愚黠，親欲為賊。寡人承天之神靈，前王之遺德，誅討越寇，囚之石室。寡人心不忍見，而欲赦之，於子奈何？」太宰嚭曰：「臣聞無德不復。大王

---

40. The ode "Bozhou" 柏舟 (The Cypress-Wood Boat) includes the line: "I am hated by a host of small-minded people" (*yun yu qunxiao* 慍于群小); see *Shijing*, 116. Zheng Xuan glosses *qunxiao* as meaning specifically: "the host of small-minded people in attendance beside the ruler" (*zhong xiaoren zai jun ze zhe* 眾小人在君則者). This criticism is specifically aimed at Wu Zixu, whose position as prime minister demanded that he spend much time with King Fuchai.
41. Zhang Jue (2006): 189 n. 15 argues that the word *gongshi* 宮室 (palace) in the original text should read *shishi* 石室 (stone cell). The problem with this reading is that it does not explain why King Goujian should need to be secreted there.

king of Yue failed to respond to your commands, Your Majesty, and raised an army to fight against you—he committed a terrible crime that led to ruler and ministers all surrendering to you.[42] Thanks to your enormous generosity, we have been able to survive. Therefore, if I am summoned, I am prepared to perform the most menial tasks for you, and if you send me away, I will go as quickly as I can. This is my wish."

All this time, the king of Yue was lying face down on the floor and crying, for he was sure that he was about to lose Fan Li. The king of Wu realized that Fan Li would not agree to become one of his ministers, so he said: "If you do not change your mind, I will return you to your stone cell."

"I will do as you command," Fan Li replied.

The king of Wu stood up and went into the palace. The king of Yue and Fan Li got back to their stone cell as quickly as they could.

The king of Yue then wore a sarong and wrapped his hair in a turban.[43] His wife wore an unornamented skirt and a shirt tied on the left.[44] The husband chopped hay to feed the horses; the wife brought water, shoveled out manure, and cleaned the stables.[45] For three years they showed no sign of resentment, nor did they allow their faces to wear an angry expression. The king of Wu climbed the Yuan Tower, and looking out in the distance, he spotted the king of Yue and his wife sitting together with Fan Li at the side of a pile of horse manure—every ritual between ruler and

垂仁恩加越，越豈敢不報哉？願大王卒意。」越王聞之，召范蠡告之曰：「孤聞於外，心獨喜之，又恐其不卒也。」范蠡曰：「大王安心，事將有意，在玉門第一。今年十二月，戊寅之日，時加日出。戊，囚日也。寅，陰後之辰也。合庚辰歲後會也。夫以戊寅日聞喜，不以其罪罰日也。時加卯而賊戊，功曹為騰蛇而臨戊，謀利事在青龍。青龍在，勝先。而臨酉，死氣也。而剋寅，是時剋其日，用又助之。所求之事，上下有憂。此豈非天網四張，萬物盡

---

42. This translation reads *jin* 今 (now) in the original text as *ling* 令 (which led to), following the commentary by Zhang Jue (2006): 190 n. 1.

43. The term translated here as "sarong" is *dubi* 犢鼻; according to *Shiji*, 117.3000, this was a kind of trouser. However, other accounts make it clear that this garment was more like a sarong; see *Fangyan*, 4.35.

44. In antiquity, non-Chinese people were conventionally said to wear their clothes fastened on the left; see, for example, *Lunyu*, 151 ["Xianwen" 憲問]. This detail emphasizes the foreign origins of the Yue ruling house.

45. These kinds of activities were commonly carried out by slaves in the early imperial period; see Hulsewé (1955): 131–32 and Chen Zhi (1958).

vassal was observed, and every courtesy between husband and wife was maintained. The king glanced back at Chancellor Pi and said, "The king of Yue is an honorable man, and Fan Li is a fine gentleman. Even though they find themselves humiliated, and in difficult circumstances, they have not failed to observe the proper ritual between ruler and subject. I find this painful to watch."

"I hope that Your Majesty will find it in your sagacious heart to feel sorry for these poor and lonely men," Chancellor Pi said.

"For your sake, I will pardon them," the king of Wu said.

Three months later, he selected an auspicious day and was about to release them. He summoned Chancellor Pi and discussed the situation with him.

"Yue and Wu occupy the same area of land and border on one another," His Majesty said. "King Goujian proved to be a stupid man, who decided of his own accord to act in a criminal manner. Thanks to the numinous powers of Heaven and the accumulated virtue of our former kings, I was able to punish this Yue bandit and imprison him in a stone cell. However, I cannot bear to see this, and I want to pardon him. What do you think I should do?"

"I have heard that every act of virtue has its own reward," Chancellor Pi replied. "If Your Majesty behaves with kindness and generosity to Yue, how can they fail to repay you? I hope you will stick to your intention."[46]

The king of Yue heard about this and called Fan Li to tell him about it. "When I heard about this around and about, I was indeed very happy about it, but I am afraid that it will not come to pass."

"Calm down, Your Majesty, for there are reasons to be concerned about this matter," Fan Li said, "since it pertains to the first part of the *Jade*

傷者乎！王何喜焉？」果子胥諫吳王曰：「昔桀囚湯而不誅，紂囚文王而不殺，天道還反，禍轉成福。故夏為湯所誅，殷為周所滅。今大王既囚越君而不行誅，臣謂大王惑之深也。得無夏、殷之患乎？」

吳王遂召越王，久之不見。范蠡、文種憂而占之，曰：「吳王見擒也。」有頃，太宰嚭出見大夫種、范蠡而言越王復拘於石室。伍子胥復諫吳王曰：「臣聞王者攻敵國，克之則加以誅。故後無報復之憂，遂免子孫之患。今越王已

---

46. This translation follows the commentary by Xu Tianhu (1999): 115 in understanding *zu yi* 卒意 in the original text as meaning *zhong qi yi* 終其意 (stick to your intention).

Gate.⁴⁷ Right now it is Wuyin Day in the twelfth month, and the time is sunrise. Wu is an 'imprisoned' day, and Yin is a position that has already been passed by Counter-Jupiter. The 'matching day' is Gengchen Day, which also corresponds to a celestial position whereby Counter-Jupiter has passed. However, you have heard good news on a Wuyin Day, which does not fit since this is a day appropriate for punishments. It is now Mao hour, which compromises Wu.⁴⁸ Furthermore, since *Gongcao* is in the constellation *Tengshe* and encroaches on Wu, when plotting to benefit yourself, success rests in the Green Dragon.⁴⁹ When the Green Dragon is located at the meridian and encroaches on Chou, it is 'dead' and 'kills' Yin; therefore, not only does the hour 'kill' the day but these movements further reinforce the inauspiciousness.⁵⁰ As for what Your Majesty so desires, there are concerns in both Heavenly Stems and Earthly Branches. Surely in this situation the Heavenly Net is spread in the four directions, and the myriad life-forms all suffer damage! What is there for Your Majesty to be happy about?"

As he had anticipated, [Wu] Zixu remonstrated with the king of Wu: "In the past, King Jie imprisoned Tang and did not execute him, and King Zhou imprisoned King Wen and did not kill him. Therefore, the Heavenly Way changed direction, and disaster was transformed into good luck. Accordingly, the Xia ended up being butchered by Tang, and the Yin dynasty was destroyed by the Zhou kings. Today you have imprisoned the ruler of

入石室，宜早圖之。後必為吳之患。」太宰嚭曰：「昔者，齊桓割燕所至之地以賜燕公，而齊君獲其美名。宋襄濟河而戰，春秋以多其義。功立而名稱，軍敗而德存。今大王誠赦越王，則功冠於五霸，名越於前古。」吳王曰：「待吾疾愈，方為大宰赦之。」後一月，越王出石室，召范蠡曰：「吳王疾，三月不愈。吾聞人臣之道：主疾臣憂。且吳王遇孤，恩甚厚矣。疾之無瘳，惟公卜焉。」范蠡曰：「吳王不死，明矣。到己巳日，當瘳。惟大王留意。」越王曰：「孤

---

47. It is now not known what exactly the *Yumen* or *Jade Gate* was; Zhang Jue (2006): 193 n. 4 suggests that it was either a divination text or a method of divination that is today lost.
48. As stated in *Huainanzi*, 269 ["Tianwen xun"], Mao corresponds to the element Wood and Wu to the element Earth; therefore, the former succeeds the latter.
49. *Tengshe* consists of twenty-two stars in the constellation Lacerta; see Sun and Kistemaker (1997): 150. The Green Dragon here represents the collective term for the asterisms located in the seven eastern lunar lodges.
50. Chou corresponds to the element Metal and, therefore, "kills" Wood; see *Huainanzi*, 269 ["Tianwen xun"].

Yue, Your Majesty, but you have not executed him: I think that you are deeply deluded. How can you avoid the same disaster that overtook the Xia and Yin dynasties?"

The king of Wu then summoned the king of Yue, but even after waiting for a long time, he had not been called for an audience. Fan Li and Wen Zhong were worried about this and performed a divination, which said: "The king of Wu has been captured." After yet another wait, Chancellor Pi emerged, and when he saw Grandee Zhong and Fan Li, he said that the king of Yue had been arrested and confined to the stone cell again. Once more, Wu Zixu remonstrated with the king of Wu: "I have heard that if a king attacks an enemy country and conquers it, he kills as many people as he can, for that way he does not have to worry about them taking revenge in the future, nor will there be any trouble from sons or grandsons of the royal family. Now the king of Yue has already been confined in a stone cell, and you should deal with him as soon as you can, because otherwise, there will definitely be problems for Wu in the future."

"In the past, Lord Huan of Qi partitioned off the land that he had traveled through and gave it to the ruler of Yan," Chancellor Pi said, "and the ruler of Qi was much acclaimed for this.[51] Lord Xiang of Song waited until the enemy had crossed the river and then fought a battle with them: the *Spring and Autumn Annals* contain many references to his strong sense of justice.[52] When great things are accomplished, you become famous, but

所以窮而不死者，賴公之策耳。中復猶豫，豈孤之誌哉！可與不可，惟公圖之！」范蠡曰：「臣竊見吳王真非人也，數言成湯之義，而不行之。願大王請求問疾，得見，因求其糞而嘗之，觀其顏色，當拜賀焉，言其不死，以廖起日期之。既言信後，則大王何憂。」越王明日謂太宰嚭曰：「囚臣欲一見問疾。」太宰嚭即入言於吳王。王召而見之。適遇吳王之便，太宰嚭奉溲惡以出，逢戶中。越王因拜請嘗大王之溲，以決吉兇。即以手取其便與惡而嘗之，因

---

51. Lord Huan of Qi 齊桓公 ruled from 685 to 643 BCE. His generosity to the ruler of Yan, who had appealed to him for assistance, is mentioned in a number of ancient texts; see, for example, *Shiji*, 32.1488, and *Guanzi*, 460 ["Baxing" 霸形].

52. Lord Xiang of Song 宋襄公 ruled from 650 to 637 BCE, and in 638 BCE, he fought a disastrous battle with the kingdom of Chu at the Hong 泓 River, where he refused to take advantage of their dangerous position to attack them. These events are recorded in many ancient texts; see, for example, *Zuozhuan*, 397 [Xi 22]. Lord Xiang of Song is often presented as exceptionally stupid and arrogant; however, some texts do praise him; see, for example, *Gongyang zhuan*, 246 [Xi 22]. It is thought that the *Wu Yue chunqiu* is referring to this text rather than to the *Chunqiu* itself.

even if your army is defeated, you can remain virtuous. Today His Majesty has decided in all sincerity to pardon the king of Yue, which means that his achievements are even more glorious than the Five Hegemons, and his fame will exceed all those who have gone before."

"Wait until I have recovered from my current illness," the king of Wu said, "and I will pardon [King Goujian of Yue] for the chancellor's sake."

Another month passed, and the king of Yue came out of his stone cell and summoned Fan Li.[53] "The king of Wu is very ill," he said, "and even after three months, he still has not recovered. I have heard that it is proper for a vassal to be worried when his lord is unwell. Furthermore, the king of Wu has treated me with great generosity. As to whether or not he will recover from this disease, I would like you to perform a divination about it."

"Today the Heavenly Stems and Earthly Branches, *yin* and *yang*, are all in harmony, and there is none in contradiction to another," Fan Li replied. "As the divination manual says: 'When Heaven itself saves you, what is there to worry about?'[54] It is clear that the king of Wu will not die. On Jisi Day, he will recover. All you have to do is be careful."

"The only reason I am still alive is that I have been relying on your advice," the king of Yue said. "Now you hesitate again and have failed to come up with any suggestions; is this what I want? As to whether this is possible or not, all will depend on your plans!"

"I have carefully observed the king of Wu," replied Fan Li, "and he is a nasty piece of work: he talks about emulating the same judicious acts as Tang but never actually does anything of the kind. I hope that you will beg to see him and ask after his health, and when he gives you an audience, you should request a sample of his stool and taste it. Observe his face carefully, then bow and congratulate him, and say he will not die—indeed, you can

入曰:「下因臣勾踐賀於大王。王之疾,至已巳日有瘳。至三月壬申,病愈。」吳王曰:「何以知之?」越王曰:「下臣嘗事師聞糞者,順穀味,逆時氣者死,順時氣者生。今者臣竊嘗大王之糞,其惡味苦且楚酸。是味也,應春夏之氣。臣以是知之。」吳王大悅,曰:「仁人也。」乃赦越王,得離其石室,去就其宮室,執牧養之事如故。越王從嘗糞惡之後,遂病口臭。范蠡乃令左右皆食岑草,以亂其氣。其後,吳王如越王期日疾愈,心念其忠,臨政之後,大縱

---

53. Xu Tianhu (1999): 116 suggests that *chu* 出 (to come out) in the original text should be read as *zuo* 坐 (to sit). Zhang Jue (2006): 196–97 n. 1 sees no reason to change the original text here.

54. Not all editions of the text include these two lines; see, for example, Huang Rensheng (1996): 250.

give him the date on which he will recover. If you say this and it does indeed prove true, what more is there for you to worry about?"

The following day, the king of Yue said to Chancellor Pi: "Your humble servant would like to ask after His Majesty's health."

Chancellor Pi then went into the palace and mentioned this to the king of Wu, and the king summoned him for an audience. When the king of Wu then needed to relieve himself, Chancellor Pi took up the container with his discharge to remove it, but just as he was going through the door, the king of Yue bowed and said: "Let me taste the king's dejections to determine his fate." Then with his hand, he took his urine and stool and tasted it. Afterward, he went in and said: "Let your humble servant, Goujian, congratulate you, Your Majesty. You will recover from this disease on Jisi Day, and by Renshen Day in the third month, you will be fully back to normal."

"How do you know that?" the king of Wu asked.

"I once learned from a person good at smelling feces that it should accord with the taste of grain," the king of Yue replied. "Where the *qi* goes against the season, the sufferer will die; where the *qi* accords with the season, the sufferer will live. Just now I personally tasted Your Majesty's feces—your diarrhea was bitter and strongly sour in flavor. This taste accords with the *qi* of the spring and summer seasons. That is how I know this."

The king of Wu was delighted. "What a wonderful man!" he said. Then he pardoned the king of Yue and allowed him to leave his cell—he went to live in the palace, though he carried on looking after horses like before. After the king of Yue tasted the stool and urine, he suffered a disease that made his breath stink, so Fan Li ordered his entourage to all eat fishwort to mask the smell.55

酒於文臺。吳王出令曰：「今日為越王陳北面之坐，羣臣以客禮事之。」伍子胥趨出，到舍上，不禦坐。酒酣，太宰嚭曰：「異乎！今日坐者，各有其詞。不仁者逃，其仁者留。臣聞同聲相和，同心相求。今國相剛勇之人，意者內慙至仁之存也，而不禦坐，其亦是乎？」吳王曰：「然。」於是范蠡與越王俱起，為吳王壽。其辭曰：「下臣勾踐，從小臣范蠡，奉觴上千歲之壽。辭曰：皇在上令，昭下四時，並心察慈仁者。大王躬親鴻恩，立義行仁。九德四塞，

---

55. Fishwort (Houttuynia cordata) is identified according to Gao Mingqian et al. (2006): 334. This plant is noted for its strong and, to many people, unpleasant "fishy" smell, earning it another common name: *yuxingcao* 魚腥草 (fish-stink plant).

Afterward, the king of Wu did indeed get better on the day that the king of Yue had predicted, and he was very much touched by his loyalty. After having dealt with the business of government, he held a great banquet at the Wen Tower. The king of Wu gave the following orders: "Today I would like the king of Yue to sit facing north, and all of my ministers should greet him as if they are his guests."

Wu Zixu rushed out, and when he arrived at his residence, he refused to even sit down.

After the wine was drunk, Chancellor Pi said: "How strange! Of those sitting here today, each has their own opinion. Let the unkind leave; let the benevolent remain. I have heard it said that similar sounds harmonize, just as those who share the same principles help each other out. Now the prime minister is a hard and brave man; it seems that he is put to shame by the very existence of this most benevolent man, and therefore, he has refused to sit in attendance. Am I right?"

"That is true," the king of Wu said.

At that moment, Fan Li and the king of Yue stood up together and toasted the king of Wu, wishing him a long life. They said: "Your vassal, Goujian, and his humble servant, Fan Li, lift their goblets to wish Your Majesty one thousand years of longevity." Then they continued:

How splendid is the government of our king,
Which shines through the four seasons,
Uniting all who are benevolent and kind.[56]
Your Majesty has personally shown great magnanimity:
You have established justice and shown benevolence!
Your manifold virtues spread throughout the kingdom,

威服羣臣。於乎休哉，傳德無極。上感太陽，降瑞翼翼。大王延壽萬歲，長保吳國。四海咸承，諸侯賓服。觴酒既升，永受萬福！」於是吳王大悅。明日，伍子胥入諫曰：「昨日大王何見乎？臣聞內懷虎狼之心，外執美詞之說。但為外情，以存其身。豺不可謂廉，狼不可親。今大王好聽須臾之說，不慮萬歲之患。放棄忠直之言，聽用讒夫之語。不滅瀝血之仇，不絕懷毒之怨。猶縱毛爐炭之上，幸其焦。投卵千鈞之下，望必全。豈不殆哉？臣聞桀登高，

---

56. If the final *zhe* 者 in this line is removed as extraneous, then this line participates in the *-in (*zhen* 真) rhyme that features in this recitation.

Striking awe into your subjects and making them submit to your authority.
How glorious!
May your virtues be transmitted without end!
You have impressed even the sun in the sky,
And it has sent down auspicious omens one after the other.
May Your Majesty enjoy ten thousand years of long life,
May you forever protect the kingdom of Wu!
May all that is within the four seas support you,
May the lords pay court to you and obey your commands!
Our goblets of wine are already lifted,
May you forever enjoy myriad blessings![57]

The king of Wu was very happy.

The following day, Wu Zixu entered the palace to remonstrate. "Who did you see yesterday, Your Majesty?" he asked. "I have heard that he who possesses the heart of a tiger or a wolf will be sure to make every use of flattering speech. This is just a matter of surface appearance, which he does to survive. Just as a dhole cannot be accounted honest, a wolf cannot be held dear. Today Your Majesty has enjoyed listening to promises that will soon be broken, and you have not considered the terrible disaster that threatens years of worry. You have set aside words of loyal advice to listen to the facile speech of a fawning minister. You have failed to kill an enemy who spilled the blood [of King Helü] or to resolve an enmity that threatens our very heart. If you place a feather on top of burning coals, it is only by good fortune that it fails

自知危，然不知所以自安也。前據白刃，自知死，而不知所以自存也。惑者知返，迷道不遠，願大王察之。」吳王曰：「寡人有疾三月，曾不聞相國一言，是相國之不慈也。又不進口之所嗜，心不相思，是相國之不仁也。夫為人臣不仁不慈，焉能知其忠信者乎？越王迷惑，棄守邊之事，親將其臣民來歸寡人，是其義也。躬親為虜，妻親為妾，不慍寡人。寡人有疾，親嘗寡人之溲，是其慈也。虛其府庫，盡其寶幣，不念舊故，是其忠信也。三者既立，以養

---

57. This recitation features a highly complex rhyme scheme, ABCCCDCBCECF-CGCGC, where the occasional unrhymed line would have added emphasis. Here, the A rhyme is from the *eŋ (*geng* 耕) group, the B rhyme is *-ə (*zhi* 之), C is *-in (*zhen* 真), D is *-ək (*zhi* 職), E is *-aŋ (*yang* 陽), F is from the *yue-ji* 月祭 group, and G is taken from the *-əŋ (*zheng* 蒸) group.

to be scorched.[58] If you throw an egg underneath a weight of one thousand *jun*, how can you hope it will remain whole? How stupid! I have heard that when Jie climbed up high, he realized he was in danger, but he did not know how to make himself safe. When rushing forward holding naked weapons, you know that you are risking death, but you do not know how to survive. If he who has gone wrong turns back, he will not proceed far down the road of no return. I hope that you will consider this."

"I have been sick for three months, but I never heard anything from you," the king of Wu said. "This proves that you, Prime Minister, are an unfeeling man. You also did not send me any of the delicacies that you had enjoyed eating, which means that you were not thinking about me—this demonstrates that you, Prime Minister, are an unkind person. If you are unfeeling and unkind, how do I know that you are loyal and trustworthy? The king of Yue made a terrible mistake, and so he has given up trying to defend his borders, coming instead to give his allegiance to me at the head of his people. This shows that he has a sense of justice. He has humbled himself as my prisoner, and his wife serves me as my slave, yet they do not hate me. When I was so ill, he personally tasted my diarrhea. This shows his sense of kindness. He has emptied his treasuries and storehouses, giving all his valuables to me with no concern for the past enmity between us. This shows that he is loyal and trustworthy. He has done these three things to serve me. If I were now to listen to you, Prime Minister, and execute him, it would merely show my lack of judgment and allow you the gratification of a private revenge! How could I betray august Heaven in this way?"

"Why are your words, Your Majesty, the opposite of the truth?" Zixu demanded. "When a tiger hides its strength, it is so that it can make a better attack; when a fox conceals its body, it is with a view to capturing its prey.

寡人。寡人曾聽相國而誅之，是寡人之不智也，而為相國快私意耶！豈不負皇天乎？」子胥曰：「何大王之言反也？夫虎之卑勢，將以有擊也。貍之卑身，將求所取也。雉以眩移拘於網，魚以有悅死於餌。且大王初臨政，負玉門之第九，誠事之敗，無咎矣。今年三月甲戌，時加雞鳴。甲戌，歲位之會將也。青龍在西，德在上，刑在金，是日賊其德也。知父將有不順之子，君有逆節之臣。大王以越王歸吳為義，以飲溲食惡為慈，以虛府庫為仁，是故為無愛

---

58. The original text here reads *xing qi jiao* 幸其焦. Following the annotations by Xu Tianhu (1999): 126, *qi* 其 is here read as the negative *bu* 不: "it is only by good fortune that it fails to be scorched."

Pheasants are caught in nets when their eyes are distracted; fish die on the hook because it is baited. You have taken charge of the government for the first time, Your Majesty, and you have ignored the ninth precept of the *Jade Gate*: 'When something is sure to fail, you cannot stop it doing so.' Right now, it is Jiaxu Day in the third lunar month, and at this time, it is almost cockcrow. On Jiaxu Day, Counter-Jupiter is located behind in the matching position, following on. The Green Dragon is in Chou, with accretion in Wood and recession in Metal.[59] This means that this day harms accretion. Accordingly, we can know that fathers will have disobedient sons, and rulers will have rebellious vassals. Your Majesty, you state that the king of Yue is just because he has given his allegiance to Wu; that he is kind because he has drunk of your urine and eaten your shit; and that he is benevolent because he has emptied his storehouses and treasuries. However, it is because he has begrudged you nothing that he is not to be held dear—he has appeared gentle and compliant to survive. Now the king of Yue has come to Wu as a vassal; this shows that his plans are indeed deep. He has emptied his treasuries and storehouses without the slightest sign of resentment; this is because he intends to trick Your Majesty. He has drunk your urine that he may eat your heart; he has tasted your shit that he may consume your liver! How great is the respect the king of Yue has shown to Wu—Wu will be captured because of this! You are the only person, Your Majesty, who can remain clear-sighted and investigate what has happened. I would not dare betray the trust of our former ruler, even to save my own life. When the altars of soil and grain have been reduced to wasteland, when the ancestral shrines are covered in brambles and weeds, it will be too late for regrets!"

"Prime Minister, stop this!" the king of Wu said. "Do not say anything, because I cannot bear to hear any more." Then he pardoned the king of Yue

於人；其不可親。面聽貌觀，以存其身。今越王入臣於吳，是其謀深也。虛其府庫，不見恨色，是欺我王也。下飲王之溲者，是上食王之心也。下嘗王之惡者，是上食王之肝也。大哉！越王之崇吳。吳將為所擒也。惟大王留意察之。臣不敢逃死以負前王。一旦社稷丘墟，宗廟荊棘，其悔可追乎？」吳王曰：「相國置之，勿復言矣。寡人不忍復聞。」於是遂赦越士歸國，送於蛇門之外，羣臣祖道。吳王曰：「寡人赦君，使其返國，必念終始，王其勉之。」

---

59. Excavated texts provide important evidence concerning Han dynasty divination practices based on the concepts of cycles of accretion (*de* 德) and recession (*xing* 刑); see, for example, Chen Songchang (2001) and Liu Lexian (2004). For a study of the significance of this system, see Kalinowski (1998–99).

and sent him home to his own country, escorting him out of the Snake Gate. The government ministers attended a banquet in his honor. "I have pardoned you and allowed you to return to your country; you must always remember this," the king of Wu said. "I hope that you will do your very best in the future."

The king of Yue kowtowed. "Today you have shown pity for my poverty and isolation, Your Majesty, and I will be able to return safe and sound to my own country," he said. "Together with my followers, Zhong and Li, I would be willing to die beneath your chariot wheels. May the blue heavens be my witness, I would not dare to let you down."

"Ah! I have heard that when a gentleman says one thing, he never goes back on his word," the king of Wu said. "Today you will set out—I hope that you will do your best, Your Majesty!"

The king of Yue bowed twice and then fell to his knees. The king of Wu helped the king of Yue to climb into his chariot. Fan Li held the reins, and then they set off. When they arrived above the Triple Ford, [King Goujian] looked up at the sky and sighed. "Ah!" he said. "With the dangers I have faced, who would have imagined that I would survive to cross these fords again?" Then he commented to Fan Li, "Today is Jiachen Day of the third lunar month, and at this time, the sun is beginning to set in the west.[60] Thanks to the mandate bestowed on me by Heaven, I have been able to return to my home. Will there be any more trouble for me in the future?"

"Do not worry, Your Majesty!" Fan Li said. "Just look straight ahead as you continue on your road. Yue will have its blessings; it is Wu that will suffer."

When they arrived above the Zhe River, in the distance they saw the rivers and mountains of Yue looking twice as beautiful as before, the land and the sky more lovely than ever. The king and his wife sighed and said: "The

越王稽首曰:「今大王哀臣孤窮,使得生全還國,與種、蠡之徒,願死於轂下。上天蒼蒼,臣不敢負。」吳王曰:「於乎! 吾聞君子一言不再,今已行矣,王勉之。」越王再拜跪伏。吳王乃引越王登車。范蠡執御,遂去。至三津之上,仰天歎曰:「嗟乎! 孤之屯厄,誰念復生渡此津也?」謂范蠡曰:「今三月甲辰,時加日昳,孤蒙上天之命,還歸故鄉,得無後患乎?」范蠡曰:「大王勿疑,

---

60. Given the dates mentioned before in this chapter, it is not possible that the third lunar month would have had a Jiachen Day; see Zhang Jue (2006): 203 n. 9. A variety of alternative dates have been suggested for these events.

situation was hopeless—we said goodbye to our people forever. Who would have imagined that we would one day come back again and be able to return to our home country?" When they had finished speaking, they covered their faces and wept bitter tears. Just at this moment, the people all shouted their welcome, and the ministers offered their congratulations.

直視道行。越將有福,吳當有憂。」至浙江之上,望見大越山川重秀,天地再清,王與夫人歎曰:「吾已絕望【宮闕】,永辭萬民。豈料再邊,重復鄉國?」言竟,掩面涕泣闌干。此時萬姓咸歡,羣臣畢賀。

Chapter Eight

The Outer Traditions
The Story of King Goujian Returning to His Country

King Goujian of Yue returned to Yue from having been a vassal in Wu in the seventh year of his reign [490 BCE]. The common people bowed to him along the roads. "Our king has suffered bitterly!" they said. "However, now Your Majesty has received the blessings of Heaven, and you have returned to the kingdom of Yue—the path to hegemony will begin from this point."

"I did not understand the lessons of Heaven, nor did I show virtue to my people," His Majesty said. "Now my subjects have gone to the trouble of thronging in these mountain roads: with what moral transformation can I repay the people of this country?" He then turned his head to speak to Fan Li. "Today is Jisi Day in the twelfth month, and it is approaching noon," he said. "I would like to enter my kingdom now; would this be all right?"

"Please wait a moment, Your Majesty, while I perform a divination about this date," he said. Afterward, Fan Li stepped forward and said: "How

《勾踐歸國外傳》

越王勾踐臣吳至歸越，勾踐七年也。百姓拜之於道，曰：「君王獨無苦矣！今王受天之福，復於越國，霸王之迹，自斯而起。」王曰：「寡人不慎天教，無德於民今勞萬姓擁於岐路，將何德化以報國人？」顧謂范蠡曰：「今十有二月己巳之日，時加禺中，孤欲以此到國，何如？」蠡曰：「大王且留，以臣卜日。」於是范蠡進曰：「異哉！大王之擇日也。王當疾趨，車馳人走。」越王策馬飛輿，遂復宮闕。吳封地百里於越，東至炭瀆，西止周宗，南造於山，

marvelous! This is a most auspicious day for you. You should go as quickly as you can, Your Majesty. Let your chariot race and your men run."

The king whipped up his horses and sped his chariot on, heading back to his palace.

Wu had granted one hundred li of land to Yue: to the east it reached to Tandu, to the west it stopped at Zhouzong, to the south it was bordered by mountains, and to the north it ended at the sea.[1]

The king of Yue said to Fan Li: "I have suffered humiliation year after year, in a situation that could easily have led to my demise, but thanks to your stratagems, Prime Minister, I have been able to return to my southern homeland. Now I would like to establish my own kingdom and set up walled cities, but I simply do not have enough people, and so this work cannot be carried out. What should I do?"

"Tang and Yu performed divinations about the land, the Xia and Yin dynasties enfeoffed subordinate states, while the Old Lord fortified and built city walls around Zhou and Luo; thus, he struck awe into everyone and made them submit for ten thousand *li* around, and his virtue spread in every direction," Fan Li replied.[2] "Surely they did not only want to crush their powerful enemies and conquer neighboring states?"

"I have been unable to maintain the system of government established by our former rulers, and so I could not rectify my virtue and protect myself," the king of Yue said.[3] "I have [ruined my army] and brought

北薄於海。越王謂范蠡曰：「孤獲辱連年，勢足以死，得相國之策，再返南鄉。今欲定國立城，人民不足，其功不可以興，為之奈何？」范蠡對曰：「唐、虞卜地，夏、殷封國，古公營城，周錐威折萬里，德致八極。豈直欲破彊敵，收鄰國乎？」越王曰：「孤不能承前君之制，修德自守。亡眾棲於會稽之山，請命乞恩，受辱被恥，囚結吳宮。幸來歸國，追以百里之封。將遵前君之意，復於會稽之上，而宜釋吳之地。」范蠡曰：「昔公劉去邰，而德彰於夏。

---

1. Quite different dimensions are given in *Guoyu*, 635 ["Yueyu shang"], for King Goujian's kingdom at this time.
2. As mentioned in the first chapter of the *Wu Yue chunqiu*, the Old Lord refers to Zhou Taiwang, the grandfather of King Wen. Zhang Jue (2006): 207 n. 3 reads Zhou and Luo as short forms of the two place-names: Chengzhou 成周 and Luoyi 雒邑. This follows texts such as *Shiji*, 33.1519, and *Xinxu*, 1344 ["Shanmou xia" 善謀下].
3. The *Shuijing zhu*, 40.941, provides a further line here, at the beginning of King Goujian's speech: "Our former ruler, Wuyu, had his capital at the south side of Mount Nan, and the altars of soil and grain, with the ancestral shrines, were located south of the lake" (先君無餘國在南山之陽；社稷宗廟在湖之南).

about the deaths of my people, so I ended up taking shelter on Kuaiji Mountain, begging for my life and hoping for the charity of others.[4] I suffered great humiliation and was covered in shame when I was held prisoner in the Wu palace. Having been fortunate enough to return to my kingdom, I have been given a fief of one hundred *li* of land. I feel I should respect the wishes of our former ruler and return to my place on top of Kuaiji Mountain: that would make it possible for me to ruin the lands of Wu!"

"In the past," Fan Li said, "Gongliu departed from Tai, and his virtues were considered glorious by the Xia; Danfu gave up his lands to a better man, and his name was known throughout the lands of Qi.[5] Today Your Majesty wants [to establish] your kingdom and set up your capital city, unifying the territory of enemy lands under your control: should you not locate your capital on a plain, whereby you can control the lands in all four directions, so that you can establish your authority as a hegemon-king?"[6]

"My plans are not fixed," the king of Yue said. "I want to build a walled city and erect an outer city wall, establishing associated village communities in outlying locations. This task is one that I wish to entrust to you, Prime Minister."

After this Fan Li observed the constellations in the skies, and basing his design on the Purple Palace asterism, he constructed a small walled city,

亶父讓地，而名發於岐。今大王欲國樹都，並敵國之境，不處平易之都，據四達之地，將焉立霸王之業？」越王曰：「寡人之計，未有決定。欲築城立郭，分設裏閭，欲委屬於相國。」於是范蠡乃觀天文，擬法於紫宮，築作小城，周千一百二十二步，一圓三方。西北立龍飛翼之樓，以象天門。東南伏漏石竇，以象地戶。陵門四達，以象八風。外郭築城而缺西北，示服事吳也，不敢壅塞。內以取吳，故缺西北，而吳不知也。北向稱臣，委命吳國。左右易處，不得

---

4. Here the characters *pojun* 破軍 ("ruined my army") are derived from the Sibu congkan 四部叢刊 edition of the text.
5. Here Fan Li makes reference to the events described in the first chapter of the *Wu Yue chunqiu*. This text continually stresses the cultural and historical connections between the two kingdoms.
6. The character *li* 立 (to establish) is missing from the original text but is incorporated into the translation of this line according to the commentary by Xu Tianhu (1999): 130.

1,122 *bu* in diameter, with one rounded and three square corners.[7] To the northwest he established the Dragon with Wings Spread Belvedere, to correspond to the Gate of Heaven.[8] To the southwest, he placed a stone-lined canal, to carry away floodwaters, to correspond to the Door of Earth. Great gates opened in the four directions, to correspond to the eight winds. Beyond the outer city wall, he constructed a further fortification, which omitted the northwest wall—this was to show that they submitted to and served Wu; hence, they did not dare to block them. *In fact, they were planning to conquer Wu, and that is why they left the northwest out, but Wu did not know that. They faced north and called themselves vassals, obeying the orders they received from the kingdom of Wu. Furthermore, left and right changed places and did not occupy their original positions—this was done to make clear that [Yue] was a vassal state.*

Once the city wall was built, the Phenomenal Mountain came of its own accord. Phenomenal Mountain had been an island in the sea off Dongwu in Langya—one night it arrived of its own accord, and everyone thought this was really strange, so they named it the Phenomenal Mountain.[9]

"The walled city that I have constructed corresponds with Heaven," Fan Li announced. "Thus, an omen of Kunlun has appeared here."

"I have heard that Kunlun Mountain is the pillar that consolidates Heaven and Earth," the king of Yue said. "Above, it reaches to the august heavens, while its *qi* spreads to all under the empyrean; below, it is founded on Earth, encompassing everything. It has nourished sages and given rise

其位，明臣屬也。城既成，而怪山自生［至］。【怪山】者，琅琊東武海中山也，一夕自來，【百姓怪之，】故名怪山。范蠡曰：「臣之築城也，其應天矣。崑崙之象存焉。」越王曰：「寡人聞崑崙之山，乃【天】地之【鎮】柱，上承皇天，氣吐宇內，下處後土，稟受無外，滋聖生神，嘔養帝會。故帝處其陽陸，三王居其正地。吾之國也，扁天地之壞，乘東南之維，斗去極北，非糞土之城，何能與王者比隆盛哉？」范蠡曰：「君徒見外，未見於內。臣乃承天門

---

7. Sun and Kistemaker (1997): 154. See also Maeyama (2002) for a detailed study of the history of this asterism.
8. Some editions of the text omit the word *long* 龍 (Dragon) from the name of this building and add another line afterward: *wei liang liu rao dong yi xiang longjiao* 爲兩螭繞棟以象龍角 (He made two serpentine coiling pillars, to correspond to the horns of the dragon); see, for example, Zhang Jue (2006): 316.
9. The supernatural appearance of this mountain is also mentioned in *Yuejue shu*, 59 ["Jidi zhuan"].

to gods, providing support for the greatest rulers of antiquity. Therefore, the [Five] Sovereigns took their place on the south side of the mountain, while the Three Kings resided at its center.[10] Our country is situated off to one side in the divisions of Heaven and Earth, occupying a corner in the southeast, whereby the Dipper has vacated the northern pole—is this not a shitty little city?[11] How can I compare with the glory and success of those monarchs?"

"Your Majesty, you have only observed the surface situation; you do not understand the inner workings yet," Fan Li responded. "I built this city to accord with the gates of Heaven and match the *qi* of Earth, so the corresponding marchmonts have been established, and thus, Kunlun appeared: this betokens Yue's hegemony."

"If it is indeed as you, Prime Minister, have said, then this is my destiny," the king of Yue said.

He named this place Dongwu and constructed the Traveling Tower on top of it.[12] To the southeast, he built Marshal's Gate.[13] He established a multistory building there, crowning the peak of this mountain: this was the Numinous Tower.[14] He raised up a traveling palace at Huaiyang.

制城，合氣於后土，嶽象已設，崑崙故出，越之霸也。」越王曰：「苟如相國之言，孤之命也。」范蠡曰：「天地卒號，以著其實。」名東武，起遊臺其上。東南為司馬門。立增樓，冠其山巔，以為靈臺。起離宮於淮陽。中宿臺在於高平。駕臺在於成丘。立苑於樂野。燕臺在於石室。齋臺在於襟山。勾踐之出遊也，休息石室，食於冰廚。

---

10. Xu Tianhu (1999): 127 indicates that the character *wu* 五 (five) is missing from this line. Many modern editions of the text simply insert it without any comment.
11. This translation follows Xu Tianhu (1999): 127 in reading *bian* 扁 in the original text as an error for *pian* 偏 (off to one side). The seven stars of the constellation Ursa Major form the Northern Dipper constellation in Chinese astronomy. Zhang Jue (2006): 210 n. 26 suggests that in states located in the central regions, the Dipper would indicate true north. However, for a remote and off-centered location like Yue, it would appear to have moved. This reinforces the image of Yue as a backward and faraway place.
12. The construction of this tower is also mentioned in *Yuejue shu*, 59 ["Jidi zhuan"].
13. Xu Tianhu (1999): 131 names this place as Same Horse Gate (Tongma men 同馬門) rather than Marshal's Gate (Sima men 司馬門), but this is clearly a mistake.
14. This building is recorded in *Shuijing zhu*, 40.943: "Yue built the Numinous Tower on top of [Phenomenal] Mountain, and also built a multistory building, in order to inspect the clouds and [Heavenly] bodies" (越起靈臺於山上，又作三層樓，以望雲物).

Meanwhile, the Repose Tower was located at Gaoping, and the Carriage Tower at Chengqiu. He established a hunting park at Leye, and the Banqueting Tower was built at Shishi, while the Purification Tower was built at Ji Mountain. When King Goujian went out traveling, he would rest at Shishi and eat from the icehouse there.[15]

The king of Yue then summoned the prime minister, Fan Li; Grandee Zhong; and Grandee Ying and asked them: "Now I would like to ascend to the Hall of Light to oversee the government of the country, spreading kindness and issuing orders that will bring comfort to the common people.[16] What day would be appropriate for this? Only the three of you sagacious gentlemen can assist me in maintaining the warp and weft of good government."

"Today is Bingwu Day," Fan Li said. "Bing is the commander of *yang*. This is an auspicious day and also a good moment—in my humble opinion, you can proceed. We are neither at the beginning nor at the end of the cycle of days, so you have obtained central ground."

"When the chariot in front has already overturned, those in the chariot behind must take warning," Grandee Zhong said. "I hope that you will consider carefully, Your Majesty."

"Indeed, sir, you have only considered one or two matters here," Fan Li responded. "Today His Majesty makes use of a Bingwu Day to begin his government afresh, saving the very foundations [of the country]: that is the first reason why it would be appropriate. Metal controls the beginning, and Fire comes to the rescue at the end: that is the second

越王乃召相國范蠡、大夫種、大夫郢，問曰：「孤欲以今［令］日上明堂，臨國政，專恩致令，以撫百姓，何日可矣？惟三聖紀綱維持持。」范蠡曰：「今日丙午日也。丙，陽將也。是日吉矣，又因良時，臣愚以為可。無始有終，得天下之中。」大夫種曰：「前車已覆，後車必戒，願王深察。」范蠡曰：「夫子故不一二見也。吾王今以丙午復初臨政，解救其本，是一宜。夫金制始，而火救其終，是二宜。蓄金之憂，轉而及水，是三宜。君臣有差，不失其理，

---

15. This account of various buildings located in and around the Yue capital is derived from *Yuejue shu*, 59 ["Jidi zhuan"].
16. The Hall of Light was considered among the most ritually significant of buildings in ancient China, and its construction was regarded as the mark of a true king; see, for example, *Mengzi*, 36–37 ["Liang Huiwang xia" 梁惠王下], *Liji*, 839–58 ["Mingtang wei" 明堂位]; and *Da Dai Liji*, 149–52 ["Mingtang" 明堂].

reason why it is appropriate. He takes the accumulated worries of Metal and turns them to Water: that is the third reason why it is appropriate. Distinctions are maintained between ruler and vassals, and neither side has lost their principles: that is the fourth reason why it is appropriate. When the monarch and prime minister stand together, the world will be settled: that is the fifth reason why it is appropriate. I think Your Majesty should quickly ascend to the Hall of Light and oversee your government."

The king of Yue established his government on this day and was careful in all things. When going out, he did not dare to be extravagant; when coming in, he did not dare to be reckless. The king of Yue always remembered his commitment to take revenge on Wu, and this was not a new pledge. He worked himself hard and racked his brains day and night. When his eyes began to close, he would prick them with thorns; when his feet got cold, he would plunge them in water.[17] In the winter, he would hold a lump of ice to his chest, while summer would find him sitting by the fire. He suffered that he might temper his ambition: he hung a gall in the doorway that he might taste it when coming in or going out so that it would be forever in his mouth. In the middle of the night, he would weep, and having wept, he would wail.[18]

是四宜。王相俱起，天下立矣，是五宜。臣願急升明堂臨政。」越王是日立政，翼翼小心，出不敢奢，入不敢侈。越王念復吳讎，非一旦也。苦身勞心，夜以接日。目臥則攻之以蓼，足寒則漬之以水。冬常抱冰，夏還握火。愁心苦志，懸膽於戶，出入嘗之，不絕於口。中夜潸泣，泣而復嘯。越王曰：「吳王好服之離體，吾欲采葛，使女工織細布，獻之以求吳王之心，於子何如？」羣臣曰：「善。」乃使國中男女入山采葛，以作黃絲之布。欲獻之，未及遣使，

---

17. *Liao* 蓼, or *Polygonum orientale*, is otherwise known in English as knotweed. See Gao Mingqian et al. (2006): 480. However, here King Goujian seems to be using the plant specifically to prod himself with, so it has been translated as the more general thorn.

18. Some editions of the *Wu Yue chunqiu* included a further line here: "Then his ministers all said: 'Why should His Majesty suffer so greatly? Taking revenge and plotting against the enemy are not something that a monarch should be concerned with; they are important matters for his ministers and subordinates.'" (於是羣臣咸曰："君王何愁心之甚？夫復讎謀敵，非君王之憂：自臣下急務也"). See, for example, Zhang Jue (2006): 214. This is derived from a quotation preserved in the *Taiping yulan*.

"The king of Wu likes his clothing to stand away from the body," the king of Yue said, "so I want to have some kudzu vines picked and have women weave this into fine cloth.[19] Then we can present it to the king of Wu to get his favorable attention. What do you think?"

"Good!" his ministers cried.

He then ordered young men and women throughout the country to go into the mountains and pick kudzu vines, and this was used to make a cloth like yellow silk. He was just about to present it, but before he had dispatched an envoy, the king of Wu sent him a letter that increased his fief—this was because he had heard that the king of Yue was doing his very best to protect his lands: he did not eat highly flavored food, nor did he wear multicolored clothes.[20] Even though he had five towers to enjoy, he had never once spent a whole day in pleasure there.[21] His lands reached to Gouyong in the east, to Zuili in the west, to Gumo in the south, and to Pingyuan in the north: more than eight hundred *li* across. The king of Yue then sent Grandee Zhong to give thanks for this grant of land, and he was armed with one hundred thousand lengths of kudzu cloth, nine buckets of sweet honey, seven staves of finely patterned bamboo, five pairs of fox skins, and ten loads of Jin bamboo.[22]

When the king of Wu received these things, he said: "Yue is a remote and backward country without any treasures, but today you have presented

吳王聞越王盡心自守，食不重味，衣不重綵，雖有五臺之遊，未嘗一日登翫，吾欲因而賜之以書，增之以封：東至於勾、甬，西至於檇李，南至於姑末，北至於平原，縱橫八百餘里。越王乃使大夫種索葛布十萬，甘蜜九黨，文笴七枚，狐皮五雙，晉竹十廋，以復封禮。吳王得之，曰：「以越僻狄之國無珍，今舉其貢貨，而以復禮，此越小心念功，不忘吳之效也。夫越本興國千里，吾雖封之，未盡其國。」子胥聞之，退臥於舍，謂侍者曰：「吾君失其石室之

---

19. Cloth made from kudzu vine fibers was an important textile in ancient China, commonly used for light summer clothing; see, for example, Yang Chengjian (2003) and Xie Zong'an (2012).
20. This form of frugality was virtually proverbial in ancient and early imperial China; see, for example, *Zuozhuan*, 1608 [Ai 1], *Han Feizi*, 699 ["Waichushuo zuo xia" 外儲說左下], and *Hou Hanshu*, 80A.2599.
21. In fact, both the *Wu Yue chunqiu* and *Yuejue shu* name many more than five towers constructed by King Goujian of Yue.
22. Zhang Jue (2006): 216 n. 13 argues that Jin 晉 in the original text should be understood as *jian* 箭 (arrow).

these items to me as tribute, to make a return for my gift.[23] This shows that Yue is being careful and thoughtful: you have not forgotten what Wu has done for you. However, originally Yue was a kingdom possessing one thousand *li* of land. Even though I have granted you something, I have not yet returned all your territory to you."

[Wu] Zixu heard this. He withdrew and went to lie down in his residence, where he said to one of his attendants: "Our ruler has lost the prisoner that he kept in the stone cell; he has been released into the southern forests. But as long as he only makes use of his tiger- and leopard-infested wilds and overgrown wastelands, to my mind, he will not cause us disaster."

Having received this gift of kudzu cloth, the king of Wu again increased the land granted to Yue, and he bestowed [on King Goujian] a feather banner, an armrest, a walking stick, and the robes of a member of the aristocracy of the Central States.[24] The kingdom of Yue was overjoyed.

A woman who had gone out to pick kudzu vines felt great pity for the king of Yue's suffering in looking after everyone, and so she composed the "Song of Bitterness." This went as follows:

> The kudzu flowers and stems grow in a lush sprawl,
> Our lord has suffered: his destiny has changed him.

囚，縱於南林之中。今但因虎豹之野，而與荒外之草。於吾之心，其無損也。」吳王得葛布之獻，乃復增越之封，賜羽毛之飾、機杖、諸侯之服。越國大悅。采葛之婦傷越王用心之苦，乃作苦之詩，曰：「葛不連蔓棻台台，我君心苦命更之。嘗膽不苦甘如飴，令我采葛以作絲。女工織兮不敢遲，弱於羅兮輕霏霏，號絺素兮將獻之。越王悅兮忘罪除，吳王歡兮飛尺書。增封益地賜羽奇，機杖茵褥諸侯儀。群臣拜舞天顏舒，我王何憂能不移！」於是越王內修

---

23. The original text reads *di* 狄 (barbaric). This translation follows the commentary by Xu Tianhu (1999): 130 in reading this as *xia* 狋 (remote). Alternatively, Lu Wenchao, whose commentary is quoted in Zhang Jue (2006): 216 n. 15, suggests that it should be read *ti* 逖 (far away).

24. According to *Liji*, 15 ["Quli shang" 曲禮上], the armrest and walking stick were appropriate gifts to be given to someone over the age of seventy. It is, however, extremely unlikely that King Goujian of Yue was anything like this old.

When tasting gall he does not find it bitter, but as sweet as molasses,[25]
He has ordered us to pick kudzu to make cloth.
[Although hungry, there is no time to eat: their four limbs are exhausted],[26]
The women weavers work hard, not daring to delay.
It is as fine as gauze, as light as the breeze,
We call this 'Plain Vine Silk,' and we are ready to present it.
The king of Yue is delighted: he has no crime to atone for,
The king of Wu is pleased: and a letter is quickly returned.
He has given us more lands, and bestowed rare feathers,
A table and a walking stick, seating cushions in aristocratic style.
Monarch and ministers bow and dance their gratitude: the royal countenance relaxes,
What worry can our king have, that can fail to be assuaged?[27]

Then the king of Yue rectified his virtue on the inside and proclaimed his Way on the outside. The king did not think that he was "instructing" anyone,

其德，外布其道。君不名教，臣不名謀，民不名使，官不名事。國中蕩蕩，無有政令。越王內實府庫，墾其田疇。民富國彊，眾安道泰。越王遂師八臣，與其四友，時問政焉。大夫種曰：「愛民而已。」越王曰：「奈何？」種曰：「利之無害，成之無敗，生之無殺，與之無奪。」越王曰：「願聞。」種曰：「無奪民所好，則利也。民不失其時，則成之。省刑去罰，則生之。薄其賦歛，則與之。無多臺遊，則樂之。靜而無苛，則喜之。民失所好，則害之。農失其

---

25. *Yi* 飴 refers to a malt sugar derived from barley; see *Shuowen jiezi*, 5B.218, and Li Zhihuan (1990): 35–59. This term is here rendered as molasses, though this is not entirely accurate.

26. This missing line *ji bu huang shi, siti pi* 飢不遑食四體疲 is derived from the commentary on "Yingzhao shi" 應詔詩 (A Poem Written by Imperial Command), by Cao Zhi 曹植 (192–232) preserved in *Wenxuan*, 20.266. Some scholars have suggested that this line is not necessarily derived from this text, since the *Wenxuan* 文選 (Selections of Refined Literature) attributes it to a text named the *Wu Yue ji* 吳越記 (Records of Wu and Yue); however, Zhang Jue (2006): 217 n. 22 argues that it was indeed lost from this *Wu Yue chunqiu* song.

27. The rhymes in this song follow the pattern AAAA, then there are three lines where the text is generally agreed to be corrupt, then the pattern resumes as follows: ABBCCBC. In this song, the A rhymes are taken from the group *-ə (*zhi* 之), the B rhymes from *-a (*yu* 魚), and the C rhymes from *-ai (*ge* 歌).

the ministers did not imagine that they were "planning" anything, the people did not think they were "serving" the monarch, the government officials did not consider that they were "supporting" the administration.[28] The country flourished without government commands.[29] The king of Yue filled his storehouses and treasuries; his fields were under cultivation; the people were rich; and the country was strong, its populace at peace and well administered. The king of Yue then accepted advice from his eight ministers and four comrades in arms; and from time to time, he asked them about matters of state.

"You must love the people, and that is all," Grandee Zhong said.

"How?" the king of Yue asked.

"Allow them to benefit, and do not harm them; allow them to succeed, and do not ruin them; allow them to live, and do not kill them," Zhong replied. "You must give and not take."

"I would like to hear about this," the king of Yue said.

"If you do not take away the things that people like, then you have benefited them," Zhong replied. "If people have been able to keep to the seasonal cycle, then you have allowed them to succeed. If you reduce punishments and get rid of fines, then you give them a means to preserve their lives. If you lighten the taxes and levies on them, it is as if you are giving them a gift. If you do not increase the number of your towers and go on endless excursions, then you will bring joy to them. If you are calm and not harsh, then you will delight them. If people lose the things that they like, you have harmed them. If farmers cannot keep to the seasonal cycle, then you have ruined them. If those who are guilty of a crime are not pardoned, then you will end up killing them. If taxes and levies are onerous, then you

時，則敗之。有罪不赦，則殺之。重賦厚斂，則奪之。多作臺遊以罷民，則苦之。勞擾民力，則怒之。臣聞善為國者，遇民如父母之愛其子，如兄之愛其弟。聞有飢寒，為之哀。見其勞苦，為之悲。」越王乃緩刑薄罰，省其賦斂。於是人民殷富，皆有帶甲之勇。

九年正月，越王召五大夫而告之曰：「昔者，越國遁棄宗廟，身為窮虜，恥聞天下，辱流諸侯。今寡人念吳，猶躄者不忘走，盲者不忘視。孤未知策

---

28. *Jiao* 教 (instructing) has strong overtones of Confucian moral endeavor. In this passage, the author seems to be dismissing any claim of moral value or high-flown rhetoric applied to what King Goujian of Yue achieved with his government.

29. Zhang Jue (2006): 330 interprets this line as criticism of King Goujian's government; this is not the case.

are making your people suffer. Meanwhile, if you increase the number of towers you have and go on one excursion after another to the detriment of your people, you make them suffer. If you exhaust your people's strength, you will enrage them.[30] I have heard that a person who does well by his country treats his people with the same love that parents show toward their children or older brothers toward their younger brothers. When you hear that people are starving or cold, then you should feel sorry for them. When you see that they are working hard and suffering, you should feel sympathy for them."

The king of Yue accordingly relaxed punishments and reduced fines, cutting taxes and levies. Then the people flourished, and they all plucked up their courage to do battle.

In the first month of the ninth year [488 BCE], the king of Yue summoned his five grandees and informed them: "In the past, the ancestral shrines of the kingdom of Yue were abandoned, and I was taken prisoner. Our shame is known throughout the world, and my humiliation has been recounted to all the other lords. My feelings toward Wu can be compared to those of a cripple who has not forgotten that he used to be able to walk or a blind person who has not forgotten that he used to be able to see. However, I have no plan for how to proceed, so I hope that you gentlemen will instruct me."

"There is no one in the world today who is ignorant of the fact that at one time our country was destroyed and our people were forced to become refugees," Futong said. "However, if you now want to plan your revenge, it is not appropriate to speak openly of this in advance. I have heard it said that when a raptor strikes, it will first deliberately make itself appear weak; when a predator is about to attack, it will certainly appear unthreatening. When an eagle is going to attack, it will fly low with its wings close to its

謀，惟大夫誨之。」扶同曰：「昔者亡國流民，天下莫不聞知。今欲有計，不宜前露其辭。臣聞擊鳥之動，故前俯伏。猛獸將擊，必餌毛帖伏。鷙鳥將搏，必卑飛戢翼。聖人將動，必順辭和眾。聖人之謀，不可見其象，不可知其情。臨事而伐，故前無剽過之兵，後無伏襲之患。今大王臨敵破吳，宜損少辭，無令泄也。臣聞吳王兵彊於齊、晉，而怨結於楚。大王宜親於齊，深結於晉，陰固於楚，而厚事於吳。夫吳之誌猛，驕而自矜，必輕諸侯，而淩鄰國。三

---

30. As noted by Xu Tianhu (1999): 132, the parallelism of this section of the text is not complete. This may be the result of corruption.

body. When a sage makes his plans, no one can see what he is up to, and no one knows what he feels about things. When everything has been arranged and he attacks, he does not have insubordinate troops in front of him, nor does he have to worry about the threat of ambushes behind him. Today Your Majesty hopes to prepare to fight against your enemies and crush Wu, so you should speak as little as possible about this, to prevent news leaking out. I have heard that the army of the king of Wu is stronger than that of either Qi or Jin and that he has profoundly angered Chu. Your Majesty should make friends with Qi and form a strong alliance with Jin while secretly affirming your relationship with Chu and treating Wu with generosity. With the ambitions shown by [King Fuchai of] Wu, he will behave with cruelty and arrogance while being completely self-satisfied; furthermore, he is sure to treat other rulers with distain while despising neighboring states. If these three countries decide their power is such that they can go back to showing open enmity, they will certainly realize that they can fight on equal terms. Yue can take advantage of [Wu's] attention being turned elsewhere to attack them, and we will be sure to win. Even with the armies of the Five Sovereigns, it would be impossible to beat us."

"I have heard it said that when plotting against another country and wanting to crush your enemies, you should determine the moment of action by observing the auspices," Fan Li said. "At the meeting at Mengjin, the other lords said that the time was ripe, and yet King Wu refused to act.[31] It is a fact that Wu and Chu are now sworn enemies, and their hatred has not abated. However, even though Qi is not friendly with Wu, they will support them outside; even though Jin is not subordinated to them, they will still follow their lead. As long as their ministers scheme and plot against their

國決權，還為敵國，必角勢交爭。越承其弊，因而伐之，可克也。雖五帝之兵，無以過此。」范蠡曰：「臣聞謀國破敵，動觀其符。孟津之會，諸侯曰可，武王辭之。方今吳、楚結讎，構怨不解。齊雖不親，外為其救。晉雖不附，猶效其義。夫內臣謀而決讎其策，鄰國通而不絕其援，斯正吳之興霸，諸侯之上尊。臣聞峻高者隳，葉茂者摧，日中則移，月滿則虧。四時不並盛，五行不俱馳。陰陽更唱，氣有盛衰。故溢堤之水，不淹其量。燔乾之火，不復

---

31. According to various ancient texts, prior to his attack on the Shang, King Wu met with his supporters at Mengjin, a place-name that literally means "Covenant Ford" and that was so called in commemoration of this event; see, for example, *Zuozhuan*, 1250 [Zhao 4], *Shiji*, 16.759, and *Chunqiu fanlu*, 107 ["Wangdao" 王道].

enemies and as long as neighboring countries remain allied and support them, Wu will continue their hegemony, and they will be the most respected of all the lords. However, I have heard that when a mountain is too tall, it will collapse, and when leaves have flourished, they must fall. The sun reaches its meridian and then sets, the moon waxes and wanes. The four seasons cannot flourish simultaneously, while the Five Elements cannot all succeed each other. *Yin* and *yang* preside in turn; *qi* rises and falls. But the waters that overflow the dike cannot restrain their might, and the flames that lap at the dry wood cannot return to being a mere spark. If the waters are peaceful, there are no violent waves to engulf and flood the land, and if the fire has been extinguished, there is no heat to singe a feather. Today Wu takes advantage of the fears of the other lords to issue orders to the world: they have not realized that when you behave with little virtue, you will receive but small gratitude in return; limited morality generates great hostility; arbitrary powers lead to loss of good sense; exhausted strength leads to reduction of might; lax soldiers lead to the army being forced to retreat; and when officers run away, the rabble will follow. I ask permission to train up an army and wait for them to be defeated. I will follow and launch a surprise attack on them. Their troops will not fight, nor will their officers pause in their flight, and so the ruler and ministers of Wu will be our prisoners. I hope that you, Your Majesty, will keep quiet about this and not allow your actions to be observed, so that we can watch for their failure."

"Water can enable a plant or a tree to float, but it can also sink them," Grandee Kucheng said. "Land can provide sustenance for myriad life-forms, but it can also kill them. Rivers and seas can flow into gulfs and bays, but they can also flood them. A wise man can follow the masses, but he can also lead them. Today Wu enjoys the benefits of the military regulations established by King Helü, and the moral instruction offered by [Wu] Zixu; hence, the government proceeds peacefully and has not collapsed, while the army wins battles without suffering defeat. However, Grandee [Bo] Pi is a wicked and deceitful man; he is highly accomplished at his stratagems and schemes, while neglecting matters of state. Zixu's power has waxed in time

其熾。水靜則無漚瀺之怒，火消則無熹毛之熱。今吳乘諸侯之威，以號令於天下，不知德薄而恩淺，道狹而怨廣，權懸而智衰，力竭而威折，兵挫而軍退，士散而眾解。臣請按師整兵，待其壞敗，隨而襲之。兵不血刃，士不旋踵，吳之君臣為虜矣。臣願大王匿聲，無見其動，以觀其靜。」大夫苦成曰：「夫水能浮草木，亦能沉之。地能生萬物，亦能殺之。江海能下谿谷，亦能朝之。聖人能從眾，亦能使之。今吳承闔閭之軍制，子胥之典教，政平未虧，戰勝

of warfare and trouble, but he will die thanks to the unpalatable remonstrance and advice that he offers. As long as these two men hold power, there is sure to be ruin and defeat. I hope that Your Majesty will pretend to go along with them, not allowing them to perceive our plans, for then Wu can be destroyed."

"Today in Wu, the ruler is arrogant, and his ministers are extravagant, while his people are overfed and his army recklessly brave," Grandee Hao said.[32] "They have enemies ready to invade their borders outside the country, but inside, the government is rocked by disputes among ministers. They can be attacked."

"Heaven has four seasons and man has five powers," Grandee Gaoru said.[33] "In the past, Tang and King Wu took advantage of the benefits offered by the cycle of the four seasons to establish the Xia and the Yin dynasties.[34] Lord Huan [of Qi] and Lord Mu [of Qin] took control of the five powers and thus held authority over the myriad states.[35] This means that one who can take advantage of these natural cycles will be victorious."

"I have not yet been able to gain any benefit from the cycle of the four seasons, nor have things been eased for me by the five powers," His Majesty said. "Let us each return to our own work."

未敗。大夫嚭者，狂佞之人，達於策慮，輕於朝事。子胥力於戰伐，死於諫議。二人權，必有壞敗。願王虛心自匱，無示謀計，則吳可滅矣。」大夫浩曰：「今吳君驕臣奢，民飽軍勇，外有侵境之敵，內有爭臣之震，其可攻也。」大夫句如曰：「天有四時，人有五勝。昔湯、武乘四時之利，而制夏、殷，桓、繆據五勝之便，而列六國。此乘其時而勝者也。」王曰：「未有四時之利，五勝之便，願各就職也。」

---

32. Elsewhere in the *Wu Yue chunqiu*, this name is given as Grandee Hao 大夫皓.
33. The original text names this individual as Gouru 勾如; elsewhere in the *Wu Yue chunqiu*, he is called Gaoru 皋如.
34. In fact, King Wu established the Zhou dynasty, and not the Yin.
35. Lord Mu of Qin ruled from 659 to 621 BCE and is frequently numbered among the five hegemons—the most powerful rulers of the Spring and Autumn period; see, for example, *Shiji*, 5:185–95.

Chapter Nine

The Outer Traditions
The Story of King Goujian's Conspiracy

It was the second month of the tenth year of the reign of King Goujian of Yue [487 BCE]. This monarch, having thought carefully and weighed up all his options, chose to go and suffer humiliation in Wu; and thanks to the blessings of Heaven, he was able [to return] to the kingdom of Yue.[1] His ministers had received his instructions, and each came up with a plan, and having discussed them fully until they were agreed, King Goujian then respectfully followed their advice; his country had already prospered thereby. Five years after his return to Yue, however, he still did not have any comrades in arms who would risk death on his behalf. Perhaps you can

《勾踐陰謀外傳》

越王勾踐十年二月，越王深念遠思：侵辱於吳，蒙天祉福，得越國。羣臣教誨，各畫一策，辭合意同，勾踐敬從，其國已富。反越五年，未聞敢死之友。或謂諸大夫愛其身，惜其軀者。乃登漸臺，望觀其羣臣有憂與否。相國范蠡、大夫種、句如之屬，儼然列坐，雖懷憂患，不形顏色。越王即鳴鍾驚檄，而召羣臣，與之盟曰：「寡人獲辱受恥，上愧周王，下慚晉、楚。幸蒙諸大夫之策，得返國修政，富民養士。而五年未聞敢死之士，雪仇之臣，奈何而有功乎？」

---

1. This translation follows Xu Tianhu (1999): 136 in adding the character *fan* 返 (to return) to this line.

say that the various grandees begrudged their persons and did not want to risk their own lives. Therefore, His Majesty climbed the Jian Tower, and looking over his various ministers, he observed whether they seemed concerned or not.[2] The prime minister, Fan Li, and Grandees Zhong, Gaoru, and their ilk sat in strict order; although they were no doubt concerned, it did not show in their faces or manner. The king of Yue then sounded a bell and made a warning proclamation, summoning his ministers to make a covenant with him.[3]

"I have suffered humiliation and experienced great pain," he said. "I am ashamed before the Zhou king above and embarrassed before Jin and Chu below. Thanks to your plans, gentlemen, I have been able to return to my country and reform the government, enriching the people and raising up fine knights. However, even after five years, I lack any officers who would risk death in my service, not to mention ministers determined to wipe out this shame—how can you be said to be contributing anything to my cause?"

Those present were silent, and nobody replied. The king of Yue looked up at the sky, sighed and said: "I have heard that good ministers think it a humiliation that their lord should be worried and die to prevent their ruler from being shamed. Now I have personally experienced the perils of being a prisoner of war and a slave, not to mention the horrors of imprisonment and ruin, and I could do nothing to help myself. I placed wise men in positions of power and employed the benevolent, in the hope of being able to punish Wu at some point in the future: this is a heavy charge on my ministers. Why

羣臣默然莫對者。越王仰天歎曰：「孤聞主憂臣辱，主辱臣死。今孤親被奴虜之厄，受囚破之恥，不能自輔，須賢任仁，然後討吳，重負諸臣。大夫何易見而難使也？」於是，計硯年少官卑，列坐於後，乃舉手而趨，蹈席而前進曰：「謬哉，君王之言也！非大夫易見而難使，君王之不能使也。」越王曰：「何謂？」計硯曰：「夫官位、財幣、金賞者，君之所輕也。操鋒履刃，艾命投死者，士之所重也。今王易財之所輕，而責士之所重，何其殆哉？」於是

---

2. Zhang Jue (2006): 225 n. 3 suggests that Jian Towers 漸臺 (a name frequently seen in ancient texts pertaining to structures in various different countries and historical eras) referred specifically to towers built near water; see, for example, *Shiji*, 12.482, *Xinxu*, 286 ["Zashi" 2], and *Lunheng*, 158 ["Yuzeng" 語增].
3. This translation follows Xu Tianhu (1999): 136 in reading *jing* 驚 (to be frightened) as *jing* 警 (to warn).

is it that you are quick to have an audience with me, gentlemen, but unwilling to be employed in my service?"[4]

At this point Jini, a young and junior official seated in the very back row, rushed forward, raising his hands and stumbling over his seating mat.

"How wrong and stupid are your words, Your Majesty!" he said. "It is not that your grandees are happy to have an audience with you but unwilling to be employed in your service; it is that Your Majesty is incapable of using us!"[5]

"What do you mean?" the king of Yue asked.

"Rulers don't take seriously such matters as official rank, salary, and rewards," Jini replied. "On the other hand, army officers are very frightened when they have to hold lances and advance against swords, risking their very lives. Now you, Your Majesty, are trying to control unimportant matters of finance while taxing knights with very serious tasks; this is indeed dangerous!"

The king of Yue was silent and unhappy, and he looked ashamed of himself. Afterward, he dismissed his ministers and asked Jini to come forward. "How can I obtain the allegiance of knights?" he asked.

"A ruler should respect those who are benevolent and just," Jini answered. "This is the gate to good government. Officials and the people are foundation stones for the ruler. If you wish to open up this gate and make these foundation stones stand firm, you will have to rectify yourself. The way to rectify yourself lies in careful selection of those around you. The reason why a ruler flourishes or fails rests in the persons who surround him. I hope

越王默然不悅，面有愧色。即辭羣臣，進計硯而問曰：「孤之所得士心者何等？」計硯對曰：「夫君人尊其仁義者，治之門也。士民者，君之根也。開門固根，莫如正身。正身之道，謹左右。左右者，君之所以盛衰者也。願王明選左右，得賢而已。昔太公九聲而足，磻溪之餓人也，西伯任之而王。管仲，魯之亡囚，有貪分之毀，齊桓得之而霸。故傳曰：失士者亡，得士者昌。願王審於左右，何患羣臣之不使也？」越王曰：「吾使賢任能，各殊其事。孤虛心高望，

---

4. This translation follows the commentary by Yu Yue (1902): 18.6a in reading *jian* 見 (to have an audience) as *de* 得 (to obtain the services of someone; here "to come to work").

5. Again, following the commentary by Yu Yue (1902): 18.6b, *yi* 易 is read as *de* 得 in this line.

that Your Majesty will select your staff according to enlightened principles, employing the wise and no one else. In the past, Taigong [was ninety years old but had achieved nothing in his life].[6] He was starving beside the Pan Stream, and yet the Western Lord Protector gave him a job, and thus, he became king. Guan Zhong was in exile and held prisoner in Lu, his reputation in tatters thanks to his greed, and yet Lord Huan of Qi employed him. That is how he became hegemon.[7] Therefore, the saying goes: 'He who loses his knights dies; he who gains them will flourish.' I hope that you, Your Majesty, will investigate those in your personal service, for then why should you worry that your ministers will not obey your orders?"

"I have employed the wise and used the able in my service," the king of Yue said, "but each has gone his own way over what he was tasked to do. I have waited impatiently, hoping to hear news of some plan for how we will take revenge on Wu. Now everyone hushes their voices and hides their faces—I never get to hear their words. Whose fault is that?"

"When it comes to selecting wise men," Jini replied, "and discovering the true abilities of knights, it is very much the same thing. Send them far away to resolve difficult problems: then you can test their sincerity. Bring them into the palace, and inform them of secrets: then you can know whether they are trustworthy. Give them topics to debate: then you can observe their wisdom. Get them drunk on wine: then you can watch them off guard. Give them tallies when they are sent on missions: then you can check their

冀聞報復之謀。今咸匿聲隱形，不聞其語，厥咎安在？」計硯曰：「選賢實士，各有一等。遠使以難，以效其誠。內告以匿，以知其信。與之論事，以觀其智。飲之以酒，以視其亂。指之以使，以察其能。示之以色，以別其態。五色以設，士盡其實，人竭其智。知其智盡實，則君臣何憂？」越王曰：「吾以謀士效實，人盡其智，而士有未盡進辭有益寡人也。」計硯曰：「范蠡明而知內，文種遠以見外。願王請大夫種與深議，則霸王之術在矣。」越王乃請大夫種而問曰：

---

6. This line does not make sense in the original text. As indicated by Xu Tianhu (1999): 137, this is likely to be the result of textual corruption. Zhang Jue (2006): 227 n. 2 suggests replacing this with the line: *Taigong jiushi er wu fa* 太公九十而不伐 (Taigong was ninety and had achieved nothing in his life) from *Yuejue shu*, 70 ["Waizhuan Jini" 外傳計倪].

7. The difficulties of Guan Zhong's life before he was accepted into the service of Lord Huan of Qi are recorded in many ancient texts; see, for example, *Shiji*, 62.2131–32, and *Guanzi*, 330–49 ["Dakuang" 大匡].

abilities. Show them beautiful women: then you can distinguish their characters. When each characteristic has been explored, knights will appear in their true colors, your people will have put forth their best intellectual efforts, and you know that their good advice is tried and tested. Why should you be worried?"

"Even if I have discovered the true colors of my advisers and my people have put forth their best intellectual efforts," the king of Yue pointed out, "there may yet be knights who have not said everything they could concerning matters that would be of benefit to me."

"Fan Li is a clever man who knows the situation inside the country," Jini responded, "and Wen Zhong is farsighted in dealing with foreign affairs. I hope that you, Your Majesty, will invite Grandee Zhong to discuss the matter seriously with you, for then the necessary skills of a hegemon-king will be assured."

Accordingly, the king of Yue summoned Grandee Zhong and asked, "In the past, thanks to your advice, sir, I was able to extract myself from a difficult and dangerous situation. Now I hope that you can provide me with a scheme—not constrained by moral qualms—which will allow me to avenge the humiliations heaped on me. What can I do to accomplish this?"

"I have heard it said that a bird flying high up in the sky can be brought down by attractive food, while a fish at the bottom of a deep gulf can be attracted by tasty bait," Grandee Zhong answered. "Now if you want to attack Wu, you must first find out what it is that they want and investigate their desires, for after that you can obtain their property."

"When it comes to human desires, even if you know what they truly want, how can you use this to kill them?" the king of Yue asked.

"If you want to take revenge and expunge your humiliations, to destroy Wu and crush your enemies," Grandee Zhong said, "then there are nine techniques that will bring this about. Your Majesty should consider them."

"I have suffered pain and humiliation," the king of Yue replied, "being shamed before my ministers inside the country and before the other lords

「吾昔日受夫子之言，自免於窮厄之地。今欲奉不羈之計，以雪吾之宿讎，何行而功乎？」大夫種曰：「臣聞高飛之鳥，死於美食。深泉之魚，死於芳餌。今欲伐吳，必前求其所好，參其所願，然後能得其實。」越王曰：「人之所好，雖其願，何以定而制之死乎？」大夫種曰：「夫欲報怨復讎，破吳滅敵者，有九術，君王察焉？」越王曰：「寡人被辱懷憂，內慚朝臣，外愧諸侯，中心迷惑，精神空虛。雖有九術，安能知之？」大夫種曰：「夫九術者。湯、

outside—my mind is confused and my spirit lost. Even if there are these nine techniques, how can I learn about them?"

"Thanks to these nine skills," Grandee Zhong said, "Tang and Wen became kings, while Lord Huan [of Qi] and Lord Mu [of Qin] became hegemons: they make attacking cities and conquering towns as easy as kicking off their shoes. I hope that you, Your Majesty, will study them.[8] The first is respecting Heaven and serving the ghosts [and spirits], to seek blessings from them.[9] The second is giving valuable gifts to their ruler, while handing out generous bribes to delight their ministers. The third is paying a high price for grain, food, and fodder for animals to empty out their country, using their greed to weaken their people. The fourth involves presenting their monarch with beautiful women to bewitch his heart and confuse his plans. The fifth is giving them fine timbers that have been cunningly worked, to get them to build palaces and halls, thus exhausting their wealth. The sixth is encouraging sycophantic ministers, making them easy to attack. The seventh is removing ministers who offer remonstrance, placing them in positions where they will be forced to commit suicide. The eighth is enriching both Your Majesty and the country as a whole so that you can prepare your own weapons. The ninth is to stockpile good arms and armor, to take advantage of their impoverishment. With these nine techniques, as long as you keep your mouth closed and do not tell anyone, protecting this secret with your life, it would not be difficult to conquer the entire world, let alone Wu!"

"Wonderful!" cried the king of Yue.

He then employed the first technique, establishing a suburban altar in the east to perform sacrifices to *yang*, under the name "August Lord of

文得之以王,桓、穆得之以霸。其攻城取邑,易於脫屣。願大王覽之。」種曰:「一曰尊天事鬼,以求其福。二曰重財幣,以遺其君;多貨賄,以喜其臣。三曰貴糴粟藁,以虛其國;利所欲,以疲其民。四曰遺美女,以惑其心,而亂其謀。五曰遺之巧工良材,使之起宮室,以盡其財。六曰遺之諛臣,使之易伐。七曰彊其諫臣,使之自殺。八曰君王國富,而備利器。九曰利甲兵,以承其弊。凡此九術,君王閉口無傳,守之以神,取天下不難,而況於吳乎?」越

---

8. The original text here reads Dafu 大夫 (Grandee), but since Wen Zhong is speaking to King Goujian, it should be read as the epithet *dawang* 大王: "Your Majesty." See Xu Tianhu (1999): 152–53 n. 6.

9. As noted by Xu Tianhu (1999): 139, the word *gui* 鬼 (ghosts) in this line lacks its complement, *shen* 神 (spirits).

the East."¹⁰ He established a suburban altar in the west to perform sacrifices to *yin*, under the name "Queen Mother of the West."¹¹ He sacrificed to the mountains at Kuaiji; he prayed to the rivers and marshes at Jiangzhou.¹² Thus, he served the ghosts and spirits for two years, and the country did not suffer any natural disasters.

"How excellent your technique is, sir!" the king of Yue said. "I would like to hear more about the remainder."

"The king of Wu enjoys building palaces and halls, and he employs his workforce without any rest," Zhong replied. "You should select the finest timbers, Your Majesty, from the most famous mountains, and present them to him."

The king of Yue then ordered more than three thousand woodcutters to enter the mountains and cut down trees. After one year, his master craftsmen had not found one piece they liked. The woodcutters wanted to go home, and they were all angry and resentful, so they sang "The Plaint of Travelers in the Woods." One night, Heaven made a pair of miraculous trees appear, twenty *wei* in girth by fifty *xun* in length.¹³ One was a catalpa,

王曰：「善。」乃行第一術，立東郊以祭陽，名曰東皇公。立西郊以祭陰，名曰西王母。祭陵山於會稽，祀水澤於江州。事鬼神一年，國不被災。越王曰：「善哉，大夫之術！願論其餘。」種曰：「吳王好起宮室，用工不輟。王選名山神材，奉而獻之。」越王乃使木工三千餘人，入山伐木。一年，師無所幸。作士思歸，皆有怨望之心，而歌木客之吟。一夜，天生神木一雙，大二十圍，長五十尋。陽為文梓，陰為梗枏。巧工施校，制以規繩。雕治圓轉，刻削磨礱。

---

10. This appears to be the earliest reference to this deity, also known as Dong wanggong 東王公 (King Father of the East), in Chinese literature.
11. The Queen Mother of the West is an ancient deity recorded in many early texts; see, for example, *Mu Tianzi zhuan*, 3.15–16, and *Shanhai jing*, 59–60 ["Xishan jing" 西山經]. Interestingly, on Eastern Han dynasty bronze mirrors from the Wu-Yue region, there are a number of examples that show the Queen Mother of the West in conjunction with scenes from the history of these two kingdoms and one that shows both the King Father of the East and the Queen Mother of the West; see Milburn (2013): 144–68 and Chou (2000): 48.
12. As noted by Xu Tianhu (1999): 139–40, no place of this name is known within the borders of the ancient kingdom of Yue.
13. These two trees would be just under one hundred meters tall but only two meters in circumference; see Wu Chengluo (1984).

and the other a nanmu tree. Clever craftsmen measured them, shaping them with compass and plumb line, carving them into perfect shape, polishing and planning, before decorating them with brightly colored paintwork. They were adorned with patterns, inlaid with white jade discs, and encrusted with gold, in designs of dragons and serpents, so fresh that they shone. Then [King Goujian] had Grandee Zhong present them to the king of Wu, with the following words: "Your humble servant by the East Sea, Goujian, sends his vassal, Zhong, who dares to communicate with your entourage through the medium of junior officials: Thanks to Your Majesty's power, I have been able to construct a small residence for myself, and I have some leftover timbers. I respectfully bow twice and present them to you."

The king of Wu was very pleased, but [Wu] Zixu remonstrated with him: "You must not accept them, Your Majesty! In the past, Jie built the Numinous Tower and Zhou constructed the Deer Tower, and so *yin* and *yang* were not in harmony, cold weather and hot came out of season, Heaven sent down natural disasters, the people were exhausted, and the country suffered civil war; then they died.[14] If you accept them, the king of Yue will destroy you."

The king of Wu did not listen and accepted them—he built the Gusu Tower with them. It took three years to assemble the materials and a further five years to complete the construction, for it was high enough to see two hundred *li* from the top. People passing by along the roads noted the corpses by the wayside and the weeping coming from the alleys: the sound of sighing was constant. The people were exhausted, and the gentry suffered bitterly—nobody found it easy to survive.

分以丹青，錯畫文章。嬰以白璧，鏤以黃金。狀類龍蛇，文彩生光。乃使大夫種獻之於吳王，曰：「東海役臣，臣孤勾踐，使臣種敢因下吏，聞於左右：賴大王之力，竊為小殿，有餘材，謹再拜獻之。」吳王大悅。子胥諫曰：「王勿受也。昔者桀起靈臺，紂起鹿臺，陰陽不和，寒暑不時，五穀不熟，天與其災，民虛國變，遂取滅亡。大王受之，必為越王所戮。」吳王不聽，遂受而起姑蘇之臺。三年聚材，五年乃成，高見二百里。行路之人，道死巷哭，

---

14. This passage is derived from *Yuejue shu*, 83 ["Jiushu"]. As noted by all commentators, the reference to the Lingtai 靈臺 (Numinous Tower), supposedly built by the evil King Jie of the Xia dynasty, is unique to these two texts.

"How amazing is this second technique!" the king of Yue said.

In the eleventh year of his reign [486 BCE], the king of Yue, having thought deeply on the subject as he always did, was determined to attack Wu. Therefore, he invited Jini to the palace and asked him: "I want to attack Wu, but I am afraid that I will not be able to crush them. I hope to raise an army as soon as possible; therefore, I have to ask you for advice."

"If you wish to raise an army and mobilize your forces," Jini replied, "you must cultivate the five grains, stockpile gold and silver, fill your storehouses and treasuries, and improve your arms and armor. Having achieved these four things, then you must investigate the *qi* of Heaven and Earth, understand the principle of *yin* and *yang*, clarify *gu* and *xu*, and consider life and death, for then you can weigh up the enemy."[15]

"Of Heaven and Earth, life and death, which is the most important?" the king of Yue asked.

"The *qi* of Heaven and Earth is the reason why things live and die," Jini replied. "The principle of *yin* and *yang* is the reason why creatures are noble and base. Clarifying *gu* and *xu* allows you to understand connections. Considering life and death allows you to distinguish the truth from falsehood."

"What do you mean by living and dying and by truth and falsehood?" the king of Yue asked.

"In spring, you plant the eight grains; in summer, you cultivate them and let them grow; in autumn, once they are ripe, you harvest them; and in winter, you store them up," Jini said. "According to the seasons of Heaven,

不絕嗟嘻之聲。民疲士苦，人不聊生。越王曰：「善哉，第二術也！」十一年，越王深念永思，惟欲伐吳，乃請計硯問曰：「吾欲伐吳，恐不能破。早欲興師，惟問於子。」計硯對曰：「夫興師舉兵，必且內蓄五穀，實其金銀，滿其府庫，勵其甲兵。凡此四者，必察天地之氣，原於陰陽，明於孤虛，審於存亡，乃可量敵。」越王曰：「天地存亡，其要奈何？」計硯曰：「天地之氣，物有死生。原陰陽者，物貴賤也。明孤虛者，知會際也。審存亡者，別真偽也。」越王曰：

---

15. The terms *gu* 孤 and *xu* 虛 imply a rectification of the calendar. When certain Stem and Branch combinations fell within particular cycles of the ten-day *xun* 旬, it was considered to be comparatively inauspicious because the day was "incomplete"; see *Shiji*, 128.3237 n. 5.

[spring] gives life, but if you do not sow—that is the first death.[16] In summer, as the crops grow, if you prevent them from setting out shoots—that is the second death. In autumn, when the crops are ripe, if you do not harvest them—that is the third death. In winter, if your stores are bare—that is the fourth death. Even if you are as virtuous as Yao or Shun, there is no one who can escape these basic principles. To grow things in the right season, with the advice of the elderly and the manpower provided by the younger people, following what is appropriate and making sure that the right kind of plants are being cultivated properly—that is the first way to preserve life. Paying attention and looking closely, distinguishing carefully between weeds and crops, and removing the weeds so that the shoots will flourish—that is the second way to preserve life. Making preparations in advance, reaping when the time is right, so that no one refuses to pay their taxes, and no one is left without a harvest—that is the third way to preserve life. Once the granaries have been sealed with mud, once the old has been swept away to be replaced with new, then the ruler is happy, his vassals enjoy themselves, and everyone has faith in each other—that is the fourth way to preserve life. As for *yin* and *yang*, this refers to the constellation in which Counter-Jupiter rests—when it stays in the same place for three years, the noble and the base will be clearly defined.[17] As for *gu* and *xu*, these are what is called the Gate of Heaven and the Door to Earth. Meanwhile, life and death refer to the ruler's moral force and virtue."

"How can one so young know so much about things?" the king of Yue inquired.

"With a good adviser, you do not hold to issues of age," Jini replied.

"Your Way is indeed excellent!" the king of Yue said.

「何謂死生真偽乎？」計硯曰：「春種八穀，夏長而養，秋成而聚，冬畜而藏。夫天時有生，而不救種，是一死也。夏長無苗，二死也。秋成無聚，三死也。冬藏無畜，四死也。雖有堯、舜之德，無如之何。夫天時有生，勤者老，作者少，反氣應數，不失厥理，一生也。留意省察，謹除苗穢，穢除苗盛，二生也。前時設備，物至則收，國無逋稅，民無失穗，三生也。倉已封塗，除陳入新，君樂臣歡，男女及信，四生也。夫陰陽者，太陰所居之歲，留息三年，

---

16. Following the commentary by Xu Tianhu (1999): 142, *yousheng* 有生 (to have life) in the original text is understood as *chunsheng* 春生 (spring gives life).
17. This translation interprets *jian* 見 (to be seen) in the original text as *xian* 現 (to be clearly defined), following the commentary by Zhang Jue (2006): 234 n. 12.

Afterward, he raised his head to observe the heavenly constellations and investigated the movements of the five planets through the lunar lodges as that which had been low ascended. He then constructed eight granaries on an area of wasteland, taking in produce according to *yin* and sending out grain after observing *yang*, calculating everything most carefully. Over the course of three years, production quintupled, and the kingdom of Yue was gloriously wealthy.

King Goujian sighed. "Such is my hegemony!" he said. "How great was Jini's plan!"

In the twelfth year [485 BCE], the king of Yue said to Grandee Zhong: "I have heard that the king of Wu is overindulgent in sex and seeks oblivion in wine, and he does not take charge of any affairs of state.[18] If we conspire against him in this respect, will we be successful?"

"He can be destroyed," Zhong declared. "Since the king of Wu is overindulgent in sex and Chancellor Pi fawns on him to direct his thoughts, let us go and present him with beautiful women, for he is sure to accept them. You should select two beautiful women and present them, Your Majesty."

"Good!" replied the king of Yue.

He then ordered physiognomists to travel throughout the country, and they discovered the daughters of woodcutters from Zhuluo Mountain, named Xi Shi and Zheng Dan.[19] He had them dressed in gauzes and fine silks and instructed in how to make up and how to move, familiarizing them with a sophisticated lifestyle at Tucheng so that they would understand the ways of the capital.[20] After three years, their studies were completed, and he presented them to Wu.

貴賤見矣。夫孤虛者，謂天門地戶也。存亡者，君之道德也。」越王曰：「何子之年少，於物之長也？」計硯曰：「有美之士，不拘長少。」越王曰：「善哉，子之道也！」乃仰觀天文，集察緯宿，曆象四時。以下者上，虛設八倉，從陰收著，望陽出耀，筴其極計，三年五倍，越國熾富。勾踐歎曰：「吾之霸矣。」善計硯之謀也。

---

18. The unusual term used here for drinking wine is derived from *Shangshu*, 271 ["Taishi shang" 泰誓上].
19. Xi Shi is subsequently conventionally listed as one of the four great beauties in ancient China; her companion Zheng Dan is usually not mentioned.
20. The *Yuejue shu*, 59 ["Jidi zhuan"], records that this place was the site of the Meiren gong 美人宮 (Palace of Beautiful Ladies).

He ordered the prime minister, Fan Li, to step forward and say: "King Goujian of Yue has discovered these two ladies hidden away.[21] The kingdom of Yue is a remote and backward place, not to mention being extremely poor; hence, we would not dare to keep them. Therefore, he carefully instructed me to present them to Your Gracious Majesty. If you do not consider them to be too ugly and unrefined, I hope that you will employ them to hold a dustpan and brush."[22]

The king of Wu was very pleased. "Yue presents these two women—this is the proof of Goujian's total loyalty to Wu," he proclaimed.

"You cannot do this!" [Wu] Zixu remonstrated. "You must not accept them, Your Majesty! I have heard that the five colors blind the eyes, while the five notes make the ears deaf. In the past, Jie underestimated Tang and was destroyed; Zhou thought little of King Wen and died. If you accept them, you are sure to suffer disaster. I have heard that the king of Yue spends his day in study and never gets tired, and during the hours of darkness, he recites through the night—furthermore, he has gathered together tens of thousands of soldiers who will risk their lives for him: if this man does not die, he is sure to achieve his ambitions. The king of Yue acts with sincerity and treats others with benevolence; he listens to remonstrance and promotes wise men in his service: if this man does not die, he is sure to become famous. The king of Yue is wrapped in a fur cloak in the summer and wears coarse kudzu cloth in

十二年，越王謂大夫種曰：「孤聞吳王淫而好色，惑亂沉湎，不領政事。因此而謀，可乎？」種曰：「可破。夫吳王淫而好色，宰嚭佞以曳心，往獻美女，其必受之。惟王選擇美女二人而進之。」越王曰：「善。」乃使相者［工］【索】國中，得苧蘿山鬻薪之女，曰西施、鄭旦，飾以羅穀，教以容步，習於土城，臨於都巷，三年學服，而獻於吳。乃使相國范蠡進曰：「越王勾踐竊有二遺女。越國涔下困迫，不敢稽留。謹使臣蠡獻之大王不，以鄙陋寢容，願納以供箕

---

21. The term *yinü* 遺女 might also imply that the two women are being presented to the king of Wu as King Goujian's half sisters; there is considerable evidence that the text was read this way during the imperial era; see, for example, Zhang Chenshi et al. (1994): 157 ["Shibie" 施別].

22. Exactly the same term, *jizhou* 箕帚, was earlier used to describe King Goujian's service in the Wu palace; this emphasizes the way in which Yue people, from the monarch downward, used their acceptance of humiliation as a way to seek revenge.

the winter: if this man does not die, he will take his revenge."[23] I have heard it said: 'A wise knight is a national treasure, but a beautiful woman can destroy the country.' The Xia dynasty was destroyed by Mo Xi; the Yin dynasty collapsed thanks to Da Ji; and the Zhou dynasty fell because of Bao Si."[24]

The king of Wu paid no attention to him and accepted the women. "This third technique is wonderful!" the king of Yue said.

In the thirteenth year [484 BCE], the king of Yue said to Grandee Zhong, "Thanks to your techniques, every plan has gone well, and there has not been a single problem. Now I would like to proceed further with this conspiracy against Wu; what should I do?"

"Your Majesty should proclaim that the kingdom of Yue is poor and backward and that this year the grain did not ripen," Zhong said. "I suggest that you ask for famine relief to get their sympathy. If Heaven has abandoned Wu, they will certainly agree to Your Majesty's request."

Yue then sent Grandee Zhong as an ambassador to Wu, where he begged for an audience with the king of Wu through the good offices of Chancellor Pi.

"The kingdom of Yue is a remote and backward country and suffers from immoderate flooding and drought," he said. "This year, the crops did not ripen, and our people are starving—the roads are crowded with the hungry and indigent. I hope that I may request grain from Your Majesty;

帛之用。」吳王大悅，曰：「越貢二女，乃勾踐之盡忠於吳之證也。」子胥諫曰：「不可，王勿受也。臣聞五色令人目盲，五音令人耳聾。昔桀易湯而滅，紂易文王而亡。大王受之，後必有殃。臣聞越王朝書不倦，晦誦竟夜，且聚敢死之士數萬。是人不死，必得其願。越王服誠行仁，聽諫進賢。是人不死，必成其名。越王夏被毛裘，冬禦絺紵。是人不死，必為對隙。臣聞：賢士國之寶，美女國之咎。夏亡以妹喜，殷亡以妲己，周亡以褒姒。」吳王不聽，遂受其女。越王曰：「善哉，第三術也。」

---

23. The habit of wearing clothes inappropriate to the season was considered a sign of remarkable abilities in ancient China; see, for example, *Gaoshi zhuan*, 565 ["Piqiu gong" 披裘公]. See also Henry (1987).

24. The belief that these women brought about the deaths of their royal husbands and the fall of the dynasties with which they were associated seems to have been common in antiquity; see, for example, *Guoyu*, 255 ["Jinyu" 晉語 1].

next year, we will return it to your granary. I hope that you will rescue our poor and needy people."

"The king of Yue has been trustworthy and circumspect, with not the slightest sign of disloyalty," the king of Wu responded. "Now in this extremity, he has come to ask for help, so how can I begrudge this wealth and crush his hopes?"

Zixu remonstrated: "You cannot do this! If Wu does not conquer Yue, Yue will conquer Wu! Once good luck has departed, evil will come; this is how you create bandits and destroy your country and your own family. If you give them relief, they will not hold you any dearer; if you do not give it, they will not hate you more than before. Furthermore, Yue has a sagacious minister in Fan Li, whose bravery is backed up by his excellent planning ability. He is using this to cover up for his attack; he is taking this opportunity to probe our internal situation. I have looked carefully at this ambassador sent by the king of Yue to beg for food aid: this is not the way you ask for grain when the country is genuinely poor and its people in trouble. He has come to our country like this to discover Your Majesty's dispositions."

"I made the king of Yue humble himself and submit to my authority, whereupon I took possession of his people and made his state altars my own," the king of Wu said. "This was done to humiliate Goujian. He surrendered to me, and when I rode in my chariot, he walked in front of the horses—among the other rulers, there is nobody who has not heard of this. Now I have sent him back to his country, restoring his ancestral shrines, returning his altars of soil and grain; surely he would not dare to even think of rebelling against me?"

"I have heard people say that when a knight is in trouble, it is not difficult for him to overcome his feelings and serve another man," Zixu said, "but later on, he will resist all attempts to control him. We have been informed that the king of Yue is suffering famine and starvation,

十三年，越王謂大夫種曰：「孤蒙子之術，所圖者吉，未嘗有不合也。今欲復謀吳，奈何？」種曰：「君王自陳越國微鄙，年穀不登，願王請糴，以入其意。天若棄吳，必許王矣。」越乃使大夫種使吳，因宰嚭求見吳王，辭曰：「越國洿下，水旱不調，年穀不登，人民飢乏，道薦飢餒。願從大王請糴，來歲即復太倉。惟大王救其窮窘。」吳王曰：「越王信誠守道，不懷二心。今窮歸愬，吾豈愛惜財寶，奪其所願？」子胥諫曰：「不可！非吳有越，越必有吳。吉往則兇來，是養生寇，而破國家者也。與之不為親，不與未成冤。且越有聖臣范蠡，勇以善謀，將有修飾攻戰，以伺吾間。觀越王之使使來請

with his people at the end of their tether—you can use this opportunity to crush them. Now you have failed to make use of the Way of Heaven or follow the principles of Earth but are going to send them food instead: you are simply confirming your fate. When the fox and the pheasant play with each other, the fox humbles itself, and the pheasant believes it. Once the fox achieves its ambitions, the pheasant is dead. How can you be so thoughtless?"

"Goujian is worried about his country, and I will give him this grain," the king of Wu proclaimed. "He who treats others with kindness and justice will have his virtues lauded to the skies. What is there to worry about?"

"I have heard that the wolf cub has a wild heart," Zixu said, "and likewise, an enemy cannot be kept close.[25] A tiger will not allow another to eat its food, and a viper cannot relax its vigilance. Today you, Your Majesty, are destroying the blessings of your country and your house to benefit an enemy without any gain to yourself—you have ignored the advice of a loyal minister to do what your enemy wishes. I am sure to see Yue destroy Wu: wildcats and deer will walk around Gusu Tower, while thorns and brambles will snake their way through your palaces and halls. I hope Your Majesty will remember how [King] Wu attacked King Zhou [of the Yin dynasty]."

Chancellor Pi responded to this from one side: "Was not [the future King] Wu the vassal of King Zhou? After he led the other lords to attack his own monarch, even though he conquered the Yin dynasty, can he be considered righteous?"

"Wu became famous because of this," Zixu said.

糴者，非國貧民困而請糴也，以入吾國，伺吾王間也。」吳王曰：「寡人卑服越王，而有其眾，懷其社稷，以愧勾踐。勾踐氣服，為駕車卻行馬前，諸侯莫不聞知。今吾使之歸國，奉其宗廟，復其社稷，豈敢有反吾之心乎？」子胥曰：「臣聞士窮非難抑心下人，其後有激人之色。臣聞越王飢餓，民之困窮，可因而破也。今不用天之道，順地之理，而反輸之食，固君之命。狐雉之相戲也，夫狐卑體，而雉信之。故狐得其志，而雉必死。可不慎哉！」吳王曰：「勾踐國憂，而寡人給之以粟。恩往義來，其德昭昭，亦何憂乎？」子胥曰：「臣聞狼子有野心，仇讎之人不可親。夫虎不可餒以食，蝮蛇不恣其意。今

---

25. The saying *langzi yexin* 狼子野心 (a wolf cub has a wild heart) was proverbial in ancient China; see, for example, *Zuozhuan*, 679 [Xuan 4], and *Guoyu*, 587 ["Chuyu xia" 楚語下].

"I personally could not bear to become famous because I had murdered my king," Chancellor Pi said.

"Steal a kingdom, and you'll be made a lord; steal some gold, and you'll get your head cut off," Zixu replied. "Now supposing that Wu had lost all sense of proper principle, then how could the Zhou dynasty have honored the Three Houses?"[26]

"Zixu believes in serving his lord by wanting to put a stop to everything that he enjoys and will only declare himself satisfied when he has contravened his lord's every wish," Chancellor Pi said. "Don't you think this is too much, Your Majesty?"

"Chancellor Pi is determined to seek the friendship [King Goujian of Yue]—in the past, he released the prisoner from the stone cell, and he accepted his gift of treasure and women," Zixu replied.[27] "On the outside, he is in cahoots with an enemy country, while on the inside, he misleads our king. Your Majesty should investigate this; do not be deceived by a host of petty-minded flatterers. Your situation now can be compared to bathing a baby; you do it even if it makes the baby cry. You must not listen to the words of Chancellor Pi!"

"Chancellor Pi is right," the king of Wu said. "You do not listen to what I say, and this is not the way that a loyal minister should behave. You are just like those liars who live by slandering others."

"I have heard that when a neighboring country has a crisis, you should hurry to rescue them, even from a thousand *li* away," Chancellor Pi said. "This is just like a king enfeoffing the descendants of the ruling house of a

大王捐國家之福，以饒無益之讎；棄忠臣之言，而順敵人之欲；臣必見越之破吳，豸鹿遊於姑胥之臺，荊榛蔓於宮闕。願王覽武王伐紂之事也。」太宰嚭從旁對曰：「武王非紂王臣也？率諸侯以伐其君，雖勝殷，謂義乎？」子胥曰：「武王即成其名矣。」太宰嚭曰：「親戮主以為名，吾不忍也。」子胥曰：「盜國者封侯，盜金者誅。令使武王失其理，則周何為三家之表？」太宰嚭曰：「子胥為人臣，徒欲干君之好，咈君之心，以自稱滿。君何不知過乎？」子胥曰：「太宰嚭固欲以求其親。前縱石室之囚，受其寶女之遺，外交敵國，

---

26. Xu Tianhu (1999): 164 suggests that the honors shown to the Three Houses represent the posthumous awards made to distinguished individuals from the late Shang dynasty government like Prince Bigan. This is not a standard usage of the term *sanjia* 三家 (Three Houses).

27. Although not mentioned in the *Wu Yue chunqiu* itself, there are other texts that state that Chancellor Pi accepted bribes from Yue; see *Guoyu*, 634 ["Yueyu shang"].

lost kingdom or the Five Hegemons supporting the last remnants of ruined or destroyed states."[28]

The king of Wu then gave Yue ten thousand bushels of grain, with the following order: "I have disobeyed the advice of my ministers in giving this to Yue; you must return it to me when you have a good harvest."

"I accept your command and now return to Yue," Grandee Zhong said. "When the harvest is ripe, we will certainly give this food back to you."

Grandee Zhong went back to Yue, and the ministers of the kingdom of Yue all shouted: "Long life!" The grain was immediately bestowed on government officials and parceled out to a myriad people.

The following year, once the crops were ripe, the king of Yue carefully selected the very best grain and had it steamed, before returning it to Wu. He handed back exactly the same number of bushels, and again he ordered Grandee Zhong to go back to the king of Wu. When the king obtained this grain from Yue, he sighed deeply and said to Chancellor Pi, "The lands of Yue are rich and fertile, and their grain is very fine—we should set this aside for our own people to plant."

Wu did indeed plant the Yue seed, but this grain had already been killed and could not produce sprouts, so the people of Wu suffered a terrible famine.

"Since they have already been reduced to misery, they can be attacked," suggested the king of Yue.

"Not yet!" Grandee Zhong said. "The country has started to become impoverished, and that is all. Their loyal minister is still present, and the

內惑於君。大王察之，無為羣小所侮。今大王譬若浴嬰兒，雖啼無聽宰嚭之言。」吳王曰：「宰嚭是。子無乃聞寡人言，非忠臣之道，類於佞諛之人？」太宰嚭曰：「臣聞鄰國有急，千里馳救。是乃王者封亡國之後，五霸輔絕滅之末者也。」吳王乃與越粟萬石而令之曰：「寡人逆羣臣之議，而輸於越。年豐而歸寡人。」大夫種曰：「臣奉使返越，歲登誠還吳貸。」大夫種歸越，越國羣臣皆稱萬歲。即以粟賞賜羣臣，及於萬民。二年，越王粟稔，揀擇精粟而蒸，還於吳，復還斗斛之數。亦使大夫種歸之吳王。王得越粟，長太息，謂太宰

---

28. The *Shiji*, 2.88 and 3.108, records that the descendants of the Xia royal family received fiefs from the Shang dynasty, and the descendants of the Shang royal family received fiefs from the Zhou. There are also various records of states that had been effectively destroyed by warfare being reestablished by the hegemons of the Spring and Autumn period.

heavenly auras have not yet been observed; you must wait a little longer for the right moment."[29]

After this, the king of Yue asked the prime minister, Fan Li: "I am planning my revenge: if we fight on water, we will need boats, while if we fight on land, we will need chariots. However, the advantages brought by chariots and boats are not as great as those of weapons and crossbows. Since you are planning this campaign on my behalf, you must not make any mistakes!"

"I have heard it said that the sage-kings were all well versed in warfare and the use of troops but that when it came to going into battle formation, marching in serried ranks, and drumming the army forward, success and failure was determined by their training," Fan Li replied. "Recently, I have heard about a maiden from the southern forests, whom the local people claim has remarkable skill; I hope that you will invite her to the palace, Your Majesty, for then we can immediately see what she can do."

The king of Yue then sent a messenger to invite her and ask about the techniques of wielding sword and halberd. The maiden accordingly went north to meet the king. On the road, she encountered an old man, calling himself Lord Yuan, who asked the maiden: "I have heard that you are good with a sword, so I would like to see something of it."

"I would not presume to hide my knowledge," she replied, "so please put me to the test."

Then Lord Yuan pulled out a stave of *linyu* bamboo.[30] The top of this branch was completely dry and desiccated, so the very tip broke off and

嚭曰：「越地肥沃，其種甚嘉。可留使吾民植之。」於是吳種越粟，粟種殺而無生者，吳民大飢。

越王曰：「彼以窮居，其可攻也？」大夫種曰：「未可。國始貧耳，忠臣尚在，天氣未見，須俟其時。」越王又問相國范蠡曰：「孤有報復之謀，水戰則乘舟，陸行則乘輿。輿、舟之利，頓於兵弩。今子為寡人謀事，莫不謬者乎？」范蠡對曰：「臣聞古之聖君，莫不習戰用兵。然行陣隊伍軍鼓之事，

---

29. The loyal minister here is Wu Zixu; however, although the *Wu Yue chunqiu* states that he was still alive at this point, according to other accounts of these events, he had already been forced to commit suicide; see, for example, *Zuozhuan*, 1664–65 [Ai 11], *Guoyu*, 650 ["Yueyu xia"], and *Shiji*, 66.2179–80.
30. Such was the fame of this story that subsequently any reference to this variety of bamboo called forth references to how it was used in the fight between Lord Yuan and the Yue maiden; see, for example, the commentary on the "Wudu fu" 吳都賦 (Rhapsody on the Wu Capital) by Zuo Si 左思 (c. 250–305), given in *Wenxuan*, 5.68.

fell to the ground. The maiden grabbed the tip. Lord Yuan had hold of the main branch and stabbed at the maiden. She dodged and then immediately lunged at him, and on the third lunge, she raised the stave and was about to strike Lord Yuan. Lord Yuan then flew high up into the trees, where he metamorphosed into a white gibbon. After this, she proceeded on her way and had an audience with the king of Yue.

"How do you use a sword?" the king of Yue inquired.

"I was born in the middle of a primeval forest and grew up in the wilds, away from other people," the maiden replied. "It was so remote that there was no way to study from a teacher, nor could I communicate with foreign lords. However, I enjoyed learning how to attack, and I have practiced without ceasing. I was not taught this by others; it came to me suddenly, of its own accord."

"What is your technique?" the king of Yue asked.

"This technique is at once most subtle and yet it is easy; its import is most secret and profound," the maiden replied. "My technique has both a main gate and a back door, and it can also be divided into *yin* and *yang*. You can open the gate while shutting the back door; and when *yin* declines, then *yang* is on the rise. There is a way to engage in hand-to-hand combat; on the inside, I make sure that I am concentrated in mind, while on the outside, I show a peaceful and composed demeanor—those looking at me then might imagine that I am a good woman, but once the fighting begins, I become like a fierce tiger. Having made my dispositions and checked my breathing, I then advance with concentrated mind; I am at once as remote as the sun and as agile as a leaping rabbit.[31] When pursuing me, they find that they are chasing my shadow; I can come and go at the speed of light. My breathing is easy and never causes me pain. I can attack from one side or the other, from front or back, and no one will ever hear me as I lunge or riposte. With this technique, one person can defeat one hundred; one thousand can defeat ten

吉兇決在其工。今聞越有處女，出於南林，國人稱善。願王請之，立可見。」越王乃使使聘之，問以劍戟之術。處女將北見於王，道逢一翁，自稱曰袁公。問於處女：「吾聞子善劍，願一見之。」女曰：「妾不敢有所隱，惟公試之。」於是袁公即拔箖箊竹，竹枝上頡〔枯〕橋〔槁〕未【折】墮地。女即捷末。袁公操其本而刺處女。處女應即入之。三入，因舉杖擊之，袁公則飛上樹，變為白猿。遂別去，見越王。越王問曰：「夫劍之道則如之何？」女曰：「妾

---

31. As noted by Xu Tianhu (1999): 149, *teng* 滕 (to bubble) in the original text should be read *teng* 騰 (to leap).

thousand. If you, Your Majesty, wish to test me, you will see what I mean when you experience it for yourself."

The king of Yue was very pleased and immediately granted her a title: she was called the "Yue Maiden." He also gave orders that the commanders of each division in the five legions and other men of ability should learn this technique to be able to instruct army officers in it. At that time, [no one was able] to beat the Yue Maiden style of swordsmanship.[32]

Subsequently, Fan Li again recommended a fine archer named Chen Yin. This Yin was a native of Chu. The king of Yue invited him to come to the palace and asked him: "I have heard that you are good at archery: where does your technique derive from?"

"I am a peasant from Chu," Yin said, "who happens to have acquired the skill of archery. I cannot be said to know all about this technique."

"That is true," the king of Yue said. "However, I hope that you can tell me a bit about it."

"I have heard that the crossbow is derived from the bow," Yin said, "and the bow derived from the slingshot, while the slingshot itself was invented in antiquity by a filial son."

"What happened with the filial son's slingshot?" the king of Yue asked.

"In the past, people lived very simple and basic lives," Yin replied. "When they were hungry, they ate birds and animals; when they were thirsty, they drank dew; and when they died, they were bundled up inside white reeds and thrown into the wilds. The filial son could not bear to see his parents eaten by birds and wild animals, so he fashioned a slingshot to protect them, to prevent them being harmed by these creatures. Therefore, the song says:

生深林之中，長於無人之野，無道不習，不達諸侯。竊好擊之道，誦之不休。妾非受於人也，而忽自有之。」越王曰：「其道如何？」女曰：「其道甚微而易，其意甚幽而深。道有門戶，亦有陰陽。開門閉戶，陰衰陽興。凡手戰之道，內實精神，外示安儀。見之似好婦，奪之似懼虎。布形候氣，與神俱往。杳之若日，偏如滕兔。追形逐影，光若彿仿。呼吸往來，不及法禁。縱橫逆順，直復不聞。斯道者，一人當百，百人當萬。王欲試之，其驗即見。」越王【大悅，】即加女號，號曰越女。乃命五校之隊長高才習之，以教軍士。當此之時，皆稱越女之劍。

---

32. Xu Tianhu (1999): 149 indicates that two characters, *moneng* 莫能 (no one was able), are missing from this line. This tradition of swordsmanship was clearly well established in the Han dynasty; see *Lunheng*, 274 ["Bietong"].

"'Cut a length of bamboo and add another length of bamboo,[33]
Then a flying clod of earth will hit flesh.'[34]

"After that, Shennong and the [Yellow] Sovereign put a string against a branch to create the bow, and they whittled at wood to make arrows; the strength of the bow and arrow struck awe into the four directions.[35] In the time after the Yellow Sovereign, there was a man named the Elder Archer in Chu. This Elder Archer was born at Mount Jing in Chu, and after he was born, he could not find his father or mother. While he was still a child, he practiced using the bow and arrow, and whatever he shot at, he would hit. He transmitted his skills to Yi, and Yi passed them on to Fengmeng, and Fengmeng passed them on to the Qin clan of Chu. The Qin clan decided that bows and arrows were not sufficient to strike awe into the world, for at that time, the lords were fighting each other, and weapons clashed—the might of bows and arrows was not enough to control the situation and make people submit. The Qin clan placed the bow sideways, attaching it to a stock, adding a trigger and a stop, making it even more powerful; afterward, the lords had to submit. The Qin clan transmitted their knowledge to the Three Marquises of Chu—that is, Judan, E, and Zhang, whom people called the Marquis of Mi, the Marquis

於是范蠡復進善射者陳音。音，楚人也。越王請音而問曰：「孤聞子善射，道何所生？」音曰：「臣，楚之鄙人，嘗步於射術，未能悉知其道。」越王曰：「然。願子一二其辭。」音曰：「臣聞弩生於弓，弓生於彈，彈起古之孝子。」越王曰：「孝子彈者奈何？」音曰：「古者人民朴質。飢食鳥獸，渴飲霧露。死則裹以白茅，投於中野。孝子不忍見父母為禽獸所食，故作彈以守之，絕鳥獸之害。故歌曰：斷竹續竹，飛土逐害之謂也。於是神農、皇帝弦木為弧，剡木為矢，弧矢之利，以威四方。黃帝之後，楚有弧父。弧父者，生於楚之荊山，生不

---

33. A number of quotations of this song give the final character as *mu* 木 (wood) rather than *zhu* 竹 (bamboo). Both of these words belong to the same rhyme group *-uk (*jue* 覺).

34. The original text gives the final character as *hai* 害 (to harm), but numerous ancient quotations attest to the final word being *rou* 肉 (flesh). This change also has the benefit of restoring the rhyme, since *rou* is also part of the *-uk (*jue* 覺) group, making this pair of lines a couplet.

35. As noted by Xu Tianhu (1999): 149, *huang* 皇 (august) in this line seems to be a mistake for *huang* 黃 (yellow). The invention of the arrow is traditionally ascribed to Yi Mou 夷牟, who served the Yellow Sovereign.

of Yi, and the Marquis of Wei.[36] From the Three Marquises of Chu, it was passed on to King Ling; that is why they themselves say that the people of Chu have used peachwood bows and arrows of thorn-wood from one generation to the next, to defend against neighboring countries.[37] After the time of King Ling, this method of shooting divided into various schools, but even though each school produced capable men, they merely used the crossbow without being able to fully appreciate the right method. My ancestors learned this skill in Chu, and after five generations, it was passed to me. Even though I do not fully understand this technique, I am willing for Your Majesty to test me on it."

"What does a crossbow look like?" the king of Yue asked.

"The stop is shaped like a square citadel, defending its subjects," Chen Yin replied.[38] "The finger trigger is the ruler, whose orders are obeyed. The nocking point is the adjutant, who takes charge of officers and men. The laminate glue is the commander in chief, who takes his place at the center. The safety mechanism is like the sentries, controlling who comes and goes. The tripod is like a body servant, obeying its master in all things. The stock is the road along which the messenger passes. The limbs of the bow are the generals, supporting their ruler. The string is the strategist, giving commands to the soldiers in battle. The arrows are assassins speeding on their way; they do as their lord commands. The arrowheads are shock troops, which keep

見父母。為兒之時，習用弓矢，所射無脫。以其道傳於羿，羿傳逢蒙，逢蒙傳於楚琴氏。琴氏以為弓矢不足以威天下。當是之時，諸侯相伐，兵刃交錯，弓矢之威不能制服。琴氏乃橫弓著臂，施機設樞，加之以力，然後諸侯可服。琴氏傳之楚三侯，所謂句亶、鄂、章，人號麋侯、翼侯、魏侯也。自楚之三侯，傳至靈王，自稱之楚累世，蓋以桃弓棘矢而備鄰國也。自靈王之後，射道分流，百家能人，用莫得其正。臣前人受之於楚，五世於臣矣。臣雖不明其道，惟

---

36. The commentary on the "Qiqi" 七啓 (Seven Enlightenments) by Cao Zhi, quoted in *Wenxuan*, 34.476, gives this line slightly differently: *Qinshi chuan Da Wei, Da Wei chuan Chu Sanhou* 琴氏傳大魏，大魏傳楚三侯 (The Qin clan transmitted their knowledge to Da Wei, and Da Wai passed it on to the Three Marquises of Chu).
37. Peachwood was traditionally regarded as having apotropaic functions; see, for example, *Zuozhuan*, 1154 [Xiang 29]. For a study of the vast number of uses of peachwood objects in early Chinese mantic practice, many of which are only recorded in excavated material, see Lü Yahu (2010): 309–18.
38. There is a passage that is closely related in theme preserved in *Sun Bin bingfa*, 84–85 ["Bingqing" 兵情].

Chapter Nine: The Outer Traditions | 195

on going whatever happens. The fletchings are the auxiliaries, keeping to the same path. The nock is the man receiving his instructions, who determines whether orders can be carried out or not. The handrest is the commandant, who controls what goes on to left and right. The arrow tips are like seasoned fighters, in that they never go astray. Before a bird can take flight, before an animal can run away, the crossbow has sounded, and they die. I am a stupid and backward man, so that is all I can say about my technique."

"I would like to hear about how to shoot properly," the king of Yue said.

"I have heard it said that there are many ways to shoot correctly, and they are very subtle," Yin replied. "The sages of antiquity could announce what they were going to hit before they even fired their crossbows. I have not been able to attain the abilities possessed by those great sages of antiquity, but I beg your permission to explain all the key points. In this method of shooting, your body must be as straight as if you were carrying a weight on your head, and your head should be held like an egg that might otherwise overbalance.[39] Your left foot should be pointing straight ahead, and your right foot should be at right angles to it, while your left hand should be held as if supporting a branch and your right hand should be held as if cradling a baby. When you raise your crossbow and aim at the enemy, you should concentrate your mind and breathe easily. Once your breath has been entirely expelled, you are at rest; when your spirit is calm and your mind is focused, you can be clear whether you should shoot or not. Your right hand should be able to trigger the mechanism without your left hand feeling the slightest thing—one body must be trained to do all these different things, and yet many people have to do them in unison! This is the right way to shoot a crossbow."

王試之。」越王曰：「弩之狀何法焉？」陳音曰：「郭為方城，守臣子也。教為人君，命所起也。牙為執法，守吏卒也。牛為中將，主內裏也。關為守禦，檢去止也。錡為侍從，聽人主也。臂為道路，通所使也。弓為將軍，主重負也。弦為軍師，禦戰士也。矢為飛客，主教使也。金為實敵，往不止也。衛為副使，正道里也。又為受教，知可否也。鏢為都尉，執左右也。敵為百死，不得駭也。鳥不及飛，獸不暇走。弩之所向，無不死也。臣之愚劣，道悉如此。」越王：「願聞正射之道。」音曰：「臣聞正射之道，道眾而微。古之聖人，射弩未發，而

---

39. The original text here reads *mao* 卯; various unsatisfactory suggestions for how to resolve this incomprehensible statement can be found in Zhang Jue (2006): 249 n. 44 and Huang Rensheng (1996): 372 n. 30. I suggest reading *mao* as *luan* 卵 (egg), which would seem to make some sense.

"I would like you to tell me about the techniques you use to remain calm when facing the enemy and to select a target for when the arrows start to fly."

"This is the Way of shooting," Yin said. "You choose your target and look at the enemy, and then you begin with a volley of shots.[40] There are weak and strong crossbows, just like there are light and heavy arrows; a bow with a pull of one *dan* requires arrows weighing one *liang*, for then they will be right for one another. You need to think about whether you will be shooting at close range or far away, upward or downward, and then select the right weight accordingly. This is the most important part of this technique, and there is nothing more to say about it."

"Wonderful!" the king of Yue said. "You have explained your Way in its entirety. I would like you to teach it all to the people of my country."

"The Way comes from Heaven," Yin responded, "but matters are decided by people. If people are prepared to study, they can achieve remarkable results."

Then [King Goujian] ordered Chen Yin to teach his army officers archery outside the northern suburbs. After three months, all the officers in his army had acquired the skills to use a bow and a crossbow. When Chen Yin died, the king of Yue was very upset and buried him west of the capital city, giving his tomb the designation: "Chen Yin's Hill."[41]

前名其所中。臣未能如古之聖人。」「請悉其要。」【音曰】：「夫射之道，身若戴板，頭若激卵。左蹉，右足橫。左手若附枝，右手若抱兒。舉弩望敵，翕心咽煙。與氣俱發，得其和平。神定思去，去止分離。右手發機，左手不知。一身異教，豈況雄雌。此正射持弩之道也。」「願聞望敵儀表，投分飛矢之道。」音曰：「夫射之道，從分望敵，合以參連。弩有斗石，矢有輕重。石取一兩，其數乃平。遠近高下，求之銖分。道要在斯，無有遺言。」越王曰：「善。盡子之道，願子悉以教吾國人。」音曰：「道出於天，事在於人，人之所習，無有不神。」於是乃使陳音教士習射於北郊之外。三月，軍士皆能用弓弩之巧。陳音死，越王傷之，葬於國西，號其葬所曰陳音山。

---

40. The term *sanlian* 參連 here refers to a technique by which a single arrow would be shot, followed by a volley of three arrows at the same time; see *Zhouli*, 352–53 ["Diguan" 地官. "Baoshi" 保氏].

41. The tomb of the great archer Chen Yin is also mentioned in *Yuejue shu*, 62 ["Jidi zhuan"].

Chapter Ten

The Outer Traditions
The Story of King Goujian's Attack on Wu

In the fifteenth year of the reign of King Goujian [482 BCE], he plotted an attack on Wu. He spoke to Grandee Zhong on the subject: "I made use of your stratagems, sir; thus, I escaped the shameful death that would have been Heaven's punishment for me and was eventually able to return home again to my country. I have already explained the situation truthfully to my subjects, and the inhabitants of my kingdom are happy and pleased![1] In the past, you said: 'If there is some sign in the heavens, I will immediately inform you.' Surely by now there ought to have been an omen?"

《勾踐伐吳外傳》

勾踐十五年，謀伐吳，謂大夫種曰：「孤用夫子之策，免於天虐之誅，還歸於國。吾誠已說於國人，國人喜悅。而子昔日云：有天氣，即來陳之。今豈有應乎？」種曰：「吳之所以彊者，為有子胥。今伍子胥忠諫而死，是天氣前見，亡國之證也。願君悉心盡意，以說國人。」越王曰：「聽孤說國人之辭：寡人不知其力之不足，以大國報讎，以暴露百姓之骨於中原，此則寡人之罪

---

1. The parallel passage in *Guoyu*, 634 ["Yueyu shang"], simply states: "King Goujian explained the situation to the people of the country" (勾踐說于國人).

"The reason why Wu was so strong was because they had Zixu," Zhong said. "Now Wu Zixu has offered loyal remonstrance and been killed for it: that means that we have seen the signs of a country being destroyed before anything appeared in the skies. I hope that you will concentrate your efforts on persuading the people of the country to support this."

"Please listen to what I mean to tell my people!" the king of Yue said. "I did not realize that I was not nearly strong enough, and so I went to take revenge on our great [neighbor]—thus, it is my fault that the bones of my people lay exposed on the Central Plains.[2] I then—with all sincerity—decided to change my approach to the government. I buried the dead and asked after the injured, I condoled with those who had suffered loss, and I congratulated those who had experienced a happy event. I saw off those going abroad and welcomed home those who returned, and I removed anything that could harm my people. Later on, I humbly served King Fuchai and sent three hundred slaves to Wu.[3] Wu enfeoffed me with a couple hundred *li* of land, and accordingly, I made an agreement with the people of Wu—young and old, senior and junior—which said: 'I have heard that people of all directions gave their allegiance to the wise rulers of antiquity in the same way as water [accumulates in the lowest place].[4] I cannot govern the country well, so let me lead my people to protect [the borders].'[5] Then

也。寡人誠更其術。於是，乃葬死問傷，弔有憂，賀有喜，送往迎來，除民所害。然後卑事夫差，往宦士三百人於吳。吳封孤數百里之地，因約吳國父兄昆弟而誓之曰：『寡人聞，古之賢君，四方之民歸之若水。寡人不能為政，將率二三子夫婦以為藩輔。』令壯者無娶老妻，老者無娶壯婦。女子十七未嫁，其父母有罪。丈夫二十不娶，其父母有罪。將免者，以告於孤，令醫守之。生男二，貺之以壺酒，一犬。生女二，賜以壺酒，一豚。生子三人，孤

---

2. The parallel line in *Guoyu*, 634 ["Yueyu shang"], reads: "I did not realize that I was not nearly strong enough, and so I became locked in conflict with our great neighbor" (寡人不知其力之不足也，而又與大國執讎).
3. This incident is also mentioned in *Guoyu*, 634 ["Yueyu shang"], and appears to have been unrelated to the time that King Goujian and Fan Li were held as prisoners of war.
4. The original text lacks the characters *zhi gui xia ye* 之歸下也 (accumulates in the lowest place). The parallel line in *Guoyu*, 635 ["Yueyu shang"], supplies the missing words here.
5. Some editions of the text conclude this line with the character *fan* 藩; some give *fanfu* 藩輔. Zhang Jue (2006): 255 n. 12 argues that this line still requires further changes to make sense.

I gave orders that strong young men should not marry elderly wives and that old men should not marry young women. If a woman reached the age of seventeen without being wed, then her parents were guilty of a crime. If a man reached the age of twenty without taking a wife, then his parents were guilty of a crime. Women who were about to give birth could report to the throne, in which case a doctor would be ordered to attend them. If she gave birth to two boys, she would be rewarded with a jug of wine and a dog. If she gave birth to two girls, she would be rewarded with a jug of wine and a pig.[6] If she gave birth to triplets, we would arrange for a wet nurse to be sent. If she gave birth to twins, we would pay an extra stipend of food. If the oldest son died, his parents would be excused from service in my government for three years; if the youngest son died, they would be excused from service in my government for three months.[7] I would be sure to weep and bury them as if it were my own child. I gave orders that orphans, widows, the terminally ill, and the sick and indigent should be assisted, and government posts found for their children. To show my appreciation of the men serving in my administration, I checked up on their housing, I improved their clothing, I made sure that they had enough to eat, and then I selected the very best for service. When a knight came from somewhere abroad, I would be sure to give him an audience at court and treat him with all due respect. I would take rice and porridge with me when traveling in the country so that if any children in the country met me while they were out playing, I would give them food and make sure

以乳母。生子二人，孤與一養。長子死，三年釋吾政。季子死，三月釋吾政。必哭泣葬埋之，如吾子也。令孤子、寡婦、疾疹、貧病者，納官其子。欲仕，量其居，好其衣，飽其食，而簡銳之。凡四方之士來者，必朝而禮之，載飯與羹，以遊國中。國中僮子戲而遇孤，孤餔而啜之，施以愛，問其名。非孤飯，不食；非夫人事，不衣。七年不收國，民家有三年之畜。男即歌樂，女即會笑。今國之父兄日請於孤曰：『昔夫差辱吾君王於諸侯，長為天下所恥。今

---

6. With this line and the previous one, there is a difference with the text found in *Guoyu*, 635 ["Yueyu shang"]. There it says that these gifts were received at the birth of each child, and not after two.

7. Zhang Jue (1994): 386 suggests that it was King Goujian who mourned other people's children for three years if an older son and for three months if younger—this would have left him with very little time to govern the country. This translation follows the parallel passage in *Guoyu*, 635 ["Yueyu shang"].

that they ate it, show them my affection, and ask their names.[8] I have eaten only my own rice, and the only clothing I have worn is that made by my wife. For seven years, I have levied no taxes, and every family in the country has enough supplies to last three years.[9] Men sing and dance; women gather happily and laugh.

"Now elders from throughout the country come every day to ask me: 'In the past, Fuchai humiliated our king in front of the other lords, and this has made us a laughingstock around the world for a long time. Now the kingdom of Yue is rich, and our king is frugal—surely we can avenge this shame?'

"I refuse, telling them: 'The humiliation that I suffered in the past was not your fault. How can someone in my position dare to put my people to the trouble of avenging such an accumulation of hatred?'

"The elders again asked: 'All within the four borders belongs to our king. A son should take revenge for this father, a vassal should requite assaults on his lord—how would we dare not to do our very best? Let us fight, that we may avenge the insults heaped on our king!' I was happy to hear this, and so I agreed to their demands."

"I have observed that once the king of Wu achieves his ambitions with respect to Qi and Jin, he claims that he will go on to enter our lands, sending his troops to put pressure on our borders," Grandee Zhong said. "However, right now his army is exhausted, and his troops have had to rest, so for a whole year he has not been able to use them—he seems to have forgotten about us. I could not be lax in this matter, so I performed a divination about

越國富饒，君王節儉，請可報恥。』孤辭之曰：『昔者我辱也，非二三子之罪也。如寡人者，何敢勞吾國之人，以塞吾之宿讎。』父兄又復請曰：『誠四封之內，盡吾君子，子報父仇，臣復君隙，豈敢有不盡力者乎？臣請復戰，以除君王之宿讎。』孤悅而許之。」大夫種曰：「臣觀吳王得志於齊、晉，謂當遂涉吾地，以兵臨境。今疲師休卒，一年而不試，以忘於我。我不可以怠，臣當卜之於天。吳民既疲於軍，困於戰鬥，市無赤米之積，國廩空虛，其民必有移徙之

---

8. The *Guoyu*, 635 ["Yueyu shang"], specifies that the asking of names took place with a view to identifying individuals for future employment by the state.
9. Zhang Jue (2006): 255 n. 28 suggests that *qi* 七 (seven) should be read *shi* 十 (ten), following *Guoyu*, 635 ["Yueyu shang"]. The concept of a well-supplied household having stocks to last three years seems to have been virtually proverbial in preunification China; see, for example, *Han Feizi*, 178 ["Shiguo" 十過].

it according to the heavens. The people of Wu are worn out with their military service, and they are sick and tired of fighting battles. In their markets, there are no stores of red rice, and the granaries across the land are empty; hence, his people must be thinking about leaving—in their poverty, they go to the seashore to seek out seaweed and whelks. When making a divination, human affairs are seen in milfoil hexagrams and oracle-bone cracks. If you were to raise an army, Your Majesty, and attacked the borders of Wu imagining that you might thereby capture much booty, you would be wrong. Since the king of Wu does not intend to attack us, it would be a mistake to move him to anger; it would be better to get close to him and find out what he intends to do."

"It is not that I want to go to war," the king of Yue said. "My people have been asking to fight in battle for three years now, so I am forced to accede to their wishes."

Having heard Grandee Zhong remonstrate about possible problems on this day, elders from Yue also remonstrated with him: "Wu can be attacked! If we win, we will destroy their country; if we do not win, then we will at least make their soldiers suffer! If the kingdom of Wu asks for a peace treaty, then you can make a blood covenant with them, and your glorious reputation will be known to all the other lords."

"Good!" said the king of Yue.

Then he had a meeting with all his ministers and issued the following order: "If anyone dares to remonstrate about attacking Wu, they will not be pardoned!"

[Fan] Li and Zhong said to each other: "Our remonstrance is unwelcome. We now have to obey His Majesty's orders."

The king of Yue met with his army officers and warned his troops concerning their duties, swearing an oath with them. "I have heard that the wise rulers of antiquity were never worried that they did not have enough soldiers; they were concerned that their thoughts and actions showed shameless self-interest," he said. "Today, Fuchai has thirty thousand soldiers wearing

心，寒就蒲嬴於東海之濱。夫占兆人事，又見於卜筮。王若起師，以可會之利，犯吳之邊鄙，不可往也。吳王雖無伐我之心，亦雖動之以怒。不如詮其問，以知其意。」越王曰：「孤不欲有征伐之心，國人請戰者三年矣，吾不得不從民人之欲。今聞大夫種諫難。」越父兄又諫曰：「吳可伐。勝則滅其國，不勝則困其兵。吳國有成，王與之盟。功名聞於諸侯。」王曰：「善。」於是乃大會群臣，而令之曰：「有敢諫伐吳者，罪不赦！」蠡、種相謂曰：「吾諫已不

armor of rhinoceros hide, but he is not concerned about their shameless thoughts and actions; he worries that he does not have enough men. Now I am going to enact the righteous wrath of Heaven: I do not want yokels showing off their petty bravery; I want officers and troops who will move forward thinking only of the rewards to come and who will retreat only when ordered to do so!"[10]

Afterward, among the inhabitants of Yue, fathers encouraged their sons, and older brothers urged on their younger brothers, saying: "Wu can be attacked!"

The king of Yue again summoned Fan Li and said to him: "Wu has already killed Zixu, and [King Fuchai] is led by a host of flatterers. The people of my country are again demanding that I attack Wu, but can such an attack be successful?"

"Not yet," Fan Li said. "You must wait until the spring of next year, and then you can invade."

"Why?" His Majesty asked.

"I have heard that the king of Wu will go north to attend a meeting with the other lords at Huangchi," Fan Li replied. "The very best of his soldiers will follow the king, and the country will be left empty, with only the old and the feeble remaining behind, the crown prince remaining to take charge of the defense. If the soldiers have just left the borders and have not yet gone far and they hear that Yue has taken advantage of this emptiness, it will not be difficult simply to turn around. You had better wait until next spring."

In the summer, in the sixth month, on Bingzi Day, King Goujian again asked about this. "You can attack," Fan Li announced.

合矣，然猶聽君王之令。」越王會軍列士，而大誡眾，而誓之曰：「寡人聞古之賢君，不患其眾不足，而患其志行之少恥也。今夫差衣水犀甲者十有三萬人，不患其志行之少恥也，而患其眾之不足。今寡人將助天威，吾不欲匹夫之小勇也。吾欲士卒進則思賞，退則避刑。」於是越民父勉其子，兄勸其弟，曰：「吳可伐也。」越王復召范蠡謂曰：「吳已殺子胥，道諛者眾。吾國之民，又勸孤伐吳。其可伐乎？」范蠡曰：「未可。須明年之春，然後可耳。」王曰：

---

10. This line literally means: "they will retreat only when they can escape punishment for doing" so (*tui ze bi xing* 退則避刑)—that is, when they have been given orders to this effect.

He sent out two thousand marines, and forty thousand trained soldiers, with six thousand of the ruler's own men, and one thousand officers.[11] They fought a battle with Wu on Yiyou Day.[12] On Bingxu Day, they captured and killed the crown prince.[13] On Dinghai Day, they entered the capital city of Wu and burned the Guxu Tower.[14] Wu reported this emergency to King Fuchai, but just at that moment, he was meeting with the other lords at Huangchi, and he was afraid that people would hear about it. He gave secret orders that this information was not to be released; he performed the blood covenant at Huangchi; and then he sent an ambassador to ask for a peace treaty with Yue.[15] King Goujian calculated that he could not yet destroy them and so made peace with Wu.

In the seventh month of the twenty-first year of his reign [476 BCE], the king of Yue again mobilized all his officers and troops for an attack on Wu. At this time, Chu sent Shen Baoxu as an ambassador to Yue. "Can Wu be attacked?" the king of Yue asked Baoxu.

"I am not at all good at stratagems and plans, so I have no idea," Shen Baoxu said.

「何也？」范蠡曰：「臣觀吳王北會諸侯於黃池，精兵從王，國中空虛，老弱在後，太子留守。兵始出境未遠，聞越掩其空虛，兵還不難也。不如來春。」其夏六月丙子，勾踐復問范蠡曰：「可伐矣。」乃發習流二千人，俊士四萬，君子六千，諸禦千人。以乙酉與吳戰。丙戌遂虜殺太子。丁亥，入吳，焚姑胥臺。吳告急於夫差，夫差方會諸侯於黃池，恐天下聞之，即密不令洩。已盟黃池，乃使人請成於越。勾踐自度未能滅，乃與吳平。

---

11. This translation here follows the commentary by Xu Tianhu (1999): 158–59. The particular problem with this line concerns the identification of the term *xiliu* 習流. The *Suoyin* commentary on *Shiji*, 41.1744 n. 3, identifies *xiliu* as criminals who have been released from custody to fight, and the kingdom of Yue was noted for its use of criminals as suicide troops in battle. However, Xu Tianhu argues that this is a mistake and that this term should be understood as specifically referring to soldiers trained in naval warfare.
12. Yiyou Day is day twenty-two in the sixty-day cycle. This account gives the same dates as *Zuozhuan*, 1676–77 [Ai 13].
13. Bingxu Day is the twenty-third day in the cycle; therefore, these events occurred one day after the battle.
14. Dinghai Day is the twenty-fourth day in the cycle, and hence, the burning of Guxu Tower occurred the day after the death of the crown prince.
15. The peace treaty between Wu and Yue, according to *Zuozhuan*, 1679 [Ai 13], was concluded in the winter of this year.

"Wu has behaved cruelly to us!" the king of Yue said. "They destroyed our altars of soil and grain and razed our ancestral shrines, turning them into flatland and preventing them from receiving blood food. Because of this, I hoped to pray for the blessings of Heaven, but although my chariots and horses, weapons and armor, officers and men are ready, I do not know how to make use of them. I would like to ask about your theories of warfare; what should I do?"

"I am very stupid," Shen Baoxu said, "so I don't know anything about this."

The king of Yue insisted on an answer, and so Baoxu replied, "Wu is a good country, which has shown its wisdom to the other lords. May I ask why you want to do battle with them?"

"The people at my side always drink the same wine and eat the same meat as I do myself. However, my food and drink is plain, and the music I listen to is simple, because I hope to take revenge on Wu—I want to fight like this!" the king of Yue said.

"If they are good, then they are good," Baoxu replied. "You cannot fight them."

"In the kingdom of Yue, I have shown my affection to my people, treating them as if they were my own children, supporting them with benevolence and wisdom," the king of Yue said. "I have reformed the legal system and reduced harsh punishments, giving the people what they want and getting rid of what they hate, encouraging good deeds and repressing the wicked, because I hope to take revenge on Wu—I want to fight like this!"

"If they are good, then they are good," Baoxu replied. "You cannot fight them."

"In the kingdom of Yue, I have made sure that the rich can live in peace and the poor receive help," His Majesty said. "I save those who are in need by taxing those who have more than enough. In this way, neither rich nor poor have failed to benefit. I did this because I hope to take revenge on Wu—I want to fight like this!"

二十一年七月，越王復悉國中士卒伐吳。會楚使申包胥聘於越，越王乃問包胥曰：「吳可伐耶？」申包胥曰：「臣鄙於策謀，未足以卜。」越王曰：「吳為不道，殘我社稷，夷吾宗廟，以為平原，使不得血食。吾欲與之僥天之中，惟是興馬、兵革、卒伍既具，無以行之。誠聞於戰，何以為可？」申包胥曰：「臣愚，不能知。」越王固問。包胥乃曰：「夫吳，良國也，傳賢於諸侯。敢問君王之所戰者何？」越王曰：「在孤之側者，飲酒食肉，未嘗不分。孤之

"If they are good, then they are good," Baoxu replied. "You cannot fight them."

"My country reaches to Chu in the south and touches Jin in the west, while to the north, we can see Qi," His Majesty said. "Every spring and autumn, I sent money, jade and silk, and men and women as tribute to be presented to them, and I have never dared to be remiss in this. I did this because I hope to take revenge on Wu—I want to fight like this!"

"Great!" Baoxu said. "If you had not done these things, it would even yet be impossible for you to do battle. The way in which a war should be fought is that you begin with knowledge, you follow that with benevolence, and you conclude with bravery. If you or your generals lack knowledge, then you cannot make plans about the changing situation or distinguish between the many and the few.[16] If you are not benevolent, then you cannot experience hunger and cold with your three armies, nor can you be with them in times of suffering or joy. If you are not brave, then you cannot make the decision about when to advance or when to retreat and cut through all debate about what to do for the best."

"I will respectfully obey your commands," the king of Yue said.

In the winter in the tenth month, the king of Yue invited his eight grandees to a meeting.[17] "In the past," he said, "Wu behaved cruelly to us: they destroyed our altars of soil and grain and razed our ancestral

飲食不致其味，聽樂不盡其聲，求以報吳。願以此戰。」包胥曰：「善則善矣，未可以戰。」越王曰：「越國之中，吾博愛以子之，忠惠以養之。吾今修寬刑，欲民所欲，去民所惡，稱其善，掩其惡，求以報吳。願以此戰。」包胥曰：「善則善矣，未可以戰。」王曰：「越國之中，富者吾安之，貧者吾予之，救其不足，損其有餘，使貧富不失其利，求以報吳。願以此戰。」包胥曰：「善則善矣，未可以戰。」王曰：「邦國南則距楚，西則薄晉，北則望齊，春秋奉幣、玉帛、子女以貢獻焉，未嘗敢絕，求以報吳。願以此戰。」包胥曰：「善哉！

---

16. Many and few (*zhonggua* 眾寡) should perhaps here be understood in a military sense; the many would be an untrained rabble army, while the few would be the elite, well-trained, and well-equipped troops. However, the parallel passage in *Guoyu*, 610 ["Wuyu"], refers to *Tianxia zhi zhonggua* 天下之眾寡 (the many and few in the world), which would appear to speak of the civilian population.

17. In the text below, only seven grandees offer advice to the king of Yue. This may indicate some textual loss or perhaps is simply a mistake; see Zhang Jue (2006): 262 n. 1. Xu Tianhu (1999): 161 suggests that the missing grandee might be Shen Baoxu, but this is unlikely, since he was not one of the grandees of Yue.

shrines, turning them into flatland and preventing them from receiving blood food. Because of this, I prayed for the blessings of Heaven, but when my weapons and armor were ready, I did not know how to make use of them. I have asked Shen Baoxu for advice, and he has already given me my instructions. Therefore, I would like to ask you gentlemen, what should I do?"

"You must rectify your rewards, and then you can do battle," Grandee Xieyong said. "When your rewards have been rectified, then it is clear that they are to be trusted; every achievement is noted, and each receives their deserved reward, so your officers and men will not be lax."

"How wise!" His Majesty said.

"You must rectify your punishments, and then you can do battle," Grandee Kucheng said. "When your punishments have been rectified, then your officers and men will respect and fear them, and they will not dare to disobey your orders."

"How brave!" His Majesty remarked.

"You must rectify things, and then you can do battle," Grandee Wen Zhong said.[18] "When things have been rectified, you will know whether they are right or wrong, and once it is clear whether they are right or wrong, people will not be mistaken."

"How discriminating!" the king murmured.

"You must rectify your preparations, and then you can do battle," Grandee Fan Li said. "When your preparations have been rectified, you can defend yourself strongly, knowing that you can deal with any unexpected event. Once your preparations are made and your defenses are strong, you will be able to cope with any problem."

"How cautious!" His Majesty said.

無以加斯矣，猶未可戰。夫戰之道知為之始，以仁次之，以勇斷之。君、將不知，即無權變之謀，以別眾寡之數。不仁，則不得與三軍同飢寒之節，齊苦樂之喜。不勇，則不能斷去就之疑，決可否之議。」於是越王曰：「敬從命矣。」冬十月，越王乃請八大夫曰：「昔吳為不道，殘我宗廟，夷我社稷，以為平原，使不血食。吾欲徵天之中，兵革既具，無所以行之。吾問於申包胥，即已命孤矣。敢告諸大夫，如何？」大夫曳庸曰:「審賞，則可戰也。審其賞，

---

18. The commentary by Huang Rensheng (1996): 347 n. 4 suggests that the *wu* 物 (things) mentioned would specifically be military supplies.

"You must rectify your music, and then you can do battle," Grandee Gaoru said.[19] "If music has been rectified, then you can distinguish between the clear and the turbid. By distinguishing clear and turbid, your reputation will be known to the Zhou royal house, and the other lords will not resent you abroad."

"How virtuous!" the king remarked.

"You must show your kindness and understand your position, and then you can do battle," Grandee Futong said. "If you show your kindness, then it must be spread wide; if you understand your position, then you will not alienate others."

"How miraculous!" the king proclaimed.

"You must observe the heavens and investigate the earth, studying how to respond to these changes, and then you can do battle," Grandee Jini said. "When three things are seen in advance—the changes of Heaven, the responses of Earth, and the actions of Man—and they are all beneficial, then you can fight."

"How enlightened!" the king exclaimed.

King Goujian then withdrew and performed a fast. He announced to the people of the capital: "I am going to come up with an unsurpassed plan; everyone will hear of me, whether they are near at hand or far away." Then he further announced to his officials and the people of the capital: "Those who obey my orders will be rewarded; you should all go to the gate of the capital city. If on the appointed day, you do not obey my order, I will kill you as an example to the rest." King Goujian was afraid that his people would not obey him, and so he informed the Zhou royal house that he was about to

明其信，無功不及，有功必加，則士卒不怠。」王曰：「聖哉！」大夫苦成曰：「審罰，則可戰。審罰，則士卒望而畏之，不敢違命。」王曰：「勇哉！」大夫文種曰：「審物，則可戰。審物，則別是非。是非明察，人莫能惑。」王曰：「辯哉！」大夫范蠡曰：「審備，則可戰。審備，慎守以待不虞。備設守固，必可應難。」王曰：「慎哉！」大夫皋如曰：「審聲，則可戰。審於聲音，以別清濁。清濁者，謂吾國君名聞於周室，令諸侯不怨於外。」王曰：「得哉！」大夫扶同曰：「廣

---

19. Again, Huang Rensheng (1996): 247 n. 6 argues for a military interpretation of this line. However, it would be equally possible to understand Grandee Gaoru's advice as pertaining to the moral transformation of people through music, which was part of a very standard discourse at this time.

go on campaign in the cause of justice, to ensure that the other lords would not feel resentful and thus cause problems abroad. He issued an order to the capital city: "If you go to the city gate within five days, then you are a good person. If you take more than five days, then you are no longer one of my subjects, and I will execute you."

Having issued these instructions, [King Goujian of Yue] then entered the palace and gave orders to his wife. The king sat with his back to the screen, and his wife stood facing the screen.[20]

"From this day on," the king said, "the management of the palace will not be discussed outside, and the government of the country will not be discussed here. Everyone should keep to their own position, in order that they may be completely trustworthy. Any problem in the palace is your responsibility; any problem up to a thousand *li* beyond the borders is my responsibility. I am having this audience with you here, to make my warning clear."

The king went out of the palace, and his wife escorted him, but she did not go past the screen. The king shut the door and sealed it with mud. The queen took out her hairpins and sat to one side of the mat.[21] Thinking the matter over, she decided to give up her makeup. Indeed, for the next three months, she did not even have the palace cleaned.

When His Majesty left the palace, he stood with his back to the enceinte, while his grandees paid their respects, facing the wall. The king ordered his grandees as follows: "It is your fault if I have problems inside the country because food is not equitably distributed and the land is not properly cultivated. It is my responsibility if we are shamed in front of the other lords and our failures are known to the entire world because the army has failed to fight the enemy and our troops have shown cowardice. From now on, internal

恩知分，則可戰。廣恩以博施，知分而不外。」王曰：「神哉！」大夫計硯曰：「候天察地，參應其變，則可戰。天變地應，人道便利，三者前見，則可。」王曰：「明哉！」於是勾踐乃退齋而命國人曰：「吾將有不虞之議，自近及遠，無不聞者。」乃復命有司與國人曰：「承命有賞。皆造國門之期，有不從命者，吾將有顯戮。」勾踐恐民不信使以征不義聞於周室，令諸侯不怨於外，令國中曰：「五日之內，則吾良人矣。過五日之外，則非吾之民也，又將加之以

---

20. This translation follows the annotations to the *Guoyu*, 623 n. 1 ["Wuyu"], where Wei Zhao suggests that the *ping* 屏 is not a screen but a physical wall.
21. As noted in *Liji*, 64 ["Quli shang"], the action of sitting to one side of one's mat was considered a sign of depression in ancient China.

affairs will only be decided within the palace, and other matters have nothing to do with you. I am warning you!"

"We will respectfully obey your commands," the grandees said.

The king then left the palace, and the grandees escorted him out of the enceinte, after which he locked the gate and sealed it with mud. The grandees sat to one side of their seating mats, refusing to eat fine foods and not responding to coaxing. King Goujian issued an order to his queen and the grandees: "The country will be left to your guardianship."

After this, [King Goujian of Yue] took his seat on top of the sacrificial altar and had the drums set up and sounded. His troops advanced and went into battle formation. His Majesty immediately had three criminals beheaded as a warning to his soldiers. He gave the following command: "Anyone who disobeys my orders will suffer the same fate!"

The following day, he advanced his army into the suburbs. He had three criminals beheaded as a warning to the troops. "Anyone who disobeys my orders will suffer the same fate!" he announced.

His Majesty then gave orders that those who would be staying in the capital should assemble so that he could say goodbye to them. "You must carry on working hard to keep the country on an even keel—I am going to go and punish our enemies on your behalf," he proclaimed.

He gave orders that the people of the capital would be allowed to escort their family members as far as the suburbs. The soldiers all said goodbye to their parents and siblings, and the people of the capital were overwhelmed with sorrow, so they composed a song in parting. This ran as follows:

> Let us move with all speed to expunge this long-standing humiliation,
> We brandish our spears; we grasp our pikes.
> Whatever disasters we encounter, we will never surrender—
> We are determined to avenge our king and restore our pride.
> Our three armies advance inexorably:
> Those in their way are all doomed.

誅。」教令既行,乃入命於夫人。王背屏,夫人向屏而立。王曰:「自今日之後,內政無出,外政無入。各守其職,以盡其信。內中辱者,則是子。境外千里辱者,則是子也。吾見子於是,以為明誠矣。」王出宮,夫人送王,不過屏。王因反闔其門,填之以土。夫人去笄,側席而坐,安心無容,三月不掃。王出,則復背垣而立,大夫向垣而敬。王乃令大夫曰:「食士不均,地壤不修,使孤有辱於國,是子之罪。臨敵不戰,軍士不死,有辱於諸侯,功隳於天下,

Each of our knights will fight to the death:
Even one hundred men are no match for him.
Heaven will help the virtuous side—
The Wu soldiers have brought this butchery on themselves!
The humiliation suffered by our king will be expunged:
His awe-inspiring might will strike terror in all directions!
Our troops are impossible to destroy,
They are as strong as leopards and wildcats.
As we advance, as we advance, each will do their very best!
Alas! Alas![22]

Everyone present was deeply moved.

The following day, [King Goujian] advanced his army as far as the border. He had three criminals beheaded as a warning to the troops. He announced: "Anyone who disobeys my orders will suffer the same fate!"

Three days later, he moved his army back to Zuili and beheaded three criminals as a warning to the troops. "Anyone who refuses to fight, who commits rape or pillage, will suffer the same fate!" His Majesty said.

King Goujian then ordered his officials to instruct the army as follows: "Anyone who is an only son, come and report to me. I am engaged in a matter affecting the fate of our country; you have left your parents' care, your family's love, to come to the aid of the state in this emergency. If your parents or siblings become sick while you are serving in the military, I will treat them as if they were my own parents or siblings. If one of them dies, I will bury them and mourn them as if it were my own parents or siblings who had passed away!"

The next day, he issued instructions to the army as follows: "If a soldier becomes sick and cannot keep up with the rest of the army, I will give him medicines and porridge, and I will share my food with him."

是孤之責。自今以往，內政無出，外政無入，吾固誡子。」大夫：「敬受命矣。」王乃出。大夫送出垣，反闔外宮之門，填之以土。大夫側席而坐，不禦五味，不答所勸。勾踐有命於夫人、大夫曰：「國有守禦。」乃坐露壇之上，列鼓而鳴之，軍行成陣，即斬有罪者三人，以徇於軍，令曰：「不從吾令者，如斯矣！」明日，徙軍於郊，斬有罪者三人，徇之於軍，令曰：「不從吾令者，如斯矣！」王乃令國中不行者，與之訣，而告之曰：「爾安土守職。吾方往征討我宗廟

---

22. This song consists of rhyming couplets, in the pattern ABBBBAB, with the rhymes taken from the *-o (hou 侯) and *-a (yu 魚) groups, respectively.

The day after that, he again issued instructions to the army as follows: "If there is someone who is not strong enough to wear armor and carry his weapons or who is unwilling to obey royal commands, I will lighten his burdens and give him a more suitable employment."

The following day, he turned his army south of the Yangtze River. Now [King Goujian] laid down the law very strictly and beheaded another five criminals. He announced: "I love my troops even more than I love my own son. However, when one of them commits a crime that merits the death penalty, even my own son could not be excused punishment."

[King Goujian] was afraid that his soldiers were merely afraid of being punished and were not really prepared for battle, so he told himself that he was not yet in a position where his troops would risk their lives in his service. On the road, he happened to see a frog with its chest puffed up with anger, as if it were about to fight, so he leaned on the bar of his chariot. One of his officers asked the king: "Why do you show such admiration for the frog, Your Majesty, that you lean on the bar of your chariot?"

"I have been thinking that although my soldiers have been angry at our situation for a long time, no one has really taken it to heart as I have," King Goujian replied. "That frog knows nothing, but it is angry when it sees an enemy—that is why I bowed to it over the bar of my chariot."

When his troops heard about this, all of them felt that they would be happy to risk their lives for such a king, and every one of them obeyed his commands.[23] The generals in command issued orders to all the troops: "Let each regiment give orders to their platoons; let each platoon give orders to their soldiers: whether it is going home or staying put, advancing, retreating, turning left, turning right—anyone who disobeys orders will be beheaded!"

之讎，以謝於二三子。」令國人各送其子弟於郊境之上。軍士各與父兄昆弟取訣，國人悲哀，皆作離別相去之詞，曰：「躒躁摧長惡兮，擢戟馭受。所離不降兮，以泄我王氣蘇。三軍一飛降兮，所向皆狙。一士判死兮，而當百夫。道祐有德兮，吳卒自屠。雪我王宿恥兮，威振八都。軍伍難更兮，勢如貙貓。行行各努力兮，於乎，於乎！」於是觀者莫不悽惻。明日，復徙軍於境上，斬有罪者三人，徇之於軍，曰：「有不從令者，如此！」後三日，復

---

23. The version of this story given in *Han Feizi*, 554 ["Neichushuo shang" 內儲說上], states that after bowing to the frog, King Goujian continued his training of the military by rewarding those who risked their lives by rushing into a burning building and advancing into the river when he drummed the army forward.

The Wu Army was all camped north of the Yangtze River, while the Yue forces were south of the river. The king of Yue divided his troops into an army of the left and an army of the right, all of them dressed in armor of buffalo hide. He also ordered the men from Anguang to carry stone-tipped arrows and equip themselves with crossbows made in Lu.[24] Meanwhile [King Goujian] took personal command of his own legion, and these six thousand men formed the central army. The following day, he intended to fight a battle at the Yangtze River. Therefore, at dusk, he ordered the army of the left to move five *li* upstream in silence and await the Wu Army there. He also ordered the army of the right to cross the river in silence ten *li* downstream, where they should lie in wait for the Wu Army. At midnight, [King Goujian] gave orders that the army of the left should cross the river, sounding their drums once they were in midstream. Then they should prepare for Wu to attack. When the Wu Army heard this, they were horrified and said to each other: "The Yue troops have been divided into two, and now they are going to be used to attack the main body of our army [in a pincer movement]."[25]

Even though it was pitch dark, they immediately divided their own troops, to encircle the Yue forces. The king of Yue gave orders that his left and right armies should pretend to be about to fight a battle with Wu: they were to make a lot of noise on their big drums. His Majesty had his own legion of six thousand men lying in ambush—they now attacked Wu in silence, not even sounding their drums. The Wu Army suffered a terrible defeat. In the wake of this, the Yue armies of the left and right attacked them,

徙軍於檇李，斬有罪者三人，以徇於軍，曰：「其淫心匿行，不當敵者，如斯矣！」勾踐乃命有司大徇軍，曰：「其有父母無昆弟者，來告我。我有大事，子離父母之養，親老之愛，赴國家之急。子在軍寇之中，父母昆弟有在疾病之地，吾視之如吾父母昆弟之疾病也。其有死亡者，吾葬埋殯送之，如吾父母昆弟之有死亡葬埋之矣。」明日，又徇於軍，曰：「士有疾病，不能隨軍從兵者，吾予其醫藥，給其糜粥，與之同食。」明日，又徇於軍，曰：「筋力不

---

24. This translation follows the commentary by Zhang Jue (2006): 268 n. 5 in reading *Lu sheng zhi nu* 盧生之弩 as "crossbows made in Lu." Sometimes, this is interpreted as a personal name "Lu Sheng's crossbows," and a person of the same name was a *fangshi* 方士 in the time of the first emperor; see *Shiji*, 6.252.
25. The original text reads *shigong* 使攻, which does not make sense, but the parallel line in the *Guoyu*, 626 ["Wuyu"], reads *jiagong* 夾攻—to attack in a pincer movement.

and the Wu Army suffered another terrible defeat at the Battle of You.[26] The Yue armies also defeated the Wu Army in battle outside the suburbs and again at the moat. Having fought three victorious battles in a row, they advanced on Wu. They laid siege to Wu at the western fortifications. The king of Wu was terrified and fled under cover of darkness.

The king of Yue set off in hot pursuit, and he attacked the Wu Army, moving through Jiangyang and Songling. He intended to enter the capital city through the Wu Gate, but when he came within six or seven *li*, looking into the distance at the southern city wall of Wu, he saw the head of Wu Zixu, as big as a cartwheel, his eyes flashing lightning, and his hair streaming in every direction, shooting out sparks for ten *li*. The Yue Army was terrified by this, and so he had to encamp his troops on the road. At midnight on the very same day, there was a violent storm with lashing rain; the thunder crashed, the lightning zigzagged, and the wind whipped up stones and sand, which struck with the force of projectiles released from a bow or crossbow. The Yue Army was thrown into complete disarray—retreating to Songling, the bodies of officers and men were left lying stiff and stark, everyone was in confusion, and nobody was able to stop their flight. Fan Li and Wen Zhong knocked their heads on the ground and bared their shoulders in apology to [Wu] Zixu, and they begged him for permission to move on. Zixu then appeared in a dream to both [Wen] Zhong and [Fan] Li, in which he said: "I always knew that Yue would one day enter Wu in triumph; that is why I requested that my head be suspended from the South Gate, so that I could watch you destroy Wu. I wanted to see King Fuchai suffer! But when I saw you enter the country, I could not bear it, and that is why I used the wind and rain to turn back your troops! However, it is by the will of Heaven that Yue attacks Wu: how can I prevent this? If you wish to proceed, you should go to the East Gate. I will open a route for you there through the city walls, and that will allow you to continue on your way."

足以勝甲兵，志行不足以聽王命者，吾輕其重，和其任。」明日，旋軍於江南，更陳嚴法，復誅有罪者五人，徇曰：「吾愛士也，雖吾子不能過也。及其犯誅，自吾子亦不能脫也。」恐軍士畏法不使，自謂未能得士之死力，道見蛋蟲張腹而怒，將有戰爭之氣，即為之軾。其士卒有問於王曰：「君何為敬蛋蟲，而為之軾？」勾踐曰：「吾思士卒之怒久矣，而未有稱吾意者。今蛋蟲無知之物，見敵而有怒氣，故為之軾。」於是軍士聞之，莫不懷心樂死，人致其命。

---

26. The *Guoyu*, 626 ["Wuyu"], names this as the Battle of Mo 沒.

The following day, the Yue Army approached from the river, traversing Meiyang via the three routes across the Di River, and arrived at the southeast corner of the city.[27] The Yue Army then laid siege to Wu.

After a siege of one year, the Wu Army was exhausted and beaten.[28] The king of Wu was pinned down on Mount Guxu. Wu sent Royal Grandson Luo to bare his shoulders in apology and walk forward on his knees to request a peace treaty with the king of Yue. "Our monarch, Fuchai, dares to reveal his deepest feelings," he said. "In the past, we committed a terrible crime against you at Kuaiji. However, today I would not dare to refuse to obey your orders—I hope to be able to make a peace treaty with Your Majesty to let us all go home. Now you have raised an army to punish me; all I can do is follow your commands. I hope that the peace treaty agreed at Guxu today will be like that agreed at Kuaiji all those years ago. If, thanks to the blessings of Heaven, we can be pardoned our terrible crimes, the people of Wu will be your slaves forever!"

King Goujian could not endure this and was going to agree to a peace treaty when Fan Li intervened. "What happened at Kuaiji is that Heaven gave Yue to Wu, but Wu did not take it. Now Heaven has given Wu to Yue: how can Yue refuse this mandate? You have been working day and night racking your brains and straining every muscle for more than twenty years—was this not for what you have achieved today? Do you really think it is a good idea to just throw away all that we have gained? If Heaven gives

有司、將軍大狥軍中，曰：「隊各自令其部，部各自令其士。歸而不歸，處而不處，進而不進，退而不退，左而不左，右而不右，不如令者，斬！」於是，吳悉兵屯於江北，越軍於江南。越王中分其師以為左右軍，皆被兕甲。又令安廣之人，佩石礛之矢，張盧生之弩。躬率君子之軍六千人，以為中陣。明日，將戰於江，乃以黃昏，令於左軍，御枚遡江而上五里，以須吳兵。復令於右軍，御枚踰江十里，復須吳兵。於夜半，使左軍涉江，鳴鼓中水，以待吳發。

---

27. The location of these places and geographical features is unknown. However, according to a quotation from the *Wudi ji* 吳地記 (Records of the Lands of Wu) preserved in the *Zhengyi* 正義 (Correct Meanings) commentary to *Shiji*, 66.2181 n. 10, the Yue Army sacrificed a white horse and poured libations of wine to Wu Zixu at a location some thirty *li* southeast of Suzhou before proceeding on their campaign; later, a shrine dedicated to his memory was constructed at this site.

28. Other accounts of these events give a siege of three years; see, for example, *Guoyu*, 655 ["Yueyu xia"].

you something and you do not take it, you will suffer disaster thereby. How can you have forgotten the horror of Kuaiji, Your Majesty?"

"I want to follow your advice," King Goujian said, "but I cannot bear to face his ambassador."

Fan Li then sounded the drums and had the army march forward. "His Majesty the king has already entrusted the government to me," he declared. "Ambassador, please leave immediately before you find yourself in trouble!"

The Wu ambassador left in tears. King Goujian felt sorry for him and [ordered a messenger to tell the king of Wu]:[29] "I will send you to live in Yongdong, and I will give you and your wife a fief of more than three hundred households to support you for the rest of your days. Would this be acceptable?"

The king of Wu refused. "Heaven has brought disaster on the kingdom of Wu; instead of coming earlier or later, it has happened during my reign," he said. "I have brought destruction on the ancestral shrines and state altars. The lands and the people of Wu will now belong to Yue. I am old, and I cannot serve Your Majesty as a vassal."

He then killed himself by falling on his sword.

Once King Goujian had destroyed Wu, he turned his army north and crossed the Yangtze and Huai Rivers, meeting the rulers of Qi and Jin at Xuzhou. He also offered tribute to Zhou. King Yuan of Zhou sent an ambassador to bestow gifts on King Goujian. Having received a mandate and title, he returned to the region south of the Yangtze River. He gave the lands in the upper reaches of the Huai River to Chu, he returned to Song the territory that Wu had captured from them, and he gave Lu one hundred square *li* of land east of the Si River. At this time, the Yue Army was on the march from the Huai to the Yangtze River, so all the other lords sent congratulations to them.

吳師聞之中，大駭，相謂曰：「今越軍分為二師，將以使攻我眾。」亦即以夜暗，中分其師，以圍越。越王陰使左、右軍與吳望戰，以大鼓相聞。潛伏其私卒六千人，御枚不鼓，攻吳。吳師大敗。越之左、右軍乃遂伐之，大敗之於囿。又敗之於郊。又敗之於津。如是三戰三北，徑至吳，圍吳於西城。吳王大懼，夜遁。越王追奔攻吳，兵入於江陽松陵，欲入胥門。來至六七里，望吳南城，見伍子胥頭巨若車輪，目若耀電，鬚髮四張，射於十里。越軍大

---

29. The original text reads: *shiling ru wei Wuwang* 使令入謂吳王 (ordered a command to enter and tell the king of Wu). This is being understood as: *shi ren wei Wuwang* 使人謂吳王 (ordered a messenger to tell the king of Wu), following the parallel line in *Shiji*, 41.1745.

The king of Yue now wanted to return to Wu. Just as he was about to set out, he asked Fan Li, "Why is it that what you say so often turns out to be the will of Heaven?"

"This is the Way of Sunü," Fan Li replied.[30] "Every word accords [with Heaven].[31] If Your Majesty is concerned about a matter of state, there are records in the *Jade Gate* and principles set out in the *Metal Casket*. Consult them; you will understand what to do."[32]

"Good!" the king of Yue said. "I have now made myself king; will everything go well?"

"No," [Fan] Li replied. "In the past, the rulers of Wu also called themselves kings and thus usurped the title of the Son of Heaven—the constellations moved against them, and the sun suffered an eclipse. Now you have usurped the title as well, so I am afraid that anomalous signs will soon be seen again in the skies."

The king of Yue [paid no attention to him] and returned to Wu.[33] He held a banquet on the Wen Tower, and all the ministers were enjoying themselves. Then he gave orders that the musicians perform a song about the attack on Wu. The music master said: "I have heard that when undertaking a great matter of state, music should be composed in the *cao* mode but that once everything has been successfully accomplished, one can sing and dance.[34] Your Majesty's respect for virtue has resulted in the

懼，留兵。即日夜半，暴風疾雨，雷奔電激，飛石揚砂，疾於弓弩。越軍壞敗松陵，卻退。兵士僵斃，人眾分解，莫能救止。范蠡、文種乃稽顙肉袒，拜謝子胥，願乞假道。子胥乃與種、蠡夢，曰：「吾知越之必入吳矣，故求置吾頭於南門，以觀汝之破吳也。惟欲以窮夫差，定汝入我之國，吾心又不忍，故為風雨，以還汝軍。然越之伐吳，自是天也，吾安能止哉？越如欲入，更從東門，我當為汝開道貫城，以通汝路。」於是，越軍明日更從江出，入

---

30. Sunü is an ancient Chinese deity. Most early references stress her association with music; see, for example, *Chuci*, 273 ["Jiuhuai" 九懷. "Zhaoshi" 昭世], and *Shiji*, 12.472. The *Wu Yue chunqiu* seems to be drawing on a different tradition.

31. This translation follows the commentary by Zhang Jue (2006): 275 n. 3.

32. Sun Yirang (1895): 3.15a–15b suggests that the text of the *Wu Yue chunqiu* is corrupt at this point and that the words *wang wen* 王問 (Your Majesty can ask) should be understood as the book title *Yumen* 玉門.

33. Most editions of the text lack the characters *buting* 不聽 (paid no attention to him); however, some do include them; see, for example, Zhang Jue (2006): 274.

34. *Cao* 操 was a kind of music played on the *qin*, which was considered appropriate for times of trouble; see *Hou Hanshu*, 35.1201 n. 4.

transformation of your country into a place where the way reigns: you have executed the wicked, you have avenged the crime committed against you and expunged the humiliations you have suffered, striking awe into the other lords and achieving the status of a hegemon-king. Your victories will be recorded in paintings; your successes will be carved into metal and stone. Paeans will be played on strings and pipes, and your name will be recorded on bamboo and silk. I ask your permission to pick up my *qin* and play for you."

Then he performed the song "Success," and the words ran as follows:[35]

How difficult! I want to attack Wu, but is it too soon? . . .

Grandee Zhong and [Fan] Li commented: "Wu killed the loyal minister Wu Zixu—why should we not attack the people of Wu?"

Grandee Zhong then stepped forward and offered a toast. He proclaimed:

> Heaven has assisted us; our king has received its blessings,
> Excellent ministers have gathered to help our virtuous monarch.
> The ancestral shrines support his rule; the ghosts and spirits protect him,
> Our king never neglects his ministers, and so they put forth their best efforts.
> The will of Heaven can neither be ignored nor withstood—
> Let me lift my brimming cup and wish His Majesty blessings without end![36]

海陽於三道之翟水，乃穿東南隅以達。越軍遂圍吳。守一年，吳師累敗，遂棲吳王於姑胥之山。吳使王孫駱肉袒膝行而前，請成於越王，曰：「孤臣夫差，敢布腹心。異日得罪於會稽，夫差不敢逆命，得與君王結成以歸。今君王舉兵而誅孤臣，孤臣惟命是聽。」意者猶以今日之姑胥，曩日之會稽也。「若僥天之中，得赦其大辟，則吳願長為臣妾。」勾踐不忍其言，將許之成。范蠡曰：「會稽之事，天以越賜吳，吳不取。今天以吳賜越，越可逆命乎？且君王早朝晏罷，切齒銘骨，謀之二十餘年，豈不緣一朝之事耶？今日得而棄之，其

---

35. According to *Fengsu tongyi*, 293 ["Shengyin" 聲音], this particular title was considered suitable for triumphal music in the early imperial era.
36. The final word of every line in this proclamation rhymes, and each of these characters belongs to the *-ək (*zhi* 職) group.

The king of Yue sat in stony silence. Grandee Zhong continued:

> Our king is wise and benevolent, he cherishes the way and virtue,
> Having taken his revenge by destroying Wu, he has not forgotten to return to us.
> He has not begrudged us our rewards: the wicked have been kept out!
> When monarch and ministers are in harmony, myriad blessings are born,
> Let me lift my brimming cup and wish His Majesty long life without end![37]

The ministers gathered together on top of the tower; all laughed heartily at this, but the king of Yue did not look pleased at all. Fan Li understood that King Goujian could not care less about the deaths of his people, but he begrudged any loss of land—now with the success of his plans and the situation in the country having been stabilized, he would be sure to want further major victories before he ever returned home. That is the reason why he looked angry and upset.

Fan Li had accompanied His Majesty to Wu, and now he wanted to leave, but he was afraid that King Goujian might then never return home and that he would be abandoning the proper relationship between a ruler and his vassal, so he followed along until His Majesty returned to Yue. As they traveled, he said to Wen Zhong: "You should leave! The king of Yue is going to have you executed!"

[Grandee] Zhong replied that this could not possibly be the case. [Fan] Li then wrote a letter, which he sent to Zhong, saying:

計可乎？天與不取，還受其咎。君何忘會稽之厄乎？」勾踐曰：「吾欲聽子言，不忍對其使者。」范蠡遂鳴鼓而進兵，曰：「王已屬政於執事，使者急去，不時得罪。」吳使涕泣而去。勾踐憐之，使令入謂吳王曰：「吾置君於甬東，給君夫婦三百餘家，以沒王世，可乎？」吳王辭曰：「天降禍於吳國，不在前後，正孤之身，失滅宗廟社稷者。吳之土地民臣，越既有之，孤老矣，不能臣王。」遂伏劍自殺。勾踐已滅吳，乃以兵北渡江、淮，與齊、晉諸侯會於徐州，致

---

37. These two recitations use the same rhyme throughout and through this rhyme are linked to the second recitation performed at the Wen Tower in the reign of King Fuchai of Wu, immediately prior to the suicide of Wu Zixu, as described in chapter 5.

I have heard that there are four seasons—in spring things are born and in the winter they die. People also have periods of success and failure; after good luck comes the bad. A wise man holds to his principles and knows when to advance and when to withdraw; that determines whether he will live or die. I may not be very clever, but I do know when it is the time to leave. When the birds have flown away, the bow is put back in its case; when the cunning hare is dead, the hunting dog will be cooked as food. The king of Yue has a long neck and a mouth like a bird; his eye is as sharp as a hawk's, and he walks like a wolf—this is the kind of person that you can go through adversity with, but you cannot share a time of happiness; you can go through danger with him, but not live in peace.[38] If you do not depart, it is clear that you will suffer disaster!

Wen Zhong did not believe what he said about the king of Yue secretly plotting against him. Fan Li discussed with him the idea of leaving and trying his luck elsewhere.

On Dingwei Day of the ninth month, in the twenty-fourth year of his reign [473 BCE], Fan Li said goodbye to the king. He told him, "I have heard it said that a vassal should work hard when his ruler is worried and a vassal should die when his lord suffers humiliation—this is the first principle of justice. Unfortunately, in serving Your Majesty, I was unable to deal in advance with the troubles that had not yet come to fruition, nor was I able to save us from disasters that had already struck. However, throughout all this, I was determined to support you and strengthen the country, so I had to go on living in spite of everything. I thought carefully about this when I had to go and serve in Wu and saw how they humiliated

貢於周。周元王使人賜勾踐。已受命號，去還江南，以淮上地與楚，歸吳所侵宋地，與魯泗東方百里。當是之時，越兵橫行於江、淮之上，諸侯畢賀。越王還於吳，當歸而問於范蠡曰：「何子言之，其合於天？」范蠡曰：「此素女之道，一言即合大王之事。王問為實，金匱之要，在於上下。」越王曰：「善哉！吾不稱王，其可悉乎？」蠡曰：「不可。昔吳之稱王，僭天子之號，天變於上，日為陰蝕。今君遂僭號不歸，恐天變復見。」越王不聽，還於吳，置酒文臺，

---

38. This remarkable description of King Goujian's appearance is at least in part derived from *Shiji*, 41.1746.

you, Your Majesty; I could not die, because I was very much afraid that you might be slandered by Chancellor Pi and suffer the same fate as that which overtook Wu Zixu. Since I did not dare to die at this point, I had to live on for a little while. It is impossible to cope with such intense shame for any length of time, and the experience of being a slave is truly unendurable. However, thanks to the numinous powers of our ancestral shrines, and your awe-inspiring virtues, Your Majesty, you have turned defeat into victory and established a dynasty just as Tang overthrew the Xia and Wu defeated the Shang. With such victories, your humiliations have been expunged; indeed, this is why I have been able to enjoy a position of power for a long time. But from this point on, let me to say goodbye to you forever."

The king of Yue was very upset, and his tears wetted his robe. "The knights and grandees of this country trust you," he said, "the ordinary people of Yue also believe in you, and I myself have placed my life in your hands and obeyed your orders. Now you talk about leaving and say that you want to go. This means that Heaven has abandoned Yue and given up on me—whom can I now rely on? Let me put it clearly: if you stay, I will divide my country with you; if you insist on leaving, I will have your wife and children tortured to death!"

"I have heard it said: 'A gentleman waits for the right moment to act, his plans are matured in advance, he would die rather than have his motives suspected, and he never lies to himself,'" Fan Li replied. "It is I who am determined to leave—what laws have my wife and children broken? You should forgive them, Your Majesty. Let me say my farewells!"

He then climbed onto a little boat and sailed out of the mouth of the Yangtze River delta, into the Five Lakes. Nobody knows where he went.

Once Fan Li had gone, the king of Yue was very upset. He summoned Grandee Zhong and asked him, "Can I bring Li back?"

"No," Zhong replied.

"Why not?" His Majesty asked.

羣臣為樂。乃命樂作伐吳之曲。樂師曰：「臣聞即事作操，功成作樂。君王崇德，誨化有道之國，誅無義之人，復讎還恥，威加諸侯，受霸王之功。功可象於圖畫，德可刻於金石，聲可託於絃管，名可留於竹帛。臣請引琴而鼓之。」遂作章暢辭曰：「屯乎！今欲伐吳可未耶？」大夫種、蠡曰：「吳殺忠臣伍子胥，今不伐吳人，何須？」大夫種進祝酒，其辭曰：「皇天祐助，我王受福。良臣集謀，我王之德。宗廟輔政，鬼神承翼。君不忘臣，臣盡其力。上天蒼蒼，不可掩塞。觴酒二升，萬福無極！」於是，越王默然無言。大夫種曰：「我

"The hexagram for the time that Li left has three *yin* lines and three *yang* lines," Zhong said.[39] "No one can control the deity Riqian.[40] When the Dark Warrior and Tiankong march forward striking awe into everyone, who would dare to stop them?[41] They cross Tianhuan, they ford Tianliang, and then they enter Tianyi, obstructing the numinous light before them.[42] Anyone who speaks of this will die; anyone who looks at them will go mad. I hope that Your Majesty will not try to bring him back, because Fan Li will not return."

The king of Yue took in [Fan Li's] wife and children, giving them a grant of one hundred *li* of land. "Anyone who dares to offend them will be punished by Heaven."

The king of Yue ordered his finest artisans to make a bronze image of Fan Li, and he placed it beside his seat, where he discussed matters of government from dawn until dusk.

After this, Jini pretended that he had gone mad, and Grandees Xieyong, Futong, Gaoru, and the others found themselves daily more alienated, to the point where they no longer bothered to attend court in

王賢仁，懷道抱德。滅讎破吳，不忘返國。賞無所悋，羣邪杜塞。君臣同和，福祐千億。觴酒二升，萬歲難極！」臺上羣臣大悅而笑，越王面無喜色。范蠡知勾踐愛壞土，不惜羣臣之死，以其謀成國定，必復不須功而返國也，故面有憂色而不悅也。范蠡從吳欲去，恐勾踐未返，失人臣之義，乃從入越。行謂文種曰：「子來去矣，越王必將誅子。」種不然言。蠡復為書，遺種曰：「吾聞天有四時，春生冬伐。人有盛衰，泰終必否。知進退存亡，而不失其正，惟賢人乎！蠡雖不才，明知進退。高鳥已散，良弓將藏。狡兔已盡，良犬就

---

39. This line refers to the two trigrams Kun 坤 and Qian 乾, which represent Earth and Heaven, respectively; see *Zhouyi*, 24 and 1, respectively. Since these two trigrams are perfectly balanced, Fan Li's actions are in accord with both Heaven and Earth.
40. Riqian is thought to be the same deity as Riyoushen 日游神, a god of ill fortune. This appears to be by far the earliest-known reference to this figure in Chinese literature.
41. Xuanwu, or the Dark Warrior, is the deity controlling the north; see Sun and Kistemaker (1997): 117–18. Tiankong is also identified as the name of a deity, but this is the first-known reference to such a god; see Zhang Jue (2006): 280 n. 4.
42. Tianhuan is the star Zeta Tauri; Tianliang is the pair of stars Xi and Tau Sagittarii; and Tianyi is the star 7 Draco; see Sun and Kistemaker (1997): 151 and 154 and *Jinshu*, 11.301.

person. Grandee Zhong was too depressed to be able to participate in government, and someone slandered him to the king: "Wen Zhong gave up his position as prime minister to make Your Majesty a hegemon-king. Now he is angry and resentful because he has not been promoted or had his fief increased. He takes his rage out on his household and cannot control his anger in public; that is the reason he no longer comes to court."

Subsequently, [Grandee] Zhong remonstrated: "The reason why I came to court early and finished late, working hard all the time, was simply because of the situation with Wu. Now they have already been destroyed, what is Your Majesty worried about?"

The king of Yue was silent.

At this time, Lord Ai of Lu was concerned about the Three Huans, and he hoped that some of the other lords would attack them for him.[43] The Three Huans were worried about the consequences of Lord Ai's anger, and so there was coup and countercoup between the former lord and his ministers. Lord Ai ended up fleeing to Jing, and the Three Huans attacked him there. The lord then fled to Wei, and from there, to Yue. The country of Lu was left empty and bare; the people of the country were deeply upset by this state of affairs. They came to welcome Lord Ai back, and he went home with them.[44] King Goujian was worried that Wen Zhong had not offered any plan to deal with this situation, and so he did not attack the Three Huans on Lord Ai's behalf.

In the twenty-fifth year of his reign [472 BCE], at dawn on Bingwu Day, the king of Yue summoned his prime minister, Grandee Zhong, and

烹。夫越王為人長頸鳥啄，鷹視狼步。可與共患難，而不可共處樂。可與履危，不可與安。子若不去，將害於子，明矣。」文種不信其言越王陰謀。范蠡議欲去微倖。

二十四年九月丁未，范蠡辭於王曰：「臣聞主憂臣勞，主辱臣死，義一也。今臣事大王，前則無滅未萌之端，後則無救已傾之禍。雖然，臣終欲成君霸國，故不辭一死一生。臣竊自惟，乃使於吳。王之慚辱，蠡所以不死者，誠恐讒

---

43. The Three Huans refer to the three major clans in Lu descended from Lord Huan 魯桓公 (r. 711–694 BCE) who dominated the political life in this state for more than a century.
44. Lord Ai's troubles with the Three Huans are documented in a number of historical texts; see, for example, *Zuozhuan*, 1735 [Ai 27], and *Shiji*, 33.1545.

asked him: "I have heard that it is easy to know another person but difficult to know yourself. What are you like, Prime Minister?"

"Alas!" Zhong said. "You know that I am brave, Your Majesty, but you do not know of my benevolence. You know that I am loyal, but you do not understand that I am also trustworthy. On so many occasions I have got rid of pretty women from your harem, stopped the performance of lascivious music, and removed persons promulgating all sorts of stories about marvels and other nonsense, but all this good advice and conspicuous loyalty has irritated Your Majesty. I have offended you—as is always the case—by going against your wishes. I would not dare to refuse to speak, even if this costs me my life; I am prepared to tell you the truth and then die. In the past, when [Wu] Zixu was serving in Wu, he was executed by King Fuchai. He told me: 'When the cunning hare is killed, the hunting dog will be cooked for food. Likewise, once the enemy state is destroyed, the ministers who planned this will be killed.' Fan Li said exactly the same thing to me.[45] Why should you be so determined, Your Majesty, to contravene the eighth section of the *Jade Gate*? I know what you intend!"

The king of Yue was silent and made no response. Grandee [Zhong] as well went no further.

[Grandee Zhong went home] and smeared excrement on the lugs [of his bronze *ding*].[46] His wife said: "You are debasing your position as prime

於太宰嚭，成伍子胥之事。故不敢前死，且須臾而生。夫恥辱之心不可以大，流汗之愧不可以忍。幸賴宗廟之神靈，大王之威德，以敗為成。斯湯、武克夏、商而成王業者。定功雪恥，臣所以當席日久，臣請從斯辭矣。」越王惻然，泣下霑衣，言曰：「國之士大夫是子，國之人民是子，使孤寄身託號，以俟命矣。今子云去，欲將逝矣。是天之棄越，而喪孤也，亦無所恃者矣。孤竊有言，公位乎，分國共之。去乎，妻子受戮。」范蠡曰：「臣聞君子俟時，計不數謀，死不被疑，內不自欺。臣既逝矣，妻子何法乎？王其勉之，臣從此辭。」乃乘扁舟，出三江，入五湖，人莫知其所適。范蠡既去，越王愀然變色，召

---

45. According to the *Wu Yue chunqiu*, this statement was in fact first addressed by the king of Wu to the two grandees of Yue and then by Fan Li to Grandee Zhong.
46. Lu Wenchao's commentary, quoted in Zhang Jue (2006): 284 n. 1, notes that the original text is corrupt at this point. Zhang Jue suggests adding the characters *gui er* 歸而 ([Grandee Zhong] went home and). Bronze *ding*s were a sign of exceptionally high status in ancient China, and hence, Grandee Zhong's behavior stresses his feeling of humiliation.

minister; is this because you think the king doesn't pay you enough? We were just about to eat, but instead of enjoying the meal, you smear [our dings] with excrement—what is that in aid of? You have your wife and children beside you; furthermore, you are the prime minister: what more can you hope for? Are you not being too greedy? Why are you behaving in this bizarre and confusing way?"

"How sad!" Zhong said, "You don't understand. Our king has now escaped from durance, and he has expunged the humiliations inflicted on him by Wu, and all I have achieved is to put myself in a position where I am sure to be killed. I offered him a plan consisting of nine techniques, which was terrible for [Wu], but which should be considered as a sign of my loyal service to His Majesty. However, our king does not think about that. He just says: 'It is easy to know another person but difficult to know yourself.' I answered him, but after that, there was no more conversation. This is a very bad sign. When I go back to the palace, I am afraid that I will never leave it alive, so I must say my final farewells to you now, for we will next meet in the Underworld."

"How do you know that?" his wife asked.

"When I had an audience with His Majesty," Zhong replied, "he contravened the eighth section of the *Jade Gate*. When the hour contravenes the day sign, then a monarch will be murdered by his ministers, for when such an evil omen appears, good men are sure to be killed.[47] However, today, the day sign contravenes the hour, which means that a monarch will kill his minister, so the end of my life is not far removed now."

大夫種曰:「蠡可追乎?」種曰:「不及也。」王曰:「奈何?」種曰:「蠡去時,陰畫六,陽畫三。日前之神,莫能制者。玄武天空威行,孰敢止者?度天關,涉天梁,後入天一,前翳神光,言之者死,視之者狂。臣願大王勿復追也。蠡終不還矣。」越王乃收其妻子,封百里之地。有敢侵之者,上天所殃。於是越王乃使良工鑄金象范蠡之形,置之坐側,朝夕論政。自是之後,計硯佯狂,大夫曳庸、扶同、皐如之徒,日益疏遠,不親於朝。大夫種內憂,不朝。人或讒之於王曰:「文種棄宰相之位,而令君王霸於諸侯。今官不加增,

---

47. Zhang Jue (2006): 284 n. 9 interprets this conversation in the light of the information given earlier about the timing of the confrontation between King Goujian and Grandee Zhong. This took place on Bingwu Day, at dawn (Mao 卯 Hour): according to *Huainanzi*, 277 ["Tianwen xun"], Bing represents the element Fire, while Mao represents Wood; hence, the hour is contravened by the day sign and is inauspicious for the minister.

The king of Yue summoned the prime minister back again and said: "Your secret planning abilities and knowledge of the military arts have served to overthrow our enemies and capture their kingdom. Out of the nine stratagems that you put forward, three were enough to destroy the powerful state of Wu—the remaining six you still have in reserve. I would like you to take those remaining techniques to the Underworld and plot against the ancestors of the people of Wu there, on behalf of our former kings."

[Grandee] Zhong looked up at the sky and sighed. "Alas!" he said, "I have heard people say that the greatest kindnesses go unrequited, and the greatest successes are never rewarded; is this not one of those instances? How much I regret not following Fan Li's advice, for now I find that the king of Yue wants to execute me! Because I failed to take in good advice, I feel as if I have been daubed in excrement."

The king of Yue presented the sword named Shulu to Wen Zhong.[48] When Zhong took hold of the sword, he sighed again and said: "The prime minister from Nanying is now the king of Yue's prisoner."[49] Laughing to himself, he continued: "For centuries to come, any loyal ministers are sure to want to compare themselves to me!" Then he fell on this sword and died.

The king of Yue buried Zhong at Mount Xi in the capital. He had more than three thousand soldiers from his battleships build a ding-shaped tomb. Some people say that he was interred below the Three Peaks.[50] One year after the funeral, Wu Zixu came from the sea to collect Zhong, cutting

位不益封，乃懷怨望之心，憤發於內，色變於外，故不朝耳。」異日，種諫曰：「臣所以在朝而晏罷，若身疾作者，但為吳耳。今已滅之，王何憂乎？」越王默然。時魯哀公患三桓，欲因諸侯以伐之。三桓亦患哀公之怒。以故君臣作難，哀公奔陘。三桓攻哀公。公奔衛，又奔越。魯國空虛，國人悲之，來迎哀公，與之俱歸。勾踐憂文種之不圖，故不為哀公伐三桓也。

二十五年丙午平旦，越王召相國大夫種而問之：「吾聞知人易，自知難。其知相國何如人也？」種曰：「哀哉！大王知臣勇也，不知臣仁也。知臣忠也，不知臣信也。臣誠數以損聲色，滅淫樂，奇說怪論，盡言竭忠，以犯大王。逆心咈耳，必以獲罪。臣非敢愛死不言。言而後死，昔子胥於吳矣。夫差之

---

48. This is the same sword as that which Wu Zixu was given when he was ordered to commit suicide, highlighting the parallels between their experiences.
49. The original text reads Nanyang 南陽; however, commentators agree that this should be understood as Nanying 南郢.
50. In the *Yuejue shu*, 62 ["Jidi zhuan"], it says that Grandee Zhong was buried at a place named Sanpeng 三蓬 by his own request.

through the heart of the mountain—together they floated out to the sea. Thus, the waves that come before the sweep of the tide are governed by Wu Zixu; the floodwaters behind, by Grandee Zhong.[51]

Having executed his loyal minister and made himself hegemon over the lands east of the [Hangu] Pass, the king of Yue moved his capital to Langya and erected the Viewing Tower, with a circumference of seven *li*, to look out over the Eastern Sea.[52] He had eight thousand suicide troops and three hundred war boats there. A short time later, he began to recruit wise men. Confucius heard about this and went to present the *yaqin* and the ritual and music of the former kings to Yue, followed by his disciples.[53] The king of Yue donned his Tangyi armor, buckled the sword Buguang to his belt, and grasped the spear called Qulu: he ordered three hundred suicide troops to go into battle formation below the pass. A short time later, Confucius arrived. The king of Yue said: "I am honored, sir. What have you got to teach me?"

誅也，謂臣曰：『狡兔死，良犬烹，敵國滅，謀臣亡。』范蠡亦有斯言。何大王問犯玉門之第八，臣見王志也。」越王默然不應。大夫亦罷。哺其耳以成人惡。其妻曰：「君賤！一國之相，少王祿乎？臨食不亨，哺以惡何？妻子在側，匹夫之能自致相國，尚何望哉！無乃為貪乎？何其志忽忽若斯？」種曰：「悲哉！子不知也。吾王既免於患難，雪恥於吳。我悉徙宅，自投死亡之地，盡九術之謀，於彼為佞，在君為忠，王不察也，乃曰：『知人易，自知難。』吾答之，又無他語。是兇妖之證也。吾將復入，恐不再還，與子長訣，相求於玄冥之下。」妻曰：「何以知之？」種曰：「吾見王時，正犯玉門之第八也，辰剋其日，上賊於下，是為亂醜，必害其良。今日剋其辰，上賊下，止吾命

---

51. There are numerous references in ancient and medieval Chinese texts to the importance of Wu Zixu as a water deity; see Yuan Ke (1991): 178.
52. Numerous texts record King Goujian's move of his capital city to Langya; however, this event has been the source of much controversy among historians; see Xin Deyong (2010) and Gu Jiegang (1987): 32. However, recently discovered bamboo texts suggest that Yue was significantly involved in the politics of the Shandong peninsula in the early Warring States era, making it much more likely that this move did indeed take place; see Li Xueqin (2011): 192.
53. The *yaqin* is a type of musical instrument particularly highly prized in ancient China. Unfortunately for the historicity of this story, the *Zuozhuan*, 1698 [Ai 16], records the death of Confucius in 479 BCE, some eight years before the death of Grandee Zhong.

Confucius said: "I can instruct you in the Way of the Five Sovereigns and the Three Kings; that is why I have brought this *yaqin* to present to Your Majesty."

The king of Yue sighed and said: "It is the nature of the people of Yue to be feeble and stupid; furthermore, we live amid mountains and travel everywhere by water. Boats are our chariots, and oars are our horses—we travel as if we are blown by the winds; once we have left a place, we rarely go back. Furthermore, it is the custom in Yue to enjoy fighting and to be willing to risk death. What have you got to say to us, sir? In what do you want to instruct us?"

Confucius made no response. Instead, he said goodbye and left.

The king of Yue sent someone to go to Mount Muke and collect the body of King Yunchang, for he wanted to move his tomb to Langya.[54] Three times, they dug down into the grave of King Yunchang, and each time the tomb emitted puffs of smoke, and flying rocks and sand struck the workmen, so no one wanted to go down there. King Goujian said: "Can it be that our former ruler does not want to be moved?"

He then gave up and departed.

King Goujian then sent an ambassador to order that Qi, Chu, Qin, and Jin should all support the Zhou house: having sworn a blood covenant, they departed. Lord Huan of Qin did not obey the king of Yue's orders, so Goujian then selected generals and officers from the combined forces of Wu and Yue; after which he went west and crossed the Yellow River to attack Qin.[55] His military suffered greatly on this campaign. However, Qin

須臾之間耳。」越王復召相國，謂曰：「子有陰謀兵法，傾敵取國。九術之策，今用三已破彊吳。其六尚在子。所願幸以餘術，為孤前王於地下謀吳之前人。」於是種仰天歎曰：「嗟乎！吾聞大恩不報，大功不還，其謂斯乎？吾悔不隨范蠡之謀，乃為越王所戮。吾不食善言，故哺以人惡。」越王遂賜文種屬盧之劍。種得劍又歎曰：「南陽之宰，而為越王之擒。」自笑曰：「後百世之末，忠臣必以吾為喻矣。」遂伏劍而死。越王葬種於國之西山，樓船之卒三千餘人，造鼎足之羨，或入三峰之下。葬七[一]年，伍子胥從海上穿山脅而持種去，與之俱浮於海。故前潮水潘候者，伍子胥也。後重水者，大夫種也。越王既

---

54. The burial of King Goujian's father at this site is also mentioned in *Yuejue shu*, 62 ["Jidi zhuan"].
55. At this point, Lord Huan of Qin had been dead for over 160 years. The ruler actually involved in these events was Lord Ligong of Qin 秦厲共公 (r. 476–443 BCE).

was terrified, and they admitted that they had brought this on themselves by their own ill-considered actions, so Yue was able to simply turn the army around. The soldiers were delighted, and they composed "The Song of the River Bridge." This went as follows:

> There is a bridge over the river, and we cross by the river bridge,
> Having raised an army, we attacked the king of Qin.
> At the beginning of winter, in the tenth month, there is much snow and frost,
> The bitter cold on our journey is indeed hard to bear.
> We went into battle formation: before we had crossed swords, the Qin Army surrendered,
> The other lords are scared—they are all terrified.
> Our fame has spread throughout the [four] seas, we strike awe into distant countries,
> Our king is a hegemon, like Lord Mu [of Qin], Lord Huan of Qi, or King Zhuang of Chu.
> The world is at peace; people live long,
> How sad that as we went and returned, there was no bridge across the Yellow River![56]

After Yue destroyed Wu, the Central States were all afraid of them.

In the twenty-sixth year of his reign [471 BCE], the king of Yue decided that the Viscount of Zhu was behaving in a wicked manner; he arrested him

已誅忠臣，霸於關東，從琅邪起觀臺，周七里，以望東海。死士八千人，戈船三百艘。居無幾，射求賢士。孔子聞之，從弟子奉先生雅琴禮樂，奏於越。越王乃被唐夷之甲，帶步光之劍，杖屈盧之矛，出死士，以三百人為陣關下。孔子有頃到，越王曰：「唯唯，夫子何以教之？」孔子曰：「丘能述五帝、三王之道，故奏雅琴，以獻之大王。」越王喟然歎曰：「越性脆而愚，水行山處，以船為車，以楫為馬，往若飄然，去則難從，悅兵敢死，越之常也。夫子何說而欲教之？」孔子不答，因辭而去。越王使人如木客山，取元［允］常之喪，欲徙葬琅邪。三穿元［允］常之墓，墓中生熛風，飛砂石以射人，人莫能入。

---

56. The final character in each line of this song would have rhymed—ŋ in Later Han Chinese; however, in terms of rhyme scheme, the song follows a pattern AAAABACAA. The rhymes are taken from the *-aŋ (*yang* 陽), *-uŋ (*dong* 冬), and *-oŋ (*dong* 東) groups, respectively.

and took him back home. Meanwhile, he established the heir to the title, He, in his place.[57] That winter, Lord Ai of Lu was forced into exile by the Three Huans. The king of Yue wanted to attack the Three Huans on his behalf, but the other rulers and grandees refused to agree to this, so in the end nothing happened.

In the winter of the twenty-seventh year of his reign [469 BCE], King Goujian was lying sick in bed, and he was about to die.[58] He told his crown prince, Xingyi:[59] "As a descendant of Yu, having received the virtue of King Yunchang, with the help of Heaven and the spirits and the blessings of the gods, even though I was cooped up in the poverty-stricken and remote lands of Yue, I was able to help out the vanguard of the Chu Army and destroy the forces of the king of Wu. I have traversed the Yangtze River and crossed the Huai; I have taken my troops into the lands of Jin and Qi. My success has been truly overwhelming! Having achieved such heights, how can others not take warning? It is very difficult to remain long in power as the descendant of a hegemon; you must be very careful!"

After this, he passed away.

Xingyi was on the throne for one year, and then he died, to be succeeded by his son Weng.[60] When Weng died, he was succeeded by his son, Buyang. When Buyang died, he was succeeded by his son, Wujiang. When [Wu]jiang died, he was succeeded by his son, Yu. When Yu died, he was succeeded by his son, Zun. When Zun died, he was succeeded by his son,

勾踐曰：「吾前君其不徙乎？」遂置而去。勾踐乃使使號令齊、楚、秦、晉，皆輔周室，血盟而去。秦桓公不如越王之命，勾踐乃選吳越將士，西渡河以攻秦。軍士苦之。會秦怖懼，逆自引咎，越乃還軍。軍人悅樂，遂作河梁之詩曰：「渡河梁兮渡河梁，舉兵所伐攻秦王。孟冬十月多雪霜，隆寒道路誠難當。陣兵未濟秦師降，諸侯怖懼皆恐惶。聲傳海內威遠邦，稱霸穆桓齊楚莊。天下安寧壽考長，悲去歸兮何無梁。」自越滅吳，中國皆畏之。

---

57. King Goujian's involvement in the political problems in Zhu is described in *Zuozhuan*, 1719 [Ai 22] and 1723 [Ai 24].
58. In fact, King Goujian of Yue did not die until the thirty-second year of his reign, which is 464 BCE.
59. The name of King Goujian's son and heir is given in different forms in different texts. The *Shiji*, 41.1747, names him as Shiyu 鼫與; the *Yuejue shu*, 58 ["Jidi zhuan"], as Yuyi 與夷; and the *Zhushu jinian*, B.19a, as Luying 鹿郢.
60. Alternative genealogies for the later kings of Yue are given in *Shiji*, 41.1747, and *Yuejue shu*, 58 ["Jidi zhuan"]; see also Henry (2007) for a comparison.

Qin. From Goujian to Qin, there were eight kings who all called themselves hegemons, over a period of 224 years. [Qin] lost the support of both his family and the people, and so he abandoned Langya and moved the capital back to Wu.[61] There were ten generations from the Yellow Sovereign to Shaokang, and there were six generations from the time when Yu accepted the abdication [of Yao] to Shaokang taking the throne—this makes 144 years. Shaokang took power 424 years after the accession of Zhuanxu:

Yellow Sovereign
Changyi
Zhuanxu
Gun
Yu
Qi
Dakang
Zhonglu
Xiang
Shaokang
Wuyu
Wuyù [came to power] ten generations after Wuyu.[62]
Wutan
Fukang
Yunchang

　　二十六年，越王以邾子無道，而執以歸，立其太子何。冬，魯哀公以三桓之逼，來奔。越王欲為伐三桓，以諸侯大夫不用命，故不果耳。
　　二十七年冬，勾踐寢疾，將卒，謂太子與夷曰：「吾自禹之後，承元［允］常之德，蒙天靈之祐，神祇之福，從窮越之地籍，楚之前鋒，以摧吳王之幹戈，跨江涉淮，從晉、齊之地，功德巍巍，自致於斯。其可不誡乎？夫霸者之後，難以久立，其慎之哉！」遂卒。興夷即位一年，卒，子翁。翁卒，子不揚。不揚卒，子無彊。彊卒，子玉。玉卒，子尊。尊卒，子親。自勾踐至於親，其歷八主，皆稱霸，積年二百二十四年。親眾皆失，而去琅邪，徙於

---

61. The move of the Yue capital city from Langya to Wu is mentioned in the *Zhushu jinian*, B.19a, which dates these events to 379 BCE.
62. The name of this individual is given as Wuren 無壬 rather than Wuyù 無玉 in some early editions of the *Wu Yue chunqiu*. This is thought to be a graphic error; see Yu Yue (1902): 18.8a.

Goujian
Xingyi
Bushou
Buyang
Wujiang
Lumuliu used the name Lord You.[63]

Wanghou merely entitled himself a lord.[64] After Zun and Qin lost Langya, it was destroyed by Chu. From Goujian to the reign of King Qin, there were eight monarchs, and they called themselves hegemons for a total of 224 years. From the time when Wuyu was first enfeoffed with the kingdom of Yue to the time when King Yushan [of the Eastern Yue] rebelled and the kingdom of Yue was completely destroyed, 1,922 years went by.[65]

吳矣。自黃帝至少康，十世。自禹受禪至少康即位，六世，為一百四十四年。少康去顓頊即位，四百二十四年。

　　黃帝→昌意→顓頊→鯀→禹→啟→太康→仲盧→相→少康→無余→無玉去無余十世）→無疇→夫康→元［允］常→勾踐→興夷→不壽→不揚→無彊→魯穆柳有幽公為名→王侯自稱為君。

　　尊、親失琅邪，為楚所滅。勾踐至王親，歷八主，格霸二百二十四年。從無余越國始封，至餘善返，越國空滅，凡一千九百二十二年。

---

63. The text appears to be so garbled at this point that it is impossible to understand.
64. The *Yuejue shu*, 58 ["Jidi zhuan"], gives the name of Wanghou as Zhihou and identifies him as King Wujiang of Yue's son. The *Shiji*, 41.1747, on the other hand, gives Zhihou as Wujiang's father.
65. The rebellion of King Yushan refers to the events of 111–110 BCE. At this time, the Han Empire was engaged in a massive attack against the kingdom of Nanyue 南越. King Yushan of the Eastern Yue initially promised military assistance, then delayed, and then declared independence from the Han and was killed. According to *Hanshu*, 95.3859, King Yushan claimed descent from King Goujian of Yue.

Appendix: The Chinese Text

A Note on the Chinese Text

The text given here is the standard transmitted version of the *Wu Yue chunqiu*. There are certain passages that are universally agreed to be corrupt and missing one or more characters; where there is general agreement on the basis of early quotations as to what has been lost, the characters being added are placed within 【】. Instances in which the text is garbled or corrupt, and where there is not an agreed solution, are discussed in the footnotes to the translation. There are also some instances in which an individual word in the transmitted text is known to be incorrect, where the right character is indicated within []. The most significant instance of this correction concerns the name of King Goujian's father: King Yunchang 允常 of Yue. The transmitted text of the *Wu Yue chunqiu* consistently refers to him as King Yuanchang 元常 of Yue. This designation was intended to avoid contravening the name taboo (*hui* 諱) on the personal name of the father of Emperor Yingzong of the Song dynasty 宋英宗 (r. 1063–67): Zhao Yunrang 趙允讓 (969–1059).

Bibliography

Ancient Texts and Dynastic Histories

Boshu Laozi jiaozhu 帛書老子校注. Annot. Gao Ming 高明. Beijing: Zhonghua shuju, 1996.
Chuci buzhu 楚辭補注. Annot. Hong Xingzu 洪興祖. Beijing: Zhonghua shuju, 1963.
Chunqiu fanlu yizheng 春秋繁露義證. Annot. Su Yu 蘇輿. Beijing: Zhonghua shuju, 1991.
Chunqiu Gongyang zhuan zhushu 春秋公羊傳注疏. Annot. He Xiu 何休 and Xu Yan 徐彥. Beijing: Beijing daxue chubanshe, 1999.
Chunqiu Guliang jingzhuan buzhu 春秋穀梁經傳補注. Annot. Zhong Wenzheng 鐘文烝. Beijing: Zhonghua shuju, 1996.
Chunqiu jingzhuan jijie 春秋經傳集解. Annot. Du Yu 杜預. Shanghai: Shanghai guji chubanshe, 2007.
Chunqiu Zuozhuan zhu 春秋左傳注. Annot. Yang Bojun 楊伯峻. Beijing: Zhonghua shuju, 1981.
Da Dai Liji jiegu 大戴禮記解詁. Annot. Wang Pinzhen 王聘珍. Beijing: Zhonghua shuju, 2008.
Erya zhushu 爾雅注疏. Annot. Guo Pu 郭璞 and Xing Bing 邢昺. Taipei: Taiwan guji chubanshe, 2001.
Fangyan zhu 方言注. Annot. Guo Pu. Beijing: Zhonghua shuju, 1985.
Fengsu tongyi jiaozhu 風俗通義校注. Annot. Wang Liqi 王利器. Beijing: Zhonghua shuju, 2000.
Gaoshi zhuan 高士傳. Annot. Huangfu Mi 皇甫謐. Beijing: Zhonghua shuju, 1985.
Gongyang zhuan; see *Chunqiu Gongyang zhuan zhushu*.
Guanzi jiaozhu 管子校注. Annot. Li Xiangfeng 李翔鳳. Beijing: Zhonghua shuju, 2004.
Guliang zhuan; see *Chunqiu Guliang jingzhuan buzhu. Guoyu* 國語. Annot. Shanghai shifan daxue guji zhenglizu 上海師範大學古籍整理組. Shanghai: Shanghai guji chubanshe, 1978.

Han Feizi jishi 韓非子集釋. Annot. Chen Qiyou 陳奇猷. Beijing: Zhonghua shuju, 1958.
Han Shi waizhuan jishi 韓詩外傳集釋. Annot. Xu Weiyu 許維遹. Beijing: Zhonghua shuju, 2005.
Hanshu 漢書. Comp. Ban Gu 班固 et al. Beijing: Zhonghua shuju, 1962.
Hou Hanshu 後漢書. Comp. Fan Ye 范曄 et al. Beijing: Zhonghua shuju, 1965.
Huainanzi jishi 淮南子集釋. Annot. He Ning 何寧. Beijing: Zhonghua shuju, 1998.
Jinshu 晉書. Comp. Fang Xuanling 房玄齡 et al. Beijing: Zhonghua shuju, 1974.
Jiu Tangshu 舊唐書. Comp. Liu Xu 劉昫 et al. Beijing: Zhonghua shuju, 1975.
Laozi; see *Boshu Laozi jiaozhu*.
Lienü zhuan buzhu 列女傳補注. Annot. Wang Zhaoyuan 王照圓. Shanghai: Huadong shifan daxue chubanshe, 2012.
Liji jijie 禮記集解. Annot. Sun Xidan 孫希旦. Beijing: Zhonghua shuju, 2007.
Lunheng jiaozhu 論衡校注. Annot. Zhang Zongxiang 張宗祥. Shanghai: Shanghai guji chubanshe, 2010.
Lunyu yizhu 論語譯注. Annot. Yang Bojun. Beijing: Zhonghua shuju, 2008.
Lüshi chunqiu xin jiaoshi 呂氏春秋新校釋. Annot. Chen Qiyou. Shanghai: Shanghai guji chubanshe, 2002.
Mengzi yizhu 孟子譯注. Annot. Yang Bojun. Beijing: Zhonghua shuju, 2005.
Mingshi 明史. Comp. Zhang Tingyu 張廷玉 et al. Beijing: Zhonghua shuju, 1974.
Mu Tianzi zhuan jiaozhu 穆天子傳校注. Annot. Guo Pu and Hong Yixuan 洪頤煊. Beijing: Zhonghua shuju, 1985.
Qianfu lun jianjiaozheng 潛夫論箋校正. Annot. Wang Jipei 汪繼培. Beijing: Zhonghua shuju, 1985.
Shangshu zhengyi 尚書正義. Annot. Kong Anguo 孔安國 and Kong Yingda 孔穎達. Beijing: Beijing daxue chubanshe, 1999.
Shanhai jing jiaozhu 山海經校注. Annot. Yuan Ke 袁珂. Chengdu: Ba-Shu shushe, 1996.
Shiji 史記. Comp. Sima Qian 司馬遷 et al. Beijing: Zhonghua shuju, 1959.
Shijing zhengyi 詩經正義. Annot. Zheng Xuan 鄭玄 and Kong Yingda. Beijing: Beijing daxue chubanshe, 1999.
Shiyi jia zhu Sunzi 十一家注孫子. Annot. Cao Cao 曹操 et al. Taipei: Huazheng shuju, 1991.
Shuijing zhu jiaozheng 水經注校證. Annot. Chen Qiaoyi 陳橋驛. Beijing: Zhonghua shuju, 2007.
Shuowen jiezi zhu 説文解字注. Annot. Duan Yucai 段玉裁. Taipei: Dingyuan wenhua shiye, 2003.
Shuoyuan jiaozheng 説苑校證. Annot. Xiang Zonglu 向宗魯. Beijing: Zhonghua shuju, 2000.
Suishu 隋書. Comp. Wei Zheng 魏徵 et al. Beijing: Zhonghua shuju, 1973.
Sun Bin bingfa jiaoli 孫臏兵法校理. Annot. Zhang Zhenze 張震澤. Beijing: Zhonghua shuju, 2007.

Sunzi; see *Shiyi jia zhu Sunzi*.
Wenxuan 文選. Annot. Li Shan 李善 et al. Taipei: Zhengzhong shuju, 1971.
Wenzi shuyi 文子疏義. Annot. Wang Liqi. Beijing: Zhonghua shuju, 2000.
Wu Yue chunqiu jijiao huikao 吳越春秋輯校匯考. Annot. Zhou Shengchun 周生春. Shanghai: Shanghai guji chubanshe, 1997.
Xin Tangshu 新唐書. Comp. Ouyang Xiu 歐陽修 et al. Beijing: Zhonghua shuju, 1975.
Xinxu jiaoshi 新序校釋. Annot. Shi Guangying 石光瑛. Beijing: Zhonghua shuju, 2001.
Xunzi jijie 荀子集解. Annot. Wang Xianqian 王先謙. Beijing: Zhonghua shuju, 2008.
Yantie lun jiaozhu 鹽鐵論校注. Annot. Wang Liqi. Beijing: Zhonghua shuju, 1996.
Yili zhushu 儀禮注疏. Annot. Zheng Xuan and Jia Gongyan 賈公彥. Beijing: Beijing daxue chubanshe, 1999.
Yuejue shu 越絕書. Comp. Yuan Kang 袁康 and Wu Ping 吳平. Shanghai: Shanghai guji chubanshe, 1985.
Zhanguo ce jizhu huikao 戰國策集注匯考. Annot. Zhu Zugeng 諸祖耿. Nanjing: Fenghuang chubanshe, 2008.
Zhouli zhushu 周禮注疏. Annot. Zheng Xuan. Beijing: Beijing daxue chubanshe, 1999.
Zhouyi zhengyi 周易正義. Annot. Wang Bi 王弼 and Kong Yingda. Beijing: Beijing daxue chubanshe, 1999.
Zhuangzi jishi 莊子集釋. Annot. Guo Qingfan 郭慶藩. Beijing: Zhonghua shuju, 2004.
Zhushu jinian 竹書紀年. Annot. Hong Yixuan. Sibu beiyao edn. Shanghai: Zhonghua shuju, 1936.
Zuozhuan; see *Chunqiu Zuozhuan zhu*.

Works Cited

Barbieri-Low, Anthony. 2007. *Artisans in Early Imperial China*. Seattle: University of Washington Press.
Bowie, E. L. 1985. "The Greek Novel." In *The Cambridge History of Classical Literature, 1: Greek Literature*, edited by P. E. Easterling and B. M. W. Knox, 683–99. Cambridge: Cambridge University Press.
Cao Jinyan 曹錦炎. 2007. "Wuwang Shoumeng zhi zi jianming kaoshi" 吳王壽夢之子劍銘考釋. In *Wu Yue lishi yu kaogu luncong* 吳越歷史與考古論叢, edited by Cao Jinyan, 14–26. Beijing: Wenwu chubanshe.
———. 2013. "Wuwang Guang tong daigou xiaokao" 吳王光銅帶鈎小考. *Dongnan wenhua* 東南文化 2:90–93.
Cao Lindi 曹林娣. 1982. "Guanyu *Wu Yue chunqiu* de zuozhe ji chengshu niandai" 關於吳越春秋的作者及成書年代. *Xibei daxue xuebao (Zhexue shehui kexue ban)* 西北大學學報 (哲學社會科學版) 4:68–73, 89.

———. 1984. "Shilun *Wu Yue chunqiu* de ticai" 試論吳越春秋的體裁. *Suzhou daxue xuebao (Zhexue shehui kexue ban)* 蘇州大學學報 (哲學社會科學版) 1:86–89.

———. 1986. "*Wu Yue chunqiu* wenxue chengjiu chutan" 吳越春秋文學成就初探. *Suzhou daxue xuebao (Zhexue shehui kexue ban)* 1:56–59.

Chen Huixing 陳惠星. 1995. "*Wu Yue chunqiu* de moulüe sixiang" 吳越春秋的謀略思想. In *Wu wenhua ziyuan yanjiu ji fazhan* 吳文化資源研究及發展, edited by Gao Xiechu 高燮初, 63–75. Vol. 2. Suzhou: Suzhou daxue chubanshe.

Chen Peifen 陳佩芬. 2004. *Xia Shang Zhou qingtongqi yanjiu: Shanghai bowuguan zangpin* 夏商周青銅器研究: 上海博物館藏品. Shanghai: Shanghai guji chubanshe.

Chen Pengcheng 陳鵬程. 2014. "*Wu Yue chunqiu* siwang xushi de wenhua neihan ji yishu gongneng" 吳越春秋死亡敘事的文化內涵及藝術功能. *Qinzhou xueyuan xuebao* 欽州學院學報 29 (4): 23–27.

Chen Qiaoyi 陳橋驛. 1982. *Shaoxing shihua* 紹興史話. Shanghai: Renmin chubanshe.

———. 1984. "*Wu Yue chunqiu* ji qi jizai de Wu Yue shiliao" 吳越春秋及其記載的吳越史料. *Hangzhou daxue xuebao* 杭州大學學報 1:91–97.

Chen Qiaoyi 陳橋驛 and Yan Yuehu 顏越虎. 2004. *Shaoxing jianshi* 紹興簡史. Beijing: Zhonghua shuju.

Chen Songchang 陳松長. 2001. *Mawangdui boshu: Xingde yanjiu lungao* 馬王堆帛書: 刑德研究論稿. Taipei: Taiwan guji chubanshe.

Chen Ying 陳穎. 1998. *Zhongguo yingxiong xiayi xiaoshuo tongshi* 中國英雄俠義小說通史. Nanjing: Jiangsu jiaoyu chubanshe.

Chen Zhi 陳值. 1958. "Guanyu Liang Han de tu" 關於兩漢的徒. In *Liang Han jingji shiliao luncong* 兩漢經濟史料論叢, edited by Chen Zhi, 259–70. Xi'an: Shaanxi renmin chubanshe.

Chou, Ju-hsi. 2000. *Circles of Reflection: The Carter Collection of Chinese Bronze Mirrors*. Cleveland: Cleveland Museum of Art.

Clunas, Craig. 1996. *Fruitful Sites: Garden Culture in Ming Dynasty China*. London: Reaktion Books.

Cohen, Paul. 2009. *Speaking to History: The Story of King Goujian in Twentieth-Century China*. Berkeley: University of California Press.

Dalby, Michael. 1981. "Revenge and the Law in Traditional China." *American Journal of Legal History* 25 (4): 267–307.

Despeux, Catherine. 1999. "Le dévoreur dévoré: De l'émincé de poisson, de ses délices et de ses méfaits." *Études chinoises* 18 (1–2): 81–120.

Dong Chuping 董楚平. 1992. *Wu Yue Xu Shu jinwen jishi* 吳越徐舒金文集釋. Hangzhou: Zhejiang guji chubanshe.

Dong Chuping 董楚平 and Jin Yongping 金永平. 1998. *Wu Yue wenhua zhi* 吳越文化志. Shanghai: Shanghai renmin chubanshe.

Doody, Margaret Anne. 1996. *The True Story of the Novel*. New Brunswick, NJ: Rutgers University Press.

Eichhorn, Werner. 1969. *Heldensagen aus dem unteren Yangtze-Tal*. Wiesbaden: Franz Steiner Verlag.

Feng Kunwu 豐坤武. 2000. "*Wu Yue chunqiu* 'dai fei quan shu' bianshi" 吳越春秋 "殆非全書" 辨識. *Lishixue* 歷史學 131 (3): 82–84.

Feng Puren 馮普仁. 2007. *Wu Yue wenhua* 吳越文化. Beijing: Wenwu chubanshe.

Fu Zhenzhao 傅振照. 2002. *Shaoxing shigang: Yueguo bufen* 紹興史綱：越國部分. Shanghai: Baijia chubanshe.

Futre Pinheiro, Marília P. 2014. "The Genre of the Novel: A Theoretical Approach." In *A Companion to the Ancient Novel*, edited by Edmund P. Cueva and Shannon N. Byrne, 201–16. Oxford: Wiley-Blackwell.

Gan Bao 干寶. 1979. *Soushen ji* 搜神記. Beijing: Zhonghua shuju.

Gao Mingqian 高明乾, Lu Longdou 盧龍鬥 et al. 2006. *Zhiwu gu Hanming tukao* 植物古漢名圖考. Zhengzhou: Daxiang chubanshe.

Gu Jiegang 顧頡剛. 1987. *Suzhou shizhi biji* 蘇州史志筆記. Suzhou: Jiangsu guji chubanshe.

Guangzhoushi wenwu guanli weiyuanhui 廣州市文物管理委員會, Zhongguo shehui kexue xueyuan kaogu yanjiusuo 中國社會科學院考古研究所, and Guangdongsheng bowuguan 廣東省博物館, eds. 1991. *Xi-Han Nanyue wangmu* 西漢南越王墓. Beijing: Wenwu chubanshe.

Guanxiu 貫休. 1985. *Chanyue ji* 禪月集. Beijing: Zhonghua shuju.

Guo Yingde 郭英德. 1998. "*Huansha ji*: Lishiju de xinbian" 浣紗記：歷史劇的新編. *Jiamusi daxue shehui kexue xuebao* 佳木斯大學科學學報 3:8–11.

Guojia wenwu ju 國家文物局, ed. 2008. *Zhongguo wenwu ditu ji: Jiangsu fence: xia* 中國文物地圖集：江蘇分冊：下. Beijing: Zhongguo ditu chubanshe.

Hägg, Thomas. 1987. "Callirhoe and Parthenope: The Beginnings of the Historical Novel." *Classical Antiquity* 6:184–204.

Hargett, James. 2013. "會稽: Guaiji? Guiji? Huiji? Kuaiji? Some Remarks on an Ancient Chinese Place-Name." *Sino-Platonic Papers* 234:1–32.

Hayashi Minao 林巳奈夫. 1975. *Chūgoku In-Shū jidai no buki* 中國殷周時代の武器. Kyoto: Kyoto daigaku jimmin bungaku kenkyūsho.

He Jianjun. 2021. *Spring and Autumn Annals of Wu and Yue: An Annotated Translation of Wu Yue chunqiu*. Ithaca: Cornell University Press.

Henry, Eric. 1987. "The Motif of Recognition in Early China." *Harvard Journal of Asiatic Studies* 47 (1): 5–30.

———. 2007. "The Submerged History of Yuè." *Sino-Platonic Papers* 176:1–36.

Hu Wenhui 胡文輝. 1995. "Juyan Xinjian zhong de rishu canwen" 居延新簡中的日書殘文. *Wenwu* 文物 4:56–57.

Huang Rensheng 黃仁生. 1994. "Lun *Wu Yue chunqiu* shi woguo xiancun zuizao de wenyan changpian lishi xiaoshuo" 論吳越春秋是我國最早的文言長篇歷史小説. *Hunan shifan daxue shehui kexue xuebao* 湖南師範大學學報 3:81–85.

———. 1996. *Xinyi Wu Yue chunqiu* 新譯吳越春秋. Taipei: Sanmin shuju.

Huang Shengzhang 黃盛璋. 1983. "Tongqi mingwen Yi Yu Ze de diwang ji qi yu Wuguo de guanxi" 銅器銘文宜虞夨的地望及其與吳國的關係. *Kaogu* 考古 3:295–305.

Huang Wei 黃葦. 1983. "Guanyu *Yuejue shu*" 關於越絕書. In *Fangzhi lunji* 方志論集, edited by Huang Wei, 106–20. Hangzhou: Zhejiang renmin chubanshe.

Hubeisheng wenwu kaogu yanjiusuo 湖北省文物考古研究所 and Suizhoushi kaogudui 隨州市考古隊. 2006. *Suizhou Kongjiapo Hanmu jiandu* 隨州孔家坡漢墓簡牘. Beijing: Wenwu chubanshe.

Hulsewé, A. F. P. 1955. *Remnants of Han Law*. Leiden: Brill.

Ji Yun 紀昀 et al. 2000. *Siku quanshu zongmu tiyao* 四庫全書總目提要. Shijiazhuang: Hebei renmin chubanshe.

Jin Qizhen 金其楨. 2000. "Shijie *Wu Yue chunqiu* de bukexiao zhi mi" 試解吳越春秋的不可曉之謎. *Shixue yuekan* 史學月刊 2000 (6): 42–47.

Jin Yong 金庸. 1996. *Yuenü jian* 越女劍. Taipei: Yuanliu chubanshe.

Johnson, David. 1980a. "The *Wu Tzü-hsu Pien-wen* and Its Sources: Part I." *Harvard Journal of Asiatic Studies* 40 (1): 93–156.

———. 1980b. "The *Wu Tzü-hsu Pien-wen* and Its Sources: Part II." *Harvard Journal of Asiatic Studies* 40 (2): 465–505.

Kalinowski, Marc. 1998–99. "The *Xingde* 刑德 Texts from Mawangdui." *Early China* 23–24:125–202.

Kern, Martin. 2005. "The *Odes* in Excavated Manuscripts." In *Text and Ritual in Early China*, edited by Martin Kern, 149–93. Seattle: University of Washington Press.

Knechtges, David R., and Hsiang-lin Shih. 2010–14. "*Wu Yue chunqiu* 吳越春秋 (Annals of Wu and Yue)." In *Ancient and Early Medieval Chinese Literature: A Reference Guide*, edited by David R. Knechtges and Taiping Chang, 1385–89. Leiden: Brill.

Lagerwey, John. 1975. "*The Annals of Wu and Yüeh*, Part I, with a Study of Its Sources." Unpublished PhD diss., Harvard University.

———. 1993. "Wu Yüeh ch'un ch'iu." In *Early Chinese Texts: A Bibliographical Guide*, edited by Michael Loewe, 473–76. Berkeley: Society for the Study of Early China and the Institute of East Asian Studies, University of California.

Lee, Jen-der. 1988. "Conflicts and Compromise between Legal Authority and Ethical Ideas: From the Perspectives of Revenge in Han Times." *Journal of Social Sciences and Philosophy* 1 (1): 359–408.

Li Jifu 李季甫. 2005. *Yuanhe junxian zhi* 元和郡縣志. Beijing: Zhonghua shuju.

Li Shoukui 李守奎. 2017. "*Yuegong qishi* yu Goujian mie Wu de lishi shishi ji gushi liuchuan" 越公其事與勾踐滅吳的歷史事實及故事流傳. *Wenxian* 文獻 6:75–80.

Li Xueqin 李學勤. 1993. "Yi Hou Ze *gui* de ren yu di" 宜侯夨簋的人與地. In *Chuantong wenhua yanjiu* 傳統文化研究, edited by Suzhoushi chuantong wenhua yanjiuhui 蘇州市傳統文化研究會, 87–89. Vol. 2. Suzhou: Guwuxuan chubanshe.

———, ed. 2011. *Qinghua daxue cang Zhanguo zhujian* 清華大學藏戰國竹簡. Vol. 2. Shanghai: Zhongxi chubanshe.

Li Zhihuan 李治寰. 1990. *Zhongguo shitang shi gao* 中國食糖史稿. Beijing: Nongye chubanshe.

Liang Chenyu 梁辰魚. 2010. *Liang Chenyu ji* 梁辰魚集. Beijing: Zhonghua shuju.

Liang Qi 梁琦. 2006. "Guiqi yu kangxia: *Wu Yue chunqiu* chuanqixing qianlun" 瑰奇與伉俠: 吳越春秋傳奇性淺論. *Xi'nan nongye daxue xuebao (Shehui kexue ban)* 西南農業大學學報 (社會科學版) 4 (3): 165–69.

Liang Zonghua 梁宗華. 1988. "Xianxing shi juan ben *Wu Yue chunqiu* kaoshi" 現行十卷本吳越春秋考識. *Dongyue luncong* 東嶽論叢 1:54–57.

———. 1993. "Lun *Wu Yue chunqiu* de zuozhe he chengshu niandai" 論吳越春秋的作者和成書年代. *Suzhou daxue xuebao (Zhexue shehui kexue ban)* 3:93–97.

Lin Xiaoyun 林小雲. 2009a. "*Wu Yue chunqiu* de xieren yishu" 吳越春秋的寫人藝術. *Qinzhou daxue xuebao* 欽州大學學報 24 (2): 18–20.

———. 2009b. "Yuanshi de shengming benxing he langman jiqing: Xi *Wu Yue chunqiu* de beiju secai" 原始的生命本性和浪漫激情:析吳越春秋的悲劇色彩. *Luoyang shifan xueyuan xuebao* 洛陽師範學院學報 28 (4): 58–61.

———. 2012. "*Wu Yue chunqiu* de xushi celüe" 吳越春秋的敘事策略. *Nanhua daxue xuebao (Shehui kexue ban)* 南華大學學報 (社會科學版) 13 (3): 97–100.

Liu, James C. Y. 1967. *The Chinese Knight-Errant*. Chicago: University of Chicago Press.

Liu Lexian 劉樂賢. 2004. *Mawangdui tianwenshu kaoshi* 馬王堆天文書考釋. Guangzhou: Zhongshan daxue chubanshe.

———. 2011. "Shuihudi 77 hao Hanmu chutu de Wu Zixu gushi canjian" 睡虎地77號漢墓出土的伍子胥故事殘簡. In *Jiandu yu gudaishi yanjiu* 簡牘與古代史研究, edited by Wu Rongceng 吳榮曾 and Wang Guihai 汪桂海, 190–94. Beijing: Beijing daxue chubanshe.

Liu Wei 劉瑋. 2008. "Ping xinbian kunju *Xi Shi*: Yi Xi Shi xingxiang wei zhongxin" 評新編昆劇西施:以西施形象爲中心. *Suzhou jiaoyu xueyuan xuebao* 蘇州教育學院學報 25 (2): 21–23.

Liu Xiaozhen 劉曉臻. 2009a. "*Wu Yue chunqiu* zhong de shige bianyuan" 吳越春秋中的詩歌辨源. *Xinan nongye daxue xuebao (Shehui kexue ban)* 西南農業大學學報 (社會科學版) 7 (3): 128–32.

———. 2009b. "*Wu Yue chunqiu* zhong de zhanbu fangshi ji tedian" 吳越春秋中的占卜方式及特點. *Wenzhou daxue xuebao (Shehui kexue ban)* 溫州大學學報 (社會科學版) 1:48–53.

Loewe, Michael. 1994. *Divination, Mythology and Monarchy in Han China*. Cambridge: Cambridge University Press.

Lu Guangwei 陸廣微. 1999. *Wudi ji* 吳地記. Nanjing: Jiangsu guji chubanshe.

Lu Xun 魯迅. 1973. "Zhujian" 鑄劍. In *Gushi xinbian* 故事新編, in *Lu Xun quanji* 魯迅全集, 533–60. Beijing: Renmin wenxue chubanshe.

Lü Yahu 呂亞虎. 2010. *Zhanguo Qin Han jianbo wenxian suojian wushu yanjiu* 戰國秦漢簡帛文獻所見巫術研究. Beijing: Kexue chubanshe.

Maeyama, Y. 2002. "The Two Supreme Stars, Thien-i and Thai-i, and the Foundation of the Purple Palace." In *History of Oriental Astronomy*, edited by S. M. Razaullah Ansari, 3–18. Dordrecht: Springer Science.

Mair, Victor. 1983. *Tun-huang Popular Narratives*. Cambridge: Cambridge University Press.

Milburn, Olivia. 2009. "Image, Identity, and Cherishing Antiquity: Wang Ao and Mid-Ming Suzhou." *Ming Studies* 60:95–114.

———. 2010. *The Glory of Yue: An Annotated Translation of the Yuejue shu*. Leiden: Brill.

———. 2011. "*Gai Lu*: A Translation and Commentary on a Yin-Yang Military Text Excavated from Tomb M247, Zhangjiashan." *Early China* 33:101–40.

———. 2013. *Cherishing Antiquity: The Cultural Construction of an Ancient Chinese Kingdom*. Cambridge, MA: Harvard University Asia Center.

Neimenggu zizhiqu wenwu kaogu yanjiusuo 內蒙古自治區文物考古研究所. 1978. *Helin'ge'er Hanmu bihua* 和林格爾漢墓壁畫. Beijing: Wenwu chubanshe.

Ouyang Xun 歐陽詢, ed. 2007. *Yiwen leiju* 藝文類聚. Shanghai: Shanghai guji chubanshe.

Owen, Stephen. 1986. *Remembrances: The Experience of the Past in Classical Chinese Literature*. Cambridge, MA: Harvard University Press.

Pan Zhonggui 潘重規. 1994. *Dunhuang bianwen ji xinshu* 敦煌變文集新書. Taipei: Wenjin chubanshe.

Pokora, Timoteus, and Michael Loewe. 1993. "*Lun heng*." In *Early Chinese Texts: A Bibliographical Guide*, edited by Michael Loewe, 309–12. Berkeley: Society for the Study of Early China and the Institute for East Asian Studies, University of California.

Qian Gu 錢穀, comp. 1935. *Wudu wencui xuji* 吳都文粹續集. Shanghai: Shangwu yinshuguan.

Qian Peiming 錢培名. 1956. *Yuejue shu zhaji* 越絕書札記. Shanghai: Shangwu yinshuguan.

Qinghua daxue chutu wenxian yanjiu yu baohu zhongxin 清華大學出土文獻研究與保護中心 and Li Xueqin 李學勤, eds. 2017. *Qinghua daxue zang Zhanguo zhujian (qi)* 清華大學藏戰國竹簡 (柒). Shanghai: Zhongxi shuju.

Ren Guiquan 任桂全. 2011. "Yizuo Zhongguo chuantong chengshi de 2500 nian: Shaoxing chengshi shi gaishu" 一座中國傳統城市的 2500 年: 紹興城市史概述. In *Zhongguo Yuexue* 中國越學, edited by Wang Jianhua 王建華, 8–18. Vol. 3. Beijing: Zhongguo bianyi chubanshe.

Rouzer, Paul. 1993. *Writing Another's Dream: The Poetry of Wen Tingyun*. Stanford: Stanford University Press.

Ruan Rongchun 阮榮春. 1996. *Shen Zhou* 沈周. Changchun: Jilin meishu chubanshe.

Schafer, Edward. 1977. *Pacing the Void: T'ang Approaches to the Stars*. Berkeley: University of California Press.

Schipper, Kristopher, and Franciscus Verellen. 2004. *The Daoist Canon: A Historical Companion*. Chicago: University of Chicago Press.

Schuessler, Axel. 2009. *Minimal Old Chinese and Later Han Chinese: A Companion to Grammata Serica Recensa*. Honolulu: University of Hawaii Press.

Shao Hong 邵鴻. 2007. *Zhangjiashan Hanjian Gailu yanjiu* 張家山漢簡蓋廬研究. Beijing: Wenwu chubanshe.

Shao Yiping 邵毅平. 2009. *Lunheng yanjiu* 論衡研究. Shanghai: Fudan daxue chubanshe.

Shen Zhou 沈周. 1991. *Shitian shixuan* 石田詩選. Shanghai: Shanghai guji chubanshe.

Song Lian 宋濂. 1983. *Wenxian ji* 文憲集. Taipei: Taiwan shangwu yinshuguan.

Stephens, Susan A., and John J. Winkler. 1995. *Ancient Novels: The Fragments*. Princeton: Princeton University Press.

Su Tie 蘇鐵. 1990. "Wu Yue wenhua de tancha" 吳越文化的探查. In *Wu Yue wenhua luncong* 吳越文化論叢, edited by Wu Yue shidi yanjiuhui 吳越史地研究會, 372–83. Shanghai: Shanghai guji chubanshe.

Sun Xiaochun, and Jacob Kistemaker. 1997. *The Chinese Sky during the Han: Constellating Stars and Society*. Leiden: Brill.

Sun Yirang 孫詒讓. 1895. *Zhayi* 札迻. n.p.: Chengfangao.

Swain, Simon. 2011. "A Century or More of the Greek Novel." In *Oxford Readings in the Greek Novel*, edited by Simon Swain, 1–35. Oxford: Oxford University Press.

Thompson, Lydia. 1999. "Confucian Paragon or Popular Deity? Legendary Heroes in a Late Eastern Han Tomb." *Asia Major* 12 (2): 1–38.

Tian Xudong 田旭東. 2002. "Zhangjiashan Hanjian *Gailu* zhong de bing yin-yang jia" 張家山漢簡蓋廬中的兵陰陽家. *Lishi yanjiu* 歷史研究 6:167–71.

Tian Yiheng 田藝蘅. 1992. *Liuqing rizha* 留青日札. Shanghai: Shanghai guji chubanshe.

van Ess, Hans. 1994. "The Old Text/New Text Controversy: Has the 20th Century Got It Wrong?" *T'oung Pao* 80 (1–3): 146–70.

Wagner, Donald. 1993. *Iron and Steel in Early China*. Leiden: Brill.

Wang, Eugene Yuejin. 1994. "Mirror, Death, and Rhetoric: Reading Later Han Chinese Bronze Artifacts." *The Art Bulletin* 76 (3): 511–34.

Wang Guangyang 汪廣洋. 1991. *Fengchi yin'gao* 鳳池吟稿. Shanghai: Shanghai guji chubanshe.

Wang Hengzhan 王恒展. 1999. *Zhongguo xiaoshuo fazhanshi gailun* 中國小說發展史概論. Ji'nan: Shandong jiaoyu chubanshe.

Wang Sanxia 王三峽. 2008. "'Ri you ba sheng' yu 'Tian zhi bashi': Hanjian *Gai Lu* ciyu xunshi erti" '日有八勝' 與 '天之八時:' 漢簡蓋廬詞語訓釋二題. *Changjiang daxue xuebao (shehui kexue bao)* 長江大學學報(社會科學報) 31 (5): 17–19.

Wang Yaochen 王堯臣. 1985. *Chongwen zongmu* 崇文總目. Beijing: Zhonghua shuju.

Wang Yu 王宇. 2007. "*Wu Yue chunqiu* yu Wu Yue min'ge" 吳越春秋與吳越民歌. *Dongnan wenhua* 3:66–68.

Wei Desheng 魏德勝. 2000. "Juyan Xinjian, Dunhuang Hanjian zhong de rishu canjian" 居延新簡敦煌漢簡中的日書殘簡. *Zhongguo wenhua yanjiu* 中國文化研究 1:65–70.

Wei Qiao 魏橋, Wang Zhibang 王志邦, Yu Zuoping 俞佐平, and Wang Yongtai 王永太. 1980. *Zhejiang fangzhi yuanliu* 浙江方志源流. Hangzhou: Zhejiang renmin chubanshe.

Whitmarsh, Tim. 2008. *The Cambridge Companion to the Greek and Roman Novel*. Cambridge: Cambridge University Press.

Wu Chengluo 吳承洛. 1984. *Zhongguo duliangheng shi* 中國度量衡史. Shanghai: Shanghai shudian.

Wu Congxiang 吳從祥. 2013. *Handai nüxing lijiao yanjiu* 漢代女性禮教研究. Ji'nan: Qi-Lu shushe.

Wu Enpei 吳恩培. 2010. "Chunqiu Wu juewei kaoshi" 春秋吳爵位考釋. *Jiangsu shehui kexue* 江蘇社會科學 3:237–43.

Xia Tingnan 夏廷楠. 1995. *Fan Li* 范蠡. Beijing: Jiefangjun chubanshe.

Xiao Fan 蕭璠. 1990. "Zhongguo gudai de shengshi roulei xizhuan: kuaisheng" 中國古代的生食肉類餚饌：膾生. *Zhongyang yanjiuyuan lishi yuyan yanjiusuo jikan* 中央研究院歷史語言研究所集刊 71 (2): 247–366.

Xiao Jun 蕭軍. 1980. *Wu Yue chunqiu shihua* 吳越春秋史話. Harbin: Heilongjiang renmin chubanshe.

Xie Chen 謝忱. 2000. *Gouwu shi xinkao* 勾吳史新考. Beijing: Zhongguo wenlian chubanshe.

Xie Naihe 謝乃和. 2020. "Shilun Qinghua jian *Yuegong qishi* de sixiang zhuti ji qi wenben xingzhi—jian shuo Yin-Zhou zhi ji bingxue guannian de liubian" 試論清華簡越公其事的思想主題及其文本性質—兼說殷周之際兵學觀念的流變. *Hangzhou shifan daxue xuebao (Shehui kexue ban)* 杭州師範大學學報 (社會科學版) 6:102–13.

Xie Zong'an 謝宗安. 2012. "Lüelun Baiyue minzu ji qi houyi de gezhi gongyi" 略論百越民族及其後裔的葛織. *Guizhou minzu yanjiu* 貴州民族研究 4:84–87.

Xin Deyong 辛德勇. 2010. "Yuewang Goujian xidu Langya shi xiyi" 越王勾踐徙都瑯邪事析義. *Wenshi* 文史 1:1–44.

Xiong Xianpin 熊賢品. 2018. "Lun Qinghua jian qi *Yuegong qishi* Wu-Yue zhengba gushi" 論清華簡七越公其事吳越爭霸故事. *Dong-Wu xueshu* 東吳學術 1:86–98.

Xu Bohong 徐伯鴻. 1991. "Chengqiao sanhao Chunqiumu chutan pan yi fu mingwen shizheng" 程橋三號春秋墓出土盤匜簠銘文釋證. *Dongnan wenhua* 1:153–59.

Xu Diancai 許殿才. 2007. "*Wu Yue chunqiu* shuolüe" 吳越春秋說略. *Shixue shi yanjiu* 史學史研究 1:18–23.

Xu Fuguan 徐復觀. 1989. *Liang Han sixiang shi* 兩漢思想史. Vol. 3. Taipei: Xuesheng shuju.

Xu Haoran 許浩然. 2004. "Nongyu Ziyu chuanshuo yunhan de lishi yuanjing" 弄玉紫玉傳說蘊含的歷史遠景. *Gudai wenming* 古代文明 3 (2): 106–10.

Xu Jian 徐堅, comp. 2004. *Chuxue ji* 初學記. Beijing: Zhonghua shuju.

Xu Jianchun 徐建春. 2005. *Zhejiang tongshi: Xian-Qin juan* 浙江通史：先秦卷. Hangzhou: Zhejiang renmin chubanshe.

Xu Naichang 徐乃昌. 1906. *Wu Yue chunqiu zhaji* 吳越春秋札記. Nanling: Xushi congshu.

Xu Tianhu 徐天祐. 1999. *Wu Yue chunqiu yinzhu* 吳越春秋音注. Nanjing: Jiangsu guji chubanshe.

Yan Kejun 嚴可均, comp. 1985. *Quan Hou-Han wen* 全後漢文. In *Quan shanggu sandai Qin Han Sanguo Liuchao wen* 全上古三代秦漢三國六朝文, edited by Yan Kejun. Beijing: Zhonghua shuju.

Yang Chengjian 楊成鑒. 2003. "Yuezu xianmin he Yuyue fushi wenhua" 越族先民和於越服飾文化. *Ningbo fuzhuang zhiye jishu xueyuan xuebao* 寧波服裝職業技術學院學報 4:16–19.

Yang Jialuo 楊家駱. 1985. *Quan Yuan zaju chubian* 全元雜劇初編. Vol. 7. Taipei: Shijie shuju.

Yang Shen 楊慎. 1985. *Danqian zalu* 丹鉛雜錄. Beijing: Zhonghua shuju.

———. 1993. *Sheng'an ji* 升庵集. Shanghai: Shanghai guji chubanshe.

Yang Yi 楊義. 1995. *Zhongguo gudian xiaoshuoshi lun* 中國古典小說史論. Beijing: Zhongguo shehui kexue chubanshe.

Yao Pinwen 姚品文. 2010. *Taihe zhengyin pu jianping* 太和正音譜箋評. Beijing: Zhonghua shuju.

Ye Mingsheng 葉明生. 2017. *Zhongguo kuileixi shi: Gudai, jin xiandai juan* 中國傀儡戲史: 古代近現代卷. Beijing: Zhongguo kexue chubanshe.

Ye Wenxian 葉文憲. 2007. *Wuguo lishi yu Wu wenhua tanmi* 吳國歷史與吳文化探秘. Beijing: Wenwu chubanshe.

Yin Zhiqiang 殷志強 and Ding Bangjun 丁邦鈞. 1993. *Dong-Zhou Wu Chu yuqi* 東周吳楚玉器. Taipei: Yishu tushu chubanshe.

Yinqueshan Hanmu zhujian zhengli xiaozu 銀雀山漢墓竹簡整理小組. 1976. *Sunzi bingfa* 孫子兵法. Beijing: Wenwu chubanshe.

Yu Shujuan 于淑娟. 2010. "Handai yuedi Chu geshi ji Yue wenhua de zouxiang: Yi Wu Yue chunqiu wei zhongxin" 漢代越地楚歌詩及越文化的走向: 以吳越春秋爲中心. *Zhejiang shifan daxue xuebao (Shehui kexue ban)* 浙江師範大學學報 (社會科學版) 6:41–46.

Yu Yue 俞樾. 1902. *Quyuan zazuan* 曲園雜纂. n.p.: Chunzaitang.

Yuan Ke 袁珂. 1991. *Zhongguo shenhua shi* 中國神話史. Taipei: Zhongyang tushuguan chubanshe.

Zhang Chenshi 張忱石, Zhong Wen 鐘文, Liu Shangrong 劉尚榮, and Lou Zhiwei 樓志偉. 1994. *Huansha ji jiaozhu* 浣紗記校注. Beijing: Zhonghua shuju.

Zhang Chouping 張丑平. 2005. "Lun Handai zashi xiaoshuo de fuchou yishi yu xiayi jingshen" 論漢代雜史小說的復仇意識與俠義精神. *Guangxi shifan xueyuan xuebao* 廣西師範學燕學報 2:96–98.

Zhang Honglin 張宏林. 2011. "Yi shi wei jian de Wu Zixu huaxiangjing" 以史爲鑒的伍子胥畫像鏡. *Shoucangjia* 收藏家 3:49–54.

Zhang Jinwu 張金吾. 1999. *Airi jinghu zangshu zhi* 愛日精廬藏書志. Shanghai: Shanghai guji chubanshe.

Zhang Jue 張覺. 1994. *Wu Yue chunqiu quanyi* 吳越春秋全譯. Guiyang: Guizhou renmin chubanshe.

———. 2006. *Wu Yue chunqiu jiaozhu* 吳越春秋校注. Changsha: Yuelu shushe.

Zhang Yi 張義. 2004. *Zhongguo xushi xue* 中國敘事學. Beijing: Renmin chubanshe.

Zhangjiashan ersiqi hao Hanmu zhujian zhengli xiaozu 張家山二四七號漢墓竹簡整理小組. 2006. *Zhangjiashan Hanmu zhujian: Ersiqi hao mu: Shiwen xiuding ben* 張家山漢墓竹簡: 二四七號墓: 釋文修訂本. Beijing: Wenwu chubanshe.

Zhao Gang 趙岡. 2006. *Zhongguo chengshi fazhan shi lunji* 中國城市發展史論集. Beijing: Xinxing chubanshe.
Zhong Sicheng 鐘嗣成. 2002. *Lugui bu* 錄鬼簿. Shanghai: Shanghai guji chubanshe.
Zhong Zhaopeng 鐘肇鵬. 1983. *Wang Chong nianpu* 王充年譜. Ji'nan: Qi-Lu shushe.
Zhou Shengchun 周生春. 1991. "*Yuejue shu* chengshu niandai ji zuozhe xintan" 越絕書成書年代及作者新探. In *Zhonghua wenshi luncong* 中華文史論叢, edited by Qian Bocheng 錢伯成, 121–39. Vol. 47. Shanghai: Shanghai guji chubanshe.
———. 1996. "Jinben *Wu Yue chunqiu* banben yuanyuan kao" 今本吳越春秋版本淵源考. *Wenxian* 文獻 2:215–26.
Zhu Changwen 朱長文. 1999. *Wujun tujing xuji* 吳郡圖經續記. Nanjing: Jiangsu guji chubanshe.
Zhu Zhaoju 祝兆炬. 2006. *Yuezhong renwen jingshen yanjiu* 越中人文精神研究. Nanchang: Baihuazhou wenyi chubanshe.

Index

Ailing, Battle of, 96, 105, 109
armor, 33–34, 87–88, 106, 109; armor and helmets, 54; buffalo hide armor, 212; rhinoceros hide armor, 202; Tangyi armor, 226
arms (weaponry), 178, 181. *See also* weapons

Bao (hereditary ministerial house of Qi), 79, 101
belt (clothing), 41, 114, 116, 226; belt–buckles, 42–43
birds, xlvi, 16, 50, 121, 124; birds and animals, 192; bird fields, 125–128; flocks of birds, 2, 45; flying birds, 140–143, 177, 195, 219; singing birds, xxviii
blood, xliii, 42–43, 139, 152; blood feud, xlii; blood food, 204, 206; blood sacrifice, 38, 119
Bo Zhouli, 43–44, 56, 72
boats, 25–25, 63–64, 91, 120n10, 122, 140, 190, 227; Great Boat of Wu, 15, 105; little boats, xxvii–xxix, 220; war boats, 226
Book of Changes, xxxv, 133n12, 135
Book of Songs, xv–xvi, xlv, 120. See also *Shijing*

bow (weapon), 88n17, 109, 192–194, 219, 196, 213; bow and arrows, 21–22, 193
bronze (metal), 41; bronze coffin, xlvi; bronze dings, 58, 223; bronze drums, 106; bronze image, 221; bronze mirrors, xin7, 179n11; bronze vessel inscriptions, xi, xlix, 7n16, 10n6
Buguang (sword name), 88, 226

Central Plains, 109, 198. *See also* Central States
Central States, 7, 10, 77, 85, 118, 123, 228; aristocracy or lords of, 5, 165; as synonym for Zhou confederacy, lii
Chang Gate, xlvi, 39, 58, 74
Chen Yin, xxxiv, 192, 194, 196
Chu Army, 13, 63, 70, 229; defeat of, 31, 61, 64, 109
Chu, Crown Prince Jian of, 18, 22–24, 31, 67
Chu, King Ling of, 13, 16–17, 194
Chu, King Ping of, xli, 17–19, 22, 43–44, 60n35, 65, 68; death of, 32; desecration of corpse of, 66, 71
Chu, King Zhao of, 18n6, 57–62, 65–66, 70–73, 109

Chu, King Zhuang of, 10, 15–17, 56n2, 103n36, 228
Chu, kingdom of, 16, 20n8, 32, 44, 56–57, 76n74, 148n52; escaped prisoners from, 37, 45
Chu, Prince Nangwa of, 58n25, 61–62. *See also* Zichang
Confucius, xxxii, 79–80, 104, 226–227
Counter-Jupiter, 94, 147, 154, 182
covenants, xxxi, 174; blood covenants, xxix, 61, 66, 96, 201, 227; blood covenant at Huangchi, 105n39, 108–109, 203; Covenant Ford, 169n31
cranes (bird), 58, 68
crossbow, xxxiv, 192, 194–195, 213; bow and crossbow, 109, 196

dogs, 3, 76, 89–90, 92, 199; hunting dogs, 113, 219, 223
Door of Earth (mantic position), 39, 160
dragons, 40, 133n12, 160, 180; Green Dragon (asterism), 147, 154; yellow dragon, 122
dreams, xxxvii, xlviii, 89–91, 213
drums (military), 54–56, 209, 212, 215; drums (musical), 16

Earthly Branches (dating system), 20n10, 40, 147, 149

Fei Wuji, 17–19, 44, 56–57, 72
Feng Huzi, 58–60
Five Sovereigns, 134, 161, 169, 227
fish, 124, 154, 177; fish and turtles, 84–85, 87, 102; fish stew, 25; sashimi fish, 74; steamed fish, xlvi–xlvii, 57–58; roast fish, 31, 34
fisherman, 24–26, 67
frogs, xxxiv, 211

Gate of Heaven (mantic position), 39, 160, 182
Gan Jiang (person), xxiiin43, 40–42, 88n17; Gan Jiang (sword), 40, 42
Gongsun Sheng, xlvii, 102n34, 111, 113, 116; death of, xlviii, 93n21, 112; dream divination by, 90–92
Grandee Bei Li, 45–46, 95, 100, 102
Grandee Futong, 131, 168, 207, 221
Grandee Gaoru, 136, 139, 171, 174, 207, 221
Grandee Jini, 136–137, 140, 175–177, 181, 207, 221
Grandee Kucheng, 132, 138, 170, 206
Grandee Xieyong, 105, 206, 221
Grandee Yeyong, 136, 138
Grandee Zhong (also known as Wen Zhong)
Gun (culture hero), 117–118, 119n7, 230
Gusu Tower, xiiin13, xxix, 76, 180, 187. *See also* Guxu Tower
Guxu Tower, 89–91, 105, 203

Heaven, 39, 41, 91–92, 141–143, 149, 160; august Heaven, 113, 129, 153; blessings of, 97, 157, 204, 206, 214; changes of, 207; Heaven and Earth, 39, 95, 122, 130, 160–161, 181, 221n39; help of, 229; lessons of, 157; Mandate of Heaven, 34, 114, 128, 155; powers of, 146; seasons of, 181; Way of, 187; will of, 46, 62, 113, 119, 125, 213, 216–217; wrath of, 202
Heavenly Stems (dating system), 147, 149
hegemon-king, 37, 97, 99, 159, 177, 217, 222
hexagram (divination method), 201, 221, 135

Houji (Lord Millet; culture hero), xxxii, 1–3, 117n3
Huai River, 47, 56, 63, 109, 119, 229; Yangtze and Huai Rivers, 96, 100, 105, 215
Huangchi (covenant and battle?), xxxi, 103, 108–109, 113n50, 202–203

jade, 3, 31, 60, 119–120, 133; jade cups, 58; jade deposits, 121; jade discs, 133n13, 180; jade pendants, 62; jade and silk, 205
Jade Gate (mantic text?), xxxvii, 146–147, 154, 216, 223–224
Jin, Lord Ding of, 88–89, 105, 107–108, 113n50
Jin, state of, 82, 107
Jupiter, 40n3, 94

Kuaiji, Commandery, xv–xviii, xxxv
Kuaiji, Mount, ix, xii, xxii, 82, 124n19, 216, 127n22; peaks of, 84, 87
kudzu cloth, 164–166, 184
Kunlun, Mount, 123, 160–161

Lai River, 26–27, 73
Lu, Lord Ai of, 79n8, 222, 229

Metal Casket (mantic text?), xxxvii, 94, 216
Ming dynasty, xxiii, xxviii–xxx, xxxiii
Mo Ye (person), xxiiin43, 40–41; Mo Ye (sword), 40, 42

omens, 17, 121, 160, 197, 135; auspicious omens, 126, 128, 136, 140, 152; evil omens, 224
oracle-bones, 66, 201
Ou Yezi, 40, 59–60

pearls, 24, 31, 58, 60, 133

qi, xxxvii, 20, 114, 132, 135; movements of, 39, 59, 160, 170; *qi* of Earth, 161; *qi* of Heaven, 41; *qi* of Heaven and Earth, 181; *qi* of spring and summer, 150
Qi Army, 96, 105, 109
Qi, Great Lord of (also known as Taigong), 131, 137n26, 176
Qi, Lord Huan of, 148, 171, 176, 178, 228
Qi, state of, 79n7, 82–83, 89
Qian Fu, xxiin39, xxxi–xxxiii
qin (musical instrument), 72–73, 216n, 217; *yaqin* (a type of *qin*), 226–227
Qin Army, 70, 228
Qin, Lord Huan of, 68–69, 227
Qin, Lord Mu of, 171, 178, 228
Qinyuhang, Mount, 93n21, 111–112, 116

rape, xlvii, 66–67, 72, 210

Shang, King Zhou of, 46, 100n33, 132n8, 147, 187
Shang dynasty, 46, 47n15, 100n33, 132n8, 188n26, 189n28. *See also* Yin dynasty
Shaoxing, xvi, lin97, liiin99
Shen Baoxu, xxxiii, 22–23, 68–70, 203–206
Sheng (son of Crown Prince Jian of Chu), 24, 32
Shiji, xxxv, xxxviii, xli, lii
Shijing, xxxv, 9n2
slaves, xlv, 134, 142, 145n45, 153, 174, 198, 214, 220; slavery, 144
Son of Heaven (royal title), 109, 118, 124, 126, 132; Son of Heaven (title of Wu kings), 11, 216; Son of Heaven (title of Zhou kings), xxiii, xxxi, 85n15, 106, 109

Song, state of, 12n8, 19, 22–23, 108, 215
Shulu (sword), 100. *See also* Zhanlu
Shun (sage king), 118–119, 124, 132, 182
slingshot, 103–104, 192
swords, xii, liii, 25–26, 42, 48–49, 97, 191; falling on sword, 52, 215, 225; fine swords, 86; making swords, 41; suicide using swords, xliv; using sword and halberd, 190; using sword and shield, 54
Sun Wu (also known as Master Sun), x, xxxiii, 53–56, 61–62, 67, 70–72, 76

Tai, Lake, xiiin13, xxxn59, xxxii, 31
Tang (culture hero), 149, 158, 184; held captive, 131, 137, 147; Tang and King Wen as dynastic founders, 132–133, 178; Tang and King Wu as dynastic founders, 171, 220
Tang, state of, 62–63, 70
Three Kings, 132, 161, 227
tigers, 153, 165, 187; physical features like a tiger, 29, 46, 54, 152, 191; White Tiger (asterism), 95
torture, 22, 38, 51, 63, 112, 220

weapons, 41, 54–55, 89, 92, 178, 190, 193, 181; magical weapons, xxiii; naked weapons, 153; weapons and armor, 80, 106, 204, 206, 211; weapons and provisions, 67
Wen Tower, 98, 151, 216, 218n37
wine, 33, 44, 151, 176, 183, 199; drinking wine, 62, 204; goblet of, 130–131, 152; jug of, 25–27, 199; libation of, 214n27
wolves, 93, 152, 187, 219
Wu Army, 32, 64–67, 73, 76, 106; defeat of, ix, 10, 15, 70–71, 110, 212–214
Wu, Crown Prince You of, 103, 105

Wu, Great Lord Protector of, 1, 4–7
Wu, King Liao of, xiii, lv, lvii, 14–15, 27–29, 40n5; murder of, xiii, 31–35, 46, 59
Wu, King Shoumeng of, xxxix, lii–liii, lv, lvii, 9–11, 128
Wu, King Yuji of, lv, 11, 13–15
Wu, King Yumei of, lv, 11, 13n9, 14, 30
Wu, King Zhufan of, lv, 11–13, 30, 128
Wu, kingdom of, xix, xxiii, xxxviii–xxxix, xlix, 32, 53, 57, 61n37, 78n3; asks for peace treaty, 201; crushing of Chu, 76; destruction of, x, 71, 92, 97, 99, 104, 215; establishment of, 101; government of, xliv, 51; help for, 96; orders received from, 160; protection of, 152; rise (and fall) of, xxv, xl; traditions of, 75
Wu, Prince Fugai of, 64, 70
Wu, Prince Gaiyu of, 32, 35, 56
Wu, Prince Guang of, lvii, 15, 28–35
Wu, Prince Jizha of, xxxix, xliii, 1n2, 11–14, 30, 32–34
Wu, Prince Qingji of, xin7, xxxvi, 46, 50–52
Wu, Prince Zhuyong of, 32, 35, 56
Wu, Royal Grandson Luo of, 90, 92–93, 102, 105, 111; ordered to apologize to Yue, 111, 214; sent to report to Zhou, 108
Wu Shang, 15, 19–22
Wu She, 17–19, 22, 56, 72

Xi Shi, xi, xiii, xxiin39, 183
Xia dynasty, 2–3, 100n33, 117, 126, 180n14, 185; Xia and Yin dynasties, 101, 148, 158
Xu Tianhu, xxvii, xxxi–xxxii, li, 203n11

Yangtze River, 22, 24, 38, 50, 119, 123, 211–212; crossing the Yangtze, 51, 65, 229; delta of, xlix, 104–105,

108, 122, 220; throwing self into, 52; Yangtze and Huai Rivers, 96, 100, 109, 215
Yao (sage king), 2, 118, 123–124, 132, 182, 230
Yao Li, xxxvi, 47–52
Yellow Sovereign, 132, 193, 230
Yin dynasty, 147, 185, 187; Xia and Yin dynasties, 101, 148, 158
Yu (sage king), xxxii, 117–128, 132, 158, 230; as ancestor to Yue royal house, 229
Yuan dynasty, xii–xiii, xxviii, xxxi, li
Yuchang (sword), 34, 59
Yue Army, xlviii, 92, 112–215
Yue, King Yunchang of, ix, lv, 59, 61, 128, 230; anger of, 70; taboo on name of, 59n31, 233; tomb of, 227; virtue of, 229
Yue, kingdom of, xi, xxxviii, xli, xliv, 165, 189, 204; ancestral shrines of, 168; backwardness of, 184–185; borders of, 179n12; destruction of, 39, 231; King Goujian's return to, 131, 157, 173; use of suicide troops by, 203n11; wealth of, 183, 200
Yue Maiden, xii, xxxiv, 190n30, 192
Yue, queen of (wife of King Goujian), xlvn85, 134n14, 142n36, 208–209

Zhanlu (sword), 58–60. *See also* Shulu
Zhe River, 129, 140, 155
Zheng, Lord Ding of, 24, 67
Zheng, state of, 23–24, 31, 64, 67–68, 100
Zhou confederacy, xxxin62, lii
Zhou dynasty, xxxii, 12, 171n34, 185, 188
Zhou, King Wen of, 131–132, 135, 137n26, 147, 158n2, 184
Zhou, King Wu of, 46, 196, 171, 187
Zhuan Zhu, xii, 29–31, 33–34, 46
Zichang, 56–57, 60–64, 67. *See also* Prince Nangwa of Chu
Zigong (disciple of Confucius), 79–84, 86–89
Zuili, xxix, 164, 210; Battle of Zuili, ix, 61, 70, 110

www.ingramcontent.com/pod-product-compliance
Lightning Source LLC
Jackson TN
JSHW022255171224
75524JS00002B/31